NIGHTINGALE 2

NINE JACK NIGHTINGALE SUPERNATURAL SHORT STORIES

By

STEPHEN LEATHER

CONTENTS

KNOCK KNOCK 5
WATERY GRAVE 51
THE CARDS 87
POSSESSION 123
CLAWS 157
THE ASYLUM 227
THE DOLL 281
THE MANSION 313
WRONG TURN 349

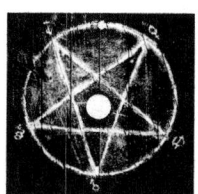

KNOCK KNOCK

Jack Nightingale stepped out onto the pavement, shivered against the cold, and lit a Marlboro. It was ten o'clock in the morning and he knew he was going to get a baleful look from Jenny McLean for being late so he figured he'd make a detour by Starbucks and pick her up a coffee and a muffin. There was a black Porsche Cayenne with near-impenetrable tinted windows parked on the other side of the road. The door opened and as Nightingale blew smoke up at the gunmetal grey sky, a large black man climbed out. Nightingale smiled as he recognised T-Bone, but the smile hardened a little as he realised that there was no obvious reason why he would be there. It could have been a coincidence, but Nightingale tended not to believe in coincidences. In his experience things, both good and bad, tended to happen for a reason. T-Bone was an enforcer for a South London gangster by the name of Perry Smith, and he didn't tend to make social calls.

T-Bone was wearing a black Puffa jacket and a black wool cap pulled low over his ears. He had his hands thrust deep into his jacket pockets which could have meant that he was trying to keep them warm or was hiding a handgun. The top of his jacket was open revealing a fist-sized gold medallion hanging on a thick gold chain around his neck. 'Yo, Birdman,' said T-Bone. 'How's things?' He wasn't smiling but his tone wasn't hostile, so swings and roundabouts.

'All good, T-Bone,' said Nightingale. A handgun was unlikely, he figured. If T-Bone was planning on shooting him, there were better places to do it than a Bayswater street in daylight. 'Were you waiting for me? You could have rung the bell.'

'I didn't want to disturb you.' He reached Nightingale but kept his hands in his pockets.

'So how long have you been there?'

T-Bone shrugged. 'Let's just say the early worm catches the bird.'

'T-Bone, mate, I've got work to do.'

'Perry has a job for you.'

Nightingale frowned. 'What sort of job?'

'The sort that needs your skill set, Birdman. Perry says I'm to bring you to him, come what may.'

'Come what may?'

'By hook or by crook, come hell or high water, whatever cliché rings your bell, he wants to see you.'

'He knows where my office is. Tell him to drop by. We've got cookies.'

'He can't travel at the moment. He says the mountain has to come to Mohammed.'

Nightingale looked at his watch. It was after nine but he didn't have anything on. It had been a quiet week. Truth be told, it had been a quiet month. 'And when you say job, you mean a paid-for job, right?'

T-Bone nodded. 'He'll pay.' He took his right hand out of his jacket and waved at the SUV. 'Time's a wasting.'

They walked over to the car. Nightingale phoned his assistant as T-Bone drove south, across the river. 'Jenny, something's come up and I'll be in late.'

'Nothing new there, then,' said Jenny.

'Ha ha,' said Nightingale. 'I'm going to see a guy called Perry Smith in Clapham, just in case they find my body down there riddled with bullets.'

'I'll make a note,' said Jenny.

Nightingale ended the call and put his phone away.

T-Bone shook his head admonishingly. 'See now, that's not funny,' he said.

'Just trying to lighten the moment,' said Nightingale, folding his arms.

'What if the cops are listening in?'

'To me? They're not.'

'You don't know that. GCHQ, they listen to everything. And you used Perry's name and said where he was. He won't like that.'

'Then let's keep it our secret,' said Nightingale.

'I don't work for you.'

'No, but we're friends.'

T-Bone frowned. 'We ain't friends.'

'T-Bone, I wouldn't have gotten into the car if I didn't trust you.'

'Trusting people and being their friend ain't the same thing, innit?'

'I'll put you on my Christmas card list, how about that?'

T-Bone's face finally cracked into a smile. 'Just be careful with Perry's name, that's all I'm saying.'

'Message received and understood. So we're good?'

'As good as we're gonna be,' said T-Bone.

They drove south across the Thames. Perry Smith lived in a terraced house in a quiet street, two stories high and with railings around steps leading to a basement. Two big black men in heavy coats were standing outside the house, stamping their feet against the cold. They looked over as T-Bone parked and nodded as he climbed out of the SUV.

The two heavies watched Nightingale with impassive eyes as he followed T-Bone into the house. T-Bone took him along the hallway to the stairs. They walked by a large room filled with three large sofas around a coffee table that was piled high with drugs paraphernalia. A big man in an LA Lakers shirt and baggy jeans was sitting on one of the sofas, a Glock in his hand. He nodded at T-Bone and T-Bone nodded back.

They went slowly up the stairs and they creaked under T-Bone's weight.

Perry Smith was in a bedroom at the rear of the house. All the furniture had been cleared out except for a two-seater sofa and a small glass coffee table. Perry was sitting on the sofa and tucking into a carton of Chinese food, something and rice. There was a bong on the table and a can of beer. A protective circle had been drawn on the bare floorboards with chalk. Nightingale frowned at the circle but before he could say anything Perry put down his chopsticks and stood up, He was wearing a navy blue Nike tracksuit and gleaming white Nike trainers. There was a thick gold chain hanging around his neck and another around his right wrist, presumably to provide balance for the huge diamond-studded gold watch on his left. 'Birdman, thanks for coming.' He spread out his hands. 'I'd shake or hug or some shit, but I have to stay where I am for the moment.'

'Says who?'

'Says who?' repeated Perry, frowning.

'Who says you've got to stay in the circle, Perry? Has someone threatened you?'

Perry pulled a face. 'Not a verbal threat, as such, but four of my associates have been killed and I was never slow at adding two and two together.'

'And we're not talking criminal elements, are we?'

'We're talking demon and devil shit, Nightingale, which is why I need you. You're the go-to man for that, right?'

'I've had a few supernatural cases, yes,' said Nightingale. 'Where did you get the design of the pentagram from?'

Perry frowned. 'Pentagram?'

Nightingale pointed at the circle on the floor. 'The drawing on the floor.'

Perry nodded. 'The internet. It's a protective circle, right? It stops demons getting to me, right?'

Nightingale tilted his head to the side. 'Sort of,' he said. 'It's more of a protective circle for when you summon a demon. But yeah, it might protect you against other entities. I suppose.'

'You suppose? What the fuck do you mean, Birdman? I don't want suppose. I want definite.'

'Well, you've got the letters in the wrong place.' Perry had written three groups of capital letters in chalk. EL, HA and MIC.

'Yeah, I couldn't make that out.'

'It's supposed to say MICHAEL,' said Nightingale. 'The archangel.'

'That's how it looked on the internet.'

'Yeah, well the internet's wrong. And the sigils, several of them are off.'

'Sigils?' repeated Perry,

'Those squiggly things between the circles,' said Nightingale. 'Some of them are off.'

'Is that a problem?'

'It doesn't seem to be so far,' said Nightingale. He shrugged. 'Time will tell. So what the hell happened, Perry? How did you get yourself into this? Why do you need occult protection?'

Perry rubbed the back of his neck. 'We were playing around with a Ouija board. Seven of us.'

'Seriously?'

Perry shrugged. 'It wasn't my idea. One of the girls wanted to do it.'

'And she just happened to have a Ouija board hanging around?'

Perry flashed him a withering look. 'No, of course not. It was an App.'

'A what?'

'An App. On her phone. It looks like a Ouija board and you type in your question and the board answers it.'

'That's bollocks, Perry. You know that.'

Perry frowned. 'Mate, it's an App. I thought it was a game, I thought we were just pissing around. But then it all turned to shit.'

'So what happened?'

'It was Micky's bird who had it. She was playing around on her iPad and Micky asked her what she was doing with it.'

'Do I know this Micky?'

Perry glared at him. 'Are you going to let me tell you what happened or not?'

'You're not the world's best storyteller, Perry. And me being a former cop, I thought a few pertinent questions might speed things up. Micky who?'

'Micky the Glass, they call him, because of his weapon of choice in a scrap. Micky's a Scouser who brings hash in from Europe, big time. I've known him for years.'

'And where is this Micky now?'

'He's dead,' said Perry. 'Can you just let me tell you the fucking story my way, Birdman?'

Nightingale raised his hands in surrender.

'So Micky is over in Spain talking to a few of his guys there. A bit of a meet and greet, pressing the flesh, no business being discussed because walls have ears, right, but sometimes you need the personal touch, you know, to check that everything's as it should be.'

Nightingale nodded but didn't say anything.

'So I went over with Micky and a couple of the guys, just for R&R,

have a few beers, hit a few of the local brothels, blow off some steam.'

'Sounds fun,' said Nightingale.

'I know, I know, you're waiting for the point, but bear with me, Birdman.' Perry sat down and ran his hands over his head. 'So the guy we're there to see, the main guy, is an Algerian, Mo his name is. Mo Money they call him because he's always saying he's got no money on him. Mo has this big fuck-off villa outside Fuengirola so we all stayed there. Anyway, Mo has this girlfriend, I forget what her name was. Fit as fuck, though. Anyway, the girlfriend has this Ouija board App on her iPad and while everyone is puffing away on some of the best, hash I've ever smoked, she shows it to Micky. Micky told her it was a load of crap. She said it answered all sorts of questions so Micky said he'd have a go and ask it if Five-0 were on his case. She gave it to him and he typed in to ask if there was anyone there. It spelled out Knock Knock.'

'Knock knock?' repeated Nightingale.

'Yeah, Knock Knock. So Micky is laughing and saying that he'll play along so he types in "who's there?", like you do.'

'Okay.'

'And quick as a flash he gets the answer. "AMY." In capital letters.'

'Amy?'

'Yeah. The girl's name. So Micky wonders what the fuck is going on and types in "Amy who?" and he gets the answer back. "AMY GONNA KILL YOU," again in capital letters which Micky thinks is funny.'

'That doesn't make sense,' said Nightingale.

'Tell me about it. We thought it was a joke.'

'Perry, I don't think demons from Hell bother with Apps.'

'I'm just telling you what happened,' said Perry. 'So Micky types in "FUCK YOU" and he gets back "NO MICKY YOU ARE THE ONE WHO'S GOING TO BE FUCKED". It knew his name. It knew his fucking name.'

Nightingale frowned. 'Are you sure?'

'What do you mean, am I sure? It called him Micky. It knew his name.'

'Did Micky type his name in? Did the girl who had the iPad?'

'She says no. It fucking shocked Micky, I can tell you. Dropped the iPad like it was red hot.'

'This sounds like a joke, Perry. A wind-up.'

'Like I said, Micky's dead, Birdman. He died two days ago.'

'Dead how?'

'Drowned in his Jacuzzi. Here in London. With a bottle of shampoo shoved up where the sun don't shine.'

'And Micky was a drug dealer, right?'

'So he had enemies, is that what you're saying? His bathroom door was locked and there was no one else downstairs. Two of his crew were playing with their Xbox downstairs and they went up when the Jacuzzi overflowed.'

'Accidents happen,' said Nightingale.

'Micky isn't the type to drown in his bath and he wasn't the type to stick a bottle of shampoo up his arse,' said Perry. 'He was fucked, Birdman. Just like the App said.'

'Where did she get the App from?' asked Nightingale.

'How the fuck would I know? Where does anyone get Apps from? The App store, I guess.'

'And why do you think it's the App that's after you?'

'What else could it fucking be?' asked Perry. 'Four of us came back to London and three of them are dead.'

'Dead how?'

'Dead how? What the fuck do you mean, dead how? Dead dead.'

'I mean how did they die, Perry? Micky died in the bath. What about the others? You sure they weren't accidents?'

'How do bodies accidentally get ripped apart and thrown around the room? Blood everywhere, guts slapped up against the wall.'

'So why hasn't it been in the papers or on TV?'

'Because the guys I run with don't go running to the cops. Little Pete was killed with twenty kilos of hash in his house. So his crew cleaned it up and dumped the pieces out in the New Forest. Smokey Joe was also killed in his bathroom. His girlfriend called me in hysterics.'

'Did she see what happened?'

'No, but she heard it. She was downstairs watching Netflix and getting stoned. She heard a kafuffle upstairs but she was pretty much out of it. When she eventually went upstairs there was blood oozing from under the door. She called me and me and T-Bone went round.'

'And?'

'And? What the fuck do you mean, and? Smokey Joe was in a dozen pieces and whoever did it had scrawled AMY on the mirror with his blood.'

'And just to be clear, Smokey Joe and Little Pete were with you and Micky in this place… what was it called?'

'Fuengirola. It's about half an hour's drive from Malaga. Yeah, Smokey Joe and Little Pete are in the distribution business. They bring in fruit and vegetables in trucks that have been adapted to hold a little extra, if you get my drift. Most of their stuff ends up in the North West, mainly Manchester.'

'And you think that something has come out of the iPad and is killing your friends? You can see how ridiculous that sounds?'

Perry scowled at Nightingale, then gestured at T-Bone. 'Show him.'

T-Bone pulled an iPhone from the pocket of his Puffa jacket, tapped on the screen and showed it to Nightingale. It was video, shot in a bathroom. There was blood all over the floor and body parts scattered around. A leg. A hand. A jaw. An ear. Nightingale grimaced.

'Smokey Joe,' growled T-Bone. 'Not smoking any more. Obviously.'

Nightingale stared at the phone. The camera moved to show the writing on the mirror. AMY. T-Bone was reflected in the mirror, his face impassive despite the carnage around him. The video ended and Nightingale gave the phone back to T-Bone. 'The Colombians can get creative when it comes to disposing of their rivals,' said Nightingale.

'Smokey Joe had no beef with the Colombians, and they would have kicked the door in, not locked it from the inside,' said Perry. 'Something ripped him apart. And why would Colombians write AMY on the mirror?'

'Why would anyone?' said Nightingale. He took out his cigarettes and he held up the pack. 'Do you mind?'

'Second-hand cigarette smoke is the least of my worries, Birdman.'

Nightingale lit a Marlboro and blew smoke before speaking. 'What do you want from me, Perry?'

'I want you to deal with this thing, whatever it is,' said Perry. 'I can't stay in here for ever pissing into bottles and shitting into plastic bags.'

'You and me both,' muttered T-Bone.

Nightingale blew smoke. 'Have you seen anything, anything outside the circle?'

Perry shook his head.

'Maybe it's run its course, whatever it is.'

'Yeah? And maybe it's just waiting for me to step out of this circle before it rips me apart, innit?'

'So what do you want me to do?'

'I've tried calling Mo Money but his phone's off. I'm assuming the worst. So I need you to go to the villa and see if he's OK or in bits. If he'd dead...' Perry shrugged. 'Then I don't know what. Find the iPad, maybe, and do whatever it is you do to stop it.'

'Stop what?' asked Nightingale. 'This is totally new ground to me, Perry. I've no idea what it is.'

'You have to help me, Birdman. I don't have anyone else I can turn to.'

Nightingale blew smoke up at the ceiling, then nodded slowly. 'Okay.'

* * *

As T-Bone drove his SUV over the Thames towards North West London, Nightingale toyed with his pack of cigarettes. 'What do you think, T-Bone?' he asked. 'What do you think killed Smokey Joe?'

T-Bone shrugged his massive shoulders. 'Beats the fuck out of me.'

'The body, how was it pulled apart? Brute force?'

'There were teeth marks.'

'Teeth marks?'

T-Bone bared his teeth in a snarl.

'Right,' said Nightingale. 'I get it. So an animal, maybe?'

'It was no animal ripped Smokey Joe apart. And don't forget the writing on the mirror.'

'So you believe Perry?'

'Perry don't scare easily,' said T-Bone. 'He's faced down some very heavy shit in the past without blinking an eyelid but this is different.'

'But you haven't seen anything?'

'I wasn't playing around with that Squeegee thing, was I?'

'Ouija.'

'Ouija, Squeegee. Potato, tomato. Who gives a fuck? All I know is that Smokey Joe, Micky and Little Pete are all dead and that nothing has happened to Perry since he drew that circle thing. Does that mean I believe in all that mumbo jumbo?' He shrugged. 'Maybe I do, maybe I don't. But I'm not going to be the one to try to talk him out of that circle.'

Nightingale nodded slowly.

'There is some weird shit out there, isn't there?'

'Allegedly.'

'You know what I mean. People get possessed, right.'

'There's evil in the world, that's true. Some of it is homegrown and some of it comes from outside. But a possessed iPad, I've got to be honest,

T-Bone, that's a first for me.'

'The world moves on, right? People adapt. Maybe demons and devils adapt too.'

Nightingale turned to look at T-Bone. 'You're the last person I'd think would believe in demons and devils.'

T-Bone shrugged. 'I believe in God, and if you believe in God you have to believe in all the stuff that comes with it.' He shrugged again. 'There's evil in the world, Birdman, and that's a fact that no one can argue with.'

'You're a Christian?'

'Baptist. ' He grinned. 'Down to my mum, that is. My dad left when I was still in nappies.'

'I am genuinely shocked, T-Bone.'

'Because?'

'Because of your line of work. How do you rationalize what you do with your religion?'

'There's plenty of violence in the Bible, Birdman. But yeah, I tend not to turn the other cheek. But sure I believe that something from the dark side killed Smokey Joe. I saw that with my own eyes. And whatever it is, if it's after Perry, then fuck, we've gotta do something.'

'I guess so,' said Nightingale.

'He's depending on you, Birdman. He can't stay in that circle forever.'

Nightingale nodded but didn't say anything.

He stared out of the side window as they drove west towards Bayswater.

'Amy means something to you, doesn't it?' asked T-Bone eventually.

Nightingale turned to look at him. 'Why do you say that?'

'Your face. When Perry mentioned the name.'

Nightingale looked out of the side window again.

'Come on, Birdman, spill the beans,' said T-Bone. 'Who is she?'

Nightingale sighed. 'Amy isn't a she. It's a demon, also known as Avanas, one of the meanest sons of bitches in Hell. It usually appears as a fire but it can take human form. Amy's in charge of 36 legions in Hell and likes to torture souls.' He forced a smile. 'Allegedly.'

'So this Amy is working through the iPad?'

Nightingale held up his hands. 'T-Bone, mate, I've no idea. I've never heard of anything like this. But I have heard of Amy.'

'This Amy, it could rip a body apart?'

'If it took human form, sure.'

'And can you kill it?'

'That remains to be seen, mate,' said Nightingale.

* * *

T-Bone dropped Nightingale outside his office and sped off down the street. Nightingale went up to the first floor and opened the door to find Jenny McLean just finishing making herself a coffee.

'I was going to bring you a coffee, and a muffin,' said Nightingale, taking off his raincoat and hanging it on the back of the door.

'I was going to thank you,' said Jenny, dropping down onto her chair. 'But as you didn't, I won't.' She sipped her coffee.

'Do we have much on?'

'Mrs Dawson wants you to see what her husband gets up to at his conference in Bournemouth. But that's next week. And I've a landlord who wants us to check if his staff are on the fiddle, but there's no rush on that because he hasn't sent the deposit I asked for.'

Nightingale sat down opposite her and put his feet up on her desk. She flashed his stained Hush Puppies a disapproving look and he put them back on the floor. 'You ever heard of Fuengirola?' he asked.

'Sure. My parents have a place in Marbella, just down the coast.'

'How's your Spanish?'

'Comme ci, comme ca.'

Nightingale frowned. 'Isn't that French?'

Jenny grinned. 'I'm impressed that you spotted that.'

'But you can speak Spanish?'

'Bien sur,' she said.

'Please stop doing that,' said Nightingale. 'Look, I need to head down to the Costa for a day or two. Can we use your parents' place?'

'We?'

'I'm going to need someone who speaks Spanish, in case I have to talk to the locals. And If you've got a place we can crash if we need to, even better.'

'I'll have to speak to mum,' said Jenny.

'They'll do anything for you, you know that,' said Nightingale.

'And what are we doing in Spain?'

'It's complicated.'

'It always is with you, Jack.'

'Can you book us on the first flight out?'

'I hear and obey.'

* * *

The EasyJet flight from Gatwick was full and Jenny and Nightingale were sat in the middle. Passengers poured out of the front and rear doors and hurried across the Tarmac to the terminal. They were the last off the aircraft and as they had been late getting to the airport there had been no room for their bags in the cabin and so they had been put in the hold so they were in no rush to get through Immigration. There were two immigration lines and the Spanish immigration officers were only glancing at the passports presented to them so Jenny and Nightingale were standing at the luggage carousel less than twenty minutes after the plane had touched down.

It was after nine-thirty pm when they walked out of the terminal. It was still ten degrees hotter than it had been in London, and the sky was only just darkening. Jenny had arranged a hire car in her name and he figured that as she was familiar with the area he'd leave the driving up to her, all the more so because the Spanish insisted on driving on the wrong side of the road.

The car was a white four-door Seat, functional and characterless. 'So what's the plan?' asked Jenny as she started the engine. 'It's about an hour and a half to my parents place so we could go straight there and grab a bite and head to Fuengirola first thing.'

Nightingale grimaced. 'Perry's living in a protective circle and pissing in bottles,' he said. 'The sooner we get him out, the better. How much daylight is left?'

'An hour or so.'

'Do you think we can get to the villa before it gets dark?'

'Probably.' She handed him the SatNav that the car rental company had given her. 'Key in the address and we'll head off.'

'Come on Jenny, you know me and SatNavs. If I start playing around with it, we'll end up in the Med.'

Jenny shook her head in disgust and took it from him. He showed her the address Perry had given him and she entered it. She attached it to the windscreen as the device calculated the route. 'Forty minutes,' she said. 'It'll be dark by the time we get there.'

'Have you got a torch?'

'Sure. Along with my coil of camping rope, my portable stove and my tent and sleeping bags.'

'There's no need to be sarcastic,' said Nightingale.

'Jack, seriously? We flew over with hand baggage. Why would I have packed a torch?'

'That old girl scout thing.'

'Girl guide. But no, I didn't pack a torch. But they have electricity here in Spain, so it shouldn't be a problem. Unless you're scared of the dark.'

'I'm good.'

She frowned as she looked across at him. 'You have told me everything about this job?'

'Sure.'

'We're going over to check that this Mo Money is alive and well?'

'That's it. In a nutshell.'

'You never said why he might not be alive and well.'

'It's complicated.'

'And it's why you're suddenly worried about night falling.'

Nightingale looked pained. 'Jenny…'

'Don't you "Jenny" me, Jack. What's the story?'

Nightingale sighed. 'A couple of people have died violently. They were playing around with an Ouija board on an iPad at Mo Money's villa. We need to check that he's OK. If he is, all well and good. If he's not…' He shrugged. 'No point in counting chickens.'

'Not dead ones, anyway.' She sighed, put the car in gear and drove out of the airport car park. 'A haunted Ouija board, is that what this is about?'

'Allegedly.'

'I just hope the client's cheque has cleared.'

Nightingale looked uncomfortable.

'Jack… please tell me we've been paid for this.'

'He'll pay.'

'How much?'

Nightingale grimaced. He'd forgotten to raise the matter of a fee with Perry Smith. 'I'm not sure,' he said.

Jenny threw him a look of disgust and concentrated on driving.

* * *

The SatNav took them to a villa that was surrounded by a high wall which had been painted a canary yellow. The villa was on a hill overlooking the apartment blocks of Fuengirola and the sea beyond. There was only one villa higher up the hill, shielded by a grove of orange trees. Night had now well and truly fallen but the moon was full, staring down at them like a baleful eye, giving them more than enough light to see by. Jenny kept the engine running and the headlights on full beam. 'Maybe we should wait until tomorrow,' she said.

'We should strike while the iron's hot,' said Nightingale.

'If by "we" you mean "you" then by all means,' said Jenny.

'Let's at least ring the doorbell,' said Nightingale. 'If he's in there then job done.'

'I'll wait here,' said Jenny. She waved at the gates. 'Be my guest.'

Nightingale sighed and climbed out. He lit a cigarette and blew smoke up at the moon. He walked over to a set of double wrought iron gates. They were locked. He peered through. There was a concrete driveway leading up to the two-storey villa. Several lights were on in the villa and a large swimming pool was also illuminated. There were two trees dotted with hundreds of tiny white lights, and a large statue of a tiger picked out with spotlights. Nightingale flicked away what was left of his cigarette and then carefully climbed the gate. Getting over the top was problematical and he took care not to snag his raincoat as he lowered himself over and dropped onto the driveway. He looked over at the car and flashed her a thumbs-up but she just shook her head scornfully.

His Hush Puppies crunched on the driveway as he walked up to the villa. Something flew overhead, something small and black and silent, either a bat or a bird. He turned to look at it but whatever it was had already disappeared behind the villa.

The front door was huge, dark wood criss-crossed with black metal strips. There didn't seem to be any CCTV or alarms. There was a brass doorbell set into the wall and Nightingale pressed it. He could hear a bell ring inside the villa. He pressed it again. And again, then stood back and waited. He looked over towards the gates but they were hidden from view and all he could see was the pool and the wall beyond. He turned and looked across the lawn towards Fuengirola. The tower blocks were dotted with lights. It was still warm but Nightingale shivered. He tried the door and to his surprise it opened. He stepped into the hallway and jumped when he saw a figure a few feet away. It took him less than a second to realise it was his reflection in a large mirror opposite the door but his pulse was still racing. 'Hello!' he called, and his voice echoed off the marble walls.

He walked through to a large sitting room, his eyes getting used to the darkness. There was just enough moonlight coming in from the windows for him to look around. Two large sofas, a dining table to seat eight, and a big screen television with huge speakers either side of it.

The kitchen was sparklingly clean, with stainless steel appliances and marble worktops glistening in the moonlight.

It was as he headed up a marble staircase that he heard the buzzing sound, quiet at first but louder as he climbed the stairs. The smell hit him about halfway up the stairs. It was a smell he'd come across several times when he was a police officer. The smell of dead flesh.

The smell and the buzzing was enough to tell him that Mo Money was dead, but he knew he had to see it for himself to be a hundred per cent sure. He found Mo Money in the bedroom. And in the bathroom. And in the bath. Bits of him, anyway, covered in flies and crawling with maggots. There was part of his arm on the bed, a hand on a dressing table, a chunk of flesh in the washbasin and a foot on the toilet seat. And scrawled on the wall above the king-size bed the word 'AMY'.

Nightingale had seen dead bodies before, but this was a whole different experience. Mo Money had been ripped apart, by something that had claws or teeth or both. There were sprays of blood all around the bedroom which suggested that was where he had died but whatever had killed him had ripped him apart and thrown the pieces around. He found the head in a wastepaper bin, the eyes wide in fear and the mouth open in a silent scream.

Nightingale hurried down the stairs and let himself out, wiping his fingerprints off the door handle before he left. He climbed back over the gate and jogged over to the car. 'Let's go,' he said as soon he sat down and slammed the door shut.

'Is he okay?' asked Jenny as she put the car in gear.

'No,' said Nightingale. 'He's in pieces. Literally. Forgive the pun.'

As Jenny drove to Marbella, Nightingale called Perry Smith on his mobile. 'Mo Money's dead,' he said as soon as Perry answered.

'Yeah, I'd figured as much,' said Perry. 'Was it bad?'

'As bad as it gets,' said Nightingale. 'And whatever it was had written AMY on the wall in blood.'

'Whatever it was? You know what the fuck it is, Birdman. And it's coming for me, innit?'

'You've been safe in the circle, Perry. I don't see that changing.'

'Yeah, well I can't stay here for ever, can I?'

'I'm on the case, Perry. Look, you said it was Micky's girlfriend that had the iPad. Where is she?'

'I was maybe pushing it calling her his girlfriend,' said Perry. 'She was an escort.'

'A hooker?'

'Money would have changed hands, yeah. We had dinner that night, then we went to a cat house that Mo Money uses, and we took a group of girls back to the villa for party time.'

'Do you remember the girl's name?'

'She was a hooker, Birdman. Who remembers the name of a hooker? Candy or Sandy or Mandy, who the fuck knows?'

'How about a description?'

'Big busty blonde. Legs that went on for ever. Micky said she gave the best blow jobs he'd ever had.'

'Spanish?'

'Eastern European. Polish or Bosnian or something. Who the fuck knows?'

'You're a real gent, Perry.'

'So what's the plan, Birdman? How are you gonna get me out of this?'

'I'll try to get the iPad,' said Nightingale. 'Which means I need to find Candy-Sandy-Mandy. Where is the cat house?'

'Just outside Fuengirola. Place called Club Isabella.'

'Isabella's the boss?'

'Isabella's just the name. The woman who runs it is Valentina. Val. In her sixties but was probably a looker back in the day.'

'I don't suppose you've got a number?'

'You suppose right. '

'You're going to have to help me here, Perry.'

'Everyone knows it in Fuengirola,' said Perry. 'It's up from the west end of the main beach. Ask any local guy, he'll know it.'

Nightingale ended the call and put his phone away. 'We need to visit a whorehouse,' he said to Jenny.

'There's that "we" again,' said Jenny. 'It's eleven o'clock at night, I haven't eaten anything since lunch and I'm tired. So the last thing I need to do right now is to visit a whorehouse. I need food and I need a good night's sleep. And even then, I'm not going anywhere near a whorehouse.'

Nightingale looked at his watch. 'Okay, eat and sleep and I'll pay the place a visit tomorrow.'

'I hope it's case-related.'

Nightingale opened his mouth to reply but then saw from the glint in her eyes that she was joking and he just smiled.

* * *

They arrived in Marbella just before midnight. Jenny's parents owned a pretty whitewashed townhouse on three floors in the old part of the town. Parking was difficult but after ten minutes of driving she managed to squeeze the Seat in between a convertible Rolls Royce and a gleaming red Ferrari. They walked to the house and Jenny let them in. There was a kitchen on the first floor with a small sitting room lined with bookshelves. 'Daddy's den,' she said. 'Let me just check the bedrooms. Mummy said the cleaner was in yesterday but I'll check that the bedding's been changed.'

She disappeared upstairs. Nightingale dropped down onto a sofa and surveyed the books. There were a lot of thrillers and spy stories and about half were Spanish editions. The classics were there too, with what looked like complete sets of Shakespeare and Dickens. Jenny appeared in the doorway. 'Bedrooms are fine,' she said. 'Yours is the one on the right. Are you hungry?'

'Sure, but it's late.'

She laughed. 'This is Marbella,' she said. 'It doesn't really get going until the early hours.'

She took him downstairs and out onto the street. Jenny was right, most of the restaurants and bars were still open, with well-dressed middle-aged couples sitting outside drinking wine and nibbling tapas. There were half a dozen restaurants in the street and all were busy.

Jenny took Nightingale to a small restaurant where she was greeted like a long-lost daughter by a balding man in his sixties who hugged her tightly and kissed her on the cheeks. He spoke to her in rapid Spanish and she answered and nodded at Nightingale. Then they both laughed. He looked at them in confusion. He'd never been good at languages. 'What?' he said.

'I was just telling Juan that you're my boss and he said that he thought you worked for me.'

'Well tell him that it feels that way to me sometimes,' said Nightingale.

Juan held out his hand. 'You can tell me yourself,' he said, in heavily accented English.

Nightingale shook. 'Sorry,' he said. 'And sorry I don't speak Spanish.'

Juan took them over to a table. 'Paella?' he asked Jenny.

'You read my mind, Juan,' she said. 'And that Rioja we love.'

'Of course,' said Juan, and he hurried away.

'How many languages do you speak?' asked Nightingale.

'Did you even look at my CV?' she said.

'Your Spanish is fluent, is it?'

Jenny shrugged. 'It depends on what the subject is,' she said. 'General chit-chat and conversation is fine, I can understand the TV news and read a newspaper, but I probably couldn't chat about string theory and black holes.'

Nightingale laughed. 'That applies to me and English, just about.'

Carlos returned with a bottle of Rioja and two glasses. He opened the bottle and poured it for them, then disappeared into the kitchen.

Nightingale sipped the wine and nodded his approval. 'I'm not a big wine drinker, but this is good.'

'You've never been to Spain before?'

Nightingale shook his head. 'I've never been a fan of the sun.'

'It is a shit newspaper.'

Nightingale laughed. 'I mean hot weather. My parents were the same, we never went abroad.'

'My parents took me everywhere,' said Jenny. 'School holidays were always spent travelling. They still do, but these days it tends to be cruises. Though they still manage to get out here at least once a month during the summer.'

They had worked their way through two-thirds of the bottle by the time Carlos brought over a huge plate of paella packed with chicken, chorizo, mussels and prawns and laid it theatrically between them. Jenny clapped her hands together in delight and thanked him in Spanish before heaping it onto Nightingale's plate and then her own.

'His food is the best in Andalusia,' she said. 'My parents eat here all the time. His sons do most of the cooking these days but he did this for us.'

Nightingale nodded as he chewed on a mouthful of succulent prawn and perfectly-cooked rice.

'So what's your plan?' Jenny asked him.

'I need to talk to a hooker. Probably best to do it sooner rather than later.'

Jenny's fork stopped on the way to her mouth. 'Excuse me?'

'I was thinking I might take a cab back to Fuengirola. I'm guessing I'll have more luck at night than the daytime.'

'That's probably why they call them ladies of the night,' said Jenny.

'I'll cab it there and back. I worry that if we leave it until tomorrow they'll just tell us to come back in the evening and we'll have lost a day.'

'Your call,' said Jenny. 'I'll be tucked up in bed anyway. Just be careful, Jack.'

He smiled brightly. 'I always am.'

Nightingale paid the bill with his credit card, Carlos hugged Jenny again and shook hands with Nightingale, then he walked her to the house. She unlocked the door and then handed him the key. 'Let yourself in,' she said.

'Sweet dreams.'

She disappeared inside and closed the door. Nightingale walked down a sloping street to the main road where there were three taxis lined up. The drivers were standing together smoking cigarettes and they looked over as he approached.

'Taxi?" said one, a tall man with jet black hair wearing a Real Madrid football shirt.

'I need to go to Fuengirola,' he said. 'Do you know a place called Club Isabella?'

The man laughed. 'If you want a girl, there are places in Marbella. Very pretty girls. Russians, Africans, Vietnamese. Whatever you want.' He said something to his companions in Spanish and they all laughed.

'Nah, it has to be Club Isabella. Can you take me?'

The man shrugged. 'Sure, of course. What is it you English say? The customer is always right? Even when he is wrong.'

He waved for Nightingale to get into the taxi. 'You okay if I smoke?' asked the driver as he got into the front seat and started the engine. He held up his cigarette.

'Sure,' said Nightingale. He took out his pack of Marlboro and his lighter. 'So long as you don't mind if I join you.'

Nightingale lit up as the taxi headed towards Fuengirola. The driver was fanatical about football and talked non-stop about the game as he drove, constantly checking in his mirror that he had Nightingale's attention and jabbing at his reflection with his cigarette.

Club Isabella was a yellow villa surrounded by a high stone wall, on a hillside overlooking the sea. There was no sign on the wall, just an intercom. The taxi pulled up outside. 'You want me to wait?' asked the driver.

'I don't know how long I'll be,' said Nightingale.

The driver gave him a business card. 'Call me if you want me to take you back to Marbella.'

Nightingale took the card, paid the fare and climbed out. As the taxi drove off down the hill, he pressed the button on the intercom. There was a CCTV camera looking down at him from the top of the wall and he obviously passed muster because the lock clicked and the gates swung open.

There was a short driveway leading to the house with orange trees draped with small lights. As he got closer to the house he heard music inside. There was another CCTV over the door. It opened just as he was reaching out to knock. A pretty girl with long dark hair wearing a red and gold Chinese-style cheongsam dress smiled at him. Nightingale was expecting to be quizzed about who he was but she just opened the door wide and beckoned for him to go inside. He wondered if it was because he looked like the sort of man who would frequent a brothel, or if they just didn't care and everyone was welcome.

She closed the door. They were in a marbled hall with a staircase that curved up to the upper floor. A man and woman were kissing on the stairs and through an open doorway to his left he could see a man sitting on a sofa with a blonde girl either side. He was kissing one of the girls while the other was watching and rubbing his thigh. Hip hop was playing on a stereo system and he heard the pop of a bottle of champagne opening. 'Please,' said the girl, gesturing at the door.

Nightingale walked in. To his left was a bar with a line of chrome and leather stools, and there was a pool table off to the right. There were half a dozen black and white sofas, two of them occupied. There were floor-to-ceiling sliding windows that opened onto a patio on which there was a cluster of small tables. Several were occupied by casually-dressed men drinking cocktails. Beyond was a large flood-lit pool.

The girl in the cheongsam waved at the bar. 'Would you like to sit here and I will introduce you to our girls,' she said.

'Is there a girl working here called Candy? Or Sandy? Mandy maybe?'

The girl frowned.

'She's blonde, big breasts.'

The girl giggled. 'Most of the blonde girls here have big breasts,' she said.

Nightingale looked around. She was right. The two did seem to go together. 'I guess so,' he said. 'Is Valentina here?'

She frowned. 'You know Val?'

'I know a friend of hers. Can you tell her I'd like to say hello.'

'Is there something wrong?'

Nightingale patted her on the arm. 'I was just asked to say hello to her, that's all. Tell you what, darling, bring Val over and I'll buy you a bottle of champagne.'

'A bottle?'

'Cork and all. Okay?'

She nodded, then turned and walked back across the room towards the pool table. Nightingale went over to sit at the bar. The girl went by the pool table and knocked on a door.

'What can I get you?' asked the bartender, an Asian girl wearing a black halter top and white shorts that looked as if they had been sprayed on.

'Corona?'

'Lime or lemon?'

Nightingale grinned. 'Lime.'

'Bottle or glass?'

'Bottle, of course.'

'A purist.'

She had an Australian accent, Nightingale realised. 'I wouldn't have it any other way,' he said.

She laughed as she popped the top off a bottle of Corona, stuck a slice of lime into the neck, and handed it to him. As he pushed the lime further into the bottle, the girl in the cheongsam opened the door and went inside.

Nightingale sipped his Corona. A black girl with huge, pendulous breasts walked by and flashed him a beaming smile. She stopped and reached out to touch his shoulder but he shook his head. 'I'm spoken for, baby,' he said.

Her smile widened. 'One guy, two girls, fantasy time,' she said in a heavy African accent.

'You'd kill me, baby,' said Nightingale.

'My name's Sheba if you change your mind.'

Nightingale raised his bottle. 'You're top of my list.'

Her eyes sparkled. 'That's good to hear because I love to be on top,' she said.

The door beyond the pool table opened and the blonde reappeared with a small woman with jet black hair cut short, wearing a blue Japanese kimono with herons dotted over it. Sheba saw him looking over at the door and she moved away, still smiling.

The woman walked towards him, followed by the girl in the cheongsam. From a distance the woman in the kimono looked quite young but as she got closer he realised she was in her sixties, but still very attractive with high cheekbones and unlined skin. Whether that was the result of good genes or a skilled surgeon, Nightingale had no way of knowing, but either way she looked bloody good. She smiled as if she realised what he was thinking, and held out her hand. He took it and kissed it. The skin was liver-spotted and wrinkled, her nails painted a blood red. Her face was still youthful but her hands betrayed her real age. 'Val?'

She nodded. 'And you are?'

'Jack. I'm a friend of Mo Money. Well, a friend of a friend.'

'How is he? I haven't seen him for a few days.'

Nightingale ignored the question. 'Can I buy you a bottle of champagne?'

She held his look. Her eyes were dark brown and there was an amused twinkle that suggested she found him amusing. Maybe she looked at all her customers that way, but it was very effective, as if he had become the centre of her world. 'And a bottle for Sarah, you said?' gesturing at the girl in the cheongsam.

Nightingale found himself frowning in her eyes and realised he was nodding along with her. 'Yes, sure, of course.'

Val snapped her fingers and spoke to the bartender in Spanish. She went over to a fridge and took two bottles of Moet et Chandon. Nightingale remembered that he hadn't changed any money, he only had sterling in his wallet. And almost certainly not enough cash to buy two bottles of expensive French champagne.

'Val, I can use my credit card, can't I?'

'Of course,' she said, and spoke to the bartender again. She picked up a credit card reader and Nightingale handed over his company American Express card. The bartender slotted it into the reader, Nightingale tapped in his four-digit pin number and tried not to think about what Jenny would see when the bill arrived.

The bartender gave Nightingale his card and popped the corks on the two bottles. Val slid onto the stool to Nightingale's right while Sarah pressed herself against him and slid her hand between his thighs.

When the bartender had filled two glasses, Val took hers and held it up. 'To new friendships,' she said, once again fixing him with her hypnotic eyes.

'I'll drink to that,' said Nightingale and clinked his bottle against her glass before drinking.

'So Sarah tells me you are looking for a particular girl,' said Val.

Nightingale nodded. 'Mo Money recommended her, but I can't remember if he said Mandy or Candy or Sandy. Beautiful girl, blonde and with....'

'Large breasts?'

'I was going to say long legs, but yes...'

'Mandy,' said Val. 'You would like to see her?'

'If possible, yes. Mo Money said she is...' Nightingale shrugged and feigned embarrassment.

'Accomplished?'

'Yes, exactly. Accomplished.'

Val looked at her watch, a diamond-encrusted Rolex. She will be available in forty-five minutes,' she said. 'Why not let Sarah take care of you until then.' She patted Nightingale on the cheek, then gently scraped the skin with her nails. 'And don't worry, Jack, you can pay for the companionship with your card.'

She slid off the stool and walked slowly back to the door, her hips swinging hypnotically. As she reached for the door handle she turned to look over her shoulder and she smiled when she saw that Nightingale was watching her. She gave him a small wave, blew him a kiss, and then she was gone.

Nightingale realised that Sarah's hand was still between his legs.

The bartender placed two ice-filled buckets onto the bar and put a bottle of Moet and Chandon in each. He knew it would be churlish to point out that Val was no longer with them so he just smiled and thanked her.

Sarah poured champagne and the two clinked glasses. He sipped the champagne and couldn't help but grimace. He had never been a fan of white wine, especially white wine with bubbles in it.

'You don't like it?' asked Sarah.

'I'm not really a champagne type of guy,' said Nightingale. 'I prefer Corona. He put down the glass and picked up the bottle.

'That's okay,' she said. 'All the more for me.' She drained her glass and refilled it. 'So what is so special about this Mandy?' she asked, rubbing her hand up and down his thigh.

'She was recommended,' said Nightingale.

'A lot of my clients recommend me,' she said.

Nightingale laughed. 'I'm sure they do.'

'What about two girls?' she asked. 'I've worked with Mandy before.'

'Really? What is she like?'

'Blonde hair and....' She mimed holding her breasts.

Nightingale laughed. 'No, I mean what sort of person is she?'

Sarah shrugged. 'Who knows what anyone here is really like,' she said. 'No one shows their real self here. It's all a fantasy.'

'In what way?'

She laughed. 'I shouldn't say. It'll destroy the fantasy.'

'Go on. I'm interested. Really.'

She leaned towards him so that her lips were just inches from his cheek. 'Any man who comes here believes he's fitter and younger and more handsome than he is outside. Here he's a movie star, a king, whatever he wants to be. The girls will adore him and hang on his every word.' He could feel her warm soft breath on his cheek.

'But it's an act?'

'Of course it's an act,' she said. 'This is our job, to make them feel good, to make them believe that they are the best lovers in the world, even when they are fat and ugly and their breath stinks.'

Nightingale grinned. 'I hope you don't mean me.'

She shrugged and sat back. 'It doesn't matter who you are or what you look like, providing you pay you'll be treated like a king. We all wear masks here. So no, I can't tell you what sort of person Mandy is. She has blonde hair and large breasts and she could twist men around her little finger, that's all I know.'

'It sounds as if you don't enjoy the job.'

She shrugged again. 'It's better than working in a factory or tele-sales. I earn thirty thousand Euros in a good month.'

'Bloody hell,' said Nightingale. 'Can I leave my CV?'

She laughed and patted him on the leg. 'Darling, I don't think anyone would ever pay you for sex.'

'Yeah, I think you're right,' said Nightingale. He took a long pull on his Corona and wiped his mouth with the back of his hand. 'I'm told I'm a selfish lover.'

'Most men are,' she said. 'That's why places like this are so busy. It's all about satisfying the customer, making sure that his needs are met.'

Sarah was surprisingly good company, and they spent the next half hour chatting and putting the world to rights. Most of the time she had her hand on his thigh and occasionally she would stroke his cheek. He really couldn't tell if she honestly liked him or if it was all an act, but he suspected the latter. She drank her bottle of champagne and was on her third glass from the second bottle when she nodded over at a busty blonde girl in a leopard-print dress who was heading in their direction. 'Mandy,' she said.

Mandy was already smiling when she reached Nightingale. 'Val says you've heard good things about me,' she said.

She offered him her hand and he kissed it. 'Mo Money speaks very highly of you,' he said.

'And I of him,' she laughed. 'He's a very generous man.' She looked around. 'He isn't with you?'

'I'm flying solo,' he said.

'Val said you were buying me champagne?'

'Of course.' The bartender was already taking a bottle from the fridge. She deftly popped the cork, poured a glass which she handed to Mandy, then put the bottle in an ice bucket.

Mandy raised her glass and Nightingale clinked his bottle against it. 'You don't like champagne?' she asked.

'The bubbles get up my nose.'

'I love the bubbles,' said Mandy, and drank half her glass. 'So, you want to take me upstairs? Why not bring Sarah, too. We could make your world spin.'

'I bet you could,' said Nightingale. Sarah's hand had moved to his groin and he shifted on his stool as he felt himself grow hard. 'But I'm not here to have my world spun. Or span.'

Mandy frowned. 'No? So what do you want... what was your name again?'

'Jack,' he said.

'So what is it you want, Jack?'

'This is going to sound crazy, but Mo Money said you had an App that allows you to talk to the dead. Like a Ouija board. But on an iPad.'

'He told you about that, did he?'

'He said it was quite something. I'll be honest, I've tried Ouija boards but I've never had any luck. Someone always pushes, right?'

'Why are you so interested in talking to spirits?' asked Mandy.

'Not just any spirit,' said Nightingale. 'My dad. He passed away six months ago. He was a builder and a lot of his work was cash. When he died my mum discovered that he had almost no money in the bank. We think he stashed it away, maybe in a safety deposit box.'

'So you want to talk to your dad and find out where the money is?'

'Do you think I'm crazy?'

Mandy sipped her champagne, then shook her head. 'It makes perfect sense, Jack.'

'Do you think the App will work?'

'We can try. But I don't have it here. It's in my flat.'

'Can we go and get it?'

She smiled sweetly. 'We can, but you'll have to buy me out from the house.'

'How much is that?'

'A thousand Euros. That's for all night.'

'Can I use my credit card?'

'Absolutely.' She refilled her glass. 'Are you sure you don't want to buy Sarah out, too. I have a mirror over my bed and we will blow your mind.'

Sarah's hand was back rubbing Nightingale's groin.

'Just the App,' said Nightingale.

Sarah pouted, drained her glass and slipped off her stool. 'I'll leave you two alone,' she said.

'Sorry,' said Nightingale.

She pouted again and walked away.

'You don't know what you're missing,' said Mandy. She held out her hand. Nightingale frowned in confusion and she laughed. 'Your card,' she said.

Nightingale gave her his credit card. The bartender was already there with the card reader and he tapped in his four-digit code again. He'd spent close to fifteen hundred Euros in less than an hour and he knew that Jenny wasn't going to be happy.

The bartender gave his card back and Nightingale got off his stool. 'How do we get to your place?' he asked.

'My car's outside,' said Mandy, linking her arm through his.

'But you've been drinking.'

She laughed. 'Two glasses,' she said.

She took him out into the hallway. Sarah was sitting on a chair looking at her smartphone. She grinned up at Nightingale. 'Have a great time,' she said. 'If you change your mind about a threesome, Mandy has my number.'

Mandy opened the front door and they walked around to the rear of the house where there was a parking area with a dozen or so cars. Mandy's was a two-seater BMW convertible that looked brand new. 'Nice,' said Nightingale. 'Business must be good.'

She laughed. 'Business is always good for me,' she said.

She eased herself into the driving seat. Nightingale sat next to her. It was a nice car, but he preferred his own MGB. It had character and despite its foibles it was fun to drive. Sitting in the BMW he felt as if he was in the cockpit of a fighter plane that would leave the ground at any moment and begin strafing civilians.

Mandy had a remote control unit that opened the gates and she drove down the hill towards the sea. Her apartment was in a modern block overlooking the beach, with parking underneath.

She took him over to the lifts. 'Do you mind if I take the stairs?' he asked.

'I'm on the twelfth floor,' she said.

'I don't like lifts.'

'Scared of heights?'

He shook his head. 'No, it's not that. I'm fine with heights. It's lifts I don't like.'

'Seriously? You want to climb twelve flights of stairs?'

'I'm good,' he said. 'I do it all the time.'

The lift arrived. The doors opened. 'I'll see you up there,' she said. She got in, the mirrored sides reflecting her tanned flesh and blonde hair from all angles.

As the door closed, Nightingale headed for the emergency exits and went up the concrete stairs, initially two at a time but slowing once he passed the halfway mark. He was panting when he finally reached the twelfth floor. He pushed open a fire door and stepped into a corridor with purple carpet and dimmed lighting. Mandy was waiting. She grinned when she saw how tired he was. 'Glad you made it,' she said. She walked ahead of him to her apartment, her backside twitching from side to side, and he was pretty sure that she knew he was watching her by the way she kept flicking her hair.

She unlocked the door and he followed her inside. Her apartment was large and open plan, with a small kitchen area to the left and ahead of them floor-to-ceiling windows that opened on to a large balcony overlooking the sea. 'Would you like a drink?' she asked.

'I don't suppose you have a Corona?'

'I've got San Miguel, which I'm told is just as good.'

'That'll be fine,' he said. She slid open the window and waved for him to go out on the balcony. He stepped out into the warm evening air. Out at sea were the dark shapes of boats dotted with navigation lights, and he could hear the slap of waves beating against the beach.

'Here you are,' she said and he turned to see her holding out a bottle of beer. He took it and thanked her. She was holding a glass of white wine. 'Cheers,' she said, and clinked her glass against his bottle. 'Let me get the iPad,' she said. 'And we can get started.' She ran her hand down his arm, then went back into the flat. Nightingale sipped his beer.

'Come here, Jack,' she said. He went inside. She was sitting on the sofa, holding an iPad. Her dress had been unbuttoned to reveal her impressive cleavage and had ridden up her legs so that he caught a glimpse of her underwear. She patted the sofa.

He sat next to her. She was holding an iPad and she gave it to him. The screen was filled with a picture of a traditional Ouija board, with all the letters of the alphabet and the words YES and NO.

'You just tap on the letters and what you write will appear in that box in the bottom,' she said. 'When there is a reply, it comes in the box.'

'So what do I do?' asked Nightingale.

'Same as if you were using a Ouija board,' she said. 'Just ask if there's anyone there.'

Nightingale tapped out 'IS ANYONE THERE?'

After a few seconds the words 'KNOCK KNOCK' appeared, letter by letter.

'Knock knock?' he said.

She laughed. 'It's playing with you,' she said. 'That's a good sign.'

'Who's playing with me?'

'Whatever spirit you've connected to.'

'But I want to talk to my dad.'

'It doesn't work like that. The spirits line up to contact the living. You have to talk to whoever comes through and ask them to reach out to the person you want to talk to.'

'My dad?'

'Exactly.'

The words KNOCK KNOCK appeared again.

'You have to ask it who's there?' said Mandy.

'Why?'

She frowned. 'What do you mean? That's the game. The knock knock game. Knock knock. Who's there?'

There was an intense look in her eyes now, almost manic, and her lips were curled back into a savage snarl. He held out the iPad. 'Show me,' he said.

'You have to do it,' she said.

'Why? Why can't you do it?'

'Because you're the one who wants to contact your dad. What's wrong, Jack? Scared?'

'Scared of what?'

'Exactly. Come on, Jack. Don't be a scaredy cat.' She pushed the iPad back towards him. 'Come on,' she said. Her breath smelled foul, as if something had crawled into her mouth and died. The whites of her eyes had gone yellow and her nails looked longer and were curled into talons. 'Just ask who's there?'

Nightingale forced a smile. He knew that without a shadow of a doubt that if he did interact with whatever was trying to communicate with him, it would end badly. And he was equally certain that Mandy knew that, too. He put the iPad down on the coffee table and picked up his beer. 'Dutch courage,' he said, and took a sip.

'There's nothing to be scared of, Jack,' she said, running her hand along his thigh. 'Just ask who's there. Then when you've contacted your father I'll take you into the bedroom and fuck you like you've never been fucked before. Free of charge.'

'Why would you do that?' asked Nightingale.

'Because I like you, Jack.' She ran her hand up his thigh. The skin was gnarled now, almost scaled. 'Come on, just ask who's there.'

Nightingale's mind raced as he took another sip of his beer.

Mandy's nails dug into his leg. 'Just do it, Jack. Come on. Do it.'

'Maybe let me finish my beer,' he said.

'Do you want to do this or not, Jack?' she said. 'I hope you're not wasting my time.'

'Maybe I should use the bathroom first,' he said. He held up his bottle. 'The beer is going right through me.'

She pointed to a corridor. 'Down there,' she said. 'First door on the right.'

He stood up, pretending to be drunker than he was, and made his way unsteadily down the corridor to the bathroom. He closed the door behind him, splashed water on his face and then stared at his reflection in the mirror. He was in deep trouble, and was running out of options. Mandy clearly knew that there was something evil about the App, and the physical changes she had undergone suggested that she was either in some way possessed, or was herself something inhuman. Nightingale wanted to get the hell out of the flat and back to England but if he did that Perry Smith would have to spend the rest of his life inside his protective circle. He needed to get the iPad away from Mandy and then find someway of dealing with it and with whatever was coming through the App. And if that proved to be the demon called Avanas then he was going to have a real fight on his hands. He splashed more water on his face, then flushed the toilet. He took a deep breath, then opened the door and walked back to the sofa. He frowned when he saw that Mandy was no longer on the sofa. The iPad was, still showing the Ouija board on the screen. He looked to his right, towards the balcony, wondering if she had stepped outside. He walked towards the balcony, catching sight of his reflection. 'Mandy?' he called.

He saw a blur in the window, the reflection of something moving behind him. He whirled around and saw Mandy coming at him with a large knife. He managed to get his arm up to block the blow and the knife missed his neck by inches. She swung again and he stepped back. The knife brushed his sleeve and he tried to grab her arm but she was too quick for him. He backed away. Her eyes were completely red now and she was snarling like an animal, her nostrils flaring as she breathed. 'Calm down,' was all he could think of saying as he kept his hands up and backed away from her.

She lashed out with the knife again and he ducked to the side. During his years as a police negotiator one thing he had learned was that sometimes there was nothing you could say to calm somebody down, nothing less than a Taser or a bullet would stop them. Unfortunately he had neither and he was running out of options.

He kept backing away, waiting for her next attack. The open window was behind him and he felt the warm night breeze blowing against his back. He looked around for something, anything, to use as a weapon. There was a brass lamp on a table against the wall but as he reached for it she lunged with the knife, catching him on the back of the hand and drawing blood. She laughed when she saw the damage she'd done. Nightingale licked the back of his hand and tasted blood. He was on the balcony now and could hear a motorcycle drive by, far below.

Mandy was breathing heavily, her neck bent forward at an unnatural angle, the knife gripped in a hand that had become like a deformed claw. Her breasts had swung free from her dress and she was snarling in triumph, knowing that there was nowhere for him to go. She raised the knife above her head and charged towards him. Nightingale stood his ground, then at the last second twisted to the side and stuck out his leg, catching her just below the knees. She pitched forward and her momentum took her over the balcony rail. She fell without a sound and a couple of seconds later he heard a dull thud as she hit the road followed by horns blaring and a woman screaming.

Nightingale backed away from the balcony into the room. He saw the knife and realised Mandy had dropped it before she had fallen. He picked it up and took it through to the kitchen area and wiped it clean with a dishcloth before putting it into a knife block. He looked around the room and spotted his glass. He washed it and put it into one of the cupboards. When he was satisfied that there was no evidence of him ever having been in the flat, he picked up the iPad and let himself out, wiping the door handle clean as he left.

The traffic had stopped in the road and half a dozen people were standing around the body, which had hit the pavement and then rolled into the gutter. No one paid Nightingale any attention as he slipped out of the building and headed along the seafront. He took out his phone and called Jenny, who answered sleepily. 'What time is it?' she asked.

'It's either very late or very early, depending on whether you're a half-full or half-empty sort of girl.'

'Don't mess around, Jack, what do you want?'

'I've got a bit of a problem,' said Nightingale. He explained about meeting Mandy and going back to her apartment, how she'd attacked him and fallen off the balcony.'

'Bloody hell, Jack, did you push her?' asked Jenny, now fully awake.

'Of course not. She charged at me with a knife and fell over the railing.'

'And you're sure she's dead.'

'It was a long way down, Jenny. I'm sure. On the plus side, I've got the iPad. Look, I don't think anyone saw me go into her flat or leave and there's nothing in the flat to show I was there. She'd been drinking so if I'm lucky they'll just assume she was drunk and took a flyer. The one downside is that the place she works will know she left with me. They don't know my name but they could give a description to the police.'

'The Spanish cops aren't the most efficient,' said Jenny.

'I know that, but I thought better safe than sorry. Look, Gibraltar's only an hour and a half away. I'm going to catch a cab there and book into a hotel, then take the first flight out in the morning. I figure that even if the cops do start looking for me, I'll be well gone.'

'So you want me to meet you in Gibraltar?'

'No need,' he said. 'I'll go back on my own, you fly out of Malaga as and when. Enjoy yourself. Have a bit of a holiday. You deserve it.'

'What are you up to, Jack?'

'Nothing.'

'I can hear it in your voice. You're up to something.'

'Okay, yes, I'm going to need help. And there's only one person I can turn to.'

'Proserpine?'

'She's the only one who can fix this.'

'Be careful, Jack.'

'I always am.'

* * *

Nightingale stood looking down at the pentagram, checking that everything was as it should be. The main circle was about twelve feet in diameter, not that the size mattered. He was in the master bedroom in Gosling Manor, where his father – his genetic father – had blown his own head off with a shotgun. Ainsley Gosling was a Satanist who had offered up Nightingale's soul in exchange for wealth and power, only to commit suicide when he tried and failed to back out of the deal. Nightingale had managed to get his soul back, but he knew that every time he summoned a demon he risked losing it again. He'd caught the first flight out of Gibraltar and taken a taxi from the airport straight to the house.

The room was now bare and the carpet had long ago been stripped out to reveal the bare floorboards. He had stripped a birch twig from a tree in the garden and he had used it to outline the circle. Then he had drawn the pentangle – the five pointed star – within the circle, with two points at the top and one at the bottom. Then he had drawn a triangle enclosing the circle. The demon, once summoned, was forced to stay in the apex of the triangle.

After he had used the birch twig, he had sprinkled consecrated salt water around the perimeter of the circle, then he had written MI and CH and AEL at the three points of the triangle. The final stage had been to place candles at the points of the pentangle and bowls of herbs in the centre, along with his cigarette lighter. He nodded to himself. Everything was as it should be.

He went into the bathroom and took off all his clothes. He had already filled the bathtub. He climbed in, lay back, and slid under the water. He stayed under for as long as he could, then scrubbed himself with a small plastic brush and a brand new bar of Johnson's Baby Soap. He washed and rinsed his hair twice, then got out and towelled himself dry before changing into clean clothes – jeans and a yellow polo shirt.

He went back into the bedroom, picked up his lighter and lit the five candles. Once in the centre of the pentagram he went over the perimeter of the circle again with the birch branch, and again with consecrated sea salt.

He used the lighter to ignite a mixture of wood chips, herbs and spices in a lead bowl. The contents hissed as they burned, filling the room with acrid smoke.

Nightingale knew the Latin words by heart, and he recited them from memory, slowly and clearly, and above all, confidently. Demons respected strength and preyed on weakness.

The smoke got thicker and his eyes began to water, and as he continued the incantation the smoke began to whirl around, forming a circle above the pentagram. The final words – 'Bagahi Laca Bacabe' – he shouted at the top of his voice.

The smoke was so thick now that he could only see a few feet in front of him, and it was whirling around so quickly that he felt dizzy. He took a deep breath and focussed on not losing his footing. Then there was a dazzling flash of light and a crack as if a tree had split in half and space seemed to fold in on itself and the smoke vanished. Proserpine was standing in the apex of the triangle, a look of disdain on her face. She appeared as a young girl in her early twenties, pale skinned and with jet black hair and eyes like circles of polished coal. Her hair had been pulled up into a jagged Mohican and hanging from each ear were small black inverted crucifixes. She had a white t-shirt with a black pentagram design, black leather jeans and black high heels, and sitting obediently next to her on a chain leash was a black and white collie dog.

'You had better not be using me as your phone-a-friend again, Nightingale,' she said. 'You know how I hate that.'

'I'm happy to see you too, Proserpine,' he said. 'It's been a while.'

'I've told you before, we don't have the same perception of time,' she said. 'Why am I here? Why have you summoned me?'

'You know of a demon by the name of Avanas?'

'Of course.'

'Avanas is a she, right? Also uses the name Amy?'

'He, she, it means nothing.'

'I know, but "it" also sounds so rude, don't you think?'

'You are rambling, Nightingale. What about Avanas?'

'Avanas has being causing havoc,' said Nightingale. 'She's been killing people, ripping them apart.'

Proserpine shook her head. 'Impossible,' she said. 'Avanas is in Hell.'

'Torturing souls?'

'Fulfilling her obligations.'

'Well, she has been using an App to connect to victims in the real world. She was using a Spanish hooker to pull in victims, getting them to play on the App and then killing them.'

'An App?'

'A program on an iPad.'

'I know what an App is, Nightingale. What does it do?'

'It mimics an Ouija board. You are supposed to be able to talk to spirits, but the only thing that comes through is Amy. Who I'm assuming is Avanas. She's killed four people that I know about. A friend of mine is in a protective circle and so far it's held. I wanted to see if you know what Avanas was up to, and if you approve. I know the Devil likes the world to think that he doesn't exist. Avanas is upsetting that apple cart. No pun intended.'

Proserpine frowned. 'What pun?'

'Apple. It's an iPad.'

'That's not a pun, Nightingale.' She glared at him and the dog growled softly. 'And you are telling me this because?'

'Because I assumed that you'd want to stop Avanas doing what she's doing. And I can help you.'

'Help me, how?'

'I've got the iPad here. I can play with the App and when Avanas comes to do what she does, you can stop her.'

'I can't do anything while I am trapped within the pentagram,' she said. 'You know as well as I do that I have to stay within the triangle.'

'I would release you.'

She grinned. 'That is very trusting of you, Nightingale. You realise that releasing me means that I can enter the pentagram with impunity?'

'You don't want to hurt me, Proserpine,' he said.

'What makes you think that?'

'Because I amuse you.' He shrugged. 'But this isn't about me. Avanas is breaking the rules and you can set her straight.'

The dog growled and Proserpine rubbed it behind the ear. 'It's okay baby. He was a police negotiator when he had a job. It's what he does. He negotiates.' The dog licked her hand. Proserpine nodded at Nightingale. 'Okay. It's a deal.'

'We don't have to sign anything?'

She laughed and the whole room shook. Dust cascaded down from the ceiling. 'In blood, you mean?' She laughed again and the floorboards rattled. 'No, Nightingale. My word is my bond.'

Nightingale picked up the iPad and opened the Ouija board App. He took a deep breath and said the words that would release Proserpine from the triangle. As he said the final words – 'tu dimisit in partes triangulo oppositas' – Proserpine smiled and stepped out of the pentagram. She smiled at him like a cat studying a mouse and for a moment he wondered if he had made the biggest mistake of his life, but then her smile widened and she waved at the iPad. 'Go ahead,' she said. 'Don't keep a girl waiting.'

Nightingale tapped out 'IS ANYONE THERE?'

Nothing happened for several seconds, then slowly, letter by letter, 'KNOCK KNOCK' appeared.

Nightingale tapped in 'WHO IS THERE?'

There was a longer pause. Then three letters appeared. 'AMY'.

'AMY WHO?' tapped in Nightingale.

Letter by letter the reply came back. 'AMY GONNA KILL YOU'.

Nightingale held up the iPad so that Proserpine could see what was written on the screen. Proserpine smiled and shook her head. 'It's a bit juvenile, isn't it?'

'It might be, but the end result isn't childish at all,' said Nightingale. He typed in 'YOU CAN TRY,' he wrote. 'I AM READY AND WAITING'.

There was a pause and then letters started appearing. 'HA HA HA HA HA.' Then the room began to shake and the written laughter became a sound, a deep throbbing roar that made Nightingale's stomach lurch. The floor seemed to shift under Nightingale's feet and he had trouble keeping his balance. He staggered to the edge of the pentagram and held out the iPad for Proserpine. He knew he was risking everything because the pentagram was no longer a barrier, he was totally at her mercy. She had given her word that she wouldn't harm him, but he had no way of knowing whether the word of a princess of Hell meant anything. She reached out a slim white hand, the nails painted black and pointed, and took it from him.

The room tilted and Nightingale staggered. One of the candles fell over and went out. Nightingale picked it up and tried to relight it but there was now a strong foul-smelling wind blowing through the room and the lighter clicked without producing a flame.

There was an ear-splitting crack as one of the window panes shattered into a hundred shards that tinkled onto the wooden floor like wind chimes.

There was a second crack, louder even than the first, and then something rose up from the floor, something covered in scales with a pointed jaw and huge yellow eyes. It roared and the stench from its maw made Nightingale wretch. It reached out with taloned claws and roared again. It took two steps forward on huge scaled legs, its feet slapping against the wood. It reached the edge of the pentagram, then stopped. Nightingale backed away as far as he could without leaving the protective circle. He had no way of knowing whether it would hold Avanas now that he had released Proserpine.

The demon stepped forward so that its clawed feet were up against the chalk mark, then it roared and stepped over the circle.

'Avanas!' shouted Proserpine, and the demon stopped in its tracks. It turned and saw Proserpine. Proserpine raised the iPad in the air and it burst into flames. She tossed the burning plastic at the demon. It threw back its head and roared again, but this time the sound was different, more a roar of fear than of triumph. 'You should not be here, Avanas!' shouted Proserpine. She pointed at Avanas and snarled. 'You need to stay in your place.'

The demon moved towards Proserpine and lashed out, but Proserpine was too fast. She stepped to the side and did something with her hands that produced a blast of energy that hit the demon in the centre of its chest.

The dog moved, leaping towards the demon. As it leapt it changed, the cute collie dog became a huge black beast with three snarling heads. The dog, or what ever it had become, hit the demon hard sending it sprawling against the wall. The dog pounced, its three jaws snapping and biting. The demon shrieked and a green fluid trickled from its wounds.

'Princess, please, have mercy!' the demon screamed.

Proserpine clicked her fingers and the dog immediately backed away, its hackles up.

'You will return willingly?' asked Proserpine.

'Yes, mistress,' said the demon, cowering from the dog.

Proserpine waved her hand in the air. There was a blast of heat and a black circle framed with flames appeared behind the demon. 'I will see you in Hell,' said Proserpine.

The demon turned and fell into the circle, which immediately sealed up with a loud popping sound. The dog was back to being a dog again and it ambled over to Proserpine, its tongue lolling from the side of its mouth.

'So was that pun intended?' asked Nightingale, taking his pack of Marlboro from his pocket and lighting one.

'What pun?' said Proserpine.

'You said you'll see Avanas in Hell, and you actually will.'

Proserpine frowned. 'Exactly. So it was a statement of fact, not a play on words. You're not very good at puns, are you, Nightingale?'

'I've had a rough couple of days,' he said. He blew smoke up at the ceiling. 'So are we good?'

'We're good.'

'I did you a favour, right? I helped you return a demon to where it belongs, so you owe me now, right?'

'Don't push your luck, Nightingale,' she said. Time and space folded in on itself and she and the dog vanished.

Nightingale took another long pull on his cigarette. He sighed and took out his mobile phone and called Perry Smith. 'Perry, mate, you're good to go.'

'You're sure?' asked Perry.

'It's sorted.'

'Thanks, Birdman,' said Perry. 'I owe you one.'

'My bill will be in the post,' said Nightingale. 'Be lucky.' He ended the call and then sat down with his back to the wall, stretched out his legs, and sighed. It had been one hell of a day. No pun intended.

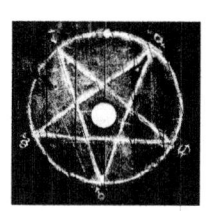

WATERY GRAVE

Nightingale kept nodding as Jenny talked, in between nibbling at his chocolate chip muffin and sipping his coffee. Jenny had brought the muffin and the coffee so he knew that she wanted something, and the least he could do was to sit and listen. He put on the face he used when a client came to tell them what was troubling them, the face that said he cared and wanted to help and would do whatever needed to be done to bring peace and harmony back into their lives.

'You are listening, aren't you?' she said, leaning towards him.

'Of course.'

'Because your eyes keep glazing over.'

'That's because I'm enjoying this muffin,' he said.

'So what have I told you so far?'

Nightingale sighed. 'Seriously?'

Jenny nodded. 'Seriously.'

Nightingale sipped his coffee. 'Your very good friend Laura Nicholson who you played lacrosse with at school lives in a multi million pound house in Sandbanks which she thinks is haunted because she keeps seeing wet footprints outside her house.'

Jenny tossed her blonde hair and looked disappointed that he had actually been listening.

'I didn't say haunted. She just said that the footprints keep appearing on the dock, heading towards her house.'

'So, she's complaining about wet footprints on her dock. And she lives by the sea.'

'Laura doesn't scare easily.'

'Why would anyone be scared of wet footprints, Jenny? Listen to yourself.'

Nightingale could see she was about to snap at him, but instead she took a deep breath and Nightingale was fairly sure she was counting to ten. 'She thinks it's her ex-husband and that he wants to hurt her.'

'What, it was an acrimonious divorce?'

Jenny sighed. 'Ex husband as in dead husband. Are you not listening to me?'

'I am, but I don't recall you telling me that her husband was dead.'

'Boating accident last year. They never found his body but his yacht caught fire while he was on board.'

'And why would his ghost come back to haunt her?'

'Well, that's why she wants to hire us. To find out.'

'We're not Ghostbusters, Jenny. That's who you call when you've got a ghost.'

'She's a friend, Jack.' She put up her hand as soon as he opened his mouth. 'She's a friend but she's happy to pay us. It's not Pro Bono and before you say anything, yes I know you hate U2.'

'Our normal rate?'

'Yes, our normal rate. And we can stay in her house during the investigation. And it's a lovely house, Jack. You know property down there now costs upwards of ten thousand pounds a square metre. When we get there you'll see why. It's idyllic.'

'And suppose it is a ghost and not just a trespasser with wet feet?'

'Then we exorcise it.'

'That's not what we do, and you know it. Exorcism is best left to the professionals.'

'Then we bring in experts. Look, how hard a job is it? We stay in a luxury house in a beautiful part of the world for a few days and we see whether or not she has something to worry about.' She flashed him a tight smile. 'Anyway, I've already said we'll be there this evening.'

'You what? How do you know I'm not busy.'

'Because I looked in your diary. You've got two divorce cases, neither of which are pressing.'

'Remind me again where Sandbanks is?'

'Near Poole, down in Dorset. It's a small peninsula crossing the mouth of Poole harbour. Fourth highest land value in the world.'

'How would you know that?'

'I think anyone who knows anything about house prices knows that,' said Jenny.

'As I'll never be able to afford to buy my own place, the price is pretty much irrelevant,' said Nightingale.

'Well you'll never get on the housing ladder if you keep turning down work.'

'I didn't say I was turning it down.'

'So you'll do it?'

Nightingale held up his hands in surrender. 'Yes, I'll do it. But how do we get there?'

'It's a two and a half hour drive, pretty much, less if the traffic's good. We can head down this afternoon before the rush hour.'

'I'll need a change of clothes.'

'I'll drive you to your flat and you can pick up what you need.'

'What about you?'

'My bag's in the car.'

'You knew I'd say yes.'

'I knew you'd do the right thing.'

He held up what was left of his muffin. 'Because of this?'

Jenny smiled. 'That, too.'

* * *

It took Jenny's Audi just a little over two hours to reach Sandbanks. It was clear that no matter how hard Nightingale worked, he'd never be able to afford a house there. Even if he won the lottery he might not have enough cash. 'So who lives in Sandbanks?' he asked as they drove past a house that seemed to be made entirely of glass.

'A fair few footballers and TV personalities, but mainly retired people. It's a bit of a long commute for anyone working in the City.'

'What about your friend?'

'Laura? Her family has money, they're big landowners in Hampshire, but her husband Miles was something in the City.'

Nightingale laughed. 'That always sounds so suspicious, don't you think? Something in the City. It's like saying I'm something in criminal investigations.'

'It's not suspicious, it's just hard to pin down what he did. He wasn't a banker, he didn't run an investment fund or a hedge fund, though he always said he could if he wanted to but that he couldn't be bothered. He was sort of an analyst, but not just an accountant who looked through reports and accounts.' She laughed. 'Like I said, it's difficult to say. He advised companies on their strategies, pointing out how their businesses were likely to change over the years and how they could best benefit from those changes. I guess you could say he was a consultant. And people paid him a lot for his advice. And I mean, a lot. I'll give you an example. Remember how seats used to recline on the budget airlines and it was always starting fights. It was his idea to have the seats fitted so that they couldn't recline. They were cheaper, it meant you could squeeze in an extra row of seats, and passengers stopped fighting. That one piece of advice saved the budget airlines millions.'

Nightingale nodded. 'Top bloke,' he said. 'I always hated it when some moron shoved the back of his seat in my face.'

'Well, that was Miles.'

'And tell me again how he died?'

'No one knows for sure. His boat caught fire because there was a fault in the electrics, that much they know. But they don't know if Miles died in the fire or if he drowned. He wasn't a big fan of life vests, though Laura was always nagging him to wear one.'

'So they never found the body?'

'What's left of the boat is on the sea bed still. Laura said the police sent divers down but there was no sign of his body.'

'I thought all bodies floated to the surface eventually.'

'That's what they say. But, you know, sharks and stuff.' Jenny shuddered. 'I try not to think about it.' She gestured with her chin at the house ahead of them. 'That's it.'

She pulled up in the driveway of a two-storey brick house with a gabled roof. There was a BMW Series 5 in front of the garage door and Jenny parked next to it. As they got out of the car the front door opened and a dark-haired woman wearing a green and blue dress appeared. 'That's Laura,' said Jenny.

Laura hurried over, her high heels clicking on the flagstones. 'Jenny, darling, you made it!'

'It's not the Outer Hebrides,' laughed Jenny and the two women air-kissed.

'And this must be Jack,' said Laura. 'Thank you so much for agreeing to do this,' she said. Jack was just about to hold out his hand but she beat him to it and got in two quick air-kisses, left and right. She was Jenny's age with considerably more make up and jewellery, but the make-up didn't disguise the dark patches under her eyes. Laura clearly wasn't getting much sleep.

'Come on in, it's Pimm's O'clock,' Laura laughed. She ushered them into the house and through to a large sitting room with a huge picture window looking out to the English Channel. There were two long, low sofas either side of a glass coffee table on which there was a jug of Pimm's, packed with fruit.

Jenny and Nightingale dropped down onto one of the sofas while Laura poured the drinks. She handed them their glasses and toasted them. 'Again, thank you so much for coming,' she said. 'I'm at my wit's end. Andrew says I'm being stupid, but that's Andrew.'

'Andrew?' said Jenny. 'Andrew Chapman? Estate agent Andrew?'

'Didn't I tell you? We're sort of together.'

Jenny laughed. 'Sort of?'

'Well, he stays over sometimes and I sometimes stay at his.'

'Oh my God, you kept that to yourself.'

She shrugged. 'I was worried it might be a bit soon. After what happened.'

'It's been six months,' said Jenny. 'I know you loved Miles to bits but you have to move on.'

'That's what Andrew says. It's just that much more complicated when there wasn't a funeral. And Miles still hasn't been declared dead.'

'Is there some doubt?' asked Nightingale. 'Could Miles still be alive?'

'Oh God no,' said Laura. 'He didn't fake his own death, if that's what you mean. Everything was perfectly fine between us. Better than fine. He'd booked a holiday for us in the Bahamas and he bought me this watch two days before it happened.' She held out her left hand, showing them a gold Rolex dotted with diamonds. 'The police suggested the same thing, mind, but they checked his bank accounts and credit cards and he wasn't hiding money away.' She leaned towards Nightingale. 'I loved Miles and he loved me, Jack. If he wasn't killed in the accident, he would have come back to me.'

'Unless he had amnesia,' said Nightingale.

'Jack...' protested Jenny.

'I'm just saying, it happens. People suffer trauma and they lose their memory.'

'Someone would recognise him,' said Jenny. 'Plus he'd have his wallet and his driving licence would at least tell him where he lived.'

'The police checked all hospitals in the south of England, just in case,' said Laura. 'But amnesia wouldn't explain the footprints.'

'Tell me about them,' said Nightingale.

'There isn't much to tell,' said Laura. 'They just started appearing. The first time I saw them was two weeks ago.'

'And they appear when?'

'It's better I show you,' said Laura. She stood up and led them through the sliding window onto a large deck where there was a huge gas barbecue and sturdy wooden benches either side of a teak table. Leading off the deck was a set of wooden steps that led to a pathway that led down the garden to a small dock. 'That was where Miles used to moor his boat,' said Laura. She took them along the wooden pathway to the dock. 'The first time I noticed them, they were just here, on the dock. As if someone had climbed out of the water.'

'Is that possible?' asked Nightingale. 'Maybe someone was swimming and climbed on to your dock for a rest.'

'The footprints just stopped. There were about ten. As if someone had walked along the dock and then vanished.'

'Day or night?'

'Night. It was about nine o'clock when I saw them. It was a lovely night and I brought out a glass of wine. I was thinking about Miles and picturing him tinkering on the boat. Then I saw the footprints. I was a bit worried because I thought, you know, maybe an intruder. There have been some burglaries in the area. I went back inside and locked the doors and windows but nothing happened. Just my overactive imagination.' She shrugged and sipped her Pimm's. 'I didn't think anything of it but a few nights later I saw the footprints again. This time further up the path. And the next night. And the next. Each time getting closer to the house.''

'Just wet footprints, nothing else?' asked Nightingale.

'Just footprints.'

'And they were definitely human footprints?'

Laura frowned at him. 'Jack, I wouldn't be making this fuss if it was a dog, would I? Of course they were human. And from the size of them, they belong to a man.'

'Did you actually see the footprints being made?'

She shook her head. 'No. They were just there.' She took another sip of her drink. 'I'm not crazy, Jack.'

'I didn't mean to suggest for one minute that you were,' said Nightingale.

'Is it because you don't believe in ghosts?'

'No, the contrary. I do believe in spirits, good and evil.'

'Evil? You think it wants to harm me?'

She looked so scared that Jenny hurried over and hugged her. 'Don't go putting thoughts in her head, Jack,' she admonished.

'I didn't mean to,' he said. 'It's not as if it's done any harm yet.'

'But you do believe me?'

'Of course,' said Nightingale.

'Thank goodness. Andrew thinks I'm imagining it.'

'He hasn't seen the footprints?' asked Nightingale.

Laura shook her head. 'They don't appear when he's here. It's only on the nights he doesn't stay over that I see them.'

'Maybe he should stay over all the time,' said Jenny.

'I think we might be getting to that stage,' said Laura. 'He already has a space in my wardrobe and a toothbrush in the bathroom. And we're talking about getting married.'

Jenny's jaw dropped. 'Are you serious?'

'I think so. Though the fact that Miles still isn't declared dead might hold things up. But Andrew has asked. Several times, actually.'

'So when do the footprints appear? Any particular time?'

'After the sun has gone down,' she said. 'I thought of setting up a CCTV camera or something, catch it on film.'

'That might be an idea,' said Nightingale. 'So no one else has seen them?'

Laura shook her head. 'I took some pictures on my phone,' she said. 'I'll show you when I'm back in the house.'

'And you say the prints get further up the path each time?'

She nodded. 'Yes, it's like it's getting stronger and stronger. Whatever it is.'

'Show me how far it's got,' said Nightingale.

Laura started walking towards the house. She went the full length of the pathway and then pointed at the steps leading up to the deck. 'The last time I saw them, they had reached the second step from the top,' she said.

Nightingale looked back at the deck. 'How far would you say that is?' he asked Jenny. 'Fifty yards? Sixty?'

'A bit more,' said Jenny. 'You probably aren't good at stopping distances, considering the heap of rust you drive.'

'My MGB is a classic,' said Nightingale.

'And my Audi is a miracle of German engineering and I reckon the pathway is seventy five yards.'

'If you're so fond of things German, shouldn't that be in metres?'

'If you'd prefer, sixty-eight and a half metres.'

Nightingale squinted at her. 'Are you serious?'

'I've always been good at maths.'

'She's not joking, either,' said Laura. 'I always used to try to sit next to her in maths tests.'

'Is there no end to your talents?' asked Nightingale.

Jenny laughed and went up the stairs to the deck. Laura followed her. Nightingale looked back at the dock. Seventy-five yards and it had taken two weeks to get there. His maths skills weren't as good as Jenny's, but he could still do the calculation – it was adding about five yards to its journey each night. And at that rate it would reach the window in another two nights. What then? Would it – whatever it was – continue inside the house? And if so, what did it want?

He climbed the steps onto the deck, and looked out over the water. Was it Laura's husband, back from the dead? Or something else? He'd never heard of a ghost leaving footprints before. He looked back at the house. Jenny and Laura were on the sofa and from the way they were giggling he assumed they were talking about something other than the wet footprints.

He went into the room and Laura immediately refilled his glass. 'You said you'd taken photographs of the footprints?' he said.

She nodded and picked up her phone. She tapped on the screen and handed it to him. 'This was three nights ago,' she said. The photograph showed three footprints, one left foot and two of the right foot, glistening wet on the wood. It had been taken with a flash and the prints glittered. To be honest, they looked more like splotches of water than actual footprints, but he had to admit they were at least foot-shaped. 'There's a few photographs,' she said. 'Scroll through them.'

There were four but they were all pretty much the same. Wet splotches on the pathway. One showed a long view with maybe a dozen splotches, and they were definitely spaced out as if somebody – or something – was walking along the pathway. He gave her back the phone. 'You say they only appear when you're here on your own?' he said.

'Well nothing happened the nights that Andrew was here.'

Nightingale looked at his watch. It would be dark in a couple of hours. 'How about we go and have a drink and leave Laura here alone,' he said to Jenny. 'She can phone us when the prints appear.'

Jenny looked over at Laura. 'Is that okay with you?' she asked.

'Of course,' she said. 'I don't think anything's going to happen until it reaches the house.'

'What do you think will happen then?' asked Nightingale.

'I don't know,' said Laura. 'But it wants something, obviously. It's as if it's working harder and harder to get there. There has to be some point to what it's doing.'

'Not necessarily,' said Nightingale. 'But let's take it one step at a time, if you'll forgive the pun. Let's see if the footsteps appear tonight and then we'll take it from there. Where can we get a drink?'

'Sandacres is good. They do food but I can cook for you when you get back.'

'Laura is an amazing chef,' said Jenny.

'Okay, we'll go and have a beer and you can call us once the footprints appear. We passed the Sandacres on the way here, right?'

'I know where it is, Jack,' said Jenny. 'And I'm pretty sure they have Corona.'

'This gets better and better.' He nodded at the Pimm's. 'You'd better go easy, you being the designated driver and all.'

Jenny grinned. 'One of the advantages of living on Sandbanks is you almost never see a policeman here. A lot of the houses use private security firms, so your chance of being breathalysed are pretty much zero.' She held up her glass. 'Not that I'll be over the limit, of course.'

'How does coq au vin sound?' asked Laura. 'I've got a new Jamie Oliver recipe I'm dying to try.'

'Sounds perfect,' said Jenny.

Laura took them through to a large kitchen and Jenny and Nightingale sat down at a large pine table as Laura went to work preparing their meal.

They polished off the Pimm's and Laura took a bottle of Pinot Grigio out of the fridge. 'One for the road?' she asked.

Jenny pulled a face. 'If I have a glass of wine on top of the Pimm's I really shouldn't be driving, police checks or no police checks.'

'It's a nice walk,' said Laura.

'You've talked me into it,' said Jenny.

Nightingale and Jenny left the house at six-thirty. It was a ten minute walk to the pub and they sat at the bar, Nightingale with his Corona and Jenny drinking a glass of Pinot Grigio. It was just after eight and they were on their second round of drinks when Jenny's phone rang. It was Laura. 'There are footprints on the deck,' she said. 'I didn't see them appear but they're there now.'

'We won't be long,' she said.

She ended the call. 'Footprints?' said Nightingale.

'Yup,' said Jenny. She drained her glass and stood up. Her phone buzzed again to let her know she had received a message. It was a picture and she showed it to Nightingale. Half a dozen wet footprints were clearly visible on the deck.

They walked quickly back to the house. There was a black BMW parked in front of the garage, and when they rang the bell the door was opened by a thin man with a receding hairline with what hair he had slicked back. He smiled at Jenny. 'You must be Jenny,' he said. 'I'm Andrew.' He offered his hand and she shook it. Then he flashed his smile at Nightingale. 'And you're Jack, the ghosthunter.'

Nightingale took an instant dislike to the man, but he managed to force a smile as he shook the man's hand. 'And you're Andrew, the estate agent.'

'That's me,' said Andrew. 'Come on in, Laura's in the kitchen.' He ushered them into the hall and closed the door. They could smell the results of Laura's cooking, and Nightingale had to admit that it smelled good.

'Wine?' asked Andrew.

'He does a bit, but it's just his nature,' said Jenny.

Nightingale got the joke immediately but Andrew seemed to struggle, then he forced a laugh. 'Oh, right, yes, good one,' he said. 'We've opened a bottle of Shiraz if that's okay.'

'Shiraz is fine,' said Jenny. 'Where's Laura?'

'Out on the deck,' said Andrew, handing them glasses of wine. 'Keeping her eye on the mysterious footprints.'

'I thought they didn't appear when you were here,' said Nightingale.

'They don't. She phoned me once they were there.'

'You live close by?'

'Not too far. I've got a small place on the way to Bournemouth. Come on, you can see for yourself what she's getting all worked up about.'

'You don't sound concerned,' said Nightingale as he and Jenny followed Andrew through the sitting room and out onto the deck. Laura was sitting on a wicker sofa staring at the wooden decking. She looked up and flashed them a worried smile. She was holding a glass of red wine between both hands.

'I'm not really,' said Andrew. 'I think it's some sort of natural phenomena. Something to do with condensation, maybe. The change of temperature as night falls.'

Jenny went to sit down with Laura as Nightingale walked over to the barbecue area. There were wet splotches on the steps leading up to the deck and half a dozen more crossing the deck, heading for the window.

'See what I mean?' said Andrew, lowering his voice so that Laura and Jenny couldn't hear him. 'I don't think they are footprints.'

'And you think condensation is responsible?' asked Nightingale. He pointed down the path that led to the dock. 'I don't see how it could produce something like that.'

'What's the alternative?' asked Andrew.

Nightingale shrugged and didn't answer.

'Laura thinks it's somehow Miles back from the dead,' said Andrew eventually.

'I don't think he's back from the dead,' said Nightingale. 'But maybe his spirit is still around. Maybe the spirit is trying to contact her.'

'With footprints? Where's the sense in that?'

'It looks to me as if each time the spirit, or whatever it is, is getting closer to the house. As if it's getting stronger.'

'So what can we do? Can we do an exorcism or something?'

Nightingale shrugged again. 'There's nothing to exorcise,' he said. 'It's not a possession. If it is a spirit, we need to try to talk to it. See what it wants.'

Laura stood up and came over to them. 'So what do you think, Jack?' she asked.

'They do look like footprints,' he said. 'And it looks to me as if they will reach the window tomorrow.' He rubbed his chin. 'Let me give it some thought.'

'Hungry?'

Nightingale grinned. 'I could eat.'

Laura served up the coq au vin with garlic mashed potatoes and steamed asparagus in the dining room at a table large enough to seat twelve. Laura, Jenny and Andrew drank wine but Laura had bought in bottles of Corona for Nightingale.

He had to admit that Jenny was right, Laura was an excellent cook. Nightingale had seconds and was still able to find room for dessert, a salted caramel chocolate tart. Although Nightingale didn't particularly like Andrew, he was good company over dinner, keeping them in near-fits of laughter with tales of his clients and customers and the near impossible task he had of keeping everyone happy. Laura and Jenny talked about their schooldays, but it was clear that everyone was avoiding the subject they most wanted to discuss – the ghostly wet footprints. It was as if there was an unspoken agreement not to talk about the subject at the dinner table. It was only after they were back in the sitting room drinking coffee that

Laura asked Nightingale what he thought they should do.

'That depends on who, or what, it is,' said Nightingale. 'If it's a lost spirit, then we need to find out what it wants.'

'Why would it want anything?' asked Andrew.

'It seems to be making a concerted effort to reach the house,' said Nightingale. 'Those footsteps aren't random. They are heading to the house, and each day they are getting closer.'

'Do you think it wants to hurt me?' asked Laura.

'I don't see that it can. It seems to be taking all its strength just to make it up the path. I hardly think it's going to be able to do anyone any harm.'

'You seem convinced that it's a spirit, as you call it,' said Andrew. 'I still think it's condensation. If that was grass out there instead of wooden planks, you wouldn't even notice it. And why would the spirit or whatever it is, why would it start in the water?'

'You know why, Andrew,' said Laura quietly.

Andrew threw her a look of disgust. 'You think it's him, don't you? Miles?'

'Well who else would it be?' asked Laura. 'He died in the water.'

'I know that,' snapped Andrew. 'We all know that. You have to let him go, Laura. He's dead. And the dead don't come back.'

'That's not strictly speaking true,' said Nightingale. 'Sometimes, if they have unfinished business, they do come back.'

'That's absolute bollocks!' said Andrew.

'Andrew!' said Laura.

'I'm sorry, Laura, but I'm not going to start believing in ghosts because of a few wet patches on the deck.' He threw up his hands. 'This is doing my head in.'

'Andrew, please,' said Laura. 'Don't get upset.'

Andrew took a deep breath, then forced a smile. 'I'm sorry everybody,' he said. 'I'm just finding this very frustrating.'

'Well I'm sure Jack has some ideas,' said Jenny.

'I need a cigarette,' said Nightingale, standing up.

'I'll join you,' said Andrew. They went out onto the deck. Nightingale offered a Marlboro to Andrew but he shook his head and took out a pack of small cigars. 'Laura hates them,' said Andrew. He lit one and blew smoke up at the sky. 'Sorry about before,' he said.

Nightingale lit a Marlboro. 'The supernatural can be stressful at the best of times.'

'So you really believe all this? Ghosts and things that go bump in the night?'

Nightingale shrugged. 'Not everything can be explained,' he said, non-committally.

Andrew took another drag on his cigar. 'I can't help thinking that she's using it as an excuse,' he said after he'd blown smoke.

'An excuse for what?'

'I've asked Laura to marry me. Or at least get engaged until we can get Miles declared dead. That was when the bloody footprints started to appear.'

Nightingale frowned. 'You're sure about that?'

'The day after. I took her out for dinner, popped the question, she said yes, and the next day....' He shrugged. 'Then she started to backpedal on the engagement. It's as if she doesn't want to let him go.'

'How long were they married for?' asked Nightingale.

'Just over ten years. I don't think she was that happy with him, truth be told. I always thought she was too good for him.'

'So you knew Miles?'

Andrew nodded. 'I sold them this house. I became a family friend, though to be honest I always liked her more than him.'

'So when Miles died, you made your move?'

Andrew looked at him sharply. 'It's been six months. That's a long time. Laura needs to move on.'

'I get that, but you can see that the footprints would upset her. Especially if they are a sign from Miles.'

'Bullshit,' said Andrew. 'If you ask me, she's doing it herself.'

'What?' Nightingale's jaw dropped in astonishment.

'Maybe not consciously,' said Andrew. 'But subconsciously?' He shrugged. 'Who knows?'

'You think she's faking the footprints to get out of marrying you? How does that make any sense? She could just turn you down, surely.'

'Like I said, maybe it's a subconscious thing. It would explain why the footprints only appear when there's no one else here. That sounds a lot more likely than a ghost, doesn't it?'

Nightingale didn't answer.

'Well, doesn't it?' pressed Andrew.

'I don't know,' said Nightingale. 'But we can always ask someone who might know.'

'Who would that be?' asked Andrew.

Nightingale looked around for an ashtray. There was one on the wicker table and he stabbed out his cigarette. Andrew was still staring at him. Nightingale forced a smile. 'Miles,' he said. He turned and walked back into the house before Andrew could reply.

* * *

'And you think this will work?' asked Laura, looking down at the circle of cards that Nightingale had prepared. They were sitting at the dining table. Nightingale had written the letters A to Z on pieces of cards, plus the numbers one to ten and the words YES, NO, and GOODBYE. The three words were at the top of the circle facing Nightingale. In the middle of the circle was an upturned wine glass.

'It's a bloody kids game,' said Andrew dismissively.

'Do you have any candles?' Nightingale asked Laura. 'Blue would be best but white or yellow would do.'

'Of course,' said Laura, and she headed for the kitchen.

Jenny was sitting at the table holding a glass of wine and watching Nightingale with an amused smile on her face. 'I don't know why you don't go the whole hog and use an Ouija board,' she said.

'Because Laura doesn't have one and I can't be bothered driving all the way to Gosling Manor and back,' said Nightingale.

'Gosling Manor?' asked Andrew.

'Jack is a man of property,' said Jenny. 'His father left him a country pile. Nice place but a bit spooky.'

'If you ever want to sell, let me know,' said Andrew. 'There are always foreign buyers with more money than sense who want a place in the country.' He took out his wallet and gave Nightingale a business card.

'Andrew!' exclaimed Laura, returning with half a dozen blue candles. 'I'm sorry, Jack, he's always working. Where do you want these?'

'Two on the table, the rest around the room,' said Nightingale. 'Spirits are more restful around candles.'

'Spirits,' said Andrew scornfully.

'Okay, everyone needs to be positive about this,' said Nightingale. 'Negativity can kill the process stone dead. Everyone has to be optimistic and be thinking good thoughts.' He waved at a chair. 'Sit down, Andrew. Please.'

Laura placed two candles in glass holders on the table and lit them, then placed another four candles around the room.

'Lights off, please,' said Nightingale.

Laura switched off the lights and took her place at the table.

'Right,' said Nightingale. 'I know Jenny has done this before, but have you?' he asked Andrew and Laura.

They shook their heads. 'What exactly are we doing?' asked Andrew.

'It's a séance,' said Nightingale.

'It comes from the French word for seat,' said Jenny.

'Basically we allow a spirit to communicate by moving the glass to the letters, thus spelling out a message,' said Nightingale. 'But before we do that, we need to carry out two things – grounding and protection. Grounding is effectively earthing your own personal energy to the energy field of the earth. You all have to imagine a ball of pure white energy inside your head, then you have to visualise it moving down through your body to your feet. As it passes through you, the ball of light has to collect all your negative energy. Don't rush it, take your time. Once the ball of energy has reached your feet, you imagine roots sprouting from your feet into the floor and you let the energy flow through it.'

Laura was nodding enthusiastically, but Andrew had a look of disbelief on his face.

'Once the negative energy is out, you pull in positive energy, drawing it up through your feet and into your body and then up into your head. Okay?'

Laura nodded, then looked over at Andrew. She narrowed her eyes and he nodded. 'Okay,' he said, but Nightingale could hear the reluctance in his voice.

'Once we've all grounded ourselves, we need to form a psychic shield to protect ourselves,' said Nightingale.

'From what?' asked Andrew.

'Once we open ourselves up to communicating with the spirit world, it's possible that we might be approached by a negative spirit.'

'What the hell's that?' asked Andrew.

'Not all spirits are well-meaning,' said Nightingale. 'But providing we set up a protective shield, they won't be able to approach us.'

Andrew looked at Laura. 'Are you sure you want to do this?'

Laura nodded. 'I want to know if it's Miles, and if it is Miles I want to know what he wants.'

'I think it's a complete waste of time, if you ask me,' said Andrew.

'Mate, you need to think positively,' said Nightingale.

'Please, Andrew,' said Laura.

'Okay, okay,' said Andrew.

'Right, once we've all grounded ourselves, we need to set up a psychic protective shield. The best way to do that is to imagine a bubble in the middle of the table and then expand that bubble until it is large enough to contain us all. No matter what happens you have to keep the image of the bubble in your mind.'

He looked around the table and they were all nodding, though Andrew clearly wasn't impressed.

'The ending is important,' said Nightingale. 'Once the session is over I will thank the spirit for its help and wish it well. Then I will ask that the glass is returned to the centre of the table. When it's back in the middle we perform another grounding and only then do we take our fingers off.'

'And if we don't?' asked Andrew.

Nightingale frowned' 'What do you mean?'

'If we don't do as you say, what happens?'

'The spirit might be trapped here. Or it might fix itself on one of us.'

'Fix?'

'Attach itself. And follow that person home. Or remain here in the house. But providing we follow the rules, that won't happen.'

'It sounds like a load of bollocks to me,' said Andrew.

'Positivity, remember,' said Nightingale.

Andrew put up his hands. 'Okay, okay.'

'Right, let's start,' said Nightingale. 'Everyone put their right hand on the glass.'

They did as he said. Nightingale said a short prayer, then told them to begin grounding. They sat in silence, concentrating. It was a full two minutes before Nightingale spoke again. 'Now form the protective shield. Nod when you have visualised the bubble surrounding us all.'

One by one they nodded. Jenny first, then Laura, and finally Andrew.

Nightingale looked up at the ceiling. 'We are here to communicate with Miles Nicholson. Are you here, Miles?'

The flames of the candles on the table flickered.

'Miles? Are you there? You are among friends, Miles. This is a peaceful place, a tranquil place, a place where you can be safe.'

Nightingale felt the glass tremble but it didn't move. He took a deep breath. Truth be told he wanted a cigarette but smoking and séances didn't mix.

'Miles Nicholson, if you are here please make yourself known.'

The glass began to move. It slowly went around in a tight circle.

'Somebody's pushing,' said Andrew and Nightingale flashed him a warning look.

'Miles, is that you?' asked Nightingale.

The glass moved slowly towards NO. It stopped next to the card.

'No?' said Andrew. 'What the Hell's going on?'

'Any spirit can work through the glass,' said Nightingale. 'We don't have any say who comes through.'

He looked up at the ceiling again. 'What is your name, spirit?' he asked.

The glass began to move again. E-M-M-A.

'Emma?' said Laura. 'Who is Emma?'

Nightingale ignored her. 'Emma, we are here to talk with Miles Nicholson. Please go in peace and love, Emma.'

The glass moved again, and this time it stopped next to the card on which was written GOODBYE.

'Goodbye, Emma,' said Nightingale.

The glass slowly moved back to the middle of the table and began to form a small circle.

'And no one is pushing, seriously?' asked Andrew.

'I'm not,' said Laura.

'Me neither,' said Jenny.

The glass stopped.

'Everyone concentrate, please,' said Nightingale. 'Keep focusing on the protective bubble and think about Miles.'

Nothing happened for a couple of minutes, then the glass began to move again.

'Miles, is that you?' asked Nightingale.

The glass scraped across the table and stopped next to the card that said YES.

Laura gasped. 'Miles?'

'Let me do the talking,' said Nightingale. He looked up at the ceiling. 'Miles, what year were you born?'

The glass moved slowly, stopping at four numbers. One, Nine, Seven and finally Six. Nightingale looked at Laura and she nodded. 'Yes,' she said.

Nightingale flashed her an encouraging smile. 'Miles, is that you who has been leaving the footprints on the deck?'

The glass moved slowly towards the YES card and then stopped.

Nightingale swallowed. His mouth had gone dry. 'Why?' he said.

The glass started to move again. 'I – W-A-S'

'I was…' said Jenny.

The glass continued to move. 'K-I-L-L-E-D'

'Killed,' said Jenny. 'I was killed.'

'On the boat, was that when you were killed?' asked Nightingale.

The glass moved again, quickly this time, and went straight to the YES card.

'When you died, was it an accident?' asked Nightingale.

The glass scraped towards the NO card.

'No!' gasped Laura.

'Is that what you want to tell us?' asked Nightingale. 'You want to tell us that somebody killed you?'

The glass moved quickly to YES. And then it moved to the letter A. Then N. Then D.

'And?' said Jenny. 'And what?'

The glass began to move but then suddenly it span off the table and crashed to the floor, breaking into a dozen shards. Laura screamed and Jenny's chair crashed to the floor as she stood up.

'The bubble!' shouted Nightingale. 'Focus on the protective bubble!' It was too late. Andrew rushed over to Laura and put his arm around her and as he did he knocked over one of the candles. It rolled across the table and fell to the floor.

Jenny picked it up and looked over at Nightingale. Nightingale shrugged. The damage was done and he doubted there was anything he could do to undo it. The glass had smashed and the protective bubble had been breached.

Laura was sobbing and Andrew was trying to comfort her. Nightingale went outside and lit a cigarette. Jenny joined him, with her wine. Nightingale blew smoke up at the night sky. 'And what?' he said. 'That's what you thought? And what?'

She frowned. 'What do you mean?'

'And-rew,' said Nightingale. 'Miles was trying to give us the name of his killer.'

Her eyes widened. 'Are you serious?'

'Who do you think threw the glass off the table? It had to be Andrew.'

'I thought the spirit had gotten angry?'

'There was no reason for it to get angry,' said Nightingale. 'But every reason for Andrew to want it to stop.'

Andrew and Laura appeared on the deck. 'What happened?' asked Laura.

'Some sort of extreme reaction,' said Nightingale. 'When you're ready we need to start again.'

'Why?' asked Andrew.

'We need to say goodbye to the spirit,' said Nightingale. 'There has to be closure.'

'No,' said Andrew. 'I'm not having Laura getting upset again.'

'I'm okay,' said Laura.

'You're not okay,' said Andrew. 'I saw how shocked you were in there.'

'Andrew, remember what I said about the spirit being trapped here.'

Andrew shook his head. 'If it is Miles who is responsible for the footprints, then the spirit is already here,' he said. 'I'm going to have to insist, I'm sorry. No more séances.'

'Suit yourself,' said Nightingale. He dropped down onto one of the wicker chairs. Jenny joined him.

'Shall I stay the night?' Andrew asked Laura.

'Maybe tomorrow,' said Laura. 'I don't think I'll be great company tonight.'

Andrew put a hand on her shoulder. 'Are you sure?'

'We'll have dinner tomorrow. I'll be fine then.'

Andrew kissed her on the cheek. 'Dinner sounds good. I'll phone you before I sleep.'

He said goodbye to Jenny and Nightingale and let himself out. Shortly afterwards they heard him drive away.

'So you met Andrew when he sold you the house?' asked Nightingale.

Laura nodded. 'Miles was keener on a smaller house about half a mile away but Andrew was very persuasive.'

'And he became a family friend?'

'He was always dropping by. He plays squash and so did Miles so they had a game pretty much every week. And Andrew enjoyed sailing.'

'Does he have a boat?'

'No, but he used to go out with Miles.'

'What about the night of the accident? Was Andrew around that night?'

Laura frowned. 'What are you getting at?'

Nightingale put up his hands. 'Nothing. Just trying to get a feel of what happened.'

'Jack was a policeman so asking questions is second nature,' said Jenny. 'Sometimes he forgets that not everyone is a criminal.'

'I didn't mean to imply anything,' said Nightingale. 'He seems a really nice guy.' That was a lie but he didn't want to tell Laura that he had taken an instant dislike to her boyfriend.

'He is,' said Laura. 'He loves me to bits. That's why he's so upset about this whole footprints thing. He's suggested that I sell this place and that I move in with him.'

'And are you going to?' asked Jenny.

Laura ran a hand through her hair. 'I feel I ought to,' she said. 'I have to move on at some point, don't I? And everything here reminds me of Miles.'

'You're sure you're not rushing into this?' asked Nightingale.

'Jack!' protested Jenny.

'I'm just saying, let's get to the bottom of the wet footprints first.'

'And how do you plan to do that?' Jenny asked.

Nightingale shrugged. 'I thought we could start with the cops. See what they think.'

'About the footprints?' asked Laura.

Nightingale shook his head. 'About what happened to Miles.'

* * *

Nightingale and Jenny were at Poole Police Station at ten o'clock in the morning. Nightingale asked to speak to the detective who had investigated the death of Miles Nicholson and a bored sergeant at reception told him the officer he wanted was Detective Inspector Steve Tigwell but that he was tied up in an interview. Nightingale gave the sergeant his business card and settled down to wait on an orange plastic chair. Jenny sat next to him. 'Do you miss being a cop?' she asked.

'I used to,' said Nightingale. 'But with all the cutbacks and public scrutiny, it's not a job I'd want to do now.'

'Public scrutiny?'

'The media second-guesses everything the cops do, and social media makes it worse. And the top cops these days are all political. They have to be, to keep their jobs. The top brass used to be loyal to the cops on the beat, but those days are long gone. Too much politics and not enough thief-taking.' He shrugged. 'So no, I don't miss it.'

It was just after eleven when a side door opened and a middle-aged man in a grey suit waved them over. He took them down a corridor to an interview room with a dual tape deck on a table. 'We'll be quieter here,' said Tigwell, sitting down and waving them to chairs on the opposite side of the table. He smiled at Jenny. 'You are?'

'I'm Jack's pretty young sidekick,' she said brightly. 'Jenny McLean.' She held out her hand and the detective grinned and shook it.

'Pleasure,' he said. He looked at Nightingale. 'You're here about the Miles Nicholson case?'

Nightingale nodded. 'We just wanted some background.'

The detective was holding Nightingale's business card. 'So who would your client be? The insurance company?'

'I'm a friend of the widow,' said Nightingale. 'Well, a friend of a friend.' He nodded at Jenny. 'My pretty young sidekick is an old school friend of Laura's.'

'I've seen Mrs Nicholson twice and she didn't express any reservations about the way I dealt with the case,' said the detective.

'She's not unhappy,' said Nightingale. He hesitated, not wanting to tell the detective about the mysterious wet footprints. In his experience, police officers tended not to believe in the supernatural. 'Basically she has a new boyfriend and would like to get a death certificate so that she can remarry.'

'Without a body that's not easy,' said the detective. 'Usually it takes seven years. That time frame can be shortened in situations where death is probable but not definitive, in plane crashes for instance. We now have the Presumption Of Death Act of 2013 which basically says that an inquest can be held without a body and death certificate can be issued. That would in theory allow her to remarry, though so far as the husband's estate goes, that would still require seven years, I think.' He forced a smile. 'I'm by no means an expert,' he said. 'She really needs to get herself a good lawyer.'

'Do you think Miles Nicholson is dead?' asked Jenny.

The detective nodded. 'I'm sure of it. Mr Nicholson took his boat out, the boat caught fire and sank, the presumption is that he fell overboard and died. He often went out without a life vest.'

'And the body was never found?'

'We sent divers down and the body wasn't on board. The waters there are very busy. If the current was right the body could have drifted into a shipping lane and there wouldn't be much left if a tanker or a ferry went over it.'

'He couldn't have faked his own death?'

The detective pursed his lips as he considered the question. 'It's possible he might have faked it, if that's what you're getting at. But he had no financial problems, his marital situation was rock steady, and there was no suspicious financial activity before or after the incident. So yes, I'm sure he's dead. But without a body...' He shrugged.

'The boat caught fire?'

The detective nodded. 'It happens. There was a gas cylinder on board for cooking and there was a diesel engine.'

'Was the boat examined?'

'It depends on what you mean by examined. It's still on the sea bed and is likely to remain there. The insurance company paid out and they have no interest in salvaging it. But we sent down divers and they confirmed that there had been a fire and the hull had broken in half. There was evidence of an explosion.'

'And they looked for a body, obviously?'

'They examined the wreckage as best they could.'

'How deep is it?'

'A hundred feet or so. I'm told.' He looked at his watch. 'I'm sorry, I've got a witness statement that I have to take and I'm running late. Is there anything else you need?'

'Just one thing,' said Nightingale. 'Is there anything to stop me going down and taking a look myself?'

'Are you a diver?'

'I can dive,' said Nightingale. 'And Jenny here has all the PADI qualifications. That's what it says on her CV, anyway.'

'When did you read my CV?' asked Jenny.

Nightingale ignored the question and continued to look at the detective. 'Would it be okay?'

'Sure, if you wanted,' said the detective. 'It would be totally up to you.'

'How about finding it?'

'I can give you the GPS coordinates,' said the detective. 'But you'd need someone familiar with the waters to get you there. And like I said, it's deep.' He stood up and offered his hand. Nightingale shook it. 'What do you expect to find?' asked the detective.

'I'm not sure,' said Nightingale. 'I've just got a feeling that I need to see the boat for myself.'

* * *

'When was the last time you went diving?' asked Jenny. She was testing the regulator on her air tank. They were both wearing black wetsuits and had weight belts around their waists.

Nightingale was struggling to attach his regulator to his air tank. 'A couple of years ago,' he said.

'Where were you?'

'Spain.'

'How deep?'

Nightingale shrugged. 'Twenty feet or so. Just sightseeing.'

'This is going to be different,' said Jenny. 'A hundred feet or more and visibility will be bad. Are you sure you want to do this?'

'I'm not letting you go down on your own,' said Nightingale.

'I'm wondering if we should be bothering, that's all.' She placed her equipment on the deck and went over to help him. They had hired the dive boat for the afternoon, paying the dive boat captain, Charlie, in cash. He had tapped the GPS coordinates into the boat's navigation system and it had taken less then half an hour to reach the location. Charlie was wearing a reefer jacket and a wool cap and smoked a roll-up as he waited for his passengers to enter the water.

'We might see something the police divers missed,' said Nightingale.

'They're professionals.'

'Oh ye of little faith.'

Jenny finished attaching his regulator and then helped fasten the tank to his back. He sat down and pulled on his flippers while she went over and put on her own equipment. She picked up two powerful underwater torches and gave one to him, attaching it to his belt with a plastic line. 'Stay close, whatever you do,' she said. 'If you lose me stay where you are and wait for me to find you.'

He threw her a mock salute. 'Aye aye, sir.'

'I'm serious, Jack. This isn't a reef dive looking for pretty fish. It's a deep dive in the English Channel and if you make a mistake it can easily turn fatal.'

'I hear you,' said Nightingale, realising that she was serious.

'Good,' she said. 'And if you at any time feel light-headed or dizzy, let me know.'

'I will,' he said. He thought about throwing her another salute but he could see that she wasn't in the mood for jokes.

Jenny waved over at the captain. 'We're going in, Charlie!' she shouted. He flashed her an 'okay' sign.

Nightingale and Jenny put on their masks, inserted their mouthpieces and walked carefully to the rear of the boat. They entered backwards and bobbed to the surface. They released air from their buoyancy compensators and gradually sank under the water, facing each other.

Nightingale could see the concern on Jenny's eyes and he tried to smile to show her that he was okay, but the mouthpiece made it impossible so he nodded.

They went slowly down, bubbles streaming from their regulators and heading up to the surface.

The visibility was better than Nightingale had expected, but it was a far cry from the last time he'd gone scuba diving. Then the water had been crystal clear and he had been able to see colourful fish and crustaceans. The water of the English Channel was murkier and once they got to about fifty feet below the surface there was almost no daylight filtering through the water. They switched on their torches and tunnels of light cut through the darkness.

Jenny tapped Nightingale on the shoulder and made a patting motion with her hand. He realised that he was breathing too quickly and she wanted him to slow down. He nodded and concentrated on breathing slowly and evenly.

They continued to descend and eventually Nightingale saw the darkness of the sea bed. They shone their torches around, illuminating the sand, then Jenny pointed to the west and headed in that direction. Nightingale stayed with her. Jenny seemed to move effortlessly through the water but Nightingale had trouble staying level. One moment his fins were scraping on the sand, the next he was heading upwards and he had to fight to keep level with Jenny.

After thirty seconds Jenny changed direction. Nightingale bumped into her and she turned to look at him. He gave her an 'okay' signal.

Jenny made three changes of direction before they found the boat. It had split into two sections and they could see the fire damage in the light of their torches. They swam over to the rear of the boat. Jenny had a waterproof camera attached to her belt and she took several photographs. Nightingale moved towards the front section. The broken edges were blackened and it looked as if there had been an explosion. He kicked his fins and moved into the main cabin. He felt something grab his ankle and he turned to see Jenny. She wagged her finger at him, telling him to stop what he was doing. Then she pointed to herself. She wanted to go in first. He flashed her an 'okay' sign. She was the more experienced diver, she should lead the way. He backed out clumsily, banging his head against the roof. Jenny helped pull him out and then she went in, taking photographs. There were lockers along the sides of the boat that doubled as seats. Jenny lifted up the one on the port side. It was filled with ropes and tools. She took a photograph and closed it, then reached over to open the one on the starboard side. Nightingale felt himself floating down so he kicked his fins but did it too hard and he bumped against Jenny. The starboard locker wouldn't open and Nightingale realised that it was padlocked. He opened the port locker and took out a claw hammer and used it to prise off the padlock. Jenny pulled the locker open. She jumped when she saw what was inside. A body. Nightingale had never met Miles Nicholson but he had seen photographs of the man in Laura's house. However there was no way of telling if it was Miles, the skin was puffed up and bloated into a parody of a human being. He was holding a knife in one hand. Nightingale played the beam of his torch over the bloated body and then over the inside of the locker lid. Nightingale's eyes widened when he saw what Miles had carved into the wood with the knife. 'A-N-D-R-E.'

Jenny turned to look at him and he could see the horror in her eyes. She pointed at the carved letters and she nodded and photographed them. When she had finished they backed out of the wreckage of the boat and headed for the surface.

* * *

As soon as Charlie had brought them back to shore. Nightingale phoned Detective Inspector Tigwell and told him what they had discovered. He arranged to meet them at Andrew Chapman's house. The detective was parked outside in a blue Toyota when Jenny drove up in her Audi.

The detective was smoking a cigarette as he climbed out of his car so Nightingale lit a Marlboro. 'You're sure about this?' asked Tigwell.

'I'm afraid so,' said Nightingale.

Jenny showed the detective the photographs she had taken on her underwater camera.

'How the hell did our guys miss that?' said Tigwell.

'To be fair, they wouldn't be looking for a body in a cupboard,' said Jenny. 'They would have see the evidence of a fire and assumed that it was an accident.

She showed him the marks that Miles had carved into the wood.

'A-N-D-R-E,' said Tigwell. 'I suppose we could be looking for a Frenchman.' He smiled to show that he was joking. 'What about the knife?'

'We left it where it was,' said Jenny.

The detective shuddered. 'So Miles was stabbed and stuffed in the cupboard. Then Chapman arranged the fire and what, swam for it?'

'He's a good swimmer and he'd have been wearing a life vest,' said Nightingale. 'He must have stabbed Miles and put him in the locker, not realising that he was still alive. Miles lives just long enough to carve part of Andrew's name.' He shuddered as he imagined what Miles's last moments must have been like.

'Proving it might be difficult,' said the detective.

'Was he ever asked if he had an alibi for that night?' asked Nightingale.

The detective shook his head. 'We never suspected foul play so it wasn't an issue.' He looked over at Chapman's black BMW, which was parked outside the garage. 'Looks like he's at home.' He dropped what was left of his cigarette onto the pavement and stubbed it out. Nightingale did the same, then he and Jenny followed the detective to the front door. Tigwell pressed the doorbell, but there was no answer. He pressed it again, longer this time, but there was still no response.

'He could be playing hard to get,' said Nightingale. He headed down the side of the house.

'I think I should go first,' said the detective. 'You two are civilians, remember?'

Nightingale and Jenny stood back and the detective walked by them. There was a hot tub at the back of the house. Leading from the tub to the rear door of the house were a line of wet footprints. Nightingale felt the hairs on the back of his neck stand up as he stared at the footprints.

'Jack,' whispered Jenny, but Nightingale silenced her with a shake of his head.

Tigwell had also noticed the wet footprints, but unlike Nightingale and Jenny he didn't realise the significance. 'Looks like he's been enjoying his hot tub,' said the detective. He knocked on the back door, and when there was no response he tried the handle. The door opened. Tigwell popped his head inside. 'Mr Chapman?' he called. 'This is the police.'

When there was no reply he opened the door wide and stepped into the kitchen. Wet footprints glistened across the tiled floor to the hall. The tiles there were marble and the footprints went to the stairs. 'Mr Chapman!' called the detective. He headed upstairs and Nightingale and Jenny followed him.

Nightingale had a sick feeling in the pit of his stomach.

'Mr Chapman!' called Tigwell again, but Nightingale knew he was wasting his time.

The wet footprints led to a door and the detective pushed it open. Jenny looked over his shoulder and gasped. Andrew Chapman was lying face down in the water-filled bath, fully-clothed. Tigwell rushed over and dragged him out of the bath and onto the tiled floor then knelt down beside him. He felt for a pulse and shook his head. 'By the look of it he's been dead for a while,' he said. He stood up and frowned down at the body. 'This doesn't make any sense,' he said. 'If he was in the hot tub, why is he dressed now?'

'Maybe he dressed and then decided he wanted a bath,' said Nightingale.

The detective looked at him quizzically. 'That doesn't make any sense either. And how did he get in the bath?'

'Slipped and fell, maybe?' said Nightingale. He pointed at Andrew's face. 'Seems there's bruising there,' he said.

'I'll get Forensics to take a look,' said the detective, taking out his phone.

'Do you need us?" asked Nightingale.

Tigwell shook his head. 'No, but I'll need a statement from you both at some point.'

'We'll be with Laura Nicholson,' said Jenny. Tigwell was already talking into his phone so Nightingale and Jenny went outside. 'You know what happened, don't you?' Jenny asked as they climbed into the Audi.

Nightingale nodded. 'Miles got his revenge. He came back from the dead to kill his murderer.'

'But why was he at Laura's house?'

'Because that was where he belonged. I'm guessing that Miles wanted to tell Laura what had happened, but it was an effort. He was trying to reach her. Then we used the glass, which made communication that much easier. Miles was trying to tell us that Andrew had killed him but Andrew broke the glass. He thought that was the end of it, he didn't realise that by smashing the glass and not letting the spirit go, he was allowing Miles to move more freely.' He reached into his coat pocket and took out his pack of Marlboro but put the pack back when Jenny flashed him a disapproving look. 'Miles was able to go to Andrew's house and...' He left the sentence unfinished and just shrugged.

'And what do we tell Laura?'

'The truth.'

Jenny's eyes widened. 'That her husband came back from the dead to murder the man who she was about to marry?'

'That's the truth.'

'Well I'm not going to tell her that, obviously.'

'So what will you tell her?'

Jenny sighed. 'I'll think of something.' She looked over at the house. 'Is it over, now?'

Nightingale nodded. 'Miles got what he wanted. He'll be at peace now. Or at least he will be once he's had a proper burial.'

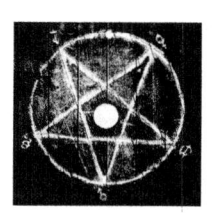

THE CARDS

Jack Nightingale knew he was going to be asked for a favour when Jenny McLean put a cup of coffee and a banana chocolate muffin on his desk and smiled at him perkily. 'And how are you this bright and sunny morning?' she asked.

'It's raining,' he said. 'The sky is grey and my MGB is playing up again. But thanks for asking.' He swung his feet off his desk, ripped off a chunk of muffin and popped it into his mouth. 'What do you want, Jenny?'

She dropped down onto the chair on the other side of his desk and tucked her blonde hair behind her ears. 'You're so suspicious.'

'I know you.' He sipped his coffee. 'Come on. Spill the beans.'

'It's a long story.'

Nightingale shrugged. 'It's not as if I've much on today. And I am enjoying this muffin.'

Jenny sat back in her chair. She was wearing a white linen dress with a blue jacket over it and had a thin string of pearls around her neck. There was a gold Rolex on her wrist. Nightingale had realised years ago that Jenny didn't need the money he paid her every month. Well, most months, anyway.

'I've got a maid,' she said.

'That's nice.'

She raised an eyebrow archly. 'This will take forever if you keep on interrupting.'

Nightingale smiled and popped another piece of muffin into his mouth.

'Her name is Maria and she's a Godsend. She was born in Chile and came over here as a student. She married a British guy after she left university and they had two kids. They got divorced about five years ago and he was a lawyer so knew what strings to pull to get custody of the kids. He remarried and they moved to Sussex. Maria had almost no money and only got to see the kids every second weekend, so she took any work she could. Two years ago her ex-husband was killed in a car accident. She assumed that she would get her children back but the world being the way it is, the new wife kept custody of the children and wouldn't give them up.'

'Bloody hell, this is messy,' said Nightingale. 'Domestics always end badly.'

'I haven't even started the story yet,' said Jenny.

'You know this isn't the sort of work we normally do?'

'Stick with me,' she said. She reached over and stole a piece of his muffin. 'So, Maria is obviously depressed. Her two kids are now ten and eight and they're living with a woman who isn't related to them, and she only gets to visit them twice a month. She's at the end of her tether. Then one day someone tells her about this guy and how he might be able to help her. His name's Mason Castle, and he reads Tarot cards. So Maria goes to see him and he does a reading. He seems to know everything about her and the cards say that nothing will change, that she has lost her kids for ever.'

'Nice.'

'But then Castle says that he can help. That the cards can change the future.'

Nightingale frowned and sipped his coffee. 'That's not how Tarot cards work, is it?'

'You're asking me?'

'They're used to foretell the future. End of.'

'Well, this guy tells Maria that his cards can change things. And that he can get her children back for her.'

Nightingale scowled. 'A con man.'

'You'd think so, yes. He makes her sign a contract. And here's the weird thing. He makes her sign it in blood.'

Nightingale's jaw dropped. 'No way.'

She nodded. 'The thing is, she didn't read the contract. She just signed it.'

'And she didn't think it strange that he wanted her to sign in blood?'

'He told her it had to be that way. It made the contract unbreakable.'

'And what did it say, this contract?'

'Like I said, she didn't read it. Her English isn't great, but then as it turned out, that didn't matter because it was written in Latin.'

'This just gets better, doesn't it?'

'I've not finished yet,' said Jenny. 'So he persuades her to sign the contract, then he plays around with the cards and tells her to go home and that he'll be in touch. Two days later the new wife kills herself. Hangs herself in her bedroom. Leaves a note saying she couldn't live without her husband. Maria is going to get her kids back.'

'Okay,' said Nightingale hesitantly. 'I'm guessing that all isn't well that ends well.'

'The day after the new wife's body is found, Maria gets a phone call. Castle says he needs to see her. She goes. He shows her the contract and explains that she has agreed to give him one of her children.'

Nightingale's jaw dropped. 'No.'

Jenny nodded. 'Yes. As soon as she gets the children back, she has to give the youngest – the girl – to him.'

'So she just goes to the cops.'

'He told her that if she did, she would be dead. The cards would kill her.'

'Bollocks,' said Nightingale.

'The new wife died, remember? Castle says Maria will go the same way. A contract signed in blood is inviolable, he said.'

Nightingale sat back in his chair. 'Wow,' he said.

Jenny nodded. 'Yeah. We need to help her, Jack. And we need to do this Pro Bono.' She held up her hand. 'And no cracks about how you hate U2 and why does he never take his sunglasses off.'

'My Bono jokes are funny.'

'The first time, maybe,' said Jenny. 'Look, Maria doesn't have much money, she's the best maid ever and I want to help her.'

'What if she takes the kids back to Chile and you never see her again?'

'I don't think that will happen. The kids have spent all their lives here and don't even have Chilean passports. And Maria loves London. But that's not the point. She needs help. And we're going to help her.'

'We are?' asked Nightingale, amused by her sudden seriousness.

'We are,' she said. 'And that's the end of it.'

* * *

Nightingale didn't know much about Tarot cards, but he knew the basics. They were originally created for playing card games across Europe in the fifteenth century, but it was a French occult practitioner by the name of Jean-Baptiste Alliette who produced the first true Tarot deck. He made a living telling fortunes using the cards he'd designed. There were – and still are – 78 cards in the deck. There are 22 trump cards including all the famous ones – The Magician, The Lovers, The Hanged Man, Death and The Fool. Then there are 56 lesser cards, the Minor Arcana, Alliette called them. Like the playing cards that are in use today, each suit had a King, a Queen and a Jack, but also a Knight. The suits in Alliette's deck were swords, wands, coins and cups. Each card had a meaning, and skilled users were supposed to be able to see the past and forecast the future depending on how the cards were dealt. Did Nightingale believe that cards could be used to predict the future? Truth be told, probably not. But he had seen enough strange things over the years to know that pretty much everything was possible.

'You look nervous,' said Jenny. They were sitting in her Audi, parked across the road from the house in Marylebone where Mason Castle had his 'consulting rooms.' Nightingale had laughed when he'd seen that on the man's website.

'Didn't Sherlock Holmes have consulting rooms?' he'd asked Jenny.

'I think he did.'

'Maybe we should have consulting rooms?'

'Maybe not.'

The website had been a relatively simple affair, a brief CV of Mason Castle and a booking page. There was no picture of the man and Google didn't turn up anything. There had been an hour-long slot available that evening and they had booked it using a false name and e-mail address. Nightingale was going to be John Dawson, and he'd prepared a backstory about being a painter and decorator who was being ripped off by his business partner. Jenny had driven him from Bayswater and had agreed to wait for him.

'Are you nervous?' pressed Jenny.

Nightingale took out his cigarettes but put them away when he saw her icy look. 'Apprehensive,' he said. 'It's a lion's den thing.'

'You'll be fine,' she said. 'Just don't go signing any contracts in blood.'

'Why does he insist on seeing people one-on-one?'

'It's his thing. It says so on the website and Maria said he was insistent. He only sees one person at a time.'

Nightingale sighed. 'Okay.'

She patted him on the leg. 'Time to go,' she said.

'If I'm not out within the hour…'

'I know, I'll call the police.'

'Actually I was going to say kick the door down and come in and rescue me, but yeah, call the cops.' He climbed out of the car, shut the door, and walked across the road.

There was a brass speakerphone to the side of a black door and he pressed the button. 'Who is it?' A woman's voice.

'John Dawson,' said Nightingale. 'I have an appointment.'

The door lock buzzed and Nightingale let himself into an impressive hallway with high ceilings and delicate mouldings. There were framed oil paintings on the wall, bleak landscapes mainly. He closed the door and headed down the hall, his Hush Puppies squeaking on the highly-polished parquet flooring. A door to the left was open and a middle-aged woman with a Botoxed face and over-plumped lips sat behind a Regency desk. 'Mr Dawson?' she said. She was smiling but her forehead was porcelain smooth.

'Yes,' he said.

'If you could pay your fee now, that would be perfect,' she said.

Nightingale took out his wallet and handed over five twenty-pound notes. She didn't offer him a receipt but put the money into a silver box. Then she stood, walked around the desk and across the hall. She was wearing a pale blue Chanel suit and Chanel shoes. Her hair was unnaturally black, almost certainly dyed. She knocked on the door opposite, opened it and spoke to whoever was inside. 'Mr Dawson is here,' she said, then stepped aside to let Nightingale walk in.

Mason Castle was sitting behind a huge desk in a high-backed Louis IV chair. He was a dwarf. Or a midget. Or a little person. Nightingale had lost track of whatever the politically-correct term was for an adult under three-feet tall, but whatever the word, that's what Mason Castle was.

His head seemed too big for his body, with bushy brown eyebrows that were at odds with a mane of grey hair, swept back over his shoulders. He was wearing a black jacket with a blood-red bow-tie and he had chunky gold rings on most of his fingers. 'It's a pleasure to meet you, Mr Dawson,' said Castle. 'Please take a seat at the table over there.' He gestured to Nightingale's left. There was a circular table with two wooden chairs either side of it. Nightingale took off his raincoat and sat down.

Castle pushed himself off his chair and walked around the desk He picked up four black candles and took them over to the table. In the centre of the table was a wooden box with small brass studs dotted around it.

'Have you had your cards read before, Mr Dawson?' asked Castle as he placed the candles around the box. The candles were a bad sign, Nightingale knew. In a regular Tarot reading white candles were lit, and sage was burnt to cleanse the room.

'No. Never.'

Castle nodded. 'It's very straightforward,' he said. He took a gold cigarette lighter from his pocket and lit the four candles. 'Can I ask you how you found out about my services.'

'Google,' lied Nightingale.

'I wasn't recommended then?'

Nightingale shook his head. 'I just saw your website.'

Castle smiled thinly, put his lighter away, walked over to the door. The light switch was just four feet off the ground and he switched off the lights and climbed back onto the chair. He grunted as he leaned over and opened the box. Inside was a deck of cards and he took it out and closed the lid. He held the deck with both hands and closed his eyes for several seconds, muttering under his breath.

Nightingale looked around. There were thick curtains over the window, heavy rugs on the floors and more oil paintings in gilded frames on the walls. The pictures were landscapes, but unlike the ones in the hall they seemed unreal, visions of dark gloomy places. A fire flickered in a Victorian cast iron fireplace. At first Nightingale thought it was a gas fire with fake coal but next to the fireplace there was a brass scuttle full of coal and a rack of brass implements and pokers. To the left of the desk was an oak filing cabinet. Was that where Castle kept his contracts, wondered Nightingale. The ones signed in blood.

'Please focus on the table, Mr Dawson,' said Castle. He had opened his eyes and was now staring at Nightingale.

'Sorry,' said Nightingale.

Castle handed the pack to Nightingale. 'Please shuffle the cards until you feel happy with them,' he said. 'It doesn't matter how long it takes. You will know when the time has come.'

Nightingale did as he was told. He shuffled for a couple of minutes and then stopped. 'Could I possibly have a drink of water,' he said. 'My throat is really dry.'

Castle frowned. 'Can't you wait?'

'I can't swallow,' said Nightingale. 'I'm nervous, I suppose.'

'You need to relax.'

'I know. But a drink of water would help.'

Castle tutted with annoyance but stood up and went over to a sideboard. As he opened a bottle of Evian water and poured it into his glass, Nightingale slid a card from the bottom of the pack and put it into his pocket. By the time Castle returned to the table, Nightingale was shuffling again. He stopped, took a drink of water, smiled gratefully, and continued to shuffle. As he looked down at the pack in his hands, he realised they were unlike any Tarot deck he had ever seen. The backs were jet black and there was a pentagram in the middle, with strange runes at the five points. There was no writing on the faces of the cards, and as he slowly shuffled he didn't see any pictures that he recognised. There was no hanging man, no priestess, no kings or queens. On some of the cards there were just symbols, on others there were animals but unlike any animals that Nightingale had ever seen. There were demons on some, horned and malevolent, there were body parts on others, and some were of strange things fighting or copulating, it was difficult to tell.

'Now you need to think about your problem,' said Castle. 'Focus on that. Focus on the issue that you want resolving. And as you shuffle, I want you to repeat to yourself the following words. "Electus Ad Veritatem Servandam". Do that now.'

Nightingale repeated the four words.

'Keep going, keep saying the words as you shuffle the cards.'

Nightingale did as he was told.

'When you feel happy with the cards, hand them back to me,' said Castle.

Nightingale gave him the deck and Castle placed it between his hands and closed his eyes, whispering to himself. After a few seconds he began to lay cards onto the table. Nightingale knew there were three main ways of laying out the cards for a Tarot reading. The simplest was a three-card spread. From left to right the three cards represented the past, the present and the future. A common method was the five-card horseshoe spread where five cards are laid out on an upright arc. From left to right the cards represent the Present, Present Desires, the Unexpected, the Immediate Future and the Outcome.

The layout used by most professional Tarot readers was the Celtic Cross, where ten cards are placed in the shape of a cross. In that layout the ten cards represented the Present, Immediate Influences, Life, Root of the Reading, Past Influences, Future Influences, Feelings, Outside Influences, Hopes and Fears, and the Outcome.

Castle didn't use any of the three methods. He laid five of them out as if they were at the points of a pentangle. He stared down at them. 'The problem you want resolving,' he whispered. 'Tell me what it is.'

'My business partner has been stealing from me,' said Nightingale. 'He is taking money from the company bank account without telling me.'

Castle nodded as he stared at the cards. 'And he will continue to do so,' he said.

He laid out five more cards on top of the first. He frowned as he stared at them. 'That is strange,' he said.

'What?'

Castle looked up at him, his eyes narrowed. 'Has Dawson always been your name?'

'Sure. Why?'

'The cards are telling me about a bird. That your name is a bird's name. How can that be?'

'John Dawson's my name. My mother was Eileen Dawson and my dad was Tom.'

Castle stared at the cards and nodded. 'They are dead now, your parents. They both killed themselves. But again I get a bird. A different bird. That's very strange.'

Nightingale said nothing.

Castle dealt five more cards. He rubbed his chin as he studied them. 'Your business partner. You know where he is?'

'Still in London, I think.'

'His name?'

'Eric Pierce.'

Castle frowned. 'I don't see an Eric Pierce in the cards.'

Nightingale took a drink of water. Now his throat was genuinely dry. 'That's his name.'

'How much did he steal from you?'

'A lot,' said Nightingale. 'Hundreds of thousands. And I think my wife helped him.'

Castle's frown deepened. 'You have a wife? I do not see a wife in the cards.'

'Yes,' said Nightingale. 'Well, in name only. We've been separated for a while. She got the house and the kids. And now it looks as if she's got all my money, too. I think she'd been fucking my partner behind my back for years. More fool me.'

Castle dealt five more cards, stared at them for several seconds, then sat back in his chair and linked his fingers over his stomach. He fixed Nightingale with an unblinking stare. 'You came here to know if your partner was stealing from you. But you already knew he was.'

'I wanted confirmation.'

'You have it,' said Castle. 'And yes, your wife is helping him. The question is, what are you going to do about it?'

'I'm not sure there is anything I can do,' said Nightingale. 'I spoke to a lawyer and he said it would cost me a small fortune to get my money back. We're joint shareholders.' He shrugged. 'It's complicated.'

'It needn't be,' said Castle.

'How so?'

Castle waved a hand at the cards. 'These cards I use, they are special, Mr Dawson. 'Most Tarot cards foretell the future. These cards can change it.'

'Change the future? How is that possible?'

'How is not the point, Mr Dawson. All that it matters is that they can. Tell me, what is it you want?'

'I want my money back. I want sole control of my company. And I want my children.'

'And you can have all that.'

'How?'

Castle waved his child's hand over the table. 'The cards. You tell the cards what you want and they make it happen.'

'It's as easy as that?'

Castle chuckled. 'I never said it was easy. Nothing worth having in life comes easily. But the cards can give you what you want.'

Nightingale laughed dryly. 'I just have to pay, is that it? You're the same as the lawyers. Take, take, take.'

'I don't want your money, Mr Dawson. I just want your signature.' He slid off the chair and walked stiff-leggedly over to the filing cabinet. He pulled open the middle drawer, took out a file and walked back to Nightingale. He slid a single sheet of what looked like parchment out of the file and gave it to him.

Nightingale looked at it. It was Latin, hand-written. 'I can't read this,' he said.

'You don't have to read it. You just have to sign it.'

'Why would I sign something I can't read?'

'Because it will give you your heart's desire,' said Castle. 'You want your money back? You want your partner and your wife to get what they deserve? And you want your children.' He pointed at the sheet. 'If you sign this, the cards will give you what you want.' Castle reached into his pocket and took out a small leather pouch. Inside was a cork, and sticking into the cork was a silver needle. He pulled it out and carefully handed it to Nightingale. As Nightingale looked at the needle, Castle took a pen from his pocket and unscrewed the cap. 'There is one more thing you need to know,' he said. 'The contract has to be signed in blood. Your blood.'

Nightingale faked a surprised laugh. 'Are you serious?'

'Yes I am, Mr Dawson. Very serious. Just prick your thumb, then dip this nib in your blood and sign your name.'

'Then what?'

'Then I will lay out the next five cards and within days you will get everything you want.'

Nightingale stared at the sheet in his hands, nodding slowly. Castle sat on his chair again and waited.

Nightingale put the sheet down on the table, jabbed at his thumb with the pin, then put the pin on the table and dabbed the nib of the pen in the blood oozing from the tiny wound. He scrawled the J and the D before the nib ran dry, then he dabbed it in his blood and finished the signature. Castle nodded his approval. 'Good man,' he said.

He picked up the Tarot deck and went through it, selecting five cards and placing them on the piles. One of the cards was a doll with long hair and blank eyes. Another card had a snake coiled around a young child, squeezing the life out of it. There was a pentagram on another. One card seemed blank but as Nightingale stared at it, it flickered. The final card was of a crucified cat. Castle closed his eyes and began speaking in what sounded like Latin. After a minute or so he stopped and clapped his hands together. 'It is done,' he said.

'How long before it works?' asked Nightingale.

Castle slid off his chair and picked up the sheet of paper that Nightingale had signed. 'Not long,' he said. 'When it happens, you will know.'

'And what did I sign? What did I agree to you?'

'The contract just confirms that you wanted help from the cards,' said Castle. He slid the sheet of paper back into the file and took it over to the filing cabinet. He pulled open a drawer and put the file away. 'It is a technicality, nothing else.' He rubbed his hands together. 'Our work here is now done, Mr Dawson. I shall be in touch once your desires have been granted.'

Nightingale stood up. Castle went back behind his desk and climbed up onto his chair as Nightingale left the room. The woman in the office on the other side of the corridor nodded as he left but didn't say anything and Nightingale let himself out of the front door. He lit a cigarette as soon as he stepped onto the pavement. It was dark now and he blew smoke up at the night sky. He walked slowly over to Jenny's Audi. She wound down the window. 'How did it go?' she asked.

'Did Maria mention that Castle is a dwarf?'

'I don't think you're supposed to call them dwarfs any more.'

'Vertically challenged then. She didn't mention it?'

'I don't think so.'

'You'd remember, wouldn't you?'

'She probably didn't think it was worth mentioning.'

'I just think that's strange, that's all.'

'He's getting people to sign contracts in blood and trying to steal their children and it's the fact that he's a dwarf that you find strange?'

Nightingale took a final drag on his cigarette, flicked it into the road and climbed into the passenger seat.

'So you had a reading?' asked Jenny.

Nightingale nodded. 'It wasn't a regular reading. He used black candles, and he had me recite some Latin phrase over and over again.'

'Can you remember what it was?'

'Something like Electus Ad Veritatem Servandam.'

'Chosen to tell the truth. Are you sure?'

'Not really. You know me and Latin. I just repeated it phonetically. Thing is, it was a shit reading. He bought my story hook line and sinker and said that my partner and wife had been stealing from me. So the cards don't work. Either that or he was ignoring what he was seeing because he was too caught up in conning me.' He took the card out of his pocket and showed it to her. 'The cards he uses, they're not like any Tarot deck I've ever seen.' There was no writing on the card, just a picture. It was a creature, part dragon, part snake, with a plume of smoke oozing from between massive jaws. 'The Tarot set is traditional, there are variations but they all have the same cards, effectively. His deck was weird and I didn't recognise any of the cards.'

'What is that?' asked Jenny, staring at the card. She took it from him, frowning.

'I don't know. A dragon?'

As they stared at it the head of the dragon moved slightly.

'What the hell!' exclaimed Jenny. 'Did you see that?'

'I think so.'

'You think so? It moved, Jack. It bloody well moved.'

'It might have been the light.'

Jenny shook her head fiercely. 'It wasn't the light and you know it,' she said. 'It moved.'

Nightingale stared at the card. The smoke appeared to be feathering from the beast's mouth and the scales on its flanks glittered as she moved the card. 'I think it's the way the card has been painted. You can see it's not printed, this was painted by hand.' He turned it over to show the symbol on the back. 'This is a sigil. A devil's sigil, I think.'

'Did he give you the card?' asked Jenny.

Nightingale looked pained. 'Not exactly.'

'You stole it?' said Jenny. 'Are you serious?'

'Let's say I borrowed it.'

'Jack! He's going to know what you did.'

Nightingale shook his head. 'There are 78 cards in the deck. He only lays out 25 in five groups of five. He won't know.'

She looked at the face of the card and frowned. 'What is it?'

'Some sort of demon, I think. Or mythological creature.' He shrugged. 'I don't know. There were no titles on any of the cards. Castle knows the meaning but I haven't a clue.'

'So what are you going to do with it?'

'I need to know what's so special about these cards. I'm hoping my old friend Mrs Steadman will help.'

'And then?'

'Then we need to get Maria's contract back. I'm pretty sure Castle keeps them in a filing cabinet in his study. That's where he put mine, anyway.'

Jenny's jaw dropped. 'Excuse me?'

'I had to sign a contract, didn't I?' He held up his left hand and showed her the prick mark on his thumb. 'It was the only way to find out where he kept them.'

'Jack, you signed a contract with him?'

'Not as Jack Nightingale, no. I signed as John Dawson.'

'Yes, but using your blood.'

'It'll be fine,' said Nightingale.

'If the contract is signed in your blood, it probably doesn't matter what name you used.'

'It's irrelevant anyway,' said Nightingale. 'When I get Maria's contract, I'll get mine too.'

'And how exactly do you plan to do that?'

'There's no burglar alarm or any form of security that I can see. It'll be easy enough to break in.' He grinned. 'I know people.'

She gave him back the card. 'I just hope you know what you're doing,' she said.

'I do,' said Nightingale. 'Most of the time, anyway.'

* * *

Nightingale's MGB was still in the garage with gearbox problems so he caught a black cab in Bayswater and had it drop him outside the Wicca Woman shop in Camden. He paid the driver and pushed open the shop door. There was only one customer, a young girl with waist-length blonde hair who was buying a selection of candles of different sizes and colours. Nightingale looked around the shop's esoteric collection of New Age and Wicca items including crystals, herbs and pretty much everything a wannabe white witch would need to ply her trade. Nothing from the dark side, of course. The owner, Mrs Steadman, was not a fan of the dark side of the occult world.

After the girl had paid for her purchases and placed them in a brightly-coloured cotton shoulder bag, Nightingale approached the sales assistant, a tall, willowy redhead with alabaster white skin and several dozen white threads tied around her left wrist. She was wearing a long purple dress and was barefoot, though even without shoes she was almost as tall as Nightingale.

'Is Mrs Steadman in?' he asked.

'She's in the back room,' said the girl in an accent that sounded East European. 'Who shall I say is calling?'

Nightingale frowned. 'I'm not calling. I'm here.'

She laughed, the sound of tinkling glass. 'I'm sorry,' she said. 'I used to be a phone operator. That was what I said all day. "Who shall I say is calling?" Maybe a thousand times a day.'

'I bet working here is more fun,' said Nightingale. 'Can you just tell her I'm here?'

She looked over at a beaded curtain, then back at Nightingale. Her perfectly white forehead creased into a frown. 'What was your name again? Sorry.'

'Jack. Jack Nightingale.'

'Like the bird?'

'Exactly.'

She smiled. 'Brilliant,' she said. She pushed through the curtains. Nightingale heard what sounded like a bird squawk and then she reappeared. 'Mrs Steadman said to go through,' she said.

Nightingale went behind the counter and through the curtain. It clicked behind him as it fell back into place. Mrs Steadman was sitting at a circular wooden table with a copy of The Guardian in front of her. A gas fire hissed against one wall and next to it was a large cage in which sat a huge black bird. A raven, maybe. Or a rook. It cocked its head on one side and stared at Nightingale with unblinking coal black eyes.

Mrs Steadman took off a pair of blue tinted pince-nez glasses and let them hang on a silver chain around her neck. 'Mr Nightingale, I was so happy to hear from you,' she said. She didn't get up but offered him her hand. It was tiny and he shook it carefully as if afraid he might break it.

Mrs Steadman was wearing a black silk dress with a high collar and silver buttons down the front. She had a bird-like face with a sharp nose and inquisitive emerald green eyes. Her grey hair was loose with a slight wave. Nightingale had never been able to place Mrs Steadman's age. Her wrinkled skin was almost translucent which made him think she was in her seventies or even eighties but she had the youthful energy of a much younger woman. She waved at the chair opposite her. 'Please sit down,' she said.

'Jack!' squawked the bird.

Nightingale stared at it in amazement.

'Jack!' it said again.

Mrs Steadman saw his look of surprise and laughed. 'He doesn't know your name, Mr Nightingale,' she said. 'That's its call. Though as it's a jackdaw it's not surprising, I suppose. I'm looking after it for a friend.'

'Jack!' squawked the bird again, as if agreeing with her.

Nightingale took off his raincoat, draped it over the back of the chair and sat down.

'Would you like a cup of tea?'

'Tea would be lovely,' said Nightingale.

Mrs Steadman got up and made a pot of tea and put it and blue-and-white striped mugs on the table, along with a matching jug of milk and a bowl of sugar. She poured tea for them both, then sat straight-backed with her hands together in her lap. 'So, how can I help you?'

Nightingale reached into his jacket pocket and pulled out the card. He held it out and she took it. Almost immediately she yelped and dropped it onto the table. She stared at her right hand, her eyes wide. There were blisters on her thumb and first two fingers and Nightingale could smell burned flesh.

'Mrs Steadman…' he began but before he could finish the sentence she had jumped to her feet and hurried out through the beaded curtain. As Nightingale picked up the card he heard her talking to the assistant. Not long afterwards she reappeared, holding a pale blue crystal between her thumb and fingers. The crystal was attached to a thin silver chain. She rubbed her fingers and thumb against the crystal as she sat down. She forced a smile. 'You must be careful with that,' she said, nodding at the card.

'I've handled it all day,' said Nightingale, putting it back into his pocket.

'You and I are not the same, Mr Nightingale. I'm, how shall I say, less contaminated than you are.'

'Contaminated?'

'I don't mean to offend, but my aura is pure, Mr Nightingale. Something as evil as that… it has an effect on me.'

'But it's used by a Tarot reader. He gives it to his customers to shuffle.'

'And again, those customers will have been contaminated. It's the way of the world.'

'Sinners, you mean? Everyone sins?'

'I wouldn't call it sinning exactly. But if you gave that card to a young child, for instance…'

'Or a priest?'

Mrs Steadman looked at him with a sly smile. 'That would depend on the priest,' she said. She took the crystal away from her finger. The burn had gone. She showed her hand to him. 'There you are, as good as new,' she said. 'So, you want to know about the card?'

'Please,' said Nightingale. 'I didn't know who else to talk to.'

'You know about Tarot cards, I assume?'

'Only that they are used to forecast the future. Do you believe in it, Mrs Steadman?'

'Whether or not I believe in the Tarot matters not one jot,' she said. 'What matters is whether or not it works.'

'And does it?'

'Sometimes,' she said. 'It depends more on the person using the cards than the cards themselves. But that card, that card belongs to a very special deck. You've heard of Aleister Crowley, of course.'

'Of course,' said Nightingale. Crowley was labelled as the 'Wickedest Man In The World,' by the British Press. He was a Satanist, one of the highest profile Satanists ever to have walked the Earth who called himself The Great Beast 666. There was also a rumour that Crowley had bedded Barbara Bush's mother – Pauline Pierce - in Paris in the 1920s and gotten her pregnant, which would have made the Satanist the grandfather of George W Bush and Jeb Bush. Crowley was long dead, of course. But his reputation lived on.

'Well, Crowley commissioned his own Tarot deck, containing astrological, zodiacal, elemental and Qabalistic symbols. The deck has the traditional order of the trumps but he changed some of the words. So Crowley changed The Magician to The Magus, The World to the Universe, Strength to Lust, Justice to Adjustment, and so on.'

'So the card I have is from an Aleister Crowley deck?'

Mrs Steadman shook her head. 'It's more complicated than that, Mr Nightingale. Crowley commissioned the artwork from a famous artist of the time, Lady Frieda Harris. She did as asked and created the cards and ended up getting quite close to Crowley and when he died in 1947 she was one of the executors of his will. In 1952 her husband died and she moved to India, where she passed away ten years later.' She sipped her tea. 'This is what is generally not known, Mr Nightingale. While she was in India she was approached by an Indian gentleman, a middleman who wanted another set of cards designed. The middleman had very specific requirements for the cards and the designs. And she was supplied with the inks and paints to be used.' She nodded at his pocket. 'The card you have is from that set. And it was just one set. She designed and painted the 78 cards herself and when she had finished they were taken from her.' She grimaced. 'What Lady Frieda Harris didn't know was that the middleman was acting for a demon from Hell. The paints she was given....' She shuddered. 'They contained more than just paint.'

'So they are special?'

'They are cursed, Mr Nightingale. Usually with Tarot cards, the power lies with the person using them. The cards are a tool to help bring out the forecasting ability of the person who uses them. The users have their favourite decks, but the cards are a means to an end. But with the second Harris deck, the power lies within the cards.'

'They're possessed?'

'Worse than that,' said Mrs Steadman. 'They are pure evil.' She sipped her tea again and this time her hand trembled. 'Truly evil, Mr Nightingale. You need to be careful. Very, very careful. Regular Tarot cards can be used to analyse the past and forecast the future. But these cards, these cards can change the future. And not in a good way.'

'What about the sigil on the back? Do you know what it represents?'

Mrs Steadman shook her head. 'I'm not an expert on sigils,' she said. 'It's not my field.'

Nightingale could feel a warmth spreading around the pocket where he'd put the card and he shifted in his chair. 'What do you think I should do, Mrs Steadman?'

'That is up to you,' she said. 'You only have the one card?'

Nightingale nodded.

'And may I ask how it came into your possession?'

Nightingale smiled uncomfortably. 'I borrowed it.'

'And does the person you borrowed it from, know that you have it?'

'I hope not.'

Mrs Steadman shook her head sadly. 'Oh Mr Nightingale, what have you done?' she sighed.

Nightingale figured the question was rhetorical. She knew exactly what he had done. The question was, what should he do next. He smiled and waited patiently.

'It seems to me you have two choices,' she said eventually. 'You could return the card, and hope that the owner doesn't realise what has happened. But that option might already be too late.'

'Why's that?'

'Because it is not the owner who is the danger. It is the cards themselves. And the cards will already know that one of their number is missing. And they will want the deck restored. The question is, will they be satisfied with the return of the card? Or will they want something more?'

Nightingale frowned. 'Such as?'

'Revenge, Mr Nightingale. They might want revenge.'

Nightingale's mouth had gone suddenly dry and he had trouble swallowing. 'You said I had two choices. What is the second choice?'

She leaned forward and fixed him with her beady stare. 'You could destroy the cards,' she said. 'Destroy the cards before they destroy you.'

* * *

It was rush hour and the traffic in Camden was horrendous so Nightingale caught the Tube back to Bayswater. He was less than a hundred yards from his office when he saw the two men. They were black and wearing hoodies and low-slung jeans. The taller of the two spotted him first and he jabbed his companion in the ribs. The smaller one looked at Nightingale and nodded. They started walking towards Nightingale with the confident swagger of predators who knew they were stronger than their prey. Both men reached into the pockets of their hoodies. They made no attempt to disguise their intentions and started walking faster. Nightingale took a quick look around but there was as much chance of seeing a policeman as there was of catching a glimpse of a leprechaun guarding his pot of gold.

The road was to his left, a row of shops to his right. There was a butchers just ahead of him and he ran in. A red-faced butcher in a black and white striped apron was handing a bundle of something to a pensioner wearing a heavy wool coat and a headscarf. Nightingale smiled and nodded at the old lady as she left the shop.

'Yes, Sir, what can I get you?' asked the butcher.

'This is going to sound crazy, but I need a knife.'

The butcher frowned. 'A knife.'

A bell buzzed as the door opened. The two hoodies walked into the shop. They were glaring menacingly at Nightingale. One of them pulled out a knife. 'Give us the card!' he snarled.

The butcher picked up a cleaver and slapped it onto the counter. Nightingale picked it up. The second hoodie had also pulled out a knife.

'I'm calling the police,' said the butcher. He grabbed at a phone mounted on the wall. Nightingale ignored him. By the time the police arrived it would be over, one way or another.

The two hoodies stared at him with blank eyes. 'The card,' said the taller one.

'The card,' repeated his companion. They both took a step towards Nightingale.

Nightingale lashed out with the cleaver, slashing the knife arm of the nearest hoodie. The hoodie yelped and life returned to his eyes. He blinked and he frowned at his injured arm. The knife clattered to the tiled floor. 'What the fuck?' he muttered. He took a step back, clutching his injured arm. 'What the fuck?' he repeated.

The second hoodie didn't seem to be aware of what had happened and continued to walk towards Nightingale, the knife twitching in his outstretched hand. He was walking stiffly as if he was having trouble controlling his legs.

The butcher had taken the phone away from his head and was staring at the two hoodies, open-mouthed.

The hoodie that Nightingale had hit turned and ran out of the shop.

'What the fuck is going on?' said the butcher.

'The card,' said the remaining hoodie. 'Give us the card!'

Nightingale waved the cleaver around but the hoodie paid it no attention, he was staring straight ahead. Nightingale raised the cleaver and thwacked it into the hoodie's right elbow. The knife fell to the floor and the hoodie started blinking. 'Huh?' he grunted. He looked up at Nightingale's face and frowned as if seeing it for the first time. Maybe he was. 'Bruv?' said the man. Then he looked at the blood that was seeping into his right sleeve. 'Bruv?' he repeated.

'You need to go now,' said Nightingale quietly.

The hoodie looked at Nightingale, then at the cleaver, then back at his arm. He frowned. 'I'm cut, Bruv,' he croaked.

'You cut yourself,' said Nightingale. 'You should go.'

The hoodie took a step back, then another, then he turned, pulled open the door and ran out. The door banged shut behind him.

The butcher replaced the receiver. 'What the hell just happened?' he asked.

Nightingale placed the cleaver on the counter. 'Attempted mugging,' he said. 'All good, now.' He smiled brightly. 'While I'm here, how about a pound of pork sausages?'

* * *

Jenny looked up from her computer as Nightingale walked into the office. 'I come bearing gifts,' he said and placed a plastic bag on her desk.

She frowned and peered into the bag. 'Sausages?'

'Breakfast of champions,' he said.

'How did it go with Mrs Steadman?'

Nightingale reached into his jacket pocket and took out the Tarot card. He placed the card on her desk, face up. The dragon moved and flame flickered from between its jaws. Nightingale turned the card upside down. 'Okay, so now here's the thing,' he said. 'Taking the card might not have been the smartest move.'

Jenny raised her eyebrows. 'Do you think?'

He ignored her sarcasm. 'Mrs Steadman basically gave me two choices. Either give the card back, or destroy the deck.'

'What about just throwing away the card you have and pretending it never happened?'

He shook his head. 'So long as the deck is incomplete, I'm in danger.'

'By "I" do you mean "we" because if you do I'm not going to be a happy bunny, Jack.'

Nightingale held up a hand. 'I'm the one who took it. You were just an innocent bystander.'

'Just so long as the forces of darkness understand that.' She frowned and leaned forward. 'Is that blood on your coat?'

He looked down at a few spots of blood on his right sleeve. 'It's nothing,' he said. He took off his raincoat and hung it on the back of the door.

'Please don't tell me you cut yourself shaving,' she said.

Nightingale sighed. 'A couple of muggers tried to take the card from me. It was… weird.'

'Weird?'

'Like they were possessed. They ran off.'

'Why, because you spoke harshly to them?'

Nightingale laughed and shook his head. 'I was in the butchers. He loaned me a knife. One thing led to another…'

'And you bring me a pound of sausages? Great, Jack, that's just great.'

'They're handmade,' he said. 'Artisan.'

'You can shove them where the sun doesn't shine,' she said. She leaned back in her chair and sighed. 'So what are we going to do?'

'So now it's we?'

She flashed him a cold smile. 'You don't think you're capable of fixing this yourself, do you?'

'Thanks,' he said. 'Are you okay to give me a lift?'

'To where?'

'Gosling Manor. I need to check out the sigil on the cards. It might give us a clue as to who – or what – we're dealing with.'

* * *

Jenny brought her Audi to a halt in front of Gosling Manor's massive wrought iron gates. Nightingale climbed out and pushed the gates open so that she could drive through. He closed the gates behind her and got back into the car. She put the car in gear and drove along a narrow paved road that curved to the right through thick woodland, then parked next to a huge stone fountain, the centrepiece of which was a weathered stone mermaid surrounded by dolphins and fish. Gosling Manor was a two-storey mansion, the lower floor built of stone, the upper floor made of weathered bricks. The mansion was topped by a tiled roof with four massive chimney stacks. To the left of the house was a four-door garage and behind it a large conservatory.

Jenny switched off the engine and they both climbed out. Nightingale lit a cigarette as he looked over at the ivy-covered entrance. 'I really should see about selling this place,' he said.

'What's taking so long?'

'My father had all sort of debts against it, it's taking the lawyers forever to sort it all out.' The house had been left to Nightingale after his genetic father – a man he'd never known – had blown his head off with a shotgun in one of the manor's bedrooms. Nightingale took a key from his raincoat pocket and unlocked the massive oak door. It opened easily and without a sound, and they walked into a huge hallway with wood-panelled walls, a glistening marble floor and a large multi-tiered chandelier. There were three oak doors leading off the hallway, but the entrance to the basement library was concealed within the wooden panelling. He pulled open the hinged panel and reached inside to flick the light switch. The light flickered on revealing a flight of wooden stairs. Nightingale headed on down.

The basement ran the full length of the house and was lined with filled book shelves. Running down the middle of the basement were two lines of display cases filled with all sorts of occult paraphernalia, from skulls to crystal balls. Nightingale walked along to a sitting area with two red leather Chesterfield sofas and a claw-footed teak coffee table that was piled high with books. He stubbed out his cigarette in a crystal ashtray, then took off his raincoat and placed it on the back of one of the sofas.

'Please don't tell me we have to go through all the books,' Jenny said. 'There are thousands of them.'

'I'm pretty sure I saw a book on sigils last time I was here,' said Nightingale. He went over to one of the bookcases. 'I'm just not sure where.'

'You know the word sigil comes from the Latin sigillum, meaning seal?' asked Jenny, dropping down on a sofa.

'You mean the cute animal that claps its flippers and eats fish?'

'You know what I mean,' said Jenny.

Nightingale pulled out a leather-bound book. It was hand-written with drawings of pentagrams, not sigils. He put it back.

Sigil might have meant seal originally, but in the occult world a sigil referred to the signs and symbols that represented various angels and demons. Nightingale was fairly sure that the sigil on Castle's cards had nothing to do with angels.

Books on sigils were rare - demons and devils preferred to keep their sigils secret because, used properly, a sigil could give a Satanist a measure of control over a demon. Nightingale was by no means an expert on sigils but he knew that many sigils were created by converting the name of a devil to numbers and transferring the numbers to a magic square. The locations were then connected by lines, forming a figure which was abstract and unique.

He pulled out a thin volume, bound in scuffed black leather. There was no title on the spine or front, but when he flicked it open he smiled when he saw the words 'Secret Sigils'. There were no chapters or headings, it was just a collection of prints of sigils and underneath the name of the devil or angel it applied to, and a brief description. There was no date of publication but the pages were yellowed with age and in places the print had faded. 'Got it,' said Nightingale. He took the book over to Jenny and sat next to her. He gave her the book and fished the card out of his raincoat and placed it face down on the coffee table.

Jenny began flicking through the book. She was just over halfway through when she found a match. 'Baal,' she said. 'Also known as Bel, Bael and Baeli. Male consort to Astoreth, the Queen of Heaven. So he's an angel? That's good news, right?'

Nightingale shook his head. 'One of the Fallen,' he said. 'Read on.'

Jenny scanned the page. 'Oh,' she said. 'One of the 72 spirits of Solomon, a great and powerful king of Hell who governs the eastern infernal regions.' She grimaced. 'That's not good.'

Nightingale leaned over and read over her shoulder. 'He is said to appear in many different forms, including the body of a man with the head of a toad or a cat, and sometimes with a human head. Sometimes with all three. Baal's infernal duties include passing on all knowledge and satisfying all cravings, no matter what they be. He can also impart invisibility to his followers. He commands 68 legions of the damned.' He sat back and sighed. 'Sounds like a nasty piece of work.'

Jenny tapped at the page. 'It gets worse,' she said. 'Some of his followers burn children as sacrifices.' Her eyes widened. 'That must be why he wants Maria's daughter.'

'And why he was so interested when I said I had kids,' said Nightingale. 'What's the betting that the contract I signed was about my fictional offspring?'

'What are we going to do, Jack?'

'First things first,' he said. 'We need to get that card back. Then we need to get the contracts and destroy them. And we need to destroy the deck, if we can.'

'That's a pretty tall order.'

'One step at a time.' He picked up the card. 'I'm going to need your help.'

Jenny forced a smile. 'Nothing new there.'

* * *

Jenny parked the Audi across the road from Mason Castle's house. She sighed and switched off the engine.

'You don't have to do this,' said Nightingale.

She flashed him a tight smile. 'You can't go back in. In case he knows what you did. So if anyone is going to be able to slip the card back into the deck, it's me.'

'Just be careful.'

She looked at him scornfully. 'Do you think? Of course I'll be careful.'

'I know, I know, I'm sorry,' said Nightingale. 'I meant, you know.' He shrugged. 'I don't want anything to happen to you, that's all.'

'Well hopefully nothing will,' she said. 'He doesn't know me, he's never seen me before, I've used a fake name to make the appointment. At some point he'll give me the cards and I'll put yours in and that should be that.'

'Thanks for doing this,' he said.

'Have you thought about what happens after we return the card? Mrs Steadman said the deck was evil and should be destroyed.'

Nightingale nodded. 'One step at a time,' he said. 'Once the card is back in the deck, we should be in the clear. We can think what to do once that's done.'

Jenny took the card out of her pocket and looked at it. A forked tongue flicked out of the dragon's mouth and its tail twitched. 'How does it do that? How does it move?'

'Don't look at it.'

'It feels warm,' she said. 'As if it was alive.'

'Just keep it hidden until you're ready to put it back.'

She nodded and slipped the card into the pocket of her jacket. She took a deep breath and forced a smile. 'Into the valley of death,' she said.

'He's just a fortune teller,' he said. 'You go in, you slip the card into the deck, you listen to what he has to say, you nod and you smile and you leave.'

'I hope so,' she said. She climbed out of the car and bent down to talk to him. 'And no bloody smoking while I'm gone.'

'Cross my heart,' he said.

She slammed the door and jogged across the road. He watched her ring the bell and a few seconds later slip inside the house.

Nightingale waited. After five minutes he took out his cigarettes. When she had said 'don't smoke' he presumed she meant don't smoke in the car and that was a fair enough request, seeing as how it was hers. He climbed out of the car and lit a Marlboro. He stared over at the house as he blew smoke up at the gunmetal sky. A woman walked by, pushing a pram. Two large women wearing black burkhas, their faces covered, waddled down the pavement laden with Marks and Spencer carrier bags. A postman in a pale blue uniform pushed a trolley full of mail. Three schoolchildren with bulging backpacks laughed and joked. Two housewives in designer suits laughed with the sound of breaking glass. Just a regular day in downtown London. And on the other side of the street, Jenny McLean was trying to slip a Tarot card into a deck owned by a man who got his clients to sign contracts in blood. His phone rang and he flicked away what was left of his cigarette. He took out his phone and looked at the screen. It was Jenny. He put the phone to his ear. 'How's it going, kid?' he asked.

'Jenny McLean can't get to the phone,' said a husky voice. 'We request the pleasure of your company in our consulting rooms. Now.' The line went dead. Nightingale cursed out loud and slapped the roof of the Audi.

* * *

The lock buzzed just as Nightingale reached out to press the button on the speakerphone. He pushed the door and stepped into the hall. He walked slowly towards Castle's office. The receptionist wasn't at her desk. The door to Castle's office was closed. Nightingale turned the handle and pushed it open. He heard the crackle and hiss of the fire but nothing else. He opened the door wider. Jenny was sitting in a chair by the table where Castle laid out his cards. She twisted to look at him and he realised she had been gagged with a strip of cloth.

'Come on in, Mr Nightingale, don't keep us waiting,' said Castle.

The dwarf was standing by his desk holding a semi-automatic. The gun looked huge in his child-sized hand. The receptionist was standing at the side of his desk.

'Please close the door behind you,' said Castle.

Nightingale did as he was told. Jenny was tied to the chair. The Tarot deck was on the table. So was the card that Jenny had been trying to return.

'Did you really think you would get away with it?' asked Castle.

'Away with what?' asked Nightingale. Castle knew his name which was definitely a bad sign but he needed to play for time.

'The cards know everything,' said Castle. 'Immediately you stole one, the deck knew who you were and what you were doing.'

'To be fair, I wasn't stealing it,' said Nightingale. 'I was borrowing it. That's why Jenny here was returning it. I don't see what the problem is.'

'You know what the problem is, Nightingale.'

'I'm not sure I do. I borrowed the card, now we've returned it, all's well that ends well.'

Castle smiled thinly and gestured with the gun. 'You know this is not going to end well, obviously.'

Nightingale gestured at Jenny. 'You can let her go. None of this is her doing.'

Castle shook his head. 'She lied her way in here and tried to sneak back the card you stole. I think it's clear she's very much involved.'

'Mason, we need to get this over with,' said the receptionist. 'We have another client in fifteen minutes.'

'Look, you've got your card back, just let us go and…'

'And what?' interrupted Castle. 'You'll forget this ever happened? You won't go to the police? You won't creep in here at night and steal the contracts, the contracts I have worked so hard to acquire.'

'It's about the children, isn't it? You're taking children to sacrifice?'

'Is that what Mrs Steadman told you?' He laughed when he saw the look of surprise flash across Nightingale's face. 'How do I know about Mrs Steadman? The cards, you moron. The cards are one. They are interconnected. Whatever happens to one of the cards happens to them all.'

'They're a living thing?'

'No, they're not alive. Not in any sense of the word. But they represent something, something powerful.'

'Something evil,' said Nightingale.

'Evil is purely a point of view,' said Castle.

Nightingale walked over to the table and picked up the card in front of Jenny. 'Stay where you are!' shouted Castle.

Nightingale ignored him and took two steps to the fireplace. 'So if the cards are connected, and the cards represent something evil, what happens to that something if I destroy the card?'

'Don't do that!' shouted Castle. 'Get away from the fire!'

Nightingale knew from Castle's tone that he had made the right call.

'What happens if it burns?' asked Nightingale.

'Don't you dare!' screamed the receptionist and she ran at Nightingale, her hands screwed up into claws.

Nightingale tossed the card into the fire and picked up one of the brass pokers. He brought it crashing down on the woman's head and she fell to the floor with a dull thud. Castle screamed and ran over to the fireplace. 'No!' he shouted. He grabbed a set of brass tongs with his left hand and began to fumble for the burning card as he tried to keep the gun pointed at Nightingale.

Nightingale lashed out with the poker and hit Castle's right elbow. The gun clattered on the floor but Castle seemed more concerned about the burning card.

Nightingale kicked the gun away, then hurried over to Jenny and started to untie her gag.

Smoke was pouring from the fire, thick black smoke that rose to the ceiling and began to swirl around.

Castle managed to grip the card with the tongs and he pulled it from the fire. He dropped it on the hearth, threw the tongs to the side and began patting the card with his hands.

The smoke was whirling around the ceiling now, and the room was filled with the sound of thunder. There was a flash of lightning, and the hairs stood up on the back of Nightingale's neck.

Castle had realised what was happening and he twisted around to look at the whirling smoke. 'No!' he shouted. 'It wasn't my fault!'

The smoke was whirling faster and faster like a miniature tornado. The centre of the tornado started to harden and take shape.

'I can handle it!' shouted Castle. 'Please!' He held up the card. 'See, it's okay! I saved it.'

Lightning flashed again and the floor vibrated. There was a figure in the middle of the room. Large, scaled. With a forked tail and three leering heads. A giant toad. A green-eyed black cat. And an old man with blazing red eyes.

Castle crawled away from the fireplace and knelt in front of the figure. 'Master, I am only here to serve you!' he shouted.

The figure lashed out with a taloned claw, knocking the dwarf to the side. Castle's head cracked against the cast iron fireplace and he went still.

'I know your name, and your name has the power!' shouted Nightingale. He coughed and cleared his throat. 'You are Baal, one of the Fallen, and I command you to stay where you are!'

The demon hesitated, but then took a step towards Nightingale and the three heads roared as one.

'Jack!' screamed Jenny. 'The cards!'

Nightingale looked at her, then at the Tarot deck on the table.

The demon roared and the room shuddered, throwing Nightingale off balance. He staggered towards the table as the demon roared again. He felt a searing heat on his back but he ignored it and gathered up the cards. As he turned to face the demon a claw flashed through the air and he ducked. It missed him by inches. He dropped down onto his knees and threw the cards into the fire.

The demon shrieked and the whole building shook as if it was in the grip of an earthquake. Flames shot up the chimney and grey smoke billowed into the room making Nightingale's eyes water even more. He coughed and spluttered as tears ran down his cheeks.

The demon took a step towards the fire, all three of its heads tilted back as it shrieked in anger or pain. There was a brilliant flash from the fireplace and the roaring of the demon reached a crescendo and then there was a crack of what sounded like thunder, the room seemed to fold in on itself and the demon vanished. So did the smoke. And the fire was hissing and crackling quietly exactly as it had when Nightingale had walked into the room.

'Jack...' gasped Jenny.

Nightingale hurried over to her and undid her bonds. She stood up but almost immediately her legs gave way and he had to grab her around the waist to keep her from falling. She put her arms around his neck. 'Is it over?' she whispered.

'I think so,' he said. 'Or at least it will be when I've destroyed the contracts.'

Jenny looked down at the unconscious bodies of Castle and his receptionist. 'What about them?'

'Don't know, don't care,' he said. 'But I doubt they'll be going to the police anytime soon.'

'I thought….' She shuddered.

'Thought what? That we were in trouble. Oh ye of little faith.' He laughed and gave her a squeeze. 'I told you I knew what I was doing.'

POSSESSION

Jack Nightingale climbed the stone steps to the Church of the Holy Cross in South Boston. The air was chilly, a wind tugging at his raincoat and whipping leaves about, so he was grateful when he opened the door and slipped into the warmth of the nave. The place was massive, one of the oldest and largest stone churches in Boston. Three levels rose high above the nave to a vaulted ceiling with stained glass windows on each side. It smelled as cool and damp as a cave. Muffled whispers scuttled across the space, heads in the pews bowed low in prayer. Up above, pigeons nested in far corners, crooning in the darkness. Along the west side of the nave was a pair of confessional boxes lined against the wall. They were carved of smooth mahogany which glistened in the chamber. Nightingale made his way to them, entering one and closing the door behind him. He knelt. Through the mesh he could make out the profile of a priest. 'Welcome, my son,' said the priest in a soft voice.

'Bless me Father, for I have sinned,' said Nightingale. 'It has been four months since my last confession.' Was lying in the confessional a sin? Probably. The priest nodded, ready to hear his confession. Nightingale continued. 'Over the months I've taken a fancy to my neighbor, a beautiful young woman. It first began at a barbecue her husband invited me to. I couldn't take my eyes off her, and I gathered she felt the same because she'd catch me staring and would smile at me. We talked and flirted a bit, and before I knew it we had started seeing each other in secret. First at the Motel 6 outside of town, then later on at my flat; even in her and her husband's bed.' The priest was silent. 'I'm not in love with her,' continued Nightingale. 'It's lust, I know that, but I think she's fallen in love with me. She says she wants to leave her husband and I don't know what to do about it.'

There was a long pause. Then the priest spoke. 'You don't love her?'

'No, Father, I don't.'

'Lust,' said the priest, nodding sagely. 'My son, I shall give you counsel. I advise you to renounce this affair immediately. Tell this woman how you truly feel, and end it. Do not go back to her. You have entered the bed of another man's wife; you have committed the grave sin of adultery.'

'You are right, Father,' said Nightingale, 'I'll do as you say. It was a mistake. I have been such a fool.'

'And you must make penance, perhaps by volunteering at this very church, or at the soup kitchen down on 3rd and Roxbury. And if in the future you should feel this sin creep up on you, this devilry whispering into your ear, you must appeal to the Heavenly Father for his love and counsel.'

'Thank you, Father,' said Nightingale.

'Do not thank me, my son, thank Him. Go ahead,' the priest encouraged him. 'Express your sorrow to the Lord, so that he may absolve you of this terrible sin.'

Nightingale bowed his head. Closing his eyes, he said, 'Dear God, I am deeply sorry for my sins. In choosing to do wrong and failing to do good, I have sinned against you, whom I love above all things. I firmly intend, with your help, to do penance, and to avoid whatever leads me to sin. Our savior Jesus Christ suffered and died for us. In his name, please have mercy on my soul.'

The priest bowed his head in prayer and brought his hands together. 'God, the Father of mercies, through the death and resurrection of His Son, has reconciled the world to Himself and sent the Holy Spirit among us for the forgiveness of sins; through the ministry of the Church may God give you pardon and peace, and I absolve you from your sins in the name of the Father, and of the Son, and of the Holy Spirit. Amen.'

'Amen,' said Nightingale, crossing himself. 'Thank you, Father.'

Nightingale left the confessional. He walked down the aisle and pushed open the large wooden double doors. A gust of cold autumn air blew back his hair and ruffled his coat. He propped up his collar, took out a packet of Marlboro, and lit a cigarette. He sat on the stone steps as he smoked and watched people going about their day in the early afternoon, the sky a grey mass with dark pockets indicating rain. He smoked, and he waited.

He was halfway through a second cigarette when he heard the door open and the shuffle of footsteps. Nightingale knew that the priest was a smoker but whereas Nightingale was a fan of Marlboro, the priest preferred to roll his own. The priest stopped at the top step and looked down at Nightingale. He was wearing his robes, his large belly protruding in the midsection. His face was red and pockmarked with acne scars from a boyhood long ago. Bright blue eyes shone out brilliantly in contrast to the unhandsome face. 'You seem reluctant to leave,' said the priest, walking down the steps.

'Just admiring your beautiful city,' said Nightingale. He took out his cigarettes and offered the pack. The priest thanked him, taking the cigarette and inserting it between his lips. Nightingale leaned over and lit it for him with his old battered Zippo.

'You are not from here,' said the priest. It was a statement, not a question.

'England,' said Nightingale. The truth. 'But I've lived in the area for a few years.' A lie. There were stoplights in the square. Several cars had parked at the red light but an old beater with deafening rap music careened past the parked cars and ran the light. Several people laid on their horns.

'A beautiful city indeed,' said the priest, watching the speeding car with disapproval. 'Though there are some undesirable elements, I must say.'

'Reminds me of the quote - "What strange phenomena we find in a great city. All we need do is stroll about with our eyes open. Life swarms with innocent monsters." Says it all, really.'

The priest smiled through a puff of smoke, impressed. 'Baudelaire,' he said. 'Though I think he was talking about Paris.'

'Yeah,' said Nightingale. 'I just like the bit about innocent monsters.'

Still smiling, the priest extended his hand. 'Father O'Grady.'

Nightingale took it. 'Jack Nightingale.'

'Nice to meet you, son.'

'Same.'

A pretty young mother and her young son walked along the sidewalk. The boy, blond with blue eyes and bound head to toe in thick winter clothes, stared at them. O'Grady smiled and waved at the little boy, who turned and buried his face in his mom's stomach. 'Do you have any children, Jack?'

Nightingale shrugged. 'None that I know of.'

O'Grady laughed. 'And what do you do? A teacher of literature, perhaps? With a leaning towards the French poets?'

'Nope, not me, Father. I wouldn't have the patience to sit in some stuffy classroom and regurgitate the same thing over and over again. Nah, I'm an investigator. Eradicating evil, that sort of thing.' He blew smoke up at the leaden sky.

'A most noble profession,' said O'Grady.

Nightingale shrugged. 'Kind of my calling, you could say.'

'Good and Evil are among the oldest rudiments of creation,' said the priest, cigarette dangling between his lips, O'Grady bared two fists together, knuckle to knuckle. 'An unstoppable force against an immovable object.' He pushed his fists until one began pushing the other in the opposite direction. 'But only the good wins. It always does.'

'And which one are we?' asked Nightingale.

O'Grady stopped the display and took the cigarette back in his hand. 'I'm sorry? What do you mean?'

'We're the good, I know that. But are we the unstoppable force or the immovable object?'

'Huh,' said O'Grady, 'good question, I never really thought of that. I suppose we could be either. But I'd like to think we're the object. The object – good – is immovable, therefore we cannot lose. We do not have to emit a force *against* something, we merely have to prevent it from forcing us into submission.'

Nightingale blew out a cloud of smoke. 'I like it. But there's that other saying: "Evil prevails when good men fail to act." I can personally say I've seen it firsthand a number of times when I was a hostage negotiator. I think if all us good men fail to act, it's only natural that the evil, or the "unstoppable force" as you call it, will take over. So which one are you, Father?' asked Nightingale, watching him. 'Are you good, or evil?'

O'Grady laughed. 'Good, of course! At least I should hope so. I wouldn't be in this profession if I felt otherwise.'

Nightingale flicked the ash off his cigarette. 'I thought so. Which brings me to why I'm here today. I know someone. A boy. He needs your help.'

The priest frowned. 'My help? I thought *you* needed my help, with your confession…'

'Sure, I was overdue a confession, but I wanted to meet you. Because of the boy.'

O'Grady looked confused. 'I'm not sure I understand what you're on about.'

'To perform an exorcism, the exorcists must first go to confession to purify themselves of sin. Right?'

'I'm sorry, you said you were an investigator?'

'I investigate paranormal disturbances. A boy I know is possessed and I need the help of an able priest to exorcise him. Your help, Father O'Grady.'

O'Grady stubbed out his cigarette and put it in a receptacle. He shook his head, his cheeks quivering. 'I'm sorry, I can't help you.' He turned to leave.

'Of course you can, you're a priest. A man of God. A man who believes in the struggle between good and evil.'

The priest stopped. 'No, I mean I don't believe you've come to the right place. Try a psychiatrist. I'm certain the boy is dealing not with a demon but with some sort of mental disorder. Almost all of these cases are.' The priest started up the stairs but Nightingale grasped the man's elbow.

'Almost all of them, right,' said Nightingale. 'But not this one. I've investigated dozens of these cases, Father, read all the research, and I can assure you this is the real deal. You said you're good, otherwise you wouldn't be a priest. I believe you. But if that's true how can you let an innocent boy die in the hands of a devil?'

'The Devil or a devil?'

'A devil,' said Nightingale. 'One of Satan's minions, but a powerful one.'

'Which one?' asked the priest, frowning.

'This one calls itself Bakka.'

The priest froze. In an instant his face paled, and he leaned against the iron railing so fast Nightingale reached out because he thought the old man was falling. The priest composed himself, breathing deeply. 'Please,' he said. 'May I have another cigarette?' Nightingale quickly took out his Marlboro, gave him one, and lit it for him. The priest sucked it in, and when he blew out the smoke he seemed to be sighing with it.

'So you know that name?' said Nightingale.

The priest nodded. It seemed an eternity before he spoke. 'There are many demons and devils in the underworld, Jack,' he said eventually, his voice a low growl. 'But few are as wretched and evil as the one you just mentioned. Bakka is known by the clergy to be one of Satan's most devout servants. It was a man once, millennia ago, back in the time of Christ. As the legend goes, this man invited his family to a banquet hall. Men, women, children, his own wife and children among them, and all their relatives. While they were dining, the man slipped out and barred the doors, then splashed the building with oil and set it on fire. He burned his entire family alive, and the next morning, once the fires cleared, he used what was left of their bodies to perform Black Mass. It is not known why he did this, whether he was possessed by a demon or by Satan himself, or whether he did it of his own wickedness. But several days later he was tracked down in the remote countryside and killed. Since then it has become one of Satan's most powerful minions.' He took a long, slow drag on his cigarette and blew smoke. 'Bakka is what you might call special,' continued the priest, 'because it doesn't need to be invited by a victim; it simply chooses them. But this devil can't survive on its own; it must be inside a human. If it's exorcised from the boy it will be forced to go somewhere else, to another human nearby. If there is no human to enter, it will be vanquished.' O'Grady looked at Nightingale. 'So even if this is Bakka, there's no way to ensure anyone's safety at the exorcism. It's virtually impossible.' He drew on his cigarette again. His face was ashen.

'I happen to know a way to protect everyone present,' said Nightingale.

'Is that so?' said the priest, his voice loaded with disbelief.

'You can leave that part to me. I just need you to be there. I need a priest. Do you know how to perform an exorcism?'

'Yes, I know how, but all exorcisms must be approved by the Vatican. There are fifty exorcists in this country designated by Bishops to combat evil. Try one of them. The Vatican will supply a list. I can get it for you if needs be.'

'I've tried several. They won't return my calls. I don't need someone who has permission from the Vatican, I need someone who knows what they're doing and you seem to be the prime candidate at the moment. You know what this devil is. You know what it's capable of.'

The priest shook his head. 'It's very risky. Very dangerous. The boy could die. So could you.'

'I can't do this on my own, Father. I'm not a priest. I'm just a man.'

'As I said, there are other priests better qualified than me to assist you.'

'We don't have time, Father.'

'It's too dangerous.'

'For you? Or for the boy?'

'For everyone,' said the priest. 'Why me? Why did you come to me?' He drew on his cigarette and his hand shook.

'Because you aren't too far away from where the boy lives. I can drive you there so you can see for yourself. Look Father, I will take full responsibility for whatever happens. But one thing is for sure, if we do nothing, the boy *will* die.'

The priest grimaced. 'So you'll take responsibility for my death, will you? Or for my soul being damned to hell for all eternity. That's not much of a comfort, frankly.'

'That's not what I meant. I mean I'll make sure nothing happens to us. I have experience in these matters. I can protect you. And me. And the boy. I know a way we can cast out the devil and make sure he does not enter anyone else, and that will result in its destruction.'

The priest smoked. He thought for a moment. Storm clouds had rolled in and thunder was grumbling in the ashen sky. Rain drops started to fall. Nightingale spoke first. 'Just see the boy. That's all I'm asking, Father. See the boy and then make your decision. It's the least you can do.'

'Where is he?'

'Plymouth. Fifty minute drive south of here.'

The priest handed Nightingale his smoldering cigarette. 'All right, hold this. I'll need to get my coat.'

* * *

It rained during their drive to Plymouth, Massachusetts, site of the Pilgrims' landing on the Mayflower in 1620 and the ninth oldest city in the U.S. It wasn't far south of Salem, where in the late 17th century dozens of people were burned at the stake, stoned, and drowned for being suspected of witchcraft. Nightingale drove a rented Jeep Cherokee. He'd turned down the offer of a SatNav and instead gave the priest a map on which he had drawn their route in red ink. The priest had changed into a rumpled grey suit and packed his clerical garments in a leather holdall along with, at Nightingale's request, several bottles of Holy Water.

They pulled up to an old Victorian home with a seashell driveway and parked. The seashells were bone-white and slick from the rain that was now pouring down. Within moments of stepping out of the car they both felt it: an overwhelming sense of dread. The atmosphere suddenly felt heavy and oppressive; their rib cages felt like vises which were slowly constricting the closer they got to the house. Father O'Grady put his hand to his chest and gasped.

'You okay?' asked Nightingale.

'I'm fine,' said the priest, though he obviously wasn't.

Nightingale knocked on the front door and it opened. A small shriveled woman with dark rings around her eyes greeted them. She was young, early thirties, but she looked much older, and ill. Her blonde hair had streaks of grey in it and her skin was wrinkled. Nightingale knew that only weeks before Lisa Wilson had been quite beautiful. 'Mrs Wilson,' he said. 'I've brought help. Meet Father O'Grady.'

Mrs Wilson attempted to smile but it looked more like a grimace. She took Father O'Grady's hand in hers and kissed it. 'Thank you so much for coming, Father. Please, come inside. You're getting soaked.'

Nightingale and the priest took off their drenched coats and shoes. A fire was burning in the hearth and Nightingale gravitated towards it, warming his hands. The priest followed. 'You feel it?' said Nightingale. The priest nodded, and shuddered. They were in a living room with family photographs on the walls and in frames on the coffee table and mantelpiece. Father O'Grady examined a picture of the parents and the boy smiling into the camera. It looked like one of those family photos you see in picture frames when you buy them at shops. The perfect family. 'Beautiful boy,' O'Grady said, running a nicotine-stained finger along the glass.

'Coffee?' asked Mrs Wilson. The men nodded and she disappeared into the kitchen. They heard footsteps on the stairs. A tall, thin man in a white Oxford shirt came down the steps. He was blond like his wife but with no grey hairs, yet his eyes told it all. They were sunken and tired-looking. Empty.

'Fellas,' said the man, nodding.

'James,' said Nightingale. 'This is Father O'Grady.'

O'Grady shook Mr Wilson's limp hand. 'How do you do?' asked the priest.

'I've seen better days, Father, but I've never seen worse.' His voice was dull and flat as if he had lost all hope.

'I'm sorry to hear that. Hopefully I can help.'

He waved for them to sit. The priest took the sofa and Nightingale sat on a winged chair by the fire. Mr Wilson paced up and down. Mrs Wilson came in carrying a tray of coffee with a ceramic milk pitcher and a small jar of sugar. Nightingale noticed her hands trembling, and the contents were vibrating on the tray. Mr Wilson took it from her. 'Sit down, hun. I've got this.'

'Sorry, Father,' she said, looking apologetically at the priest. 'I haven't slept much.'

'Please, don't apologize.'

She looked at her husband seriously. 'Is he asleep?' She sat down next to O'Grady and put her hands in her lap. They were the gnarled claws of a woman twice her age.

'For now,' said her husband, pouring coffee into three mugs and handing them out.

'What is the child's name?' asked O'Grady.

'William,' said Mr Wilson. 'But we call him Billy. Everyone calls him Billy.' He pulled a chair away from an oak dining table and sat on it, his legs pressed together awkwardly.

'And what seems to be the problem with Billy?'

Mrs Wilson glanced at Nightingale. 'Hasn't he told you?'

'Yes, but I'd like to hear it from you,' said O'Grady. 'First hand, as it were. As I have explained to Mr Nightingale, often what appears to be a case of demonic possession can turn out to be a simple mental disorder.'

Mr Wilson shook his head vehemently. 'No. He's not crazy. We're not crazy.'

'No one said crazy,' said the priest, holding up a liver-spotted hand. 'But sometimes what appears to be possession can actually be a sign of an underlying mental health issue, that's the point I am making.'

'That's just another way of saying that you think Billy is crazy, and he isn't. Something has changed him. Something has done this to him.' He looked at Nightingale. 'You believe me, don't you?'

Nightingale nodded. 'Yes,' he said. 'Yes I do. I wouldn't be here if I didn't.'

Mr Wilson looked over at the priest. 'See? Billy isn't crazy.'

'I believe you,' said O'Grady. 'But I need to know exactly what has happened to Billy. From the beginning.'

'All right,' said Mr Wilson, 'it all started back at the hospital, two weeks ago. At least we think it did. Billy caught bronchitis at school and he got very sick. We took him to hospital, where he stayed for a couple of days and was given strong antibiotics. He was getting better. Then, the afternoon we took him home, all hell broke loose.' He paused. 'Sorry, I shouldn't say that. I don't want to say that.'

'It's all right,' said O'Grady. 'Go on.'

'As soon as we got home, Billy started acting... strange. He became moody. He wouldn't listen to me or his mother. He wouldn't eat. His whole demeanor changed. He was cold and mean, and his voice sounded like nothing I'd ever heard in my life, like an old woman's voice, croaky, sort of. Vicious. We put him to bed that night but he wouldn't fall asleep. We heard him pattering around the house, slamming doors and cabinets, scratching the walls. I went downstairs and found him standing in the kitchen with his back to me, in the dark. His head was craned to the side like he was looking at something on the fridge. His body was completely still, but he was whispering. I couldn't tell what he was saying because it sounded like it was in Latin, but he was whispering in rapid fire. Finally I turned him around to face me, asking what the heck was going on, and he screamed. He grabbed me by the throat and started choking me, yelling, *"Die! Die! Die!"* He was so strong I couldn't stop him. Billy is ten years old and weighs seventy-five pounds; I can pick him up and throw him if I want to. This wasn't Billy. This was something else.' He shuddered and folded his arms.

'Then what happened?' asked the priest quietly.

'Lisa came downstairs and helped me restrain him. It took both of us to stop him and get him to calm down. He just got drowsy and drifted into a weird sleep, but he was still whispering. We carried him upstairs and put him to bed.'

'Sounds like it could be night terrors,' offered O'Grady.

Mr Wilson glared at him. 'Father, with all due respect, these are not night terrors. Since that day he's been the same ever since, day and night. Sometimes he's back to his normal self, and he doesn't seem to remember any of the awful things he's said or done, he's our sweet Billy, but as soon as he comes out, that other side seems to take over, and it's real angry when it does. I don't know a whole lot about this thing, Father, but I know my son. That thing upstairs is not him.'

'Don't say that,' said Mrs Wilson, her voice trembling. 'It's Billy. He's our son.'

'Not at the moment it's not,' said Mr Wilson, shaking his head. 'You can see it in his eyes, he isn't Billy any more. Billy has gone.' He looked at the priest, tears welling up in his eyes. 'We want our son back. Please, can you help us? You're our last hope.'

'We'll do what we can,' said the priest. He looked across at Nightingale and nodded. 'I suppose it's time I met Billy.'

They set down their coffee mugs and went upstairs in single file. They stopped outside the boy's bedroom door. Nightingale took a small birch wood cross from his jacket pocket. 'You came prepared,' observed the priest dryly.

'It's not my first possession case,' said Nightingale. 'And it probably won't be my last.'

Father O'Grady took off his rosary and wrapped it around his hand, holding the small gold cross in the palm of his hand. He blessed himself and the others. Mr Wilson opened the door and were instantly met with a horrible stench of vomit, feces, and urine. It smelled like they were in a sewer. The curtains were drawn, and there were large holes in the walls. All of the furniture except for the bed and a lamp had been removed. Nightingale knew this was a safety precaution, things had been thrown around violently when the boy had first returned from the hospital.

As soon as they entered, the boy went from sleeping soundly to sitting straight up in the bed. He did this so fast that everyone in the room jumped. Mr Wilson was right: what they were looking at was not a boy at all, but a deformed, hideous representation of a boy. Billy was in his underwear and he had bruises and scratches all over his body. His hair was greasy and matted with vomit. Specks of vomit were on his face. His black eyes burned out of their sockets like coals as he watched them with predatory cunning. His purple lips had been mashed by his teeth and were bloody and plump. He opened them wide and said in a deep voice, *'Welcome to the party, priest. Are you here to fuck me? Of course you are.'*

'What?' said Father O'Grady, aghast. The thing on the bed began laughing hysterically and jumping up and down.

'The restraints,' asked Nightingale. 'Where are they?'

'I don't know,' said Mr Wilson, 'they were just...'

They saw them: the restraints were on the ground by the bed. Somehow Billy had taken them off, and now he was free. Billy jumped and whooped with joy. *'HAHAHAHAHAHA!'* In one swift motion Billy wrenched a crooked piece of wire from the box spring under the mattress and began stabbing himself repeatedly in the forearm, drawing blood. *'Die vermin! Die pig fuck! Die die die!'*

'Stop!' shouted Mr Wilson, rushing forward and trying to wrestle with the thing. Billy gave him a shove and threw him several feet in the air. He smashed against the wall. Mrs Wilson fainted. Father O'Grady took out his Bible and began reading from it in a loud voice: 'We drive you from us, whoever you may be, unclean spirits, all satanic powers, all infernal invaders, all wicked legions, assemblies and sects! In the Name and by the power of Our Lord Jesus Christ may you be snatched away and driven from the Church of God and from the souls made to the image and likeness of God and redeemed by the Precious Blood of the Divine Lamb!' Billy squealed like a stuck pig. Together Nightingale and the priest tied him up, binding his arms and feet with thick rope and then tying them off to the bedposts. Billy was crying in a high-pitched wail.

'Begone, Satan, inventor and master of all deceit, enemy of man's salvation!' shouted the priest. *'Begone!'*

Billy went completely still. His black eyes stared up at the ceiling. 'I don't think he's breathing,' said Nightingale. He went to check his pulse but Billy snapped his jaws near his throat. Nightingale moved away. 'I guess he is,' he said.

Mr Wilson was pulling himself up off the floor. He was shaking. Nightingale and O'Grady followed as Mr Wilson picked up his wife and carried her down the stairs, setting her on the sofa. As Mr Wilson tried to bring his wife back to consciousness, Nightingale clutched O'Grady's arm and led him outside. 'This isn't a mental disorder,' he said in a hushed voice. 'It's possession, and that boy in there needs your help. If you don't help him, he'll die. You understand?'

Father O'Grady nodded. 'Yes,' he said.

'So are you going to help him or not?'

The priest nodded. 'I'll do my best,' he said, his voice shaking. 'I'll perform the exorcism. Tonight. As soon as possible. But I need your assurance that the devil won't enter one of us. You said you had a way to protect us.'

'I do,' said Nightingale. 'Leave it to me.'

* * *

Dusk settled over Plymouth as Nightingale got in the Cherokee and turned the key in the ignition. He was headed for the hospital where the boy had been in hopes of learning who might have died with a devil inside them, which was the only way Bakka could have passed on to the boy. The priest had remained behind with Mr and Mrs Wilson. Nightingale had made it clear that they were to stay away from the boy until he returned.

He cracked his window in spite of the rain and lit a cigarette. Then he turned on the radio to quiet his mind. Soft jazz played as he pulled away from the kerb and drove towards the hospital, just a few miles away. A set of lights turned red and he brought the Cherokee to a halt. He tapped in time to the tune on the steering wheel, finished his cigarette and tossed the butt out into the street. The lights changed and he accelerated. As he hit thirty miles an hour the radio emitted a gut-wrenching shriek that made him wince. He cursed and switched the radio off. Except while the button clicked into the off position, noise continued to screech from the speakers. Then he heard a inhuman voice, the voice he had heard coming from the mouth of Billy back at the house. Bakka. *'Leave this place, pig. Or I shall kill you and bring you back to Hell, where you will be my slave forever.'*

Nightingale clutched the steering wheel. The radio switched over to a classical station, and classical music was blaring through the speakers, getting louder and louder. He tried to shut it off but pressing the buttons had no effect. The sound intensified, a maddened orchestra playing rapidly as if for the final time. He tried to pull over but the car was accelerating even as he eased his foot off the gas. 65 mph, 70 mph, 75 mph… He tried to brake. Nothing. The forest on the side of the road began to whirl by in a murky haze of speed and rain. The music was deafening. In a split second his mind went over his options. He could use the emergency brake, but he'd probably overturn the car. He could try running off the road but if he hit a tree even the airbag might not save him. If this was Bakka at work then he needed supernatural assistance. He screamed the words: 'Stop! In the name of the Archangel Michael, the slayer of devils and demons and the emissary of the Lord Jesus Christ, I command you to **stop!**'

The car stopped accelerating. The stereo switched back to talk radio, where a mild voice was now describing the weather. '…and that's pretty much what we have today, folks. Periodic rain, which will taper to mist in the evening with areas of dense fog along the coast. Tomorrow we can expect a few showers around the…'

Nightingale took a deep breath. His heart was racing. He pulled over to the side of the road and lit a cigarette with a shaking hand.

* * *

The receptionist on duty at the hospital was a plump brunette wearing too much red lipstick. She had red rouge on her cheeks and she resembled a giant doll. Nightingale flashed her what he hoped was his most disarming smile. He handed her a business card with his name, cell phone number and an address in New York. 'I'm a private investigator, I'm trying to get details of a death that occurred here two weeks ago.'

'So you're not a relative?' She smiled revealing a smear of lipstick across her lower front teeth,

'No, like I said, I'm a private investigator working for the parents of a young boy who was here at the same time as Billy Wilson. Billy was sick and while he was here he was comforted by a couple who came to visit someone who died. They really helped Billy and the parents want to thank them, but they never got their names.'

The receptionist nodded. 'I remember Billy. Lovely little boy.' Her face was suddenly serious. 'He was quite sick, it was touch and go for a while. Bronchitis.'

'That's right.'

'How is he now?' asked the receptionist.

'As right as rain,' lied Nightingale. 'His parents aren't sure who the couple were, but they are pretty sure they were here to visit someone who later died. They just want to take Billy to thank them. Considering they lost someone, they thought it might, you know, help them deal with their loss to know how grateful Billy is for the way they helped him.'

'That's so sweet,' said the receptionist. She looked at her computer screen and tapped on her keyboard. 'What day do you think they were here?'

'October eight,' said Nightingale. 'Or thereabouts.'

She tapped on the keyboard again, then nodded. 'Yes, we did lose a patient on October the eighth,' she said. 'Father Edward Allen Perkins.'

'Do you have an address?'

'He won't be there, will he?' said the receptionist. 'He's dead.'

Nightingale was having trouble maintaining his smile, but he did the best he could. 'Of course, but I'm assuming he lived with relatives. And Billy does really want to thank them.'

'We're not supposed to give out patients details,' said the receptionist.

'Of course not, but I'm sure Father Perkins won't complain. Seeing as how he's – you know - dead.'

The receptionist frowned, then nodded. 'I suppose so.' She peered at the screen again. '19 Dunbarrow Street, here in Plymouth.'

'Is it far?'

'About a mile. Down Main Street, left at the Burger King, right at the Taco Bell, and that's Dunbarrow Street.'

Nightingale thanked her and lit a cigarette as he headed out to the car. So the man who had died was a priest? That couldn't have been a coincidence. Maybe Father Perkins had been meddling with something he shouldn't have. He finished his cigarette, climbed into the car and followed the directions the receptionist had given him.

The Perkins house was small, with wood sides and a pitched roof. An old rotted 'For Sale' sign stuck out from the yellow lawn, which was overgrown and littered with leaves. Nightingale parked at the side of the road and walked along a paved pathway to the door. The green paint was peeling off in places. The door was locked and nobody responded to his knock. He circled around back where he found a window at eye level. He took off his coat, bunched it around his hand, and smashed the window. He cleared the glass with his coat and climbed inside. He was in the kitchen. There were dishes piled high in the sink, covered with mold. Walking down a narrow hallway he immediately became overwhelmed by the stench of feces and vomit. He entered a small living room which had newspaper clippings on the walls and books piled all over the place. There were urine stains on the carpet and Nightingale had to hold his coat over his mouth and nose to offset the stench. He checked out the newspaper clippings tacked to the walls. All of them detailed possessions, suicides and the occult.

'You were into some nasty things, weren't you, Father Perkins?' Nightingale muttered to himself. He found a small book open on the desk, a very old volume made of vellum that smelled musty with age. He turned it over to inspect the spine. *"Devils, Demons, & Exorcisms."* The copyright date on the inside said it was printed in the early 1800s. He flipped through the pages and found that it was a compilation of stories about exorcisms and various ways they can be performed. There was a wrinkled leather bookmark marking a page containing the names of several demons. One was highlighted in yellow. *Bakka.*

A loud crash upstairs made Nightingale jump. His heart thumped hard. He listened. Something was scratching the floor up there. *Scratch scratch scratch.* Three scratches in quick succession, a sign of the demonic.

'Hello?' he called.

Scratch scratch scratch.

Nightingale went slowly up a flight of creaking stairs. He heard the sound again, *scratch scratch scratch.* It was coming from the bedroom. Steadying himself outside the door, he raised his foot and kicked it in. The door smashed inward and he saw a flash as something flew in the air.

Meow-arrrt!

Nightingale staggered back, but then recovered his balance. He grinned. A bone-thin cream-colored cat was huddled in a corner, its back arched, staring at him. By the looks of it the thing hadn't been fed in a while. It was breathing heavily, as scared as he had been. Nightingale stepped to the side and the cat ran out, its ears back, clearly scared out of its wits.

* * *

The rain had slackened as Nightingale pulled in the driveway of the Wilson house, but the sky was coal black and the wind was blowing across the ocean and through the trees hard enough to make them bend. He leaned over and pulled his overnight bag off the back seat. Along with a change of clothing it contained everything he would need to perform the exorcism. Along with a pair of police-issue handcuffs and a high-powered stun gun.

He got out of the car and walked across the yard. He flinched as he heard an animal-like howl from inside the Wilson house. Followed by Mrs Wilson screaming.

Nightingale raced into the house and up the stairs, dropping his bag in the hall. He found Mr Wilson hunched up against the wall opposite Billy's room, bleeding profusely from a deep gash in the side of his head. Father O'Grady was inside the room splashing Holy water on Billy as he writhed and screamed on the bed. Red welts formed on the skin where the water touched. Billy wailed. *'Leave me you child fucker! Child fucker child fucker child fucker!'* The priest stopped spraying Holy water and froze. *'Yes, child fucker, we have reserved your place in Hell where you will be raped by eager children for all eternity! Yes! Yes! YES!'*

'Be silent!' Father O'Grady sprayed the creature again and it squealed.

Nightingale grabbed the priest and dragged him out of the room. He slammed the door shut. 'What is wrong with you?' he demanded. 'I told you not to go near the boy until I got back.'

'That thing *insulted* me!' hissed O'Grady.

'That's what it does! You need to keep your composure, you idiot! If you don't it will see your weakness and pounce on it!'

Mr Wilson was moaning on the ground. Nightingale knelt down and examined the wound on his head. It wasn't life-threatening. 'James, can you hear me?'

Mr Wilson blinked as he tried to focus on Nightingale's face. 'Uh huh...'

Nightingale looked up at O'Grady. 'Lisa, where is she?'

'I don't know.'

'What do you mean you don't know?'

'I don't know!'

'Find her!'

O'Grady trudged down the stairs while Nightingale helped Mr Wilson to his feet. Billy was laughing maniacally and shrieking that it would kill them all before the end of the night. The house vibrated. In the kitchen dishes spilled out of cupboards and smashed to the floor. Lights were blinking on and off. Nightingale helped Mr Wilson downstairs and lowered him to the sofa. He was groaning. He closed his eyes but Nightingale slapped him gently. 'Wake up, James! Don't fall asleep.' He looked up. 'Father!' he shouted. 'Father O'Grady!'

Father O'Grady appeared at the kitchen door. 'I found her.'

Nightingale rushed into the kitchen. Mrs Wilson was huddled in a small recess behind the stove, which she'd apparently dragged away from the wall. She was whimpering. Her eyes bulged out of their sockets as her mouth worked soundlessly.

'She's in shock,' said Nightingale. 'What happened upstairs?' he asked. 'When you went into the room?'

The priest was ashen and his voice shook as he spoke. 'It, uh... it attacked us.'

'The boy was in restraints. He couldn't get to you.'

'You can restrain the body but not the spirit. I told you how strong it was! We shouldn't have come. Lord, forgive me...' He crossed himself with a shaking hand.

'Get ahold of yourself,' said Nightingale. 'We need to end this before anything else happens.'

'I don't believe I can,' said the priest. He shook his head. 'It's too strong. Too powerful.'

Nightingale grabbed him by the shoulders and shook him. 'You can, and you will.'

'You can't protect us from that thing!'

'Yes I can. I'm going to draw two magic circles, one around me and the other around you. I've done it before and it works. All you have to do is stay in the protective circle. No matter what happens, stay in the circle.'

O'Grady shook his head. 'No. It's time for me to leave.' The priest went to go but Nightingale stood in the doorway.

'I don't think so,' he said. 'You started this with me, and you're finishing it. Come on. Let's go. Put on your gear. Now. There's no time to waste, we need to get this done.' The priest did as he was told, putting on a surplice and a purple stole with trembling hands.

While O'Grady blessed himself and prayed, Nightingale helped Mrs Wilson out of the kitchen and put her on the couch next to her husband, who was nodding in and out of consciousness. 'Do not leave this couch, whatever happens,' said Nightingale. 'Just stay here. Promise me.'

'I promise,' she whispered. She reached for her husband's hand and held it tightly.

Nightingale went around the couch, picking up rugs and tossing them out of the way. He took a stick of consecrated chalk from his overnight bag and drew two concentric circles around the couch. He filled the space between the two circles with protective sigils, drawn from memory.

'This circle will protect you, but only if you stay within it,' he told them. 'Okay?'

'Yes,' said Mrs Wilson, her voice a dull monotone.

Nightingale put his face close to hers. 'You must stay within the circle, do you understand, Mrs Wilson?'

'Yes,' she repeated, this time with more conviction.

'All right. Father, are you ready?' The priest was wearing his surplice and purple stole. He didn't say anything, but he nodded. Nightingale led

Father O'Grady upstairs.

Billy's room had become deathly quiet. Nightingale gently eased open the door. The air inside was so cold that their breath formed white clouds. The bed was empty. The restraints had been snapped apart. Billy was gone. Suddenly they heard a low growl coming from the ceiling. Nightingale looked up. Billy was crouched upside down on the ceiling, smiling at them with bloody teeth.

'Impossible,' whispered O'Grady.

Billy leapt from the ceiling and landed on Father O'Grady, the two of them crashing to the ground. Billy bared his teeth and went for his throat but Nightingale ripped him off the priest and hit him with the lamp. Billy grinned. *'It hits us but we feel nothing. Nothing! Ahahahaha!'*

Nightingale dropped the lamp and pulled out the stun gun. He pressed the two prongs against Billy's neck and pulled the trigger. Billy went into spasm and Nightingale kept the current surging through the boy's body until he finally went still. 'Help me!' Nightingale shouted at the priest. 'Help me get it to the bed!' Father O'Grady snapped into action, grabbing Billy's feet. Billy began to thrash around again as they carried him over to the bed. Billy kicked the priest in the nose just as they reached the bed. O'Grady fell back with a cry. Nightingale wrestled with Billy, tying his wrists in the restraints.

The bed rose from the ground, hovering. Then it catapulted upward, slamming Nightingale into the ceiling. It went into free fall, then flew up against the ceiling again. The bed repeated this movement several times until Nightingale fell off and crashed onto the floor. *'Hahahaha!'* Billy was trying to wriggle out of the restraints. As he whipped his vicious face about, blood and vomit splattered the walls and the two men. Nightingale jumped up, grabbed the restraints and tightened them, then secured Billy's feet as he continued to curse and scream.

'Ready?' asked Nightingale. The priest was hunched. He had blood all over his face, and he was wheezing. 'Ready?' repeated Nightingale. 'We need to do this now.'

The priest nodded. 'Are you sure you can protect me?'

'I'm sure,' said Nightingale. He held up the chalk. 'This chalk was consecrated by an archbishop, and I know the sigils that will protect us from Bakka.'

'He lies!' screamed Billy. 'He lies, he lies!'

'You're using black magic?' asked the priest. He shook his head fearfully. 'No.'

'It's not black magic, it's just magic,' said Nightingale. 'It will protect you.' He held up the chalk. 'This is as holy as your water.'

Billy continued to scream as Nightingale drew a protective circle around the priest, smaller than the one he'd drawn downstairs. When he'd finished he stood up. 'Stay within that circle and you'll be safe,' he said.

'Would the Holy Water help?' asked O'Grady.

'Of course,' said Nightingale. He took four white church candles from his bag and placed them around the bed, lit them with his Zippo and then sprinkled herbs over the flames as he spoke loudly and clearly. *'Ut benedicat tibi Dominus in lucem haec magia est in circulos. Nemo venit ad nocere nobis.'*

As Nightingale drew a second circle around himself, the priest sprinkled Holy Water on the floor around his circle.

'It is time, Father,' said Nightingale. 'It is time to banish the demon from the boy.'

With a trembling hand, Father O'Grady traced the sign of the cross over Billy, himself and Nightingale. Then he sprinkled Holy Water on all three of them. Billy screamed. O'Grady recited the Litany of the Saints.

'Lord, have mercy,' said O'Grady.

'Lord have mercy,' repeated Nightingale.

'Christ, have mercy.'

'Christ have mercy.'

'Christ, hear us.'

'Christ hear us.'

'NO! It burns. It BURNS!' Billy writhed in agony on the bed.

'God, the Father in heaven.'

'Have mercy on us,' said Nightingale. Then they went through all the Saints, one by one, appealing for their help to banish the demon. Billy writhed on the bed, shitting and farting. The house shook on its foundations and they could hear furniture in the next room smashing the walls.

'Let us pray,' said O'Grady. Nightingale and the priest bowed their heads. 'God, whose nature is ever merciful and forgiving, accept our prayer that this servant of yours, bound by the fetters of sin, may be pardoned by your loving kindness.'

Billy writhed in pain. *'Leave us! LEAVE US!'* The bed rose and fell rapidly, slamming into the floor so hard that the whole house shook.

'Holy Lord, almighty Father, everlasting God and Father of our Lord Jesus Christ, who once and for all consigned that fallen and apostate tyrant to the flames of hell, who sent your only-begotten Son into the world to crush that roaring lion; hasten to our call for help and snatch from ruination and from the clutches of the noonday devil this human being made in your image and likeness. Strike terror, Lord, into the beast now laying waste your vineyard. Fill your servants with courage to fight manfully against that reprobate dragon, lest he despise those who put their trust in you, and say with Pharaoh of old: "I know not God, nor will I set Israel free." Let your mighty hand cast him out of your servant, Billy Wilson, so he may no longer hold captive this person whom it pleased you to make in your image, and to redeem through your Son; who lives and reigns with you, in the unity of the Holy Spirit, God, forever and ever.'

'Amen,' said Nightingale. Billy was thumping up and down on the bed. Then he went still. Then suddenly he snorted and spat a big green mass directly at Father O'Grady's face. O'Grady took out a handkerchief, wiped it off, and continued to speak.

'Fuck you child fucker! Fuck you!'

'I command you, unclean spirit, whoever you are, along with all your minions now attacking this servant of God, by the mysteries of the incarnation, passion, resurrection, and ascension of our Lord Jesus Christ, by the descent of the Holy Spirit, by the coming of our Lord for judgment, that you tell me by some sign your name, and the day and hour of your departure. I command you, moreover, to obey me to the letter, I who am a minister of God despite my unworthiness; nor shall you be emboldened to harm in any way this creature of God, or the bystanders, or any of their possessions.'

Billy fell still on the bed, his eyes staring wide and unseeing.

Father O'Grady put his hand on Billy's ankle, saying: 'They shall lay their hands upon the sick and all will be well with them. May Jesus, Son of Mary, Lord and Savior of the world, through the merits and intercession of His holy apostles Peter and Paul and all His saints, show you favor and mercy.'

'Amen,' said Nightingale.

Billy's eyes opened wide. 'NOOOOOO! I'll kill you! I'll kill you! I'LL KILL YOU!'

Father O'Grady stood tall. 'I cast you out, unclean spirit, along with every Satanic power of the enemy, every demon from hell, and all your foul companions, in the name of our Lord Jesus Christ. Begone and stay far from this creature of God. For it is He who commands you, He who flung you headlong from the heights of heaven into the depths of hell. It is He who commands you, He who once stilled the sea and the wind and the storm. Hearken, therefore, and tremble in fear, Satan, you enemy of the faith, you foe of the human race, you begetter of death, you robber of life, you corrupter of justice, you root of all evil and vice; seducer of men, betrayer of nations, instigator of envy, font of avarice, fomenter of discord, author of pain and sorrow. Why, then, do you stand and resist, knowing as you must that Christ the Lord brings your plans to nothing? Fear Him, who in Isaac was offered in sacrifice, in Joseph sold into bondage, slain as the paschal lamb, crucified as man, yet triumphed over the powers of hell.'

Father O'Grady traced in the air the three signs of the cross, saying, 'Begone, then, in the name of the Father, and of the Son, and of the Holy Spirit. Give place to the Holy Spirit by this sign of the holy cross of our Lord Jesus Christ, who lives and reigns with the Father and the Holy Spirit, God, forever and ever.'

'I will bring you to hell, vile pig fuck priest! Leave now and I'll spare you! Oh it hurts, it HURTS!'

'I adjure you, ancient serpent, by the judge of the living and the dead, by your Creator, by the Creator of the whole universe, by Him who has the power to consign you to hell, to depart forthwith in fear, along with your savage minions, from this servant of God, Billy Wilson, who seeks refuge in the fold of the Church. I adjure you again, not by my weakness but by the might of the Holy Spirit, to depart from this servant of God, Billy Wilson, whom almighty God has made in His image. Yield, therefore, yield not to my own person but to the minister of Christ. For it is the power of Christ that compels you, who brought you low by His cross. Tremble before that mighty arm that broke asunder the dark prison walls and led souls forth to light. May the trembling that afflicts this human frame, the fear that afflicts this image of God, descend on you. Make no resistance nor delay in departing from this man, for it has pleased Christ to dwell in man. Do not think of despising my command because you know me to be a great sinner. It is God Himself who commands you; the majestic Christ who commands you. God the Father commands you; God the Son commands you; God the Holy Spirit commands you. The mystery of the cross commands you. The faith of the holy apostles Peter and Paul and of all the saints commands you. The blood of the martyrs commands you. The continence of the confessors commands you. The devout prayers of all holy men and women command you. The saving mysteries of our faith command you. Depart, then, transgressor! In the name of the Father, and of the Son, and of the Holy Spirit, I cast you out!'

The body of the boy went into spasm. Vomit bubbled to his lips and spilled out. He moved erratically, moaning and vomiting profusely. Finally he went still, his head falling to the side. He closed his eyes, and when he breathed again a black mass blew out of his mouth and filled half the room. Nightingale took out his wooden cross and gripped it tightly. O'Grady stared defiantly at the black smoke, which seemed to hover in front of him. 'You have no place here, filth.' He threw Holy Water at the mass of smoke and the air was filled with a horrendous screeching sound that made Nightingale wince.

The cloud of smoke began to harden, forming an animal-like shape some eight feet tall, with horns and a tail. It moved towards Nightingale, each step shaking the room. It stopped at the edge of the protective circle and roared.

Nightingale stood his ground, though his heart was pounding. 'No can do, mate,' he said. 'You'd be better looking elsewhere.'

The demon roared again and then turned towards the priest who was still throwing Holy Water at the apparition. It moved towards the priest. O'Grady took a step back but managed to stay inside the circle. 'Am I safe?' he shouted at Nightingale. 'For the love of God, tell me I'm safe.'

'I'm afraid not,' said Nightingale. 'I might have fucked up your circle. Sorry.'

'What?' screamed O'Grady. 'What are you saying?'

'I'm saying that better the devil resides in you than in an innocent boy,' said Nightingale.

The priest stared at him in amazement. 'What are you saying?' he shouted. 'What the fuck are you saying?'

The demon had started to turn back into smoke and Nightingale's eyes were watering. It became a mass of black cloud, then like a snake rearing its head to strike, the mass dipped backward, then sprang forth into the gaping mouth of the priest. O'Grady didn't even have time to scream. His body shuddered and he fell over. In an instant he was crouched on all fours, growling like an animal. Nightingale pulled his stun gun from his pocket, pressed the prongs against O'Grady's neck and pulled the trigger. Nine hundred thousand volts pulsed through the priest and sent him into convulsions. Nightingale kept the stun gun pressed against the man's neck and he pressed the trigger again. And again. Eventually the convulsions stopped. Nightingale put the stun gun away, pulled out the handcuffs and bound O'Grady's hands behind his back before checking on Billy.

Billy was curled up in a foetal ball, sobbing quietly. Nightingale gathered him up and carried him gently downstairs. Mrs Wilson looked up as he carried Billy into the sitting room. Her eyes widened in horror but Nightingale shook his head and smiled. 'Billy's fine,' he said. 'It's over. You can leave the circle now.'

She hurried over to him and Nightingale handed Billy over. She hugged the boy to her chest and smothered him with kisses. 'He'll need a lot of rest,' said Nightingale. 'Give him water and soup and try him on solid food tomorrow. But rest is the key. And love.'

'Thank you,' said Mrs Wilson tearfully. 'God bless you, and Father O'Grady.'

'Well, we'll see how that works out,' said Nightingale but she had already turned away and carried Billy over to her husband.

Nightingale went upstairs. O'Grady was groaning. Nightingale dragged him to his feet. '*I will drag you down to hell, Nightingale!*' The voice was Bakka's.

'Not trapped in that body you won't,' said Nightingale. He dragged the priest out of the door and down the stairs. Mr and Mrs Wilson were tending to Billy and didn't see him haul the priest out of the front door.

A police cruiser pulled up, its light flashing but its siren off. Behind it was a dark sedan.

Nightingale took O'Grady over to the sedan. The driver's side door opened and a tall, thin detective in a dark blue trench coat climbed out. He was holding a flashlight and he shone it at Nightingale. 'That you, Jack?'

Nightingale grinned. 'Who else is going to be delivering you a paedophile priest this time of night?'

The detective shone his flashlight at the priest. The priest scowled and turned away. 'Get that light out of my face!' he shouted. 'I demand to be released!'

'You don't make any demands, you child-raping bastard!' hissed the detective. He nodded at Nightingale. 'It's him,' he said. 'Father Andrew Lawston. How the hell did you track him down? We've been looking for him for five years.'

'Fuck you both, fuck you and your seed, I will bring you all to hell!' shouted the priest.

'He's not happy,' said Nightingale.

'Neither would you be if you were facing life behind bars,' said the detective. 'How did you track him down?'

Down the road a black stretch Humvee pulled up at the side of the road and its lights went dark.

'Just lucky, I guess,' said Nightingale. He pushed the priest over to the detective who slammed him up against the sedan.

'Bullshit,' said the detective. 'When you first called me to say you had a line on Lawston I assumed you were shitting me. But you delivered.' He checked the cuffs on the priest's wrists and smiled. 'And you even used police-issue cuffs.'

'All part of the service.'

'Like I told you on the phone, there's no reward out for this scumbag. But there's a lot of folk back in New York who'll owe you their thanks.'

'I'm happy to be kept out of it,' said Nightingale. 'The credit's all yours.'

The priest snarled. 'I'll kill you both, I'll rip your arms and legs from their sockets and flay the skin from your bodies. You'll die in Hell, screaming for mercy but there'll be no mercy for you. I am Bakka and I sit on Satan's left hand and you will know my power.'

The detective slapped him on the side of the head. 'Sounds to me like he's working on an insanity defence, but that's not going to work. There are plenty of witnesses in New York more than happy to give evidence about what he did and who he did it to.' The detective pulled open the door and shoved the priest onto the back seat. 'Forty-four kids,' said the detective. 'And that's just what we know of. I'm sure there's loads more who are just too afraid or embarrassed to come forth. Scum like him should face a firing squad, in my opinion.'

The detective stuck out his hand and Nightingale shook it, then the detective climbed into the front passenger seat. He waved and the car drove off. Nightingale lit a cigarette as the car headed down the road.

Two uniformed officers were standing by the patrol car and Nightingale went over to them. 'What happened in there?' asked the older of the two, gesturing at the Wilson house.

'It's complicated,' said Nightingale.

'That Wilson boy has been having problems.'

'He's okay now.'

'That priest, he didn't..?'

Nightingale shook his head and blew smoke. 'Actually, he helped.'

'Helped?'

'Little Billy was possessed. But he's okay now.'

The officer frowned. 'Possessed?'

'It's a long story. But like I said, the priest was able to help.'

'Maybe they'll take that into consideration, back in New York,' said the officer.

'I doubt it,' said Nightingale. He turned up his collar against the cold night air and walked down the road to the Humvee. The windows were heavily tinted so he couldn't see who was inside. He opened the rear passenger door and sweet-smelling cigar smoke billowed out.

'So all's well that ends well?' asked a soft Texan drawl.

Nightingale climbed in. Joshua Wainwright was stretched out with his hand-tooled lizard skin cowboy boots propped on the seat opposite him. He had a cigar in one hand and a crystal tumbler of brandy in the other. He had a NY Yankees baseball hat on back to front, tight jeans and a red-and-white checked shirt and looked more like a cowboy on his day off rather than the billionaire businessman he was.

'Worked like a dream,' said Nightingale. He sat down, leant forward and opened a small fridge. He took out a bottle of Corona and popped off the cap before raising it in salute to his employer and benefactor. 'More of a nightmare, I suppose. For Lawston anyway.'

'He had it coming,' said Wainwright. 'I don't know how many lives he ruined over the years, the ones I know about are probably just the tip of a very dirty iceberg.'

'Well, he's being punished now,' said Nightingale.

Wainwright nodded. 'Lawston is in his sixties so with any luck he'll live another twenty or thirty years with Bakka inside him. The only way that Bakka can be released is if Lawston dies and the authorities will take good care of him so that's not going to happen in the near future.'

'He could kill himself.'

Wainwright shook his head. 'He's clearly deranged so he'll be on suicide watch, in a bare cell with a cardboard mattress. No, Bakka is stuck where he is for a very long time.' He reached over and clinked his glass against Nightingale's bottle. 'Job well done, Jack.'

'Thanks,' said Nightingale. He reached into his pocket and took out the copy of *Devils, Demons, & Exorcisms* that he had taken from Father Perkins' house. 'For your collection,' he said.

Wainwright took it, examined the spine, and nodded his approval. 'A classic, and a first edition. Thank you.'

Nightingale leaned back and sighed. 'I'm knackered. Exorcising demons really takes it out of you.'

'You need a vacation,' said Wainwright. 'I'll arrange something for you.'

'You're all heart, Joshua.' He sipped his Corona. 'Can I ask you a question?'

'Sure.'

'What was your interest in Lawston?'

'What do you mean?'

'I mean how does a paedophile priest get on to your radar? And why would you want me to handle it for you?'

'It wasn't about the priest, Jack. I couldn't give a flying fuck about the priest.'

Nightingale frowned. 'So it was Bakka?'

Wainwright grinned and raised his glass in salute.

'So I'm assuming Bakka isn't on your team?'

'I don't have a team, Jack. But yes, me and Bakka have had a few run-ins in the past. Now he's not going to be bothering me, for a while at least. And I'm not the only one who has been having problems with the little shit, so this is going to win me brownie points with some very important people, so like I said, your vacation is on me.'

CLAWS

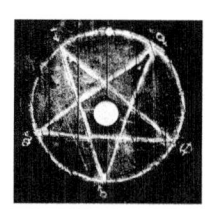

Food.

The smell of food overcame everything else, even the stench of fear that radiated from the prey. The hunter stared unblinking at it, drew air in through flared nostrils, opened its mouth, showing the huge incisors and growled menacingly.

The prey gaped, struggling to process what its pitiful small eyes saw before it, certain death standing just eight feet away, poised to strike. Its tiny mouth with its pathetic weak teeth opened and closed, and a whining noise came from it, wordless, yet eloquent testimony to the terror coursing through its veins.

The hunter breathed deeply again, drinking in the fear, and once again the smell of fresh meat. The claws protracted, the shoulder muscles tensed and the powerful thighs eased backward, poised to spring. Hunger, and hatred, contempt and anticipation mingled in the coursing blood, as it waited for the moment of truth, relishing the helplessness of its quarry.

The prey looked around helplessly for an escape route, a weapon, some forlorn hope, but there was none. Finally it seemed to accept its fate, staring submissively into the impassive and merciless eyes of its executioner, the eyes that would be the last thing it would ever see.

The hunter's muscles exploded in a frenzy of killing fury as it sprang.

* * *

'Mr Nightingale, they were the footprints of a giant cat. There is no doubt about that.'

Jack Nightingale took a long drag on his Marlboro, blew smoke up at the ceiling, raised one eyebrow and pursed his lips. 'Seems pretty unlikely,' he said.

'The police called in animal experts,' said the woman. 'The marks on the floor were definitely from giant feline paws. And the claw marks on the body fitted the same pattern.'

Nightingale looked closely at her while he thought of his next question. In her mid-thirties, obviously took good care of herself. The blonde hair was immaculately cut and colored, the black suit looked expensive, as did the open-necked white shirt. And her pearls could be real, for all he knew. If she'd been crying over her husband's death, she'd either gotten over it quickly, or hidden it very skilfully with high quality make-up.

'But how could a big cat manage to find its way up to a third-floor apartment?' asked Nightingale. 'And then got out again? You told me the front door was shut, and tigers don't do doorknobs, as far as I know.'

Her nostrils flared and her eyes narrowed. 'If that's English humor, I don't need it or appreciate it, Mr Nightingale. My husband is dead, remember?'

'I'm sorry,' said Nightingale. 'I wasn't really trying to be funny, just pointing out the facts. But the windows don't open, so how could a big cat have gotten in and out of here? And without any of the other tenants seeing anything. It makes no sense, Mrs Cresswell.'

'I never said it did. All I know is what the police told me. I was up here the whole time. Dan worked in Florida during the week and stayed in a rented apartment. I've never been near the place. I couldn't even find Gladesville on a map.'

Nightingale frowned. 'So what are the police doing about it?'

'Pretty much nothing, as far as I know. They seem to have no witnesses, no suspects, no motive and no idea how he was killed. That's why I called you.'

'Yes, you did,' said Nightingale, taking another drag on his cigarette. Vivienne Cresswell had given him permission to smoke in her home, but the slight pursing of her lips as he smoked suggested that she wasn't really all that happy about it. 'Though you haven't explained exactly how you knew where to contact me. I don't tend to advertise.'

'The person who told me about you didn't want their name mentioned, but said you'd helped them in the past. Helped with something else for which there seemed to be no rational explanation.'

Nightingale gave that one some thought. There were quite a few people who might fit that description, though several of them were dead now. Still, it seemed Vivienne Cresswell wasn't going to be satisfying his curiosity. He exhaled more smoke. 'So why would anyone want your husband dead, Mrs Cresswell?' he asked. 'Did he have any enemies?'

'Of course not, he was a businessman,' she said, frostily. 'He was CEO of Cresswell Explorations, he was down there looking for gas, he wasn't the kind of man who made enemies.'

Nightingale tried again. 'Any ex-girlfriends who might have borne a grudge?' Her eyes flashed, and he held up his hands in surrender. 'I'm sorry,' he said. 'But I have to start somewhere, and sometimes the obvious answers are the right ones. So, no exes, no current affairs, no jealous husbands?'

She pursed her lips, but gave the question a few moments thought. Finally she shook her head. 'No, not to my knowledge,' she said, her voice quieter now, and she seemed to be choosing her words more carefully. 'We never had any problems in the bedroom, but then I have a lot of friends who thought their husbands could be trusted, and were proved wrong. All I can say is that I never had any reason to doubt Dan's fidelity. On the other hand, he was a very attractive man, so I can't dismiss the possibility.'

Nightingale nodded.

'OK,' he said. 'While we're at it, I'll assume no threatening letters or e-mails, no strange phone calls, no business rivals with a grudge?'

'Again, none that I know of,' she said. 'You know, the police asked all the same questions.'

'They would,' said Nightingale. 'There are only so many questions that can be asked, and if they were stumped, chances are I will be too, unless the answer is something that the average cop wouldn't ever consider.'

'Like what?'

'I have no idea, and I won't be getting one hanging around here. If you really want me to look into it, you'll need to hire me, give me a letter of authority to act on your behalf, and I'll be needing to go down there for a while. That could work out expensive, and there's no guarantee I'd find out more than the cops. I don't want to waste your money.'

'Money's not an issue, Mr Nightingale. My husband was a very wealthy man, and my father was Webster Danforth.'

There was a silence, while Nightingale decided whether he should ask, or just look impressed. He took the riskier option. 'Sorry, I'm not from around these parts.'

She smiled, for pretty much the first time since the butler had shown him in. 'Well, I guess an Englishman might not be familiar with Danforth toothpaste, she said, 'But it was one of the leading brands up here, until my father sold out to Unilever in the eighties. He left it all to me, so, as I said, money won't be an issue. Tell me what you need and I'll have it wired to your bank today.'

Nightingale grimaced. 'I don't trust banks all that much,' he said. 'I'd prefer a cash advance.' He named a figure which was twice his usual fee, but Vivienne Cresswell didn't even blink.

'That will be fine. Kar...the person who recommended you said you could be trusted, but not instructed, and that you'd do things your own way. I'll have the money delivered to your hotel this afternoon, along with a plane ticket to Fort Myers. Apparently that's the nearest airport, I'll arrange car hire too.'

'I'll get started right away,' said Nightingale.'

She looked straight at Nightingale, and he could see her eyes starting to redden. 'Mr Nightingale, I'm not a particularly demonstrative person, but be assured that I loved my husband very much, and I'm going to miss him terribly. It might be some small consolation to me to know that whoever did this to him will be caught and punished.'

Nightingale nodded. 'Believe me, Mrs Cresswell, I'll do everything I can.'

* * *

Fort Myers Airport was the nearest major hub. The Florida summer weather was hot and dry, and the air-conditioning in Nightingale's Ford Escape had been working overtime for almost all the journey as the precise voice of the GPS system guided him to Gladesville. Vivienne Cresswell had reserved a room for him at the Plaza Hotel which seemed pretty central, and was certainly a cut above the roach motel Nightingale would probably have found if he'd been paying himself. He arrived in the early evening, treated himself to a room service dinner and showered before taking out the file that his client had given him and studying it while he lay on the bed and smoked.

Dan Cresswell had indeed been a good-looking guy in life, if the photos were to be believed, and had kept himself in shape. Somewhere just over six feet with mid-length dark blonde hair and a tan which looked as if he'd got it the natural way. He and Vivienne looked as if they belonged together and every photo she'd given him showed them smiling blissfully at the camera. Nightingale's naturally suspicious nature caused him to wonder whether it was all too good to be true. Vivienne Cresswell hadn't mentioned any problems, and Dan wasn't around to ask, but maybe he could find someone else who knew them who might open up. Assuming there was anything to open up about.

Vivienne had included copies of the local coroner's report and the information the police had shared with her, most of which just restated what she'd told him in New York. The whole thing seemed cut and dried, Dan Cresswell had been killed by a giant cat in a third-floor apartment room. Cut and dried, but completely impossible.

Nightingale could think of nothing useful to do until the morning, and badly needed rest after his journey, so found an old movie on the TV to help put him to sleep. He'd be starting with the people who so rarely seemed pleased to see a private detective. The Police.

* * *

Detective Mike Stone was probably in his early fifties, and looked every year of it and more. Nightingale guessed his weight at around two-twenty pounds, not much of it muscle, and he didn't look to be anything more than average height, as far as could be judged with him slumped back in his chair. His dark green sport jacket had probably been bought twenty pounds previously, and needed cleaning, especially around the shoulders, where the dandruff from his badly cut grey hair settled. The shirt collar, even with the top button undone, looked to be straining to cope with his neck, and his dark grey tie was loosened and bore a couple of food stains. His eyes were small and bloodshot, the lids hooded. The evidence of his teeth and fingers suggested a long-term smoking habit. He gave no sign of enthusiasm or interest as Nightingale was shown into his office, certainly not enough to get up or offer a greeting. He waved to the chair in front of his desk. Probably not a methodical man, thought Nightingale, judging from the piles of disordered papers that covered the desk.

Stone studied his visitor for a full minute before speaking.

'Front desk says you want to talk about the Cresswell case. What's your interest in him?'

'His wife hired me to look into it,' said Nightingale.

The detective's eyes narrowed. 'She not happy with the job we've been doing?'

'Her husband's dead, nobody knows how and nobody's been arrested. Maybe she thought another pair of eyes and feet might help.'

'British feet in suede shoes? What can you do that we can't?'

'Probably not that much,' admitted Nightingale. 'Maybe it just helps her feel better, to know she's doing everything possible. I don't want to get in the way of your investigation.'

Stone smiled at that. 'I'm not sure we have an investigation for you to get in the way of. Three weeks and we got no motive, no suspects and no cause of death that makes any sense at all. She wants to hire you, can't see how you could make things any worse. I got no problem with you, but anything you find out comes straight to me? Got it?'

Nightingale nodded. 'You mind if I ask you a few questions?' he asked.

Stone shrugged carelessly. 'Figured you'd want to. You need a cigarette too?'

Nightingale smiled. 'Takes one to know one, I guess. Do we go outside?'

'We can do better than that, Florida's still not fallen to the health nazis completely, we can't smoke in an enclosed workplace, but bars are still OK. There's one across the street and I'm due a break, though I'll need to keep it to coffee on duty.'

'Sounds good,' said Nightingale. 'Lead me to it.'

* * *

Nightingale followed Stone across the road into the Shamrock Bar where they took a booth and ordered two coffees. They lit cigarettes, but stayed quiet until the young waitress in tight jeans and an even tighter tee-shirt had brought the two cups. Stone took a sip, then nodded at Nightingale. 'So, what can I tell you?' he asked.

'What do I need to know?'

'From the top, and from memory. Daniel Charles Cresswell Junior, thirty-five years of age, president, CEO and sole owner of Cresswell Gas Exploration. Found deceased in Apartment 3:25 at 1435 South 12th Avenue, three weeks ago, the 15th, as far as I remember. It was Monday when the maid found him, MO said he could have been dead since late Saturday. Cause of death, massive wounds to the throat, stomach, chest and legs. Could have come in any order apparently, though they guess the throat wound was the fatal one.'

Nightingale knew most of that from the report he'd read the night before, but said nothing. He was hoping Stone could tell him things that hadn't been released to the public, but pushing too hard too soon would be a mistake. He let the man tell it at his own pace.

'All the windows were shut, the door was locked from the inside, but could have been pulled shut. Dead lock and bolt weren't on.'

Nightingale nodded.

Stone sipped his coffee. 'We did all the things you'd expect. The maid was out of it, visiting relatives in Jacksonville all weekend. Wife too, plenty of witnesses put her in New York. No sign of any marital problems.

No enemies, no death threats. No motive that we could find, no vengeful girlfriends, no wronged husbands, no disgruntled employees, nobody he owed money to, nothing seemed to have been stolen.'

Another nod from Nightingale.

'So nothing,' continued Stone. 'No leads. But that's not the worst of it, not by a long way. That came when we got the DNA results.'

Stone paused, almost inviting Nightingale to respond. Nightingale decided to decline the invite, but lit another cigarette. Stone was no stranger to the game, so lit a cigarette of his own and showed no sign of resuming. Finally Nightingale decided Stone was doing the favor so he'd play it his way and he broke the silence. 'So, you found other DNA in the room?'

'Yeah, Cresswell's, the maid's, traces of a few other people. And a whole bucket-load from our principal suspect.'

'Someone in the files?'

'Not hardly, as I guess you know. Our lab boys couldn't place it, but the zoo guys did. One hundred per cent certainty. Blood-stained paw prints, tooth and claw marks on the body to match. The guy was ripped to pieces by a Florida panther.' He sat back and watched to see how he'd react to the news.

Nightingale raised his eyebrows, but no more. The interview with Vivienne Cresswell had pretty much prepared him, though it hadn't come close to explaining it. Stone's matter-of-fact statement of the impossible made it sound even more ridiculous. 'There's no possibility that he was killed elsewhere and brought back to the room?' asked Nightingale.

'Not a one. MO said he bled out right where he was, and there were pieces of him all over the room.'

'So somebody put a panther in there with him?'

'You think? How much do you know about Florida panthers?'

'It wouldn't be my specialist subject on Mastermind.'

'What?'

'Forget it,' said Nightingale. 'English humor.'

'Yeah, I heard about that. Anyway, I know a lot more about them than I did a month ago. This is a wild animal, same as a puma, cougar or mountain lion, except down here they're always called panthers. They can get to seven feet long, weigh maybe a hundred and fifty.'

'So you don't put one in a cat basket?' said Nightingale.

Stone didn't seem to pick up on the sarcasm. 'You do not. And you don't put one on a leash and walk it through the streets. And if you do, people are going to notice. And if you put one in a crate and transport it to an apartment building by truck then get a crane to lift it to the third floor, people are going to notice that too.'

Nightingale grinned. 'But you asked around anyway?' he said.

Stone gave him a long look, as if he'd just noticed something for the first time. 'Let me guess, you were a cop once?'

'Why do you say that?' asked Nightingale.

'You got the look, plus you know when to keep quiet. Of course we asked, no surprises. People saw mailmen, paper boys, girl scouts, at least five different women they said looked like hookers, any number of people 'acting suspicious', old ladies, a guy in a wheelchair...not one of them saw a hungry wild cat. And I guess it's the sort of thing you'd remember.'

'You'd think so,' agreed Nightingale.

'So, nobody sees it going in, nobody sees it coming out and pulling the door behind it.'

'Nobody heard anything?'

'Nothing that sounded like a guy being torn apart by a big cat. Neighbors were in and out all weekend, and the walls are thick...but still...' He shrugged.

'Any chance he was killed with a rake or something, and then panther DNA left as a distraction?'

Stone snorted dismissively. 'Nice try. Someone carrying a rake around looks a little conspicuous, and they don't sell Panther DNA in drug stores.'

'It didn't really seem likely. I'm just clutching at straws.'

Stone nodded. 'After three weeks, so are we. Besides, if you want to just kill a guy, why go to that kind of trouble? They sell guns and knives down here. It's a lot less effort.'

'What did the coroner say?'

'Left it open. What else could he do?'

'So where are you with it now?'

'Nowhere,' said Stone. 'We have plenty of evidence, all of which leads us to something impossible. Chief suspect is a Florida Panther, there's no way one could have been in that room. You can't call it murder unless we can show someone put the animal in the room. I can't arrest all the local panthers.'

'There are some around?' asked Nightingale.

'Sure, zoos, sanctuaries. Nobody's missing one.'

'Private owners?'

Stone shook his head. 'Nope, they're protected animals, you can't get a license to keep one. Course, there may be some guy who's keeping one illegally, but that still doesn't explain how it got up there. Damned thing makes no sense at all. it's plain impossible.'

Nightingale nodded, that was surely the way it seemed, though these days his definition of 'impossible' was a lot more flexible than it had been.

* * *

Nightingale knew that a lot of detective work consisted of asking people questions they'd already answered, in the hope either they'd remember something new, with the off chance that maybe he'd even think of a new question. Trouble was, a lot of his questions and theories tended to make no sense to people who hadn't been through some of his experiences. Still, wearing out Hush Puppies was an occupational hazard of the job. Not that there was usually all that much walking to do in American cities - the car was king.

He drove his rental car to the Gladesville Zoo. Stone had given him the name of his contact, and a business card with a note scribbled on the back, which got him in to see Dr. Sally Taylor, head of the large feline department. She met him at reception, a tall, lithe, copper-skinned woman with short dark hair and bright yellowy-green eyes. She looked about the same age as Nightingale, and her white tee-shirt and tight jeans showed that she kept herself in excellent shape. Her handshake was firm as she introduced herself.

'Mr Nightingale? Dr. Taylor, but call me Sally.'

'Jack, please.'

'Good to meet you Jack. You come from Mike Stone, you with the police too?'

'No, I'm working for a woman called Vivienne Cresswell, in connection with the death of her husband.'

Sally nodded. 'I remember, we did a lot of lab work on it. Not usual for us to work with the police. Follow me, we can talk in my office.'

Sally's office had been adequately furnished without any unnecessary expense, the only distinguishing feature being the prints of big cats decorating the walls. She waved him to a chair, and sat in the black leather seat behind her cluttered desk, papers overflowing her IN tray and books piled up on the left.

'Sorry about the mess,' she said. 'I'm a much better animal doctor than administrator.'

Nightingale smiled. 'I was never much good at paperwork myself, seemed to breed faster than rabbits.'

She returned his smile. 'Seems that way. You've talked to Sergeant Stone, so you know what we told him. So what can I tell you?'

'OK, I'm guessing you know panther DNA when you see it and there's no possibility of a mistake.'

'Yes we do, and no there isn't.'

'So, could you actually tie the DNA they sent you to one specific panther?'

'Of course, just like with people, it's unique. And, in case you were wondering, it wasn't from one of our animals, or any one we've treated and released back into the wild.'

'You don't know of any missing panthers in the area?'

She smiled. 'It's not the kind of thing you lose. No, I know of no missing panthers.'

Nightingale thought for a few moments. This didn't seem to be getting him too far and still wasn't answering the big question of how an animal that size could have got in and out of Cresswell's apartment.

'OK, could you tell me more about the animals themselves?'

She stood up and motioned him toward the door.

'I can do a lot better than that, Jack. Why not come and visit with our cats?'

* * *

The two cats were tan colored with cream underbellies, their tails and ears tipped with black. Nightingale was fascinated by their eyes, which seemed to shift from yellow to blue, as they stared at him, The larger one, which he assumed was the male, seemed to fix its gaze right on him, without a trace of friendliness, before walking away from the bars with a contemptuous sounding hiss, and a confident roll of its shoulders. The female stood at the bars and chirped at Sally, seeming to recognize her as a friend.

'I don't think he likes me much,' said Nightingale.

'Nonsense,' replied Sally, 'I'm sure he'd find you very tasty.'

'That's reassuring, do they often attack humans?'

'Well, if you need reassurance, I can provide that easily enough. Statistically you'd be far more likely to be killed by a dog, horse, snake, bear or by bees. In fact, there's not a single documented instance of a Florida Panther attacking a human being.'

'Except Dan Cresswell?'

'Including Dan Cresswell, whatever the Police might think. It's quite impossible that one of these animals sneaked up three floors of an apartment building, knocked on the door, killed him and wandered back home again. They're hardly stalking the streets of Gladesville. Besides, they avoid contact with humans.'

'So what do they eat?'

'Hares, rabbits, waterfowl, deer, wild boar. They've even been known to eat alligators, though that can work both ways. Never people, though I wouldn't recommend climbing into the cage to prove the theory.'

Nightingale grinned. 'I'll take your word for it. How many do you have here?'

'Full time, none,' said Sally. 'These two are recovering from separate car accidents, that's one of the major threats to the animal. We also have a pair of orphaned cubs who were brought in when their mother was found dead. We're raising them here, but they'll be introduced back to the wild as soon as they're ready. In separate areas, since inbreeding is another serious problem with such a small population.'

'Are they endangered?' asked Nightingale.

'Not as much as before, but there are estimated to be only around two hundred of them left.'

'That's all?'

'That's a big success story, back in the seventies there were thought to be only twenty in the wild. Now we have a separate sanctuary and rescue centre near the Wildlife Reserve.'

'You must be doing something right.'

'We try, but we're battling on a whole load of fronts. Mostly habitat depletion, people keep building roads to fragment their habitat, every year brings more new developments, now we even have to contend with fracking.'

'Fracking?' echoed Nightingale. 'What's that?'

She frowned at him. 'Where have you been, Jack? Don't you read the papers?'

'I don't always have time to keep up with the world,' he said. 'What is it?'

'Hydraulic fracturing, basically mining for gas by smashing underground rocks with high pressure water.'

'Does it work?' asked Nightingale.

'Sure,' she said. 'It's helping solve America's energy problems. Trouble is, it makes a mess, causes endless damage to the water table and risks earth tremors. There's a company just opening up a concession on the very edge of the Florida Panther Wildlife Refuge. Going to make even more problems for the animals.'

Nightingale felt a shiver run up his spine. He had a bad feeling as he asked the obvious question. 'Which company?' he asked.

She gave him a humorless smile. 'Now I'd have thought you might have known that,' she said. 'It's Cresswell Exploration.'

* * *

Back in his car, Nightingale decided a talk to his client might be in order, and called her cell. Mrs Cresswell got straight to the point and asked him how the investigation was going.

'Slowly so far,' said Nightingale. 'Talking to the police didn't get me too far, but I know a lot more about panthers than I did this morning. Mrs Cresswell, did you know what your husband's company was doing down here?'

'Looking for gas? That's what they usually did, but we never really discussed details. We had kind of a deal, he never talked about his work, I never talked about my friends.'

'They were apparently setting up a fracking operation on the edge of the panther reserve here.'

'So? You think one of the panthers got upset about it, followed him home and killed him?' she said, her voice loaded with sarcasm. 'That the best you can do?'

'To be fair, I didn't suggest it,' said Nightingale. 'But it does seem pretty unlikely.'

'Look, Mr Nightingale, maybe I didn't tell you the whole truth, I did know he was starting up a fracking operation, it's an area he'd been moving into lately. I...I didn't...I don't entirely approve of it. It's a controversial area, people say it causes tremors, contaminates water supplies, all kinds of things. But we didn't discuss it anymore, he was my husband, it's what he did, so I just sort of put it aside and got on with my life.'

'I'm not criticizing,' said Nightingale. 'Anyway, the reason I'm calling is I'd like to take a look at the apartment, do you have any objections?'

'None at all, I assume the police have finished there now, but somebody down there probably arranged for it to be cleaned. No doubt the super has a spare key, use my name.'

'Fine. Tell me, who runs your husband's company now?'

'Well, I guess in theory I do. Dan left me everything and he owned it outright. But Chad Hutton, his director of operations, has been running things down there. Basically he's keeping things ticking over until we decide what to do.'

'Could I talk to him?'

'Sure, I'll call him, you know where the operation's located? I think most of the guys stay in a motel down there.'

'Yeah, I know where to find the operation...the lady at the zoo drew me a map.'

'Mr Nightingale...do you have any idea what happened to Dan yet?'

'None that makes any sense,' he said. 'But I'm working on it.

* * *

A call to Mike Stone confirmed that the Police had no further interest in Cresswell's apartment, and Vivienne Cresswell's name was enough to get the key from the building super. The man looked to be in his late fifties, and was adamant that he'd seen and heard nothing unusual that weekend, or any other time. Cresswell had generally come back to the apartment late and left early. No visitors that he'd ever seen. 'But I don't spend my time checking up on the tenants, boy. I turn in early and watch TV in bed, mostly I only see them if there's a problem needs fixing,' he said.

'Did you see the body?' asked Nightingale.

'Never once. That maid just called 911 straight away. First I knew was when a couple of patrol cars turned up outside, but the police went straight up, and after that they wasn't letting anybody in. I heard he was tore up pretty bad, that true?'

'So I hear,' said Nightingale. 'But I wasn't there either. I'll just take a quick look and be on my way.'

'Not much to see up there now. Cops finished, then they had the place cleaned. His clothes and such got sent back to the widow, I guess.'

Nightingale smiled. 'I shouldn't be very long at all, then.'

'Need a hand up with that bag?' he said, nodding at the case Nightingale was holding.

'Thanks, but it's fine, not heavy. Just a little photographic equipment.' Nightingale didn't waste any time looking round the apartment, which had obviously been given a thorough cleaning, and probably had several items of furniture and the carpets replaced. Blood stains weren't easy to remove, and Cresswell had bled out. Nightingale locked the door and headed to the shower, took out shower gel and a new nailbrush from his bag and cleaned himself thoroughly. He dried himself in a clean towel he'd borrowed from the hotel, then dressed in an equally clean bathrobe. He took his bag into the living-room, sat on the sofa and took out two large church candles, which he placed at either end of the coffee table, and lit with his cigarette lighter.

He took out a glass ball and placed it on the coffee table in front of him, then a small and very old leather bag, from which he took a pink crystal, hanging on a silver chain. He smiled to himself, if the Super decided to come up and check on him, he'd have plenty of explaining to do.

This was a long shot, since he had nothing to use to get vibrations from. Locating Cresswell was pointless, his ashes were at the crematorium, and whoever...or whatever...had killed him had left no trace beyond panther DNA, and he could see no way of getting hold of that. Instead he planned to use a Spell of Attunement, to try to align his vibrations to those left in the room. Any number of people would have been in here since the death, but he was hoping that the strongest emotions would have produced the longest lasting vibrations. It had been known to work for other people.

Allegedly.

Nightingale was careful not to touch the crystal itself, winding the chain round his hands like a rosary. He closed his eyes, whispered three sentences in what he had been told was Ancient Greek, and tried to clear his mind of everything except an image of the crystal, focusing in as completely as he could on the glowing pink jewel, willing himself inside it. He held himself inside, until slowly he began to expand his field of thought outwards again, still keeping his mind as empty as possible, trying to tune in to the feelings and vibrations left in the room.

There had indeed been plenty of people in the room, all of whom had left their own mark on its atmosphere, but Nightingale tuned it out, like background chatter, and focused on the strongest vibrations.

There were two...or was it three, the second seemed almost to be two people. He stretched out further and let them flow over him.

Fear.

The first was fear, blind, stomach-twisting, uncomprehending fear, then pain, appalling pain. Surprise, incredulity, fear and pain in a rapid repeating cycle. But the pain was the strongest, intensifying beyond endurance until Nightingale was forced to pull himself away from it.

It must have been Cresswell's spirit, leaving the trail of his final moments behind it. Nightingale shut his mind to it, and opened himself towards the second spirit.

This one was more confused. Nightingale sensed fear here too, but it faded into certainty, then hatred. Intense hatred, and hunger, but the hunger was never as strong as the hatred. This was a strong and certain spirit, though occasionally its certainty broke, and he sensed the fear in it again, underneath, almost in a different, gentler spirit. But always the hatred returned to strengthen it. Nightingale tried with all his power to open himself further, to see the bearer of this spirit in his crystal ball. He caught a flash of wide bright eyes, but before he could tell the color, they had gone.

He kept at it for another ten minutes, but by now he was trying too hard at a task for which relaxation was essential. Finally he gave it up, put the crystal away, blew out the candles and dressed again.

Cresswell had died in fear and agony, without understanding what was happening to him. Whoever, or whatever, had killed him had done so from pure hatred and blood-lust, though, strangely, there was softness in it too.

He glanced at his watch, and was surprised to find it was nearly eight. His stomach told him he needed to eat, but he was weary from his efforts with the crystal and couldn't be bothered with anything complicated, so he drove to the nearest branch of Domino's and ordered a pizza.

* * *

The next morning brought more people to see, more questions to ask.

The next stop needed to be the Cresswell Exploration Hydraulic Fracturing test site just on the outskirts of the Florida Panther National Wildlife reserve. He'd asked Sally to draw him a map, since the Cresswell team had made their own road, which didn't show on the Escape's GPS system. He drove out of town, along the highway some fifteen miles, and nearly missed the turn-off to the right onto a narrow gravel road. He took it slowly, since the Escape wasn't really designed for serious off-road work, and followed the track down for two miles until it ended at a large and obviously man-made clearing.

The place was littered with four-wheel drive trucks, excavators, large flat-bed wagons and tankers. There was a tall central crane or tower, maybe for a drill, a system of pipes with what looked like a very large valve in the centre. Men in Cresswell-logoed coveralls and yellow hard-hats were milling around.

He stopped the Escape next to one of the smaller trucks, got out and walked in the direction of a portakabin, which looked the nearest thing to an office that he could see. He managed to get within thirty yards of it before one of the workers challenged him. 'Help you, mister?' said the man.

The guy was well over six foot and hefty, his tone wasn't unfriendly, but Nightingale decided to stop and flash a smile. 'Hope so,' he said. 'I'm looking for Chad Hutton, your Director of Operations.'

The man nodded. 'Your name would be?'

'Jack. Jack Nightingale. Vivienne Cresswell said he'd be expecting me.'

Another nod, and a smile as the man recognized her name. 'Sure, I'm Dave Kowalski, come with me.'

Nightingale followed him round to the door of the portakabin, which Kowalski opened. Inside there was an unoccupied room with a door leading off on either side. Kowalski knocked on the right hand door, opened it without waiting for permission and put his head round the door.

'Guy here to see you, Chad. Says Mrs Cresswell sent him.'

The voice that answered him was muffled by the door and Kowalski's body. 'Yeah, she called, send him in.'

Kowalski stepped aside and opened the door wider for Nightingale to enter. Nightingale nodded at him in acknowledgment and stepped inside. The office was small, with a desk and a chair but little other furniture apart from a rack for uniforms and hard hats which took up most of the right-hand wall. Hutton rose and walked towards his visitor. He was around five-nine and Nightingale pegged him at early forties, judging from the thinning grey hair and lines around his eyes. He'd aged pretty well apart from that, the tan and the trim frame witnesses to a life of heavy work outdoors.

'You'll be Jack, I'm Chad. Not enough room to talk in here,' he said. 'Let's go outside, get a little sun. Better wear one of these.'

He took a hard hat from the rack and passed it to Nightingale, before putting on his own. 'Nothing much can fall on your head, unless the main drill tower collapses on you, and then you'll have so many broken bones it won't matter what shape your head's in. Still, rules are rules. There's a coffee machine in the rec room if you need one.'

'No, I'm fine thanks,' said Nightingale, who was no fan of machine-brewed coffee.

Hutton led the way back out through the main door, and they walked to the back of the portakabin, where there was a backless wooden bench, He waved Nightingale to sit down. Nightingale took out his packet of Marlboro and looked at Hutton hopefully.

'Sure,' said Hutton. 'Safe enough over here, not for me, gave them up twenty years ago.'

Nightingale nodded his sympathy and lit up.

'So,' said Hutton. 'Vivienne asked me to give you any help you need, and I guess she calls the shots now, so what can I tell you that I haven't told the cops?'

'What did you tell the cops?'

'Nothing much, I guess. Dan wasn't due down here that weekend, but he didn't always fly home. Nobody here had ever visited him in the apartment, if we socialized, it was in town, but that was pretty rare. We work long hours here, and it's not the kind of job you want to be showing up for hung over. Cops asked me about any enemies, death threats, suspicious characters hanging around, but there was really nothing like that. It's the hell of a thing though, they say he looked like he'd been ripped apart by a wild animal.'

'So I hear,' said Nightingale. 'You said there was "really" nothing like that, when you talked about threats and things. What did you mean?'

Hutton puffed out his lips and wiped the sweat from his brow with the back of his hand, maybe buying a little time to organize his thoughts. 'Well, we're not exactly the most popular people round here,' he said eventually. 'There's a lot of opposition to fracking, and this site is about as controversial as you can get, right on the edge of the wildlife reserve. We've had a couple noisy protests down here, and I think there's more scheduled in town. But it's a big leap from a protest march to murdering the CEO of the company. Far as I know, nobody threatened people personally.'

'So fracking is going to damage the reserve?'

Hutton took another pause. 'It can have implications, sure,' he said. 'People are worried it'll contaminate the water table, they panic that there'll be earthquakes, but it won't come to that. It's a question of priorities, I guess.'

'How do you mean?'

'Look, Americans need power, but they don't like the way it's created. There's protests everywhere about fracking, nuclear power, nobody wants a coal mine or an oil well near them. But they want to be able to drive anywhere they choose, charge up their iPad and iPhone, hit the internet and watch TV. They just don't want to know about where that power comes from, but they need more and more of it, and we need to find new sources. In the end people are going to have to decide whether they want vast tracts of beautiful untouched land, or to keep the lights on.'

It sounded like a speech Hutton had made before, and it wasn't getting Nightingale too far. He lit another cigarette, and tried to change tack. 'So, who organized the protests? Local groups?'

'Far as I know. Gladesville Against Fracking they call themselves. That woman from the Zoo's pretty involved. Tall, dark girl, short hair.'

'Dr Taylor?' said Nightingale. 'I've met her.'

'Yeah, that's her. I got nothing against her, she seems a nice lady, passionate about what she believes in. We're just on opposite sides of the fence. She's kind of vocal, but I never heard her threaten anybody.'

Nightingale nodded. 'What kind of man was Dan Cresswell?' he asked.

'My boss,' said Hutton, and pressed his lips shut.

'Look, Chad, I'm not trying to do a hatchet job on the guy, I've been hired by his wife to try to help find out what happened to him, since the cops seem stuck. I'd just like to know a bit more about him personally, might give me a lead or two. If...if there's anything you tell me that might upset Vivienne, well, it doesn't have to get back to her.'

Hutton unglued his lips and smiled a little. 'I'm sorry,' he said. 'Guess I'm confusing you with some of the reporters we had down here when it happened. Always looking for an angle, girlfriend, jealous husbands, you know.'

'I know,' said Nightingale. 'But I hope we're on the same side here. How long had you worked for him?'

'Maybe nine years, off and on, contract stuff at first, but around five years ago he made it full-time, and I've worked my way up. Not that it's a big organization, but it was well run and seemed to make a lot of money.'

'You worked pretty closely with him?'

'You could say that. He was pretty hands-on with new sites at first, but once they got properly started he tended to loosen the reins a little.

He'd trust me and the guys to get on with it and start thinking about the next thing. I was surprised he stayed as long as he did down here. It's up and running now.'

'Any particular reason he might have wanted to stay longer down here?'

Hutton pursed his lips, then puffed out some air. 'None that I know of. Look, Jack, I knew Dan Cresswell a lot of years, I can't say he was a close friend, but he was a straight-up guy to work for. Some of the things he may have done in his private life may not have been my style, but they were none of my business. I've met Vivienne quite a few times over the years, and I like her. I wouldn't want rumors and stuff to get back.'

'I told you, they won't, not unless there's a court case. Come on Chad, the guy was killed. Help me.'

Hutton nodded. 'I guess. OK, you've seen photos of Dan?'

'Yeah.'

'He was a good looking guy, he was still pretty young, he was successful, confident and he had money. There are women who find those qualities attractive. A lot of women.'

'I'd imagine so.'

'And quite a few of them weren't put off by a little thing like a wedding ring. Assuming he was wearing it when they met him, which he didn't always.'

'So he got around?' said Nightingale.

'That's what I hear, and I saw him in action, couple times.'

'Seems strange, having Vivienne at home.'

'Some guys just can't go without, maybe they like the novelty. The challenge, the danger of it. Heck, I'm not averse myself, but I don't have a wife at home.'

'And did it ever turn dangerous?'

'Not that I ever heard. Guess he had the knack of picking women who knew the score. If any of them turned nasty, he never discussed it with me.'

'You think he was seeing someone in Gladesville?'

'It wouldn't surprise me, couple of the boys said they'd seen him talking to a woman in some bar.'

'Would they have a name? A description?'

'I never heard a name. I can ask around if you think it might be useful.'

'That's half the fun of being a detective,' said Nightingale. 'You never really know what's going to turn out to be useful.'

* * *

As Nightingale drove back through Gladesville, he ran into a demonstration heading down Main Street toward the town square. It occurred to him that whoever had decided to shorten 'Hydraulic Fracturing' into 'Fracking' had played right into the hands of those opposed to it. All the protestors were wearing bright orange -shirts with 'Frack Off Out Of Gladesville' printed on them. The various signs were pretty much in the same unimaginative vein, featuring 'No Fracking Way', 'Not In My Fracking Name' 'Frack You Cresswell Explorations' 'Protect Our Panthers From The Sad Frackers'. It struck him as a little insensitive to be holding a protest march so soon after the death of the CEO, but then the operation was still going on, with all its possible environmental hazards.

Nightingale was surprised by how many people he recognized, despite his short time in the town. He spotted a waitress from the restaurant he'd eaten in the previous night, one of the hotel receptionists, two people he'd seen at the zoo and the barman from Dave's. At the front, he saw Sally Taylor, walking with a little girl around twelve, who he assumed must be her daughter.

Nightingale was out of people to talk to for the moment, and wasn't sure he was going to find answers that way, but by the time he got back to his hotel room it was probably too late for the local library so he decided to head out for an early dinner.

Gladesville was hardly the gourmet capital of Southern Florida, but Stan's Surf'n'Turf looked as if it would provide everything he needed, and it did a good job. Nightingale was intrigued enough to step a little outside his comfort zone and try the alligator steak for the first time. It wasn't bad – it tasted a little like chicken. He washed it down with a local beer.

Mary-Ann was the waitress, a woman in her early fifties, disposed to talk to a customer sitting alone, maybe from her maternal instinct, maybe just to make him feel welcome enough to come back. 'So, you be wanting dessert now?' she asked as she collected his plate. 'We got key lime pie, cherry pie, Mississippi mud pie, homemade apple pie....'

'Pie to the power of four,' said Nightingale.

She looked blank.

'Joke,' he said. 'Maths. I'll take the key lime, please.'

'Be right back,' she said, walking back to the serving hatch, returning almost immediately with a slice of pie. 'Here you go, you're new in town, ain't you? English?'

'Yes.'

'Business?'

'Sort of,' said Nightingale. 'I've been asked to look into Dan Cresswell's death.'

'The guy from the fracking company?' Boy that was a thing.'

Nightingale was about to ask another question, but she nodded at him and scooted off to another table. He took his time over the pie, which tasted as if it had come straight from the fridge, and waited till she came back.

'Coffee? Another beer?'

Nightingale settled on a beer, he wasn't planning on driving again that night, and coffee before trying to sleep wasn't always the best idea. She came back with the bottle and a fresh frosted glass. 'Thanks,' he said. 'Did Dan Cresswell ever eat in here?'

'Not that I know,' she said. 'Look, if you want to talk, I'm due a break at nine, come round the back and I'll have more time.'

She hurried off again in response to a look from a woman on the other side of the room. Nightingale finished his beer slowly, paid and went outside to smoke a cigarette while he waited for Mary-Ann's break time. At nine he walked round to the back of the restaurant, she came out, sat on a bench and lit a cigarette. She looked up at him as he walked up, and waved him to sit beside her. 'Enjoy your dinner?' she asked.

'Pretty good, so can I ask you a question or two?'

'Sure, you're not with the police are you? I guess they don't hire English guys.'

'No, I'm strictly private, working for the family. Jack Nightingale.'

'Well, you know my name from the badge. So, ask away.'

'You said Dan Cresswell never ate here?'

'Not that I know of, and if he had one of the other girls might have said something. It was pretty big news, we don't get a lot of people dying mysteriously round here.'

'Suppose not.'

'Few of the other guys from the fracking company come in from time to time. Always four or five together. They eat pretty quietly, nice enough guys, but you might guess they don't feel too welcome down here.'

'Lot of bad feeling about the fracking?'

'Enough, plus they brought in all their own guys to work here, so it's not like the town gets much from it, apart from what they spend in bars and restaurants, I guess.'

'So you never saw Cresswell?'

'Now, I didn't say that. I saw him a few times around town. Good looking guy, but I guess he knew it too. Twenty years too young for me.'

'Did you see him anywhere specific?'

'Couple of times in the Waikiki lounge down on Apache, some of us go there for a drink when we finish up here. Some nights anyway.'

'Was he with anyone?'

'Now you're asking.' She paused to light another cigarette. 'I just noticed him in passing, you know? Guess he might have been with a woman, but I didn't take enough notice.'

Nightingale nodded and lit a fresh cigarette of his own. 'So, if he didn't eat here. Where else might he have gone?'

She shook her head. 'No idea. It's a small town, but there's plenty places to eat. We got all the chains, Red Lobster, Taco Bell, Pizza Hut. Couple up-scale places, The Green Door and Maxwell's. Any amount of small places like this one. Guess the police would probably have found out.

'I guess they would,' said Nightingale.

'Anyway, I'm done out here, back to work for me. You come back any time, Jack Nightingale, with or without questions.'

* * *

Nightingale picked up a passing taxi and told him to drive to the Waikiki Lounge, which the driver seemed to know well enough. The name had warned Nightingale what to expect, and he wasn't disappointed. The bar was designed to look like an old cabin, with woven grass umbrellas covering the outside tables, and a similar grass canopy over the frontage. Tall mock-Polynesian totem-poles, topped with brightly painted heads flanked the main entrance, and waitresses wearing grass skirts and with leis round their necks were carrying trays of brightly colored drinks. He walked inside, where the Polynesian theme continued, with more carved heads, grass wall-hangings and a half coconut on each table as an ashtray. The only discordant note was the music, which seemed to be modern American, and so nothing Nightingale recognized. He took a stool at the bar and ordered a beer.

'Australian, huh?' said the barman, whose name-tag identified him as Phil. He was a heavy-set man in his late forties, a lot of hair hanging down in a pony-tail, but not much on his head. He wore a multicolored flowered beach shirt, though it was difficult to tell where the shirt ended and his arm and neck tattoos began.

Nightingale shook his head. 'English. I'm helping out on the Cresswell case.'

Phil frowned a little before he caught the reference. 'Yeah, the guy who got killed? One of those mining guys, right? He used to come in here a few times. Never knew his name, but I recognized the photo they put in the paper.'

'Not a regular then?'

'Nah, like I said, a few times. I got the feeling he was cruising, you know. Looking for chicks.'

Nightingale looked around. 'Not many in here usually?'

Phil looked slightly offended at the slur on the bar. 'Hey, it's early. We get a fine standard of young lady in here later on. Not sure they'd all be buying what he was selling though.'

'You ever see him with anyone in particular?'

Phil thought about that one for a while. 'Hmmm, we get a lot of people in here, can't keep tabs on them all. Give me a minute, I'll ask one or two of the girls.'

'You need the photo?' asked Nightingale.

'Nope, we all know what he looked like, now.' He walked to the far end of the bar, where two young waitresses were standing, taking a rest between drink orders. Nightingale watched him ask a question, saw the brunette shake her head, but the blonde gave a longer reply. Phil nodded a few times, then headed back up the bar. 'Tammy says she remembers him with a couple of girls, one short and blonde. The other one tall and black. Didn't know either of them, they weren't regulars. Looks like he varied in his tastes.'

'Could be. Did the cops come in asking questions?'

'Not yet. Lot of bars in town, maybe they'll get to us in the end. So you're not a cop?'

'No, private. Hired by the family.'

'Well, good luck with that. I hear they found the guy clawed to bits and half eaten. That right?'

'Allegedly,' said Nightingale.

* * *

Nightingale got back to his hotel room around twelve, not much wiser than he'd left it. He'd confirmed Chad Hutton's view that the workforce of Cresswell Exploration weren't Gladesville's favorite people, and also confirmed that Dan Cresswell had been a womanizer, but not much more. He'd maybe got a little further than the Police by finding out Cresswell's proclivities, since people were often wary of passing on gossip to the authorities, but it hadn't got him anywhere. The description of Cresswell's escorts was vague enough to fit hundreds of people, and he didn't relish flogging round every bar in town to see if any other waitresses could do better.

Nightingale decided to smoke a last cigarette before bed, but patted all his pockets without success. He swore to himself, could he have left his pack on the bar in the Tahiti lounge? The hotel bar was closed, he doubted they'd sell them in reception, and he couldn't face a walk to find some. Maybe there was another pack in his raincoat, or his spare suit. He opened the wardrobe and his jaw dropped. What was left of his clothes still hung on their hangers, but he wouldn't be wearing them again. Someone, or something, had slashed them to ribbons, with something extremely sharp.

Nightingale sat on the bed and cursed again. The raincoat had been an old friend, with him through some hard times, fire as well as rain, and had been on its last legs before, but it was now too far gone even for him to wear. 'Still, looks like I've rattled the bars to someone's cage,' he muttered. 'Or something's.'

* * *

Food.

The prey stood a mere ten feet away, yet knew nothing of the hunter's presence. The hunter crouched downwind, from force of habit, though the tiny nostrils and feeble sense of smell of its quarry rendered the precaution unnecessary. The darkness of the shrubbery hid the hunter's body almost completely, and it stayed motionless as its prey walked past the machine to head for its lair. This time there was no fear, just the blissful unawareness that its last moments had arrived. This would be too easy, a sudden surge, one leap to bring the creature down, one swift and savage bite to kill it, and then the feeding. The hunger and the hatred would be satisfied.

The hunter's eyes narrowed, seeing perfectly in the dim light that rendered its prey almost blind. A pause to savor the moment,

Now.

* * *

The sound of his cellphone woke Nightingale at just after eight. He didn't recognise the number but took the call. It was Sergeant Stone. Nightingale rubbed his eyes with his free hand and tried to think of a reason why he was due a wake-up call from the Police.

'You there?' said Stone.

'I'm here,' said Nightingale. 'To what do I owe the pleasure?'

'I guess you didn't see the local TV news, we got another one.'

'Another what?'

'I also guess you're still asleep. Another killing, another guy clawed to death in his own home.'

'Who?'

'Charles Lincoln Hutton it says on his driver's license, and that's about the only way to identify him. He worked for Cresswell Explorations.'

'I know, I met him yesterday.'

Stone grunted. 'Look, I got questions I need answering, and maybe you might help. Can you get down here?'

'Thirty minutes?'

'Cool. I'll have coffee for you.'

Nightingale made it to Police Headquarters in twenty-five minutes. He was shown into Stone's office, where his coffee was cooling on the desk opposite the Sergeant. Stone was looking even more disheveled than before, his shirt collar grubby and the bags under his eyes darker, probably due to a sleepless night. He waved Nightingale to the seat opposite him, raised his eyebrows at the large plastic bag Nightingale was carrying, but didn't mention it. 'Thanks for stopping by,' he said. 'I might as well get straight to the point. Where were you between eight and two last night?'

'Am I a suspect now?'

'It's routine,' said the sergeant.

Nightingale shrugged. 'Stan's Surf'n'Turf, then the Tahiti Lounge till around twelve. After that, in bed at my hotel.'

'Alone?'

Nightingale grinned. 'Even my boyish charm doesn't work that fast in a strange town. Yes, alone. The receptionist will be able to confirm what time I came in, and that I didn't go out again. So what's happened?'

'We got a dead guy, like I said, Charles Hutton, found in the drive of his rental house, throat ripped out, stomach ripped open, liver missing believed eaten, judging by the tooth marks on the rest of him. Nobody saw anything, the house is a good distance from any other ones so nobody heard anything. Not that he'd have done much screaming without a larynx.'

Nightingale shuddered. He was only glad he hadn't seen Hutton's body for himself. 'Does the ME have any thoughts?' he asked.

'Guess you know what his thoughts are,' said Stone. 'Same as the other guy. Torn to pieces by a big cat. The DNA samples are on their way to the zoo. My guess is, they'll come back panther, unless we have a whole menagerie walking the streets round here.'

'Any prints?'

'Not this time, graveled drive so the blood soaked in, nothing to leave prints on.'

'You got any ideas?' asked Nightingale.

'None worth shit, though we're just starting. From what I know now, guy didn't go out too much, few quiet beers now and then, that's all. You got anything?'

'Nothing that makes much sense,' said Nightingale. 'Except the obvious, there's a panther loose around here with a taste for human flesh.'

'Yeah, provided the human flesh works for a fracking company. I don't buy it, but I got nothing better for the moment. What's in the bag, your laundry?'

Nightingale opened the bag and took out the remains of his suit and overcoat. Stone let out a whistle. 'Well now. Tell me about it.'

'Nothing to tell, I just found them that way last night.'

'I'm assuming the receptionist didn't let any wild animals into your room?'

'She says nobody...and nothing.'

'Guess you won't be wanting to wear them for a while, mind if I get the lab boys to take a look?'

'Be my guest,' said Nightingale. 'Though I'd put money against it being a panther's claws, looks way too regular.'

'Box cutters, if you ask me. Still won't hurt to check. Looks like someone's trying to send you a message.'

'It does rather,' said Nightingale.

'Be a good plan to find out who, and why.'

'It would.'

'Before you end up as cat food.'

'That too.'

'You carrying?'

'Not at the moment, I'm not a great fan of armed civilians.'

'You might wish you'd made an exception if a panther comes at you.'

'I'll think about it.'

'You do that. Look, seriously, Jack, I've got two dead guys in a town where the murder rate is generally zero, and I don't have idea one about why, how, who or maybe even what. Seems like someone is tying you in with this and doesn't wish you well. You might want to think seriously about something to even the odds. You get a sniff of anything, you come to me. Don't try to do this alone, you get me?'

'I get you,' said Nightingale. 'But I have no ideas either.'

Nightingale never much liked lying to the police, but telling Stone his current theory would probably have gotten him committed. He drove away from Police Headquarters back towards his hotel, but stopped outside a gun store, got out and took a look in the window. There was surely plenty of choice, but he was reluctant to take that step. His time as a firearms officer in London had taught him respect for weapons, and he'd never needed to draw his own. It had also taught him that civilians who carried guns were far more likely to end up shot than those who didn't. Still, information was always useful, so he walked in.

The guy behind the counter was small and grey-haired, probably around sixty and wearing gold-rimmed glasses. If he'd worn a white coat instead of a check shirt and jeans, he could have passed for a dentist or an optician, He looked over his glasses and smiled.

'Morning, sir, how can I help you today?'

'Been thinking about buying a gun, but I don't know what the law is down here.'

The man raised his eyebrows at Nightingale's accent and gave him another smile. 'A little different from where you come from, I'd guess.

Florida's what they call a 'Shall Issue' state for carry permits, and we honor all permits from other states. Would you have one?'

'Actually I do, from Texas. Though I've never used it.'

'Then you're all set, you got the run of the store. No restriction on concealed carry, carry in the car, rifles, anything you want. Just don't take your gun into a bar.'

'Is there a waiting period?'

'No sir, nor background check either. Pay your money, take your weapon. Were you looking for something for hunting, or personal protection?'

'Could end up as both,' said Nightingale.

'Well, that could be difficult, hunting tends to mean a rifle, and they're not that easy to carry round concealed.'

'I know, I really just wanted to check on the formalities today.'

'Well we pretty much got none, Florida's a gun friendly state. Soon as you make up your mind, be sure to come on back. My name's Randy, be glad to help you any time.'

'Thanks,' said Nightingale. 'I appreciate it.'

He walked back out to the parking lot, called the zoo and was put through to Dr Taylor. Her soft voice was as seductive as ever, but he detected an undertone of stress in there. 'Jack, good to hear from you. What can I do for you? But make it quick, we're kind of under pressure here.'

'I guessed,' said Nightingale. 'I just finished talking to Sergeant Stone, he pretty much brought me up to date.'

'Well, then you'll know we have a lot of work to do today. God, I'm hoping this doesn't create some kind of panic. We have a tough enough job raising funds for the panthers as it is, without the idea of them being man-killers getting out. It's just ridiculous. They've never been known to attack a human.'

'I won't keep you,' said Nightingale. 'Just wondered if we could meet up soon, maybe compare notes, and I have a few questions I was hoping you could answer.'

'I'd like to help, but I'm going to be snowed under for a few days.'

'How about if dinner was thrown in?' he asked.

'Dinner's always good,' she said. 'And I'll have more time after work than at work. Tonight good?'

'Sure, you choose. So far I only know Stan's.'

'Stick with what you know, I say. See you there at seven?'

'Sounds like a plan.'

Nightingale hung up and checked the time on his cell, the talk with Stone had taken longer than he'd thought and it was nearly twelve. There was a Subway three doors down from the gun store, so he bought a sandwich and coffee, finished them in the car, then consulted his map and headed for the library.

* * *

The Gladesville library was housed in a large sandstone building, with a frontage resembling a Greek temple, complete with columns and a triangular pediment. Inside it was much more modern, with banks of computers and probably half as many books as twenty years before. Hardly surprising, it was far easier to find information on the internet than by wading through shelves of reference books which were outdated as soon as they were published. Nightingale paid for an hour of computer time, and started his search. After twenty minutes, he gave it up. What he'd been thinking about didn't seem to have occurred to anyone else on the internet, which was hardly a surprise, since it was impossible. Maybe he needed to find a more direct source. He'd found answers before by looking into Native American legends, and knew he wasn't far from the Florida Seminole Reserve. A glance at their website gave him a couple of useful addresses, and he made a note of them. The GPS in the Escape would guide him down there, but he noted some directions anyway. He really hoped that it was just coincidence that the route down there was known as the Devil's Garden.

He glanced at his phone to check the time, did some quick calculations and decided he wouldn't have time to get there and back today before his date at seven, and he didn't want to cancel on Sally Taylor. She didn't seem the sort of woman who needed to give a man more than one chance. Besides, he'd be needing to pick up some new clothes if he wanted to make a good impression. He was hoping she'd relax enough to answer his questions, one or two of which might be pretty far out there.

* * *

Nightingale was sitting at the bar with a bottle of Corona when Sally Taylor showed up right on seven. She'd swapped her white coat for a black jacket worn over a low-cut yellow top, and a black skirt that finished midway up her thighs. With her black heels, she was tall enough to look Nightingale in the eyes, and did so for a moment before nodding a welcome. 'Nice to see you again, Jack. I'll join you in a beer, but make it Bohemia.'

She settled onto the stool next to him, raised her bottle in salute to him, then took a long draught that half-emptied it. Nightingale gave her a quizzical look. She smiled at him.

'I needed that first one,' she said. 'Don't worry, I'll slow down now. This has been one bitch of a day. Lab tests, police questions and then the reporters. I'm sorry, I guess you don't need to hear my problems.'

'Feel free,' said Nightingale. 'I'm a good listener. What are the cops saying?'

'They're saying they want answers from me, and I don't have any. Panthers don't wander through towns, they'll do anything to avoid contact with humans. And as I keep telling them, there's absolutely no record ever of them attacking a human, much less ripping two to pieces. It's just not possible.'

'And the reporters?'

'My God, they're like vultures hovering over the carcasses. Have I lost a panther, where do I think the animal's hiding, what can people do to protect themselves? In the end, I think the cops have asked them to go easy on the whole thing, they don't want people panicking and shooting at every shadow they might see.'

'Makes sense,' said Nightingale. 'Might end up with a lot of dead cats and dogs.'

'And people.'

'Them too. Hungry?'

'As a horse. Never had time for lunch. Lead me to it.'

It was Mary-Ann who did the leading, favoring Nightingale with a wink and a knowing smile as she handed them menus. He decided not to repeat the alligator experiment and went for a medium-rare steak.

'Steak sounds good to me,' said Sally. 'But make mine extra rare, just pass it over a candle on the way to the table.'

Mary-Ann laughed. 'Maybe I'll just find a steer with a sunburn, let it walk in here by itself. Wine?'

'I'll just take another beer.'

'Me too, I'm not much of a wine man,' said Nightingale. As Mary-Ann gathered up the menus and walked away, Nightingale told Sally that he'd seen her at the protest match in Main Street the previous afternoon.

'At the protest march? I didn't see you.'

'I was driving. That your daughter with you?'

'My niece, Orisa. She's kind of passionate about panthers, I'm not sure she understands fracking, but if it's bad for the cats, she's dead set against it.'

'Unusual name.'

'It's Bantu, means 'angel on earth', suits her, she's a lovely kid. Her mother was my sister, I try to spend as much time as I can with her, her father's a great guy, but he appreciates a woman's touch.'

Nightingale had noted the 'was', but was reluctant to ask. She saved him the trouble. 'Her mother was killed, walking on the highway into town. Seemed her car broke down, her cell battery was flat, so she decided to walk. It was getting dark, the guy that hit her swore he never saw her. Anyway, Orisa lost her mother and Jerry lost his wife.'

'I'm sorry,' he said. Inadequate as ever, but what else was there to say?

She smiled weakly. 'Yeah. So, how are you finding Gladesville? The natives friendly?'

'So far,' said Nightingale, deciding to keep the overcoat business to himself. 'Not that I've had a lot of time to socialize. Spent most of my time asking obvious questions and getting nowhere.'

'So are we socializing a little now, or are you just figuring out the best time to start on your questions?'

Nightingale was saved from having to answer by the arrival of their food.

'That was fast,' he said.

'Saves a lot of time if you don't want your meat cooked,' said Mary-Ann, setting a fresh beer down by the side of each plate.

'Looks good,' said Nightingale.

'Dog food would look good right now,' said Sally, getting to work with her knife and fork.

Sally barely said another word until she'd finished, apart from a few observations about the food and the beer, both of which she judged adequate rather than special. She finished, put down the fork, wiped her mouth and looked at him.

'That's better,' she said. 'Let's wait a while before we take any dessert decisions. I have a full bottle still, so that'll keep me busy a while. You want to start in on the questions?'

'OK. You're sure those two men couldn't have been killed by a Florida Panther?'

'I'm not sure of anything any more. My experience of panthers tells me it can't be true, there's no way one could get into a room, or into a residential area. They avoid human contact. But then what other explanation can there be? They were ripped apart, panther hairs and panther DNA in the wound, panther fang and claw marks. Panther prints in the blood in Cresswell's room. But how can it be?'

Nightingale shook his head. 'I've no rational ideas at the moment.'

'Maybe we should try irrational ones,' she said.

He smiled. 'I've sort of made a specialty of that over the last few years.'

'And what does that mean?' she asked.

Nightingale shrugged. 'It's complicated. Let's just say I've seen some odd things. Maybe even odder than this.'

'So what about that irrational explanation?'

'OK. Let's try this. What about a way that panther DNA could have got onto those two men without an actual panther being involved?'

She frowned. 'Well, I guess someone could have ripped them apart, then spread panther blood and hair into the wounds, maybe used a panther claw to make tracks in the wounds...' She shrugged and smiled. 'Even as I say that, I can hear how ridiculous it sounds.'

Nightingale nodded. 'That's quite a lot of panther parts for someone to be carrying around though. And this isn't China, you can't buy them in drug stores.'

'That's not so funny,' she said. 'I'm no big fan of Chinese medicine. But you're right, there's almost no way anyone could get hold of those things. And even if they could...'

'Yeah, why? Why not just shoot them?'

'True enough.'

'Let's try another idea,' he said. 'How about some system where a human did the killing, but managed to leave Panther DNA all by himself.'

Her yellow-green eyes sparkled in amusement and she laughed. 'How does that happen?'

'I was hoping you might tell me. So, for example, what would happen if a human injected themselves with panther DNA?'

For a moment she looked stunned, then laughed again. 'What? Jack, come on, do you even know what DNA is?'

'Yeah, it's the microscopic genetic coding that makes living creatures what they are. It's in every cell of the body.'

'Now hold on to that word 'microscopic'. It's not something you can pile up and put in a bottle, much less just inject into someone.'

'Ok, maybe not DNA then. What about panther blood, what would happen to someone then?'

'In small quantities, nothing at all. In large quantities, I have no idea. I suspect if you replaced all your blood with panther blood you'd die.'

'Just that? You don't think it's possible that you might take on some of the qualities of the animal?'

'Jack, you've been watching way too many films. Of course not. If you have a blood transfusion from a woman, you don't grow breasts. They've given pig hearts to people, they don't go outside, oink and wallow in mud.'

'But they would have a pig's DNA?'

'No, they wouldn't. They'd have human DNA. Maybe if you took samples from the heart that would come up pig, but nowhere else. Not in the blood, skin or anywhere. And trust me, nobody's transplanting panther parts into humans.'

'I guess it was a wild idea,' said Nightingale. 'Just trying to eliminate the completely impossible.'

'Like Sherlock Holmes. Didn't he have a story about some guy injecting himself with monkey serum and climbing up trees? It wasn't possible then, it's not possible now.'

'So where does that leave us?' asked Nightingale.

'It leaves me exactly where I started,' she said. 'The girl from the zoo. It's the police's job to solve killings, not mine. As for you, Mr Detective, I really have no idea what to suggest, except tell your client you have no idea and no leads.'

'It might come to that,' said Nightingale. 'Though there's another wild theory I'd like to explore before I give up.'

'And what might that be?'

'I'll let you know if anything comes of it. I'm headed down to the Seminole Reservation tomorrow.'

'Big Cypress? How come?'

'Well, if I can't find a scientific explanation, I thought I might try myths and legends.'

She raised her bottle to him. 'Well, good luck with that.' She took another sip, then put the bottle back down. 'Moving back into the real world, how'd you like to see some real panthers in their natural environment?'

'Cool, how could I do that?'

'Well, first you need to be invited by the panther lady, that's me. We have a center out in the wilds where we do some observation. I can't guarantee we'll see any, but if you want to drop by the zoo on Wednesday around eleven, I can take you down there.'

'Sounds good, the more I know about them the more chance I'll think of something.'

'Be warned, it's out in the swamps. I'd lose the suit, and those suede shoes of yours won't cut it either.'

'Looks like I'll be going shopping.'

* * *

Food.

The hunter had no need of a fresh kill yet, but the danger was clear. The prey would need to be stalked, there was too much light, too many others here. No need to follow closely, the stench of the creature practically stung the hunter's sensitive nostrils, enabling it to follow far beyond range of its eyes. The soft feet padded along the hard streets, until the hunter knew for sure which way the prey was heading. Then it took a different route, running parallel to the prey to get ahead of it, to lie in wait in the darkness until it passed, so the threat could come from the direction it least expected.

Now, to wait patiently and silently for the right moment to attack. And kill.

* * *

Two beers seemed to be over Sally Taylor's driving limit, so she'd taken a taxi home, reminding Nightingale of the time for the panther visit as she waved him goodbye. Nightingale decided to leave the Escape in the parking lot and take the fifteen-minute walk back to his hotel, since he wasn't about to risk a DUI stop from Mike Stone's colleagues. Gladesville seemed like a town that went to bed early, and there were no other pedestrians about, something that Nightingale had found strange when he'd first arrived in the USA. These days he went with the flow, and almost never walked if he could drive.

He'd been walking about ten minutes when he started to feel the hairs on the back of his neck prickle and stand on end. Three years before, he'd have assumed it was nothing, but these days he paid far more attention to vibrations and feelings, something that had saved his life on more than one occasion. He stopped and looked behind him. The street lights left large parts of the sidewalk in shadow, but he couldn't see or hear anything. A dark SUV drove past, its lights showing nothing either. He shook his head and walked on, quickening his pace this time.

He hadn't gone a hundred yards more when the feeling returned, stronger this time. Again he stopped and looked behind, but saw nothing. He looked around for somewhere he could safely duck into, but he was passing a row of shops, all closed for the night. The hotel was only five minutes away, maybe a little less if he pushed. He walked faster.

He heard a whistle behind him, spun round again, but there was still nothing to see. Then an odd chirping sound came from in front of him, but again he saw nothing. He began to jog, wishing he'd taken Stone's advice about buying a gun. In the distance, he saw the lights of the hotel, but at the same time he heard a dreadful hiss and something leaped at him from behind the corner of a closed shop.

It was huge, dark and moved incredibly fast, knocking him to the ground before he had chance to react. He fell on his back, the dark shape on his chest, pinning him down with its body weight, hissing and chirping into his face, its breath hot and stinking of raw decaying meat. He felt a blow land on his left cheek, and desperately tried to get his hands up to cover his face, frantically screwing his eyes shut to protect them.

The weight was gone from his chest. He opened his eyes and the thing was gone. He heard the sound of running bare feet, or paws, and then nothing. He pulled himself to his feet and looked in every direction, but again saw nothing. He leaned against a shop doorway, lit a cigarette with shaking hands and took a long, lung-filling drag to settle his nerves. He lifted his hand to feel his cheek, which was sore, probably going to show a huge bruise, but there seemed to be no blood. His suit was a dusty mess, with a hole in the right elbow, but otherwise he seemed undamaged.

He took another long pull on his cigarette. He was alive, and that was a good thing. But why hadn't the thing killed him?

* * *

Nightingale was up early, took a taxi back to his car, and then headed to the Seminole reservation at Big Cypress. His cheek now bore a huge bruise, which the girl on reception had commented on, with what seemed like genuine concern. He gave a fairly weak explanation of having fallen while walking back from the restaurant. She seemed to accept that, probably thinking he lived up to the image of the drunk Briton abroad, but he wasn't about to tell her the truth. As he drove north, he continued to wonder why he was still alive. Assuming that the thing which had attacked him had been a panther, why hadn't it done a whole lot more damage? Could it just have been a warning, and if so why? He was pretty sure Hutton hadn't been warned, and there was no suggestion Cresswell had either. Was it because he had no connection to the fracking operation? But how could an animal know that? And if there was a human controlling it, how could the control be so perfect as to override the big cat's killing instinct? He realised he was looking a gift panther in the mouth, and he was happy enough not to have been killed, but it didn't make any sense that he had been attacked and spared.

He was hoping maybe to find some answers on the Seminole Reservation, and he gave up on thinking for a while to concentrate on his driving. The GPS guided him to the Frank Osceola Library, a low modern brick building in the center of a residential area. The only sign that he was on a Seminole reservation was the casino he'd passed a mile or so back, otherwise he could have been in any medium-sized American town. He smoked one more cigarette as he looked at the building and tried to figure out what it was he was going to be able to ask without looking a complete fool. According to a nameplate in front of her, the librarian's name was Linda Macdonald. She was young, dark-haired, friendly and keen to help, though she wrinkled her nose in puzzlement when Nightingale introduced himself and made his request.

'Panthers? Well, I guess we'd have some information, or you could rent a computer and take a look at the internet. Though if you want detailed information, you should really be asking down at the Sanctuary, over at...'

'It's not really factual information I'm looking for,' said Nightingale. 'I'm more interested in Seminole myths and legend about them. The kind of thing that might not be too easy to find in written form.'

The girl gave another puzzled look. 'Oh. Well, we do have books of old stories, you could spend some time browsing those. Or you could talk to James Jones.'

'Who's that?'

'Well, he's pretty much living history around here. Claims to be a direct descendant of Sam Jones.'

Nightingale's face must have betrayed his ignorance, and Linda Macdonald looked a little surprised. 'Sam Jones, or Abiaki to give him his Seminole name, was a medicine man. And pretty much the leader of The Seminole nation when they fought the government and managed to get themselves allocated their home in Florida.'

'So this James Jones is a medicine man too?'

She laughed. 'Hah, not unless the medicine comes in Budweiser bottles, I guess. But he spent a lot of time studying history in his younger days, claims to have a whole heap of stories handed down from his famous ancestor. We get him in here sometimes to tell stories to the kids in school holidays.'

'Where might I find him?'

She turned to glance at the clock behind her. 'Probably in Pizza Hut right now, he goes there for the lunch buffet special most days. If you buy him lunch and a beer, tell him Janice Macdonald's girl sent you, he'll be happy to talk to you.'

'Janice is your mum?'

'Exactly.'

'How will I recognise him?'

'Just ask anyone in there.'

'Great, you wouldn't have his cell number?'

'I wouldn't indeed. He'd never be seen dead with one.'

'Let's hope I'm lucky then,' said Nightingale.

She stopped smiling, and stared at him, as if weighing up what she saw in him. 'In some ways, I think you probably are,' she said. 'In others, not so much. Take care, Mr Nightingale.'

* * *

The Pizza Hut advertised an all-you can-eat lunch buffet for $9.99, and quite a few of the patrons seemed to view that as a challenge. None more so than the mountain of a man that the waitress pointed to when Nightingale asked for James Jones. He had a booth to himself and must have weighed well over three hundred pounds, sitting down behind a piled plate and a pitcher of beer. His grey hair was parted in the middle and cut short, leaving his huge, wrinkled sunburned face exposed. All Nightingale could see of his upper body was covered in a blue Jack Daniels T-shirt which was probably the largest one from the outsize store. Nightingale walked over. 'Mr. Jones? My name's Nightingale, I was wondering if I could talk to you for a few minutes.'

The man looked up from his plate, ran his eyes over Nightingale and waved him to the bench seat opposite.

'Have a seat, if you care to, though management probably appreciate it if you get yourself some lunch. Maybe a drink. I'll take another pitcher of Bud.'

Nightingale nodded and headed for the buffet, where he took a few slices of pizza. He gave Jones's drink order to a waitress, adding a beer for himself, and returned to the table.

Jones looked up again, checked Nightingale's plate and grunted. 'Guess you already ate, huh? Hey, Suze, fill this up again, will ya? You know what I like.'

Suze was a woman in her thirties, who'd just arrived with the drinks and nodded at Jones as she took his plate. 'You know I shouldn't Jimmy,' she said. 'But since it's you.'

'Yeah, saves people needing to walk round me at the buffet. So, what did you say your name is, boy?'

'Jack Nightingale.'

'No shit? You from Australia?'

'England.'

Jones sniffed. 'No shit? My daddy was over there winning the war for you guys back then. Said the girls were real friendly. I probably got some cousins over there I don't even know about. You might even be one.'

'I don't think so, it's an old English name. Anyway I'm doing a little research into Florida panthers,' he said.

'No shit? Don't follow ice hockey myself.'

Nightingale was beginning to wonder whether he could say anything that wouldn't produce 'no shit' as a response. 'No, I meant the animals. The big cats. I'm planning on writing a book. The lady at the library said you might be able to fill me in on some of the traditional stories and legends about them. '

'Janice Macdonald's girl? Yeah, her mom used to be quite something. So, you wanting to buy a little of an old man's time? I come cheap these days, lunch and the two pitchers is on you.'

Nightingale nodded. 'That sounds good to me.'

'Cool, I'll be needing dessert and coffee. Don't care to combine business with pleasure, so you won't mind if we talk outside afterward?'

Nightingale forced a smile as Suze returned with another piled plate. He realised he might be waiting quite a while.

* * *

James Jones was a dedicated eater, but not fast, and it was past two by the time he wiped the final crumbs of key lime pie from his chin, swilled down the last of his second coffee, belched and raised himself from the table. His baggy blue jeans would have held two of Nightingale, and he pulled them up under his vast stomach, picked up his enormous denim jacket and waddled toward the exit, leaving Nightingale to count out bills and leave them on the table.

There were benches and tables in the parking lot, and Jones settled himself at one of them, took a cigar from his jacket pocket and lit it. Nightingale lit a Marlboro in self-defense. Jones blew smoke upwards, gave a satisfied sigh and focused his faded brown eyes on Nightingale. 'I'm bought and paid for, boy. What can I tell you?'

'As I said, I'm interested in Seminole legends about panthers, and was told you knew more about the old stories than anyone round here.'

'Guess that's true, boy,' he said. 'Panthers, eh? Well, you know the story of when God made the world?'

'I'm a novice here,' said Nightingale.

James narrowed his eyes, maybe in concentration, maybe to protect them against the smoke. 'Well, you know the Panther was always Creator's favorite of all the animals, it's said. When the Creator was making the Earth, he called Panther to him and said "When it's complete, I would like for you to be the first to walk on the earth. You are majestic and beautiful. You have patience and strength. You are the perfect one to walk the earth first". And when the Earth was finished, Creator took all the animals and put them in a big shell.'

Nightingale wasn't sure this was what he wanted, but he doubted the old man would appreciate being stopped in mid-flow, so he said nothing and filled his lungs with smoke.

'After a while a tree grew near the shell, and then one of its roots cracked it. Finally Wind rose up, and widened the crack, and then Wind lifted Panther out and set him down on the Earth. So Panther was the first animal ever to walk the Earth, and he was still Creator's favorite. Creator spoke to him and said that Panther would be in possession of all knowledge. Panther would have the power to heal ailments and to enhance mental powers. So, you see why Panther is still a sacred animal, people still respect the Panther clan amongst the Seminoles.'

The old man stopped talking, nodded a little, yawned and closed his eyes, then shook himself awake again and puffed on his cigar.

'That the kind of thing you want, boy? You gonna put that in the book you ain't never gonna write?'

Nightingale couldn't hide his surprise. Even after two pitchers of beer, the old man had seen through him. 'Sorry,' he said. 'I just thought...'

'Never mind. You can't con a con man, son. Now suppose you tell me what really brings you down here.'

Nightingale told him. The fracking, the deaths, the panther evidence, and his wild theory. The old man listened as carefully as Nightingale had, then shook his head. 'So what do you want from me? I tell you it's 'red man's magic' and there are things no paleface can understand? Come on, man, even I moved into the 21st century. I tell stories, but that's all they are.'

'So you've never even heard of it as a legend?'

'It's not one of our legends. Though the Navajo talk about "skin walkers", but they don't turn into big cats, more like coyotes, foxes, eagles. And they have to murder a close relative to gain the power. Just a story. You ask me, sounds more like Eastern Europe. Except they don't have panthers there. Maybe Africa, plenty of big cats out there. Could be an African legend. Anyway, ain't it usually done with wolves?'

'Allegedly, though I suppose it's just as impossible.'

'Maybe. You ever seen anything happen that you plain straight-up knew was impossible?'

Nightingale smiled grimly. 'Yes, I have.'

'Well, for all I know, you might be right this time. Seems like it would fit the facts.'

'And if I am right, what do I do about it? How do I kill a were-panther?'

'Well, chances are there's no handbook for it. If I had to guess, I'd say the same way as a werewolf.'

'And how's that?'

James Jones told him.

* * *

It was mid-afternoon when Nightingale got back to Gladesville and parked the Escape in front of Randy's gun store, stubbed out his latest cigarette and prepared for yet another talk with someone who was going to think he was out of his mind. Maybe he was right too, Nightingale had no evidence at all for his theory, but then what evidence was he meant to find when the thing was impossible?

Randy was behind the counter, and looked up smiling as the doorbell announced Nightingale's arrival.

'Y'all came back then. So, made a decision?'

'Yeah, I need a handgun I think.'

'Well, you got plenty of choice, all makes, all calibers, depending on how much stopping power you need.'

Nightingale took a deep breath. 'I'll be honest, Randy, it's not a case of the gun, it's more about the ammunition.'

'That's no problem either, we got good stock of any caliber shells you need, all types.'

Nightingale forced a smile. 'I need silver bullets.'

The four words stopped Randy's flow completely, and he stood motionless behind the counter, his mouth wide open. He blinked twice before speaking, much more slowly this time. 'You want silver bullets?'

'I do.'

'What are you, the Lone Ranger?'

'Probably not, I just want silver bullets. Is that difficult?'

Randy shrugged. 'It's not difficult, it's impossible. Ain't nobody makes functional bullets out of silver. It's damned expensive, it takes a ridiculous amount of heat to melt it, it shrinks after molding, and it's not accurate at more than a foot.'

'People have tried?'

'Course people have tried, even if just to prove the Lone Ranger couldn't have done it either. Why in God's name you want silver bullets?'

Nightingale decided to stick close to the truth. 'I plan to go werewolf hunting.'

Randy leaned on the counter and laughed. 'Wow. I shoulda guessed, you headed for Transylvania?'

'Not exactly, I think that's vampires anyway.'

'Could be, well. Whatever you're planning to do, you won't be doing it with silver bullets, mister. Not unless you buy your own machine shop.'

Nightingale sighed. 'So I guess there really is no way to kill a werewolf?'

'Meh, you could try another system.'

'Like what?'

'Shotgun shells. Get yourself some scrap silver, fill a few shells with it and blast the hell out of that thing.'

'That would work?'

'How the Hell would I know? Making the shells is easy enough, I guess finding the werewolf to try it on could be the hard part, but that's up to you. My job's just to give you what you want.'

'OK, sounds good. What do we do?'

'Choose yourself a shotgun. Minimum barrel length is eighteen inches in most places, but Florida's got no restriction, so you can get a fourteen incher. Easier to carry, and conceal. Pistol grip too. There's a jeweler three doors down, I can get some scrap silver from him. How many shells you gonna need?'

'Six?'

'I can do that for you, but it ain't gonna be cheap. You wanna choose a gun?'

'A shotgun's kind of bulky, though.'

'Well, there is an alternative. This here's a Taurus Judge.'

Randy put a large revolver on the counter.

'This is the six-inch barrel version. Fires a .45 Long Colt Round, or .410 shotgun shells. Not as much stopping power as a real shotgun, but you'll be getting plenty of silver into that...er...werewolf, when you find him.'

'Sounds cool. I'll take it.'

'Drop back tomorrow morning and I'll have the shells ready. As I said, they're going to cost you.'

'Not a problem.'

Nightingale walked out to his car, wondering at how little curiosity the man had shown. It occurred to him Randy probably thought he was insane, but an insane man's dollars were worth just as much as anyone else's.

* * *

Nightingale had no plans for the evening other than dinner somewhere, since he had no idea where to look for any kind of a clue. He'd thought about looking at the scene of Hutton's death, but put it on the back burner, since the police would have found any useful evidence, and he had no reasonable excuse for getting inside the house. He'd been employed to look into Dan Cresswell's death, but that gave him no rights to look into private houses. Still, perhaps he might get a little more information by another route. He took a wild guess from his less than immaculate appearance that Mike Stone lived alone, so he called him and offered dinner. Stone seemed enthusiastic, so maybe his own cooking held no appeal. He suggested a Mexican restaurant in town, which wouldn't have been Nightingale's first choice, but he went along with it. Best to have the man comfortable.

When Stone arrived at Paco's Cantina, he'd shed the loosened tie and swapped the green jacket for a zip-up Miami Dolphins jacket, though he hadn't tried to zip it over his paunch. He joined Nightingale at his table and ordered a Corona too.

'What do you recommend?' asked Nightingale.

'Makes no difference what you order in here,' said Stone. 'Same stuff, just folded differently.'

Nightingale had heard it before, but forced a smile. 'Burritos it is then.'

They ordered and the waiter walked away. 'So how's the investigation going?' asked Nightingale.

The detective gulped down half his beer. 'We know exactly what happened. Hutton was ripped to death by a Florida Panther, apparently pumia concolor coryi if you want the official Latin name. Exactly the same as Cresswell. Classic attacks, throat and stomach torn out, signs of the animal eating parts of the body. No room for doubt, wound evidence, claw marks, prints, DNA. Open and shut case, not even a homicide matter, you can't charge an animal with murder.'

'Except...'

The detective threw up his hands. 'Except it ain't possible. Cresswell was killed in a locked apartment three floors up, no way a panther could get in or out. Hutton's death was at least possible, in the driveway of his house, but nobody's ever seen a panther anywhere near Gladesville. And what are the chances that a mysterious panther decides to feed on two guys in a town of thirty thousand and they both work for the same company?'

'Pretty remote,' said Nightingale.

'Approaching zero,' agreed Stone, gesturing at the waiter for another beer. 'So there you have it. The case is completely solved, and we only need to find our panther. So, what have you found out?'

'Nothing concrete,' said Nightingale. 'Like you said, the obvious explanation is impossible. Unless...'

'Yeah?'

'Unless something impossible actually happened. Do you have any thoughts on the supernatural?'

Stone paused in the act of raising his beer to his lips, put it down and stared at Nightingale. 'What you talking about? Ghost panthers or something? You been watching too much TV.'

'Maybe so, but I can't think of anything else at the moment.'

'Well, you keep trying, because I'm not going up to Chief Davis and telling him I got a rogue ghost cat killing people.'

'Maybe not a ghost,' said Nightingale. 'Maybe something that looks like a panther, kills like one, but really isn't fully a panther.'

'You lost me,' said Stone.

'Maybe I lost myself,' said Nightingale. 'What I'm thinking makes no sense, but it might be the only thing that fits.'

'Makes no sense, and there's no provision for it under Florida law. What, some guy who can change into a panther? Wasn't that a TV show too? Animalman?'

'If it was, then it was before my time. But you have to admit, it would answer all the questions.'

'I ain't admitting anything. It's like saying every time we get a tough case, we can solve it by blaming the Invisible Man. Sure, it fits the bill, but it ain't possible.'

'No,' said Nightingale. He gestured at the detective's beer. 'It isn't, is it? You want another one of those?'

'Nope, guess I'm done, this case won't make any more sense with a hangover. You want to share a cab?'

'No, I've got my car outside,' said Nightingale. 'Somehow I don't feel like walking round Gladesville at night anymore.'

'Can't argue with that, town's getting dangerous for strangers.'

* * *

Next morning, Nightingale stopped off at Randy's on his way to the panther center. He flashed the Texas concealed carry permit that Wainwright had provided months earlier, paid, then placed his package in the luggage compartment of the Escape. He walked a few doors down to a camping store and invested in a pair of boots that looked a little more suitable to the Everglades than his Hush Puppies, and put his favorite brown suede shoes on the back seat. He figured his black jeans and black zipper jacket would pass muster.

He showed up at the center a few minutes before eleven to find Sally Taylor waiting in the parking lot, together with her niece and a tall blonde-haired young man Nightingale hadn't seen before. They were all dressed in camouflage outfits, Sally and the girl with matching caps. Nightingale parked and got out.

'Morning,' she said. 'Jack Nightingale, this is Kyle Pollard, Kyle's just starting with us, so I thought he could use a trip out into the wilds. And Orisa never misses a chance to come out and look at animals, do you, honey?'

The girl looked up at her aunt and smiled contentedly. 'I wish I could live out there. Nice to meet you, Mr Nightingale.'

Nightingale nodded at his two new acquaintances. Sally Taylor gave him a quick appraisal. 'Yep, you'll do. Won't be cold out there, we'll be home before dark. We have supplies in our van, so hop in.'

Nightingale thought of the package in the back of the car. Better safe than sorry. 'I'd rather drive my own car,' he said. 'I'll follow you.'

'OK, but we'll only be driving around a half hour. Panthers and highways are a bad mix, so we'll be going the rest of the way by airboat. That OK, or would you rather bring your own boat and follow us then too?'

'No, I guess we can share a boat, but I'll bring my car as far as that.'

'Suit yourself,' she said and walked off in the direction of a blue van with Florida Panther Rescue Center painted on the side. Nightingale got back into the Escape and started the engine.

Sally Taylor drove carefully rather than quickly, so it was around forty minutes later that the blue van pulled off the highway at a sign for Everglade Airboats onto a narrow blacktop, which ran for a few hundred yards before opening out in front of a single story corrugated iron building about the size of an aircraft hangar. She tooted her horn and an old, grey-bearded man dressed in camouflage appeared. Everyone got out and walked toward him.

'Josh, this here's Jack and Kyle,' said Sally, by way of introduction. 'They're doing the tourist thing today.'

'Sure, Miss Sally, she's all ready for you. You want me to come along or you in the mood to drive?'

'I'll take her. You put your feet up for the day.'

They followed her down past the side of the building. The grass sloped down and started to get a little softer underfoot. An airboat was parked about ten feet from the water. It was little more than a metal sled, painted in camouflage colors and with two elevated padded seats and another half dozen lower down. Behind the seats sat an enormous gleaming engine, connected to what looked like an aircraft propeller, housed inside a giant wire cage, presumably to stop body parts or other debris flying into the prop.

'Okay, Jack,' said Sally. 'Since it's your first time, why not climb up here next to me, maybe I'll let you take a turn at driving. Orisa and Kyle, you get your turn on the way back if you're good.'

It wasn't actually Nightingale's first experience of an airboat, since he'd driven one in Louisiana, but that wasn't a story he was inclined to share with Sally at the moment, so he said nothing and climbed into the seat. Kyle arrived carrying a picnic box and a long thin brown gun case. Nightingale nodded at the case. 'Expecting trouble? I though panthers were frightened of humans.'

'Oh they are,' said Sally. 'But alligators and snakes not so much. Better safe than sorry, I guess, We always bring it, never had to use it in four years, Hope we never will.' She started up the motor, the big prop spun into action, and the boat slowly glided over the grass and down onto the water.

It took forty minutes to cruise down the waterway to the hide. The landscape was unchanging, grass, trees dipping their branches into the water and reeds clogging the water, though the airboat skimmed over them easily enough. After ten minutes, Sally let Nightingale take over the basic controls. There were only two, the gas pedal and a lever that controlled the rudders. Push forward for left, pull back for right. There were no brakes, the driver just came off the gas and waited for the craft to coast to a halt. Nightingale's previous experience gave him confidence, but he still kept it slow and steady until Sally took over again.

'Not bad for an Englishman,' she said. 'I'll take it from here, we can push on a little faster.'

Another twenty minutes and she slowed the motor to a quiet purr, then cut it altogether to allow the boat to drift in to the left hand bank. Nightingale looked around, but could see nothing but more trees, undergrowth and shrubbery.

'We're here?' asked Nightingale.

'Sure,' she said. 'You were expecting a neon sign? OK, follow me and keep it quiet. Oh, and watch where you step, we don't want to disturb any snakes today.'

She tied the boat to the trunk of a nearby tree and led the way around fifty yards inland, to where a heavily camouflaged wooden shack had been erected, overlooking a clearing which stretched out for fifty yards behind it before the trees took over again. Sally opened the door and ushered them inside. There was almost no furniture, just a long table, a camp bed and a few chairs. The walls were pretty much all windows, but with camouflage netting covering them and cutting out most of the light. 'Welcome to our observation hut,' said Sally. 'I can't offer you any entertainment, but it's just possible you may see a panther if we're lucky. We released a pair here a year or so ago, and they've made a territory for themselves, we think. Though, I've spent many a day out here and seen nothing.'

'We'll be lucky today,' said Orisa, sniffing the air. 'I can feel they're close.'

The girl had taken off her camouflage cap, and Nightingale took a careful look at her for the first time. She shared her aunt's coloring, the high cheek-bones and flawless copper skin held the promise of real beauty in years to come. Her dark hair was cut quite short, but framed her smiling face perfectly. 'You can smell them then?' Nightingale asked.

Her smile turned into a laugh. 'Not really, I just sort of get a feeling we'll be lucky.'

'Help yourself to the picnic,' said Sally. 'Keep the noise to a minimum. I'll be using the main camera, so if anyone sees anything, just point me at it.' She took the camera out of her backpack, checked the battery was fully charged, then closed the shutter again. She took a chair and sat at the window overlooking the clearing.

'Jack and Orisa, why don't you take a front window each, case one of them comes down to the water looking for baby gator,' said Sally. 'Kyle, you join me. Sorry, Jack, no smoking down here, they'd smell it from miles away.'

Nightingale gave a rueful grin. 'No problem,' he said. 'I've been thinking of cutting down.'

'Sure,' said Sally. 'For a few hours anyway.'

It occurred to Nightingale that Kyle Pollard hadn't actually said a word all day, and he gave no sign of breaking his silence now, sitting crouched forward peering out of the window, a small Sony video camera strapped round his hand. He was breathing slowly and regularly, his concentration total.

Nightingale followed his example, and gazed intently out of his window, across the short distance to the water. He could see one or two wading birds, which he couldn't identify, but not much else. He sat silently and waited.

He had no real idea how much time had passed before it happened.

The first inkling he had was a sniff from Sally behind him, and he saw out of the corner of his left eye her body tense and stiffen. Next to him, Orisa also sniffed the air and froze, her gaze fixed at a spot down by the water. A young whitetail deer was slowly and cautiously making its way down to drink, gazing in all directions with the wariness any animal shows at vulnerable times. Danger could come from any direction, from the water or the land. It sniffed the air, getting ever closer to the waterside, then finally bent its head to drink.

Nightingale sensed Sally standing behind him, and heard her press the button on the video camera, but kept his gaze fixed on the white tail, until he noticed that Orisa was looking in a slightly different direction, behind and to the left. He followed her eyes, and could just discern a slight movement in the long grass, a movement that ran contrary to the wind. The deer seemed to see nothing, and its keen sense of smell detected nothing downwind.

Nightingale heard Sally's breathing slow and become shallower, and her niece seemed to fall into the exact rhythm of the woman. Kyle had also risen, but seemed to be watching the scene far more dispassionately. As Nightingale watched, the movement in the long grass ceased, and the deer lifted its head and sniffed the air.

It was over in seconds. The panther timed its spring to perfection and the victim barely had chance to run three steps before the big cat landed on its back, dragging it to the ground, killing it with one brutal snap of its jaws to the deer's throat, and dragging its kill back into the safety of the trees.

Nightingale looked to his left, where Orisa's throat was flushed, her fingers outstretched and moving in rhythm to the soft humming sound she was making.

Sally spoke out loud. 'Orisa, essaquivo de lasto, de lasto tengra. Essequivo, tengra, tengra de lasto.'

Nightingale had no idea what language Sally Taylor had spoken in, much less what the words meant, but they seemed to break the girl's spell. The flush round her throat died down, her hands were still. She looked at her aunt and smiled. 'Wow, that's as close as we've ever seen one,' she said. 'And a kill too. She was just so fast, wasn't she?'

Nightingale was quite prepared to believe it had been a female panther, though he'd seen nothing to indicate the animal's sex.

'I got it all on film,' said Kyle, and Nightingale gave a start at hearing the unexpected voice. 'Well, on memory card, anyway.'

'Well done, Kyle,' said Sally. 'Me too. Anyway, that noise will have scared off all the locals, and the cat won't be hunting again for a day or two, so looks like our work here is done for today. Jack, thank you.'

'Me? Why?'

'As Orisa said, that's the closest we've ever seen a wild panther. Looks like you brought us luck.'

* * *

The ride back to the boatyard was uneventful, and Nightingale sat in one of the bow seats, smoking and looking at the banks. He saw a turtle or two, and a flurry of movement that might have been an alligator, but other than that there was just uninterrupted trees and vegetation. Kyle and Orisa each took a turn at handling the boat. The young girl had obviously done it before, but Kyle seemed a novice, heavy on the gas pedal and frequently forgetting which way to move the stick when he wanted to turn. It was easier on everyone's nerves when Sally Taylor took over again. She guided the craft into the bank, and there was scarcely a bump as she ran it onto the shore and back up the slope. Josh came out to take the keys and check they'd had no problems, after which the four of them walked back to their transport. They stopped next to the blue van.

'Well, now you've seen our little hidey hole out in the everglades, and even a panther in the wild.' Sally said to Nightingale. 'You see why we're so passionate about protecting that environment? The fracking threatens the stability of the whole eco-system, not just the cats. If they pollute the water table, it'll be a disaster.'

Nightingale shrugged. 'I'm just down here to find out who or what killed Cresswell, I'm no ecologist. The way I see it now, especially with Hutton going the same way, it's got to be something to do with a girl. Both of them had the reputation of womanisers, maybe there's a jealous husband around. Whatever, I'm pretty sure the police are bound to get to the bottom of it.'

'But you think the fracking will stop now?' asked Orisa. 'They'll go away and leave the cats in peace?'

'I doubt it,' said Nightingale. 'Money talks, and to be honest I see no reason why they should stop. First thing tomorrow, I plan to call Vivienne Cresswell and suggest she gets the crew back to work. She's my client, my loyalty is to her, not some bunch of cats and she's losing money all the time the men are idle.'

The little girl's face was red with fury, and she spat out her words. 'You can't do that. You just can't. Don't you care at all?'

'Sorry, love,' said Nightingale. 'It's not my job to care. Money talks.'

He turned, walked to the Escape and drove away while the other three stood and stared after him.

Nightingale drove his Escape back towards town, then let the GPS guide him to the house that Chad Hutton had rented, and outside which he'd died. He could have asked Stone for a key, but would have struggled to give the detective a sensible reason for the request. He didn't have his crystal or any of his other equipment with him, but he didn't expect to need it.

He pulled slowly onto the graveled drive, hidden from the road by the front hedge, then used the light from his cellphone screen to make his way round the side and to the back door. The lock looked pretty flimsy, but he saved himself time by wrapping a stone in his jacket and smashing a window pane to access the interior lock and let himself in. He searched the kitchen quickly, but there was almost nothing to find, Hutton had been no cook, the fridge held a few beers and a couple of Chinese take-out containers, and the cupboards nothing but a jar of coffee, a bag of sugar and a half-full box of cookies.

The living room held nothing that looked at all personal, probably it had all come as part of the rental. There were two technical magazines which Nightingale paid no attention to, as he moved on to the bedrooms. The smaller one showed no traces of occupation, and Hutton had evidently stuck to the master bedroom. The bed had been stripped, no doubt the cops looking for some stray DNA on the sheets, and the adjoining bathroom held no personal items any more.

Nightingale opened the top drawer of the nightstand and raised an eyebrow. There were enough boxes of condoms there to suggest that Hutton had been just as much of a ladies' man as his late boss.

Nightingale opened the front door from inside and walked back out. He knew there'd be nothing to find on the drive, Stone and his men weren't amateurs. Stone had assumed that the fact Hutton had been killed outside meant his killer had never been inside, but maybe he'd been wrong. Nightingale got back into the Escape and headed off to the hotel.

It all made sense now.

Except that it was still impossible.

* * *

Nightingale sat on his hotel bed and smoked a cigarette, trying to compose himself for what he was expecting to happen that evening. He had all the information he needed, but no idea what use it was going to be to him, and no idea whether he could do what needed to be done. The pizza he'd picked up on the way back was still three-quarters intact. He'd tried a few channels of the TV, but it was more an irritant than a distraction, so he'd given up. He got up and walked to the window, and looked out onto the dark street. Night fell early this close to the Tropics, and the town seemed quiet. He lay back down on the bed, and tried to empty his mind.

When the knock came, it was soft and hesitant and he almost missed it. He'd left the door unlatched, so he didn't bother moving. 'Come in, it's open.'

She came in quietly, dressed now in a Girl Scout uniform holding a cardboard box. Nightingale waved her to a chair.

'Orisa. What can I do for you?'

'Maybe open a window, for a start,' said the girl. 'It smells like an ashtray in here.'

Nightingale didn't move. 'My room, my rules,' he said. 'What brings you here?'

'I could sell you some cookies. But I wanted to make a last try to change your mind,' said Orisa. 'I know that woman, Mrs Cresswell, will listen to you. Please can't you tell her to take the men away, leave the panthers in peace?'

'Sorry,' said Nightingale. 'That's not how it's going to be.'

'I don't understand,' said the girl. 'Why are you doing this? When I met you, I thought you were a nice man. I don't believe you want to hurt the panthers.'

Nightingale shook his head. 'They're what's called collateral damage,' he said. 'It's the price of progress. Maybe you'll understand better when you grow up.'

She snorted. 'Hey, I'm grown up enough, and I don't understand you at all. What are you getting out of this?'

'Money,' said Nightingale. 'Maybe I should buy some shares in

Cresswell Explorations, they're likely to make a fortune down here.'

The girl seemed furious, rather than upset, but made an effort to control herself. 'So that's the way it is,' she said. 'I'll go now, but I'll just go to the bathroom, if that's alright with you, Mr Nightingale.'

Nightingale looked at her sadly. 'Be my guest,' he said.

Nightingale put his cigarette out in the ashtray on the nightstand and watched carefully as the girl went into the bathroom, leaving the door slightly ajar behind her. He sighed, looked at the ceiling, then fixed his attention on the door again.

Something pulled it open, and the creature walked out. It was long and lean, smaller than the one he'd seen at the hide, and it stood framed in the doorway, its yellow eyes glinting at him. Was it hatred he saw, or just hunger? The animal clicked and hissed at him, and he saw its shoulders tense. He pulled his hand from under the pillow and pointed the gun unwaveringly at the panther's head.

'I had to be sure,' he said. 'And now I am. Stop right there, Orisa.'

From the direction of the apartment door, Nightingale heard a gasp, but never took his eyes from the panther.

'Sally?'

'My God,' said the woman. 'I dropped her home, but she must have come straight out again, her father called...'

'Stop her, Sally. I don't want to have to shoot.'

'It will do no good if you do,' said the woman. 'Her gift is beyond the power of bullets.'

'This gun is loaded with a shotgun shell, full of silver. I'm told that makes a difference.'

His eyes were still fixed on the panther, which stood motionless, staring at him, but at the edge of his vision, he saw the woman nod.

'The legend says that silver is the only way, though I have never known anyone try.'

'I'm assuming you wouldn't want to take the risk?'

'You can't shoot her.'

'I'm betting I can. Two men are dead, I don't plan to be number three.'

'If you do, she will revert, the sound of the shot will attract immediate attention, and you will have to explain why you went to such lengths to murder a naked twelve-year old girl.'

'That's a fair point,' admitted Nightingale. 'But at least I'll be alive.'

'Until they can organize an electric chair.'

Still the panther glared hatred at him, but hadn't moved a muscle.

'Can she understand us,' asked Nightingale.

'I think so,' she said. 'She hasn't attacked, yet.'

'Can you stop her?'

'I could try, if I wished.'

'It would make things a lot easier. I've got what I wanted.'

'And what was that?'

'I know how Dan Cresswell was killed. That's what I came for.'

'You were never going to suggest resuming fracking at all, were you?'

'No. Just occurred to me that you might think getting rid of me would be a good idea. For a while I thought you were the killer. I needed to be sure. Now, talk to her.'

'And if I do, what happens then?'

'Not much, I suppose. I don't need to be arrested for murder, I can hardly take her down to police headquarters and tell them she killed two men because she can change into a panther. It's a stand off, but if she moves any closer, I'll shoot and deal with the consequences.'

'Can I approach her?'

'From the side, don't move in front of the gun, or I might have two bodies to explain.'

Sally knelt down, and crawled slowly across the floor until she was beside the panther, The panther kept looking at Nightingale, and gave a series of clicks. The woman placed a hand on its flank and spoke softly.

'Orisa, essaquivo de lasto, de lasto tengra. Essequivo, tengra, tengra de lasto.'

They were the same words she'd spoken in the cabin, but this time she repeated them over and over, until finally the big cat dropped its gaze from Nightingale, looked at the woman, and slowly backed into the bathroom again. Sally crawled in after her, and pushed the door shut.

It was a full two minutes before the woman spoke.

'We're coming out now. There is no danger.'

'I'm still holding the gun,' said Nightingale.

The door opened and Sally and Orisa walked out. The girl had lost her fury, and her eyes were red from crying. Sally handed her a key.

'Go and sit in the car now, little one. I won't be long, I'm sure Jack has some questions. It'll be all right now. I'm pretty sure he's a friend.'

Orisa nodded, sniffed, and went outside. 'So tell me,' said Nightingale.

'It is an ancient gift my ancestors brought from Africa. It descends through the female line, though not all of us carry it. Her mother did, and the accident which killed her happened when she was cat. The urge is strongest at our time, each month, though as we mature we learn to resist it. I recognized the signs in Orisa, but her first change came when I was unprepared. The anger burned in her, and she vented it.'

'I guessed from the cookies at Hutton's house. Stone mentioned someone had seen a girl scout at Cresswell's apartment block,'

'She used them to gain entry there too. Cresswell was a kind man, and let her in. I regret the deaths, she was not in control, not responsible in the way a human, even a child, would be.'

'Really? Not sure I believe that. I'm also not sure you didn't lend a hand. Cresswell and Hutton both seemed fond of women, and you'd have been hard to resist.'

She smiled. 'An interesting theory, though I doubt the Police would be convinced, since neither of them was killed by a woman. Perhaps I was seeking to influence them by...other means.'

'I can't prove anything, can I? The police would think I was insane. Not so sure they'd be wrong. So what happens now?'

Again the smile. 'That depends on you,' she said. 'What are your plans?'

'I don't have any, except to leave. I can't go to the police with this. I called Vivienne Cresswell and she wants no part of the fracking operation here now. She'll probably send her crew to Alaska or somewhere. I sent her fee back, told her I had no more ideas than the police. Is Orisa still a danger?'

'Not without a target for her hatred. I shall teach her to control her changes, take her into the everglades when it is her time, so she may be a cat and run free.'

Nightingale nodded. 'So that pretty much settles it. Apart from the four hundred dollars you owe me.'

She looked at him in surprise. 'I need a new suit and raincoat. That was your little attempt to discourage me?'

She nodded. 'One of them. You're not an easy man to discourage, Jack. The maid is a friend, and looked the other way for a small present. I'll send you a check.'

'Don't forget.'

She rose to go. 'Goodbye, Jack Nightingale, you are an unusual man. I wish you well.'

'Yeah, you too,' said Nightingale, though he wasn't really sure he meant it.

She'd reached the door when his voice stopped her.

'Sally.'

'Yes?'

He looked at her and rubbed his bruised cheek. 'Thanks for keeping your claws sheathed the other night.'

She smiled. 'You're welcome. It would have been a shame to spoil your boyish good looks.'

THE ASYLUM

The three teenagers sat huddled around a campfire in a vacant lot of Philadelphia, Pennsylvania. John had smuggled a bottle of vodka from his dad and he, Sally and Ronnie were drinking heartily from it, passing it around and telling stories. They were sixteen years old and it was the weekend, not that it mattered; they lived in a poor neighborhood in Philly's dilapidated outskirts and weekends weren't much different from the rest of the week. Each block boasted dozens of leaning houses where gangs organised their drug deals and the homeless squatted. Crime was rife. Rape and murder were routine. But having grown up there, the kids barely noticed the noise. The sirens, broken bottles and gunshots were part of the scenery. And if their parents cared they were out past midnight, they didn't show it.

'I hear Chelsea's pregnant,' said John proudly, smirking as he took a swig from the bottle. He was a tall muscled teenager wearing his big brother's old football jacket, his blonde hair short and spiked. It gleamed in the firelight.

'No way!' said Sally, a brown-haired girl with full lips, wearing skinny jeans and a halter top that sagged low, giving full view of her breasts.

'Swear to God,' said John, glancing slyly at her cleavage. 'It's true.'

'Who's the father?' asked Ronnie. He was the bespectacled outcast of the group, a gangly kid, and the only one with any aspirations to leave Philadelphia and attend university. Sometimes, John couldn't stand to look at him. He thought Ronnie was a real weakling with his stupid glasses and scrunched-up face.

'What's it to you?' said John. 'Jealous?'

'Oh, leave him alone,' said Sally.

Ronnie said nothing. He glanced down the street at two hoods walking under the streetlamps as if in search of something. They were inspecting the parked cars. They stopped near an old sedan, looked about, shoved a slim jim through the rubber window seam and unlocked the door.

'Anyway,' said John, rolling his broad shoulders, 'like I was saying, Chelsea's knocked up. I'll give you two guesses who the dad is, Sally.' John snatched the vodka from her hands.

'Hey!' she said. 'I wasn't finished with that.'

John smirked. 'You win, I'll give you the vodka back. You lose, you give me a blow job.'

'In your dreams,' she said.

'Fine,' said John, pleased with himself. 'Then I guess I'll be drinking this booze all by myself.' He opened the bottle and took a nice long drink, sighing and wiping his lips. They were quiet while Sally weighed her options.

Ronnie glared at John. He liked Sally. When Ronnie spoke, Sally listened, unlike John, or anyone else, for that matter. And she was sweet. One time when Ronnie's dad was on a serious bender and didn't come home for two weeks, leaving him without any food, Sally brought him meals every day even though she lived on the other side of town and faced constant harassment from the gangs on her trips to Ronnie's house. Ronnie's dad was the only family he had left; he had no idea what he would've done if Sally hadn't been there to help him. He wanted to stand up for Sally but he knew he was no match for the bigger and stronger John.

The two hoods got in the car and started the engine.

Sally crossed her arms and narrowed her eyes at John. 'Fine,' she said. 'You're on.' John hooted and clapped his hands. Ronnie looked away – he felt himself blushing with jealousy and didn't want them to see it.

'Okay…,' began Sally, 'I guess, Terrence!'

John shook his head. 'Nope! One guess left.'

Sally furrowed her eyebrows, bit her bottom lip and thought a moment. 'Hmm… is it—' 'It's Roger,' Ronnie mumbled.

'What'd you say?' asked Sally.

'It's Roger,' said Ronnie. 'He's the father.'

'Ronnie, you idiot!' said John. 'Come on, dude. What the hell?'

Sally was watching Ronnie. 'How did you know that?'

'That doesn't count!' said John. 'Not fair! I still get a BJ.'

Sally gestured for him to be quiet, still looking at Ronnie. 'Tell me,' she said. 'How'd you know?'

Ronnie shrugged as if he had just finished solving an easy math problem. 'It's not that hard, really. You ever see the way he looks at her?'

Sally shook her head. John was fuming, glancing around for something to break. He got up, found a milk bottle, and threw it over the wall where it smashed on the street. He chuckled to himself and went in search of another bottle.

'When we're in math class on Monday,' said Ronnie, 'check out the way Roger looks at her when she goes to the blackboard. Look at his eyes. You'll see what I mean – he's in love with her. I knew that already, so when John said Chelsea was pregnant I just kind of put two and two together.'

'You're an asshole,' shouted John. 'You know that? And I'm still getting my BJ.'

'No you're not,' said Sally. 'All you're getting is a swift kick in the butt if you keep being a jerk. Sit down, shut up, and hand me that vodka, will you?'

John sullenly did as he was told. Sally drank the vodka and passed it to Ronnie, who took a small sip. In the street the hoods put the car in gear and drove down the road. A man with a gun ran out of the house in his underwear, took aim at the car and fired several times. He missed. The car rounded a bend and drove off. The man screamed and cursed in the middle of the street, kicking trash.

'Not his lucky night,' Sally murmured, and the guys laughed.

'Hey,' said John, 'What say we get out of here? I know a place.'

'What kind of place?' asked Sally.

John leaned forward and whispered dramatically. 'A haunted place.'

'Wentworth Asylum?' offered Ronnie.

'Yep.'

Ronnie shook his head. 'Count me out, then.'

'Don't be such a pussy, Ronnie boy.'

'Wait, what's Wentworth Asylum?' asked Sally. 'What are you guys talking about?'

'You know,' said John, 'the haunted lunatic asylum over on Monroe Street?' Sally frowned. John said, 'I forgot you're kind of new around here. We haven't popped your cherry yet.'

'Hey!'

'Jeeze, relax, Sal, I meant your haunted house cherry.'

'So what's so special about this asylum?' asked Sally.

'Only that it's one of the most haunted places in the country, if you count that special.'

'No way,' she said, her eyes widening.

'Yeah way. It was on the History Channel a bunch of times. You know The Truth Is Out There show with Keith Harrington?'

'What!' said Sally. 'I love Keith Harrington! He went there? I didn't see that one.'

'Yeah,' said John, 'it's one of his older episodes from a few years ago. One of his team members fell eight stories off a balcony to his death. It was all over the news. Keith says it was an accident. But he's never gone back.'

'That's crazy,' said Sally.

Ronnie bristled uneasily. 'Can we talk about something else?'

'But I want to hear it!' said Sally.

John went on, 'As the story goes, Wentworth Asylum was built in the early 1800s and they say it's the most haunted asylum in the world. During the 1930s or '40s there were a bunch of cutbacks, so it filled up past capacity, but there wasn't enough staff to treat all the patients. Pretty soon there were several thousand crazies living in a place that could only house about three hundred of them. It got so bad they didn't have any clothes on them, they were totally naked, and they were sleeping in big groups in hallways full of their own shit. Thousands of them died every year. What's worse, around that time the state was sending all kinds of people to the loony bins for any reason at all. Even kids. Lots and lots of kids.'

Sally was rapt with attention. 'How do you know all this stuff?'

John shrugged. 'It's a local legend, everybody knows it. Right Ronnie boy?' Ronnie nodded. 'It gets worse,' said John. 'In the '50s there were all these new scientific advancements and shit. Because funding was so bad, a couple of big pharmaceutical companies proposed a big deal to the guys at Wentworth Asylum: they'd donate tens of thousands of dollars, which was a shitload of money back then, if they'd allow them to conduct experiments on the patients.'

'No!' gasped Sally.

John was nodding. 'Yep. And guess what? Wentworth was all too happy to oblige. So for the next thirty years these doctors tortured patients at Wentworth with all kinds of different drugs and treatments. The death rate went from two thousand a year to about five thousand a year. So on top of all the torture, rape, starvation, and the trouble of psychotic patients being mixed in with the innocent ones and killing them or doing way worse, the patients were being tortured by their own staff and couldn't do anything about it.'

'That's horrible,' said Sally, putting her hand over her mouth.

'Wait a sec, it gets better. In the late '80s they shut the place down. This is back when Wentworth proper wasn't a total shithole like it is now. But pretty soon the economy was going down the drain and everybody was skipping town. The asylum got overtaken by hobos, satanic cults, and at least one or two serial killers. The cops patrolled the grounds every night, finding all kinds of things from disemboweled cats and dogs to actual dead people. There was even a rumor that one of the patients, a really violent psychotic murderer by the name of Susan Grimes, stayed behind, living in the dark underground tunnel network connecting all the buildings, eating rats, and murdering people with an axe!' John shouted the last word and made a swooping motion with his hand, causing Sally to yelp and fall backwards. He burst out laughing.

'You're such an asshole!' said Sally when she had regained her composure.

'Sorry,' said John, grinning, 'I couldn't help myself.'

'I even believed you!' said Sally. She hit him on the arm.

'I wasn't lying,' said John. 'There are tons of stories about Susan Grimes. People go missing there all the time, never to be seen again. Others are found brutally murdered with their arms and legs chopped off. I'm not even kidding. Look it up.'

'It's true,' said Ronnie quietly. 'It has happened before.'

'See? Even Ronnie agrees with me.' John crossed his arms proudly, as if waiting to be patted on the head.

'Well, you definitely talked me out of going,' said Sally.

'Good choice,' said Ronnie.

'Oh, come on! Have a bit of fun. Probably only a tiny percentage of those stories are even true anyway!'

'I'm not going,' said Sally. 'And that's final.'

'It's a bad idea,' said Ronnie.

'All right, fine,' said John, standing up. 'I'll go by myself then.'

'Don't be like that,' said Sally. 'Just hang with us. You don't know what's out there.'

John took a long drink from the vodka and wiped his lips with his coat sleeve. 'If you pansies won't join me then you leave me no choice. I'll go alone. Besides, you're missing out. You don't even know the real reason I'm going.'

'What are you talking about?' asked Sally.

'My brother sells his weed at the asylum. He's stashed it in one of the buildings. He showed me once. Every now and then I go over and take a few buds. He never notices.'

'You're lying,' said Sally. John knew she had a weakness for smoking pot.

'I swear to God, cross my heart and hope to die,' said John. Then he shrugged. 'Whatever. I'll go have a smoke and you pansies can just play hopscotch, or whatever it is pansies do for fun.' He took the bottle and scaled the wall, landing heavily and walking across the brown grass under the glow of the street lamps.

'Hey wait up!' Sally called, climbing the wall. Sitting at the top, she turned to Ronnie. 'Ronnie, come on, let's go.'

Ronnie didn't move. 'Seriously?'

'Come on!' She hopped off the wall and followed John. Ronnie warily got up and climbed over the wall and joined them.

* * *

Sally recognized the asylum immediately when she saw it, she had passed it every day on her way to school since moving to the town of Wentworth, but she had never known what it was. She had always thought it was just another abandoned building, Lord knows there were plenty of those in Wentworth, but now she saw there were lots of buildings on the grounds, and they were all connected.

They passed the vodka bottle around on the way, getting drunk. Ronnie kept saying it was a bad idea and they should go back to town, that he knew a dealer and he'd put up the money for an eighth if that's what they wanted, but now Sally was infected with the adrenaline of a good scare and wouldn't turn back. Reluctantly, Ronnie followed.

The asylum was massive. John said it was one of the biggest in the United States. Three tall Gothic buildings dominated the front of the grounds. They stood at least a hundred feet high with windows smashed out or boarded up. Surrounding the complex were about a dozen large outbuildings that looked like Victorian military barracks. Some of the rooms had balconies. John and Sally made a game at guessing which balcony Keith Harrington's friend jumped – or fell – from, until John said she had used up all her guesses and owed him a blowjob, pointing out the correct balcony. Ronnie thought it was all a ruse; John was just trying to impress her.

At the entrance the wrought-iron gate looked as if a fleet of dump trucks had waged war with it over the years, bent inward and falling apart. Through it they glimpsed the asylum grounds, a sprawling stretch of dead grass and overgrown weeds flecked with dirt piles from animal burrows. The wind picked up a little and gave them a chill as they crossed the pebbled driveway. Their voices echoed over the emptiness. 'See that one?' John pointed at a rectangular building left of the main buildings. 'That's where we're going. That's where Bobby hides his stash.'

'Your brother must be crazy for selling weed here,' said Sally.

'What if he's here?' asked Ronnie, unable to hide the fear in his voice.

'He's not here, idiot. He's in the city. Besides, we'd know if people were here. It's so quiet you could hear a mouse fart.' Sally chuckled. Ronnie blushed – John had called him an idiot and Sally hadn't even defended him.

Getting closer, Ronnie noticed the buildings were covered in graffiti. As they reached the rectangular outbuilding he noticed it was a cafeteria. Its doors were locked but below the doorknob was a hole in the wood, as if someone had chopped their way through. John glanced at Sally and motioned her towards it. 'Ladies first.'

Sally frowned at him. 'Yeah, right.'

'How about Ronnie boy? Wanna prove you're not such a pansy after all?' Ronnie was already prepared for this; he took a deep breath, brushed past John and ducked into the hole. 'Now that's what I'm talking about!' said John.

Ronnie glanced around at the huge room full of upturned tables and chairs. The air reeked of mold, stale feces and urine. On the cafeteria's far wall in red spray paint were the words SATAN LIVES. Ronnie felt goosebumps crawl up his spine. Something clutched his arm and he jumped, stumbling over a bench. It was John, laughing. 'Take it easy, Ronnie boy. The fun's not even started yet.'

They followed John to the rear of the cafeteria, then down a long corridor that was completely dark and freezing cold. 'I wish we had a flashlight,' said Ronnie.

Sally fished out her cell phone and flicked on a flashlight, illuminating a series of upturned gurneys, yellowed walls with peeling paint and streaks of brown. Part of the walls had caved in, showing a fibrous white material. There were no windows.

'Think that's asbestos?' asked Ronnie.

'I don't know,' John shrugged. 'Who cares?'

'We shouldn't breathe that in,' said Ronnie. 'It's dangerous.'

'You and your negativity, man,' said John, leading them farther down the hallway. They couldn't see up ahead. 'Why can't you just have a good time like the rest of us humans? Is that so hard?'

Ronnie said nothing.

'Do you think anyone else is in here somewhere?' asked Sally.

John smirked. 'You mean like Susan Grimes?' Sally eyed him coolly and he changed his tone. 'No,' he said. 'Besides, why would there be?'

'We're here,' said Ronnie. 'Your brother hides his weed here. What's to stop somebody else from being here?'

'Relax, you two. We'll smoke a joint and be outta here in no time. Personally, I think it's kind of cool. These digs are like hundreds of years old.'

They entered a wide chamber with tall windows reaching high up to a vaulted ceiling. Iron bars were on the windows, and pale moonlight fell through them and pooled on the floorboards. It looked like a mausoleum. 'Which room is this?' asked Sally, shining the light around at the graffiti scrawled on the walls.

'This is the Murder Room,' said John.

'The what!'

'Take it easy, it's just a nickname from the old urban legends. When the cops used to come here they would always find bodies in this room, so they called it the Murder Room.'

'And you brought us here why?'

'Come on,' he said. 'I know a way out. The weed's right next to the exit.' They turned left down a flight of stairs ending in pitch darkness. Curse words covered the walls. The air was colder, and they smelled something rotten like old meat. Sally pinched her nose. 'Eew... what's that smell?'

'Dead animal, probably,' said John, shrugging. At the landing they turned right and went through another windowless hallway. Suddenly everyone stopped. There was a sound coming from the other end. Something squeaking. It sounded like the creaking wheel on a gurney.

'What is that?' whispered Sally. Ronnie had frozen still and was holding his breath. Sally tugged John's arm. 'Come on. Let's go back.'

'The weed is right around that corner,' John whispered.

The squeaking came again. Squeak-squeak… Squeak-squeak.

Ronnie broke out in a cold sweat. His spine tingled. He wanted to go back outside where there was cool night air and open spaces, because suddenly he felt like the walls were closing in, squeezing and suffocating them. He felt faint.

Squeak-squeak… Squeak-squeak.

'We're leaving,' said Sally in a hushed tone, but John took the phone from her hands and began walking towards the sound. It was the only light they had. Sally called to him but he kept going. They had no choice but to follow.

Squeak-squeak… Squeak-squeak.

They crept silently along the left wall, holding their breath. The sound was coming from just around the corner and was getting louder. On the floor above them a door slammed shut so hard they felt the ceiling vibrate. They jumped. 'What was that!' said Ronnie. Sally's face paled. John said nothing, walking as if in a trance. Footsteps rattled on the stairs behind them.

Squeak-squeak… Squeak-squeak.

John turned around, and for the first time they saw that he was actually terrified. 'There's an exit around the corner down the stairs,' he said. 'The weed's hidden in the wall. When we get to the corner we run, but one of us has to grab it.'

'Screw the weed!' said Sally. 'Something's in here with us, John!'

Squeak-squeak… Squeak-squeak.

The squeaking was much louder now, and much closer. Filling their noses was the acrid scent of rotten flesh, so pungent they could taste it. Ronnie threw up in his mouth and swallowed it down, grimacing. John looked like he was about to cry. 'Fine,' he said. 'Forget the weed! On a count of three we run like hell. One... Two...'

To their left a child giggled in the open doorway.

Sally screamed and bolted down the hall, crashing into pieces of hospital furniture. All around them doors rapidly opened and slammed shut. The light disappeared and reappeared in sporadic bursts. Rounding the corner, Ronnie stopped and John crashed into him, sending them both sprawling to the ground. 'Why'd you stop?' John shouted. Ronnie pointed at something in front of them. The beam from Sally's light fell on a concrete wall, stained and flecked with mold as if it had always been there, but just a second ago it was an opening to the stairs... to the exit...

Above them, doors were slamming shut and things were crashing. It sounded like a dozen strong men were picking up whatever they could find and hurling it against the walls. Echoing down the corridor was a deep, croaking laugh. John whimpered. Then a dark spot began to form on the crotch of his pants.

'Where's Sal?' Ronnie whispered, but John didn't answer. His eyes bulged and he was gasping heavily – he was in shock. 'Come on, we've got to find Sally and get out of here! Come on!' Ronnie helped him to his feet and picked up the mobile phone, shining light down the corridor. He could faintly make out an opening. He looked around for Sally but she was nowhere. 'Sally!' he whispered. 'Sal! Where the hell are you?'

The stench of rotting flesh was so strong they could taste it all the way down their throats. Doors slammed. Then opened and slammed again. They heard scuttling feet behind them, giggles in the rooms. Then something moaned in the darkness. Ronnie stopped, clutching John with his free arm. The moan came again, like someone sick or in pain, coming from a room up ahead on their right. In the same direction something started growling at them. It was unlike anything Ronnie had ever heard. Gurneys flipped over and crashed against the ceiling and walls. It was coming for them.

Terror seized Ronnie's heart and sent him pushing John into the nearest room. He closed the door and whatever it was clawed furiously at it, yapping and barking wildly like a hyena while skittering for the handle. Ronnie bolted the door just in time. The creature howled. He turned around, gasping for air, his face covered in sweat. His eyes widened. 'Oh my God,' he said. He had found Sally.

She was lying facedown in a bathtub against the windowless wall. She was wearing different clothes, a white hospital shift spattered with blood. Her breathing was labored and wheezy, and something seemed to be clicking in her throat, like phlegm. 'Sal?' Ronnie slowly went over to the bathtub, shining the light on her, but she didn't move. She kept wheezing. Her naked back was exposed through the shift, and Ronnie could see her spine and the paleness of her skin, blue veins curved and twisted around the humps of her spine. John stood motionless against the wall while the creature howled and moaned outside the door. Ronnie reached down to turn Sally's head. 'Sal, are you okay?'

John's breath caught in his throat. 'That's not Sally,' he said.

The head turned on its own, revealing a woman's rotted face with deep-set black eyes. She opened her mouth wide and cackled horribly, releasing a stench of blood and excrement and foul meat. John screamed. Ronnie fell backwards and dropped the phone, breaking it.

The room went dark.

While the woman crawled out of the tub, John opened the door and ran screaming down the hall. Sharp claws seized him by the belly and dug into his stomach, causing him to squeal frantically and choke. A mouth full of long jagged teeth clamped down on his throat and tore wildly at his flesh. Blood sprayed the wall, and the creature that held him groaned in ecstasy, snapping bones with its powerful jaws and greedily sopping up the blood with its tongue.

Cold hands had grasped Ronnie from behind, fingernails digging into his flesh as a gravelly voice spoke to him, 'Come to me come to me come to me!' Teeth sank into his neck and he screamed, struggling with the woman and kicking her in the mouth. He bolted from the room. He could hear her running after him, her bare feet padding the hospital floor. 'I'll get you and stab you and eat you and kill you!'

'Sally! Help! Somebody! Somebody help me!' He plowed through metal gurneys and furniture, cutting his forearm on something. Doors were opening and closing repeatedly. Exiting the corridor, he nearly slipped as he ran up the stairs. He took them three at a time as the voice followed close behind: 'I'll gut you and eat you and lick you and gouge you!' At the top of the stairs he tripped over something and slammed to the ground. The asylum grew deathly quiet. Moonlight fell through the barred windows. He closed his eyes and waited for the woman to grab him and drag him back to the darkness.

Nothing happened. Then someone let out a gurgled cough, as if liquid had filled their lungs. Ronnie looked around in the semi-darkness. His eyes adjusting, he saw Sally lying on the ground in a pool of blood. She had been mangled horribly by something, blood running freely from open wounds. She was choking, spitting up blood, and her eyes were pleading with him... pleading for what?

For mercy, thought Ronnie. She wanted mercy. 'Please,' she managed, blinking at him. A gouge in her throat made it hard for her to breathe. Blood poured out of it and became shiny in the moonlight as it pooled on the floor.

Ronnie shook his head. 'No,' he said. 'I'm getting us out of here.' He bent over and picked her up, but she cried out sharply, so he set her down. Ronnie caught something in the corner of his eye and froze. The mad woman, Susan Grimes, was standing at the top of the stairs with her black hair covering her pale face. In her left hand an axe was dripping with fresh blood. She did not move. 'Please,' Sally said again. 'Please don't leave me.'

'No, Sal,' he said. 'I'm not going to leave you.' Tears filled his eyes and ran down his face. But Susan Grimes stepped forward and raised the axe high above Sally's head. All at once hundreds of doors opened and slammed around them. 'Fuck off!' he screamed. Then he glanced down at Sally, her eyes wide and unseeing. She was dead.

Susan Grimes bought down the axe and Ronnie jumped backwards. A spray of warm blood hit him in the face. Sally's head rolled, then tumbled down the stairs. Susan Grimes looked at him.

Ronnie ran.

He didn't stop when he crawled through the cafeteria door and choked on the night air. He didn't stop when he reached the street. He kept running. And he kept screaming.

* * *

Jack Nightingale no longer believed in coincidence. He used to, in another life, back when he was a police negotiator and believed that sometimes people were just in the wrong place at the wrong time. That saying still held true for many cases, but not most. Most times you were at the wrong place because you were put there by some dark force or higher power, which were both deceptive and cunning. Someone got hit by a man in a truck with no alcohol in his system and with a proven track record of being an excellent driver. The pedestrian was following the rules, the driver was following the rules, and the lights hadn't changed, so what happened? Fate happened. And like death, it was always watching and waiting. That's why when Nightingale watched the newest episode of The Truth Is Out There – in which Keith Harrington and his camera crew set out to debunk supernatural myths and stories – and he received a phone call from the man himself, he wasn't totally dumbstruck. It wasn't coincidence: it was fate.

He had called Nightingale on his private mobile. It was just after 10pm in New York City. Autumn rain was pounding on the windows of his hotel room and he heard sirens outside on the street below. 'How did you get this number?' asked Nightingale. 'Who gave it to you?'

'A friend of a friend,' said Harrington. 'Someone who thinks you might be able to help me.'

Nightingale slipped into a bathrobe and cracked a window. Then he opened his packet of Marlboro and lit a cigarette, inhaling deeply. 'What is it you want, Mr Harrington?'

'I've got a case I need your help with, Mr Nightingale. Probably the worst case you'll ever see.' Nightingale suddenly pictured a nine-year-old girl slipping off a high rise balcony and falling through the air, then the sound of wet meat slapping into a fry pan. It would take a lot to beat Nightingale's worst case.

'I highly doubt that, Mr Harrington,' he said.

'Please, call me Keith. And listen to this. The case involves a centuries-old insane asylum, torture and rape over the span of seven decades, many dozens of missing persons, countless murders, and twenty-five unsolved homicides going back to the late 1970s, including one from my own crew a few years back, and, as of yesterday, two teenagers.'

Nightingale blew smoke out the window. 'You're talking about Wentworth Asylum.'

'Yes, I am.'

'I watched that episode a while back, Keith. I'm sorry about your friend. What was his name… Chris?'

Harrington was silent a moment. 'Charles,' he said. 'And thanks. Anyway, something else has happened and we want to update the story with a follow-up episode.'

'What happened ?' he asked.

'There were three of them. A girl and two boys. They decided to go to Wentworth in the middle of the night to collect some weed one of their older brothers had stashed away there. The girl was found first. Her torso, that is, all hacked up in pieces. Her head was at the bottom of the stairwell. Her bottom half still hasn't been accounted for.'

Nightingale winced. 'And the boys?'

'One of them was nailed to the wall with iron spikes. Each limb had been hacked from the body and was nailed separately. Almost looked like the Vitruvian Man, except nothing was connected. The other boy was found later that night, a bloody mess running down the streets of Wentworth screaming at the top of his lungs. He screamed all the way to the hospital until they sedated him. He's a little better now, but he's still in shock. He says his friends were killed by an axe murderer.'

'So what do you think happened?'

'We don't know. But that's why we're going back.'

'And why do you need me there?'

'I'd rather explain that when I see you.'

Nightingale thought about it for several seconds before answering. 'Okay. I'll come.'

'I already bought you a train ticket,' said Harrington. 'I'll meet you at the station.'

Two minutes later his phone rang again. It was Joshua Wainwright, the billionaire Satanist who was Nightingale's employer and protector. Again, Nightingale was sure it wasn't a coincidence. 'Hi Joshua,' he said.

'You've spoken to Keith Harrington?'

Nightingale smiled to himself. He was sure that Wainwright knew exactly who he had and hadn't spoken to. 'Just now,' he said.

'Did he tell you I own his company?'

'He didn't mention you.'

'Well that's something at least. He's got it in his head to do a live transmission from the asylum. You need to put a stop to that.'

'There is something going on there, then?'

'Yes, unfortunately. Harrington's show is supposed to prove that there is no such thing as the supernatural, but if he goes ahead and broadcasts live there's no knowing what might happen.'

'You think something might happen?'

'It's a possibility.'

'So why don't you just stop him?'

There was a short silence and Nightingale pictured the Texan drawing on one of his favourite cigars. 'I own the show but I don't interfere,' he said. 'Not overtly, anyway. If I start putting Harrington under pressure he might take the show elsewhere. At least this way I have some control. That's why I need you there.'

'I'm on it, Joshua.'

'Good to hear,' said Wainwright. 'And Jack, be careful.'

'I always am.'

'I'm serious,' said Wainwright.

'So am I,' said Nightingale.

* * *

Nightingale got off the train at Philadelphia's 30th Street Station just after eight in the morning. The station's huge coffered ceiling was lit up by dangling lights, making the scene before him seem surreal, as if he was dreaming. Adding to that was the rich sunlight pouring in through the windows on either side of the lobby, a sprawling room with a shiny marble floor that reflected Nightingale's image back at him. People were milling about, men in suits and women in blouses rushing with newspapers tucked under their arms and Starbucks coffee in their hands, seemingly racing against time.

Nightingale yawned. He hadn't slept much after Keith Harrington had called. He had known the story of Wentworth Asylum for some time. Everyone knew about Wentworth Asylum. There were some stories you just couldn't put out of your mind no matter how hard you tried. Like that of a crazed ex-mental patient roaming the haunted grounds in a white hospital shift with a bloody axe, her mouth a grinning black hole and her eyes soulless orbs from which death glimmered. And as he had told

Harrington, Nightingale saw The Truth Is Out There episode where Harrington's friend Charles had fallen off a balcony to his death. No one knew if it was an accident or if Charles had been thrown to his death. Nightingale knew enough about Wentworth to know that it was no place anyone should visit, let alone a trio of drunk teenagers in the middle of the night.

'Nightingale!' someone yelled. 'Over here!' Keith Harrington was leaning against a magazine rack with a newspaper and coffee in his hands like everybody else, which was probably why Nightingale hadn't recognized him. Harrington was wearing his customary leathers and his dark hair was held back in a ponytail. He had a neatly-trimmed goatee that glistened as if it had been oiled. Harrington was a lot shorter than he appeared in his television show, at least six inches shorter than Nightingale.

'Jack Nightingale,' said Nightingale, reaching out his hand.

Harrington shook it, then put the cup of coffee and newspaper into his hands. 'Coffee for the road,' said Harrington, ushering Nightingale towards the doors. 'And the latest news on our little debacle.'

Nightingale opened the newspaper to the front page, which showed bold headlines: DOUBLE MURDER AT WENTWORTH ASYLUM, SURVIVOR BARELY ESCAPED WITH HIS LIFE. There was a description of the grisly murder scene and a mumbled statement from Ronnie Riley of Wentworth, Pennsylvania. 'It was Susan... Susan Grimes. She murdered my friends with... an axe.'

Nightingale frowned as he read the newspaper. 'It says here there's an investigation underway?'

Harrington chuckled. 'If you can even call it that. Take my word for it, up until the other night no policeman has bothered to step foot inside the Murder Room for the last twenty years.'

'The Murder Room?'

They went through the double doors and Harrington waved over a black car with tinted windows. It pulled up next to them and a burly driver struggled out and opened the back door for them. Harrington motioned Nightingale inside. 'Yeah, that's what the press dubbed it around the time. Wentworth shut down in the early eighties, because so many murders were happening in that room, bodies being found much the same way that those two kids were killed.'

'Chopped to bits?'

'Exactly,' Harrington said. 'But they never found who was responsible. You saw the show we did on the asylum.'

'I was half watching it, Keith. I'm not a big TV watcher.'

'Well we covered the whole thing. Everyone says it's haunted but we spent a night there and didn't come across anything supernatural. We had all the equipment but there were no cold spots, no apparitions, nothing.'

'Good to know,' said Nightingale.

'But we did go through all the shit that happened there over the years. Do you remember the segment we did on Wentworth's John and Jane Doe?'

Nightingale shook his head.

'Unidentified male and female discovered in the Murder Room in 1982 by police after a handful of locals complained of screams interrupting their sleep during the night. Why they didn't dial the police till morning, I have no idea. But two police officers turned up first thing that morning and found the kids, the same age as the ones the other night, dismembered and tortured, their body parts spread all over the place like a macabre treasure hunt. Apparently, they had been tortured over a period of several hours. Some of the body parts had teeth marks and flesh gouged out, as if an animal had been eating them. Forensics matched five teeth to a Ms Susan Grimes, an ex-Wentworth patient who first appeared in the system at age five when she was sent there on account of stomach pains. This was back in the '50s.'

Nightingale gaped at him. 'You've got to be joking. Stomach pains?'

'No joke. Are you sure you were watching? We covered all this in the show. They used to send undesirables to the crazy house for literally any reason that might hold water. Grimes grew up in Wentworth, spent her entire childhood there. She pretty much went crazy while she was a resident. Over the course of ten years she killed at least five patients that we know of; she used an axe on the last three, who she killed in a frenzy on the same night. Then came the public health crisis, which rocked the nation with those films of abuse in mental hospitals across the U.S. Wentworth closed its doors because of it. They had been mired in illegal activity since they started taking bribes from drug companies in the '50s for secret human testing. Untold thousands of patients died. The number is still debated. Two thousand? Twenty thousand? It's one of the worst unsolved crimes in American history, but you won't hear any of our policy-makers talking about it, not unless it's behind closed doors and they're saying how good of a job they did in cleaning it all up. Guess what Wentworth did when they shut down?'

'Destroyed the records?'

'Yep, and they released several thousand mentally ill patients, some of them known murderers, including Susan Grimes. Grimes, along with many other patients that day, disappeared from history. After the police found those corpses in '82, several teams went in and searched the entire Wentworth complex. No sign of her.'

'Hang on, are you saying they released her into the community?'

'No one knows. Once they had identified her the cops went back and she wasn't there. Maybe she escaped. Maybe the authorities released her. Nobody knows for sure.'

'I'm sorry, Keith, that defies belief. They had a mad murderer in their care and they let her go?'

'Like I said, no one knows for sure and all the records were lost. Those two police officers I mentioned? Weeks after the investigation they both ended up dead. Their wives were found hacked to pieces in their homes. The officers' wrists were slashed so deep so as to appear chopped. No murder weapon was ever found.'

Nightingale took out a packet of Marlboro. 'You mind?' Harrington shook his head, so he took a cigarette and lit it. 'I still don't understand the significance here,' he said after he'd blown smoke out of the window. 'The police went mad, killed their wives and then themselves, right? They must've been utterly traumatized, even if they had been seasoned cops. I've seen dead bodies before, particularly of children, and I can tell you firsthand, it changes you.'

'I can respect that,' said Harrington. 'But these guys were straight edge. Didn't do drugs, didn't drink. They were honest cops who loved their families and visited their mom's for every Sunday supper, that kind of thing. And in both cases, there were signs of forced entry.'

'How so?' asked Nightingale through a breath of smoke.

'Doorknobs hacked off. Not to mention bloody footprints on the floors. You see where I'm going with this?'

Nightingale looked at him with narrowed eyes. 'The two cops who investigated the scene in '82 were murdered by the same psychopath they suspected were responsible for the deaths in the asylum. This Susan Grimes? That's what you're saying. And she's just killed again. In the asylum.'

'I think it's a possibility. Which is why we want to go back and do another show there.'

'Yes, but if Susan Grimes were still alive she'd be about seventy by now. She probably died years ago.'

'Exactly,' said Harrington. 'But what if her soul is still in there, and she's grown so powerful she can kill the living? She killed John and Jane doe, she killed the cops, Charles and those kids, and countless others over the years. She has to be stopped.'

'You believe that?'

Harrington laughed nervously. 'Our show debunks stories like this.

That's what we do. But there's something different about this story.'

He fell silent. Nightingale smoked his cigarette down to the filter and flicked it out the window. He watched the Philadelphia skyline pass by. Autumn leaves were being blown in the wind and passersby were holding their collars tight to their necks, heads dipped down to avoid the cold.

'I need your help, Jack. I think I might be in danger,' said Harrington, his voice a quiet whisper.

Nightingale turned to look at him, frowning. 'What's happened?'

'For the past week I've been having the same dream. Susan Grimes comes to me in the middle of the night holding an axe with blood all over it. I'm stuck in my bed and I can't move, and I have to watch as she chops me up, piece by piece.' Harrington was trembling. He took a few deep breaths and composed himself. 'I'm scared, Jack. Scared that she's going to come for me. I've been a sceptic all my life, but I'm starting to believe that there's something to this. You have to help me.'

Nightingale nodded. 'I'll do what I can,' he said.

* * *

Keith Harrington's production team had set up a temporary office in Philadelphia's Old City District. It was full of ornate buildings, some of them brick, with shops, fashion boutiques and art galleries studding the historic streets. Nestled in one of the quieter streets was the office of The Truth Is Out There, where a team of men and women was busy answering phone calls, dismantling green screens and packing film equipment. 'Hey, guys!' Harrington hollered, and everyone stopped what they were doing and looked at him. 'This is Jack Nightingale,' he said. 'He's going to be our special guest on show tonight.' The team nodded and quickly went back to their duties.

'Wait a second,' said Nightingale. 'What do you mean, special guest?'

'We're streaming tonight's episode live. You'll be our star guest.'

'Are you mad? I offered to investigate the asylum with you, not to be on television. What if someone dies? On live TV?'

'I'm tempted to say the ratings will go through the roof, but no one is going to die. Not with all our people there. Look, if you insist, we'll keep you off camera.'

'Not good enough.'

'We've got to think of the ratings, Jack. Doing it live gives it extra edge.'

'I get that,' said Nightingale. 'But by placing this on television for the world to see, you're opening a lot of doors best left shut.'

'Or we're closing doors that have already been opened.'

Nightingale shook his head. 'Once you start broadcasting live, you lose control. What if there is some sort of entity and it appears?'

'Then it's great TV. And if nothing happens, it's still great TV.'

'Keith, these dreams you've been having. What if Susan Grimes does appear, and what if she does attack you? You want that broadcast live? You screaming like a little girl?'

Harrington shrugged, but then he wrinkled his nose. 'Yeah, I see what you mean.' He narrowed his eyes. 'So you think it's possible? I am in danger?'

'I don't know, Keith. But why take the risk. Let's go in there with cameras, let's record what we see and take it from there.'

Harrington nodded. 'Deal,' he said.

Harrington called a group meeting and explained the plan to his production team. They were going to place motion sensor cameras throughout Wentworth Asylum, with the feeds going to a control center in the Murder Room, and three teams of four would conduct separate investigations during 'lockdown' from midnight to dawn. On one team was Father Bailey, a stout Irishman with a bulbous nose who trained as an exorcist at the Vatican, along with Keith Harrington and Nightingale. The other two teams would be headed by seasoned paranormal investigators

Ben Lee and Rachel Wood. Ben was an awkward gangly Chinese man in his thirties with jet black hair and gold-rimmed glasses in a grey sweater and jeans. Wood was Keith Harrington's assistant, and always appeared on camera with Harrington. She was also his girlfriend, a petite strawberry blonde with freckles and a ready smile. She wore black pants and a tight-fitting Rock tee-shirt that left nothing to the imagination. Nightingale wasn't introduced to the rest of the team, but from what he saw they were mostly in their mid-to-late twenties.

'I know I said I'd never go back to Wentworth, not after what happened to Charlie. I always thought that his death was just a crazy accident, but now I'm not so sure. So I want everybody to be careful, understand?'

He was faced with nodding heads. Ben put up his hand. 'The last time we pretty much proved there wasn't anything supernatural there,' he said.

'There never is,' said Wood. 'That's the point of the show.'

Ben flashed her a withering look. 'I know,' he said. 'So why are we going back?'

'Because of the recent deaths,' said Harrington. 'Deaths are always good TV, you know that. We can do a séance, try to talk to the victims. Viewers love that.' He looked around the room. 'Anyone else?' No one spoke, so Harrington clapped his hands together. 'All right, guys. We meet back here at eight o'clock, and then it's show time.'

'I'm off for a drink,' said Nightingale.

Harrington put a hand on his shoulder. 'No,' he said. 'There's someone you need to meet before we go to the asylum.'

* * *

Ronnie Riley lay tossing and turning in his hospital bed, his tired brain wracked with nightmares. In his dream he was trapped in a burning building in the midst of a scorched city. Everywhere he turned there was fire. In the walls of flame, drawing close and charring his skin, were a series of ugly demonic faces, all of them sneering and growling with long fangs and colourless eyes. Through the flames gnarled claws reached for him, but he scurried away and ran out the door, running, running, running like the coward he was.

He ran down the fiery street with its wrecked buildings. He was a coward. He'd run from Susan Grimes in the asylum and left poor Sally there to be devoured. He'd kept running until there was nothing left to do but sink to his knees and cry. And here he was, still running, and still a coward.

All around him the buildings were engulfed in flames. Some were crumbling down on their foundations and sending waves of blackened concrete into the road. He felt heat against his back, followed by low laughter and hurried footsteps from behind.

They had found him.

He came to the edge of the city, bordered by a green forest that hadn't been touched by the fire yet. This was the end of the road, he knew. If he went into the forest the demons would surely follow him, burning and killing everything in their path. Pretty soon they'd have dominion over the whole world.

Ronnie turned and faced the demons. There were hundreds, no, thousands of them, sprinting off skyscrapers and bounding down the ruined streets. Their mouths were slack and they were screaming for him. They wanted his soul. They wanted to devour his flesh. Anger flashed through him as he pictured Sally's mangled corpse. He held up his hand and yelled at the top of his lungs: 'Stop!'

To his surprise, the advancing horde stopped before him. The demons in the front seemed taken off guard, as if they'd met with an invisible wall. They peered at each other uncertainly. Then they set their vicious eyes on Ronnie and snarled at him.

'This is the end of the road for you!' he screamed. 'Go back to Hell, you bastards! You'll come no farther!'

They spat at him, they cursed him, and they threw hunks of human meat until Ronnie was covered in blood and gore. He wiped his eyes but they were already on him, snapping and biting. 'Stop!' he said, as the first demon bit a chunk out of his leg. 'No! No!' Ronnie was screaming and trying to fight them but there were too many. Scraps of bloody flesh and gore flew up around as the demons tore into his body with their teeth and claws. 'No! No! No!' That was when he woke up, still screaming. His sheets were soaked with sweat.

He looked around and realised he wasn't alone in the hospital room. There were two strangers. Two men. Then as he blinked at the figures he recognised one. 'You're Keith Harrington,' he said. 'The Truth Is Out There.'

Harrington smiled. 'That's right, kid. How're you feeling?'

'I'm... I'm okay... I guess. What're you doing here? You're here to visit me?' He realised there was also a girl in the room. He smiled as he recognised her. Rachel Wood. Keith's assistant on the show.

'Yep, and this is Jack Nightingale.'

Nightingale stepped forward and shook the boy's hand. 'Pleasure to meet you, Ronnie.'

'And this is Rachel. I'm sure you know her from the show?'

Wood gave him a big smile and waggled her fingers at him and Ronnie blushed.

'If you don't mind my asking, what were you dreaming about just now?' asked Nightingale.

Ronnie shuddered. 'I really don't want to talk about it.'

'Bad dream?' asked Nightingale, sitting on the edge of the bed.

'Yeah,' Ronnie said, wiping his forehead.

'Sounded like you were up against something frightening.'

'I was.'

'We want to help you, Ronnie, but first we have to know exactly what happened to you back at Wentworth. We haven't much time.'

Ronnie's eyes widened. 'You're going to Wentworth? Are you nuts? They'll kill you! They'll kill all of you!'

Nightingale leaned forward. 'Who will, Ronnie?' he asked. 'Tell us.'

'Those things at the asylum! The demons!'

Nightingale glanced quickly at Harrington. 'How many?'

'Thousands! You can't go there. They're everywhere, in every room and on every staircase.'

A nurse opened the door, saw the two men with Ronnie, and hurried in. She looked accusingly at Nightingale. 'He needs his rest,' she said. 'Ronnie, I heard you scream. Are these folks bothering you?'

Ronnie shook his head. 'No, it was just a bad dream is all.'

'You sure?'

'I'm sure. Really. This is Keith Harrington from The Truth Is Out There.'

The nurse frowned. 'The what?'

'It's a hit TV show.'

The nurse shrugged. 'I don't watch TV,' she said. She held up her hand. 'Five minutes,' she said, and left the room. Nightingale leaned forward. 'Go on,' he said. 'Tell us what happened.'

Ronnie breathed a deep sigh, then he told them his story. He told them about the weed and the squeaking gurney and the wall that appeared from nowhere. He told them about John getting eaten and about finding Sally on the ground in a pool of blood. And he told them about Susan Grimes attacking them with her bloody axe. Averting his eyes, he told them last about running away from Wentworth Asylum and the terrible nightmares that had plagued him ever since, the nightmares that seemed all too real.

'There was nothing you could've done,' said Nightingale. 'Anyone would've run at that point.'

Ronnie picked at his blanket and said nothing.

'Why do you suppose they let you go?' asked Nightingale.

Ronnie kept his eyes down. 'I got the impression it was me or Sally. Sally died, and if I'd stayed it would've been both of us, so I ran.' He looked up at them. 'You guys believe me? You don't think I'm crazy?'

'You're not crazy,' said Harrington. 'We know what you went through. We need to put a stop to it. We mean to exorcize Wentworth Asylum and send those demons back to Hell.'

'But what about Susan Grimes?'

'We'll send her back to wherever she came from,' said Harrington. 'Ronnie, I want to ask you a favour.'

'What?'

'We're going to be filming the show from within the asylum. What I'd like to do is to send you a feed here, in the hospital, so that you can watch what's going on.'

Ronnie shook his head fiercely. 'I'm not going back there.'

'You won't actually be going back. You can just watch it. We'll set up a screen. I'll leave Rachel here with you and she can talk to you about what you're seeing. She can record that. And you can advise us where to go, stuff like that.'

Ronnie looked over at Wood and she nodded enthusiastically. 'It'll be fun,' she said. 'I'll order pizza.'

'The hospital won't allow it, will they?'

'If we pay them enough they will,' said Harrington. 'So you're okay with that?'

'I guess so,' said Ronnie, but Nightingale could hear the uncertainty in his voice. Harrington produced his wallet and took out a card. 'Here, this is my private cell. If you need anything, and I mean anything, give me a call. All right?'

Ronnie took the card. 'Thanks, Mr Harrington.'

'Call me Keith.' Harrington nodded over at Wood. 'Do you want to pick up your equipment from the car? Then talk to Lyle about fixing up the Skype link.'

They said goodbye and went for the door. Before they closed it, Ronnie called out to them in a trembling voice. 'Hey, guys?' he said. 'I think something bad's going to happen tonight. Something very, very bad. I'm not sure what it is, but it feels… big.'

Nightingale watched the boy closely.

Harrington smiled. 'Don't worry, kid,' he said. 'We've got it covered from here on out. Get some rest. You're safe now.'

Nightingale followed Harrington out into the corridor. 'What do you mean, exorcise?'

'That's what Father Bailey is going to do. He was trained by the Vatican.'

'That's your plan? An exorcism? You said séance.'

'We'll do both. It'll make for great TV. And in the unlikely event there is a presence there, an exorcism will get rid of it.'

'If Susan Grimes is a ghost. But ghosts tend not to go around with axes. And Ronnie talked about demons.'

'I think he's just got Post Traumatic Stress Disorder. I don't believe in demons, do you?'

Nightingale didn't answer the question.

'Father Bailey was trained by the best.'

'Keith, exorcisms are for possessions. So far as I know, no one has been possessed.'

'Like I said, Jack, it'll make for great TV. And it can't do any harm.'

'Says who? Carrying out an exorcism on a demon can be like pouring gasoline on a barbecue,' he said.

Harrington patted him on the shoulder. 'You worry too much,' he said. 'Father Bailey knows what he's doing.'

* * *

Nightingale took out his packet of Marlboro and smoked as

Harrington drove back to the office. Before they had left the hospital, Wood had taken her equipment from the trunk and an orderly had helped her take it up to Ronnie's room.

'I don't think an exorcism is the way to go,' said Nightingale. 'By all means go in with your monitoring equipment and see what's there, but an exorcism might provoke a reaction.'

'So you do believe there's something there?'

'Ronnie didn't sound as if he was making it up. But it could be a copycat, someone who heard the Susan Grimes stories and wants to make them real. Or it could just be another serial killer who favours the axe. You might be able to flush whoever – or whatever – it is out into the open. But an exorcist isn't going to be any use against a human serial killer. Or a demon.'

'There's no such thing as demons,' said Harrington. 'In all the years I've been doing The Truth Is Out There I've never come across anything that couldn't be explained away by good old science.'

'But the dreams worry you?' Nightingale saw a woman standing in the center of the road. 'Hey! Watch out!' he shouted.

Harrington slammed on the brakes and spun the wheel. Tyres squealed as the car sideswiped, then flipped and rolled several times. The ceiling crumpled inwards like aluminum foil and the windows shattered. The car collided with a pole, which groaned and toppled over the car. The power lines crackled with electricity, sending up sparks.

The world had gone quiet for Nightingale. He blinked several times but heard nothing. His head was numb, and he felt queasy. He was lying upside down on the roof of the SUV's back hatch in a carpet of glass. He quickly came to his senses and started crawling on his elbows across the broken glass towards Harrington, who was unconscious and bleeding from the head. Gas was pooling on the ground, spreading towards the fallen power line. Sparks were landing on the asphalt near the spreading pool. Harrington lay tangled up in his seatbelt. He was coming round, still in shock. He seemed confused. 'Night... Nightingale,' he mumbled. Nightingale hushed him and hit the seatbelt button. It didn't work. He hit it again. Nothing. 'Did you see her? Susan Grimes.' The pool of gas was quickly flowing towards the sparks. They had moments before the fuel burst into flames. Nightingale fumbled around for something sharp, found a piece of glass and began cutting away at the seatbelt. Not fast enough. They weren't going to make it. 'Go,' said Harrington.

'Shut up and help me.'

'Huh?'

Nightingale slapped him across the face. 'Help me!' he said. Harrington's eyes glowed with sudden awareness. He grabbed a piece of glass and began cutting the opposite end of the seatbelt. A single spark shot up from the fallen power line and landed in the pool of gas, catching fire.

'Get out of here!' said Harrington.

'Hurry up!'

'Go!' Harrington shoved him, but Nightingale pressed his glass against the seatbelt and sliced it. The fire swept towards the gas tank. Nightingale took Harrington from under his armpits and trudged as fast as he could away from the car. An explosion sent them flying on top of each other and hot wind burned their skin.

'Did you see her?' said Harrington.

'I saw a girl.'

Harrington shook his head. 'It was a woman. It was Susan Grimes.'

'I don't think so,' said Nightingale.

'She was holding an axe!'

'I didn't see any axe,' said Nightingale.

'There was an axe.' Harrington looked around, frowning. 'Where is she?'

'Maybe she was never here,' said Nightingale. 'Maybe we imagined it.'

'We both imagined the same thing?' Harrington shook his head. 'I don't think so. It was Susan Grimes and she was out to get me.' He looked over at the burning car. 'She almost did.'

* * *

Harrington and Nightingale reached the office of The Truth Is Out There just shy of 8 p.m. They walked through the hall to the meeting room, their clothes burnt, torn, and flecked with blood. A thick bandage covered Nightingale's left eyebrow and Harrington's forehead was plastered with butterfly stitches. They opened the door and walked into the meeting room where a dozen voices were all talking at once. Suddenly they fell silent. The team stared speechless at them, mouths agape. Finally someone spoke. It was Harvey Cooper, one the longest-serving members of the team, heavily overweight with permanent sweat stains on his shirts. 'Holy cow... what happened to you guys?'

'Load up the vans,' said Harrington. 'We're going to Wentworth.'

Frankie Mays hurried over. 'Are you okay, Keith?' She was in her early twenties, her blonde hair tied back in a ponytail and wearing a headset.

'I'll be fine. Nothing a bit of make-up won't cover. Did you talk to Rachel?'

Frankie nodded. 'She's set up in Ronnie's room. We've run a test and it works, so we just need to set up in Wentworth.' She frowned. 'Are you sure you're okay?'

'We had a bit of a car crash,' said Harrington. 'It's not a problem.' He clapped his hands. 'Right, let's get into the vans. We want to start by midnight.' He looked around. 'Where's Father Bailey?' he shouted.

'He said he'd meet us there,' said Harvey.

Harrington groaned. 'He'd better not be at the communion wine,' he said. 'Come on, off we go.'

Half an hour later a convoy of four vans pulled up in front of the main

Wentworth Asylum building. Harrington and Nightingale were in the first van, driven by Ben. It was the first time Nightingale had seen the building and he shivered at the sight of it. There was an atmosphere of death and decay about the place, and it wasn't just the smell. The place just felt wrong.

The team pulled open the van doors and began carrying equipment inside. Nightingale lit a cigarette and blew smoke up at the quarter moon. Harrington looked at the pack and Nightingale offered it to him. 'I didn't think you smoked.'

'I gave up ten years ago,' said Harrington. He took one and Nightingale lit it for him with his Zippo. 'Though I guess you never really give up.'

A grey sedan pulled up behind the vans and Father Bailey climbed out. He was in full priest regalia and carrying a leather holdall. He waved at Harrington and walked over, the bag swinging at his side. 'I needed fresh Holy water,' he said, 'blessed by the bishop.'

Neither Harrington nor Nightingale mentioned the strong smell of booze that was coming off the priest, or that his cheeks were now several shades redder than they had been last time they'd seen him.

'Where are we setting up?' asked the priest.

'The Murder Room,' said Harrington. 'It's the first room on the left after the reception area,' he said. 'It's where they used to process the patients on arrival. That'll be our main control centre and then Lyle is fixing up sensors in more of the rooms.'

'And where will I carry out the exorcism?'

'Let's wait until we see how the sensors perform. Then we'll do a walk-through looking for cold spots or any disturbances. Anytime we find anything, you can do what's necessary. If we don't find anything, we can exorcise the Murder Room.'

When they got to the Murder Room, the priest placed his bag on a chair in the corner. Harrington's team were busy carrying out their assigned tasks with casual professionalism. They erected three tall floodlights that lit the room with fluorescent light. Camilla Garcia, a pretty Hispanic woman with dark eyes, was drawing a large salt circle around them. Father Bailey began praying and dashing holy water throughout the room.

'Are you serious?' said Nightingale, nodding at the priest.

'Father Bailey always does this,' said Harrington. 'And it gets everyone in the mood.'

A series of monitors were placed on folding tables. Two electricians ran cords along the ground to different rooms, then duct taped them, setting up cameras and motion sensors which sprang to life on the Murder Room's monitors. Nightingale watched Ben on camera, lit up green. 'Testing, one two. Testing, one two,' he said. Lyle Brooks, a short pimply kid in a tweed blazer, was wearing a headset and manning the monitors. 'Hear you, Ben. Loud and clear.'

Frankie was on a different screen adjusting the lens of a fixed infrared camera. As Nightingale watched, a chair slowly lifted from the ground and floated in the air behind her. Nightingale waved Harrington over. 'Keith, look at this!'

Harrington hurried over and stared at the screen. He was holding a radio and he put it to his mouth. 'Frankie, where are you?'

'One of the wards.'

The chair bobbed soundlessly behind her.

'Frankie, honey,' said Harrington. 'Come on back to the Murder Room now.'

'Why?' she asked, slapping duct tape on the cord below the camera. 'I haven't finished here.' Another chair rose in the air, then a squeaking gurney, causing Frankie to gasp and turn around.

'Come back now, Frankie. Quick as you can.' Harrington looked over at Lyle. 'Lyle, are we recording this?'

Lyle flashed him a thumbs up.

Suddenly the two chairs and the gurney flew at Frankie. She screamed and fell on the ground just as the furniture smashed into the wall. Still screaming, she ran out of the hall, moments later appearing in the Murder Room. The team rallied around her.

'You okay?' asked Nightingale.

'Yeah,' she said, patting herself down. 'I think so.'

Nightingale noticed three deep scratches on her forehead. 'You're bleeding.'

'Am I?' She dabbed her forehead, seeing the blood. 'Shit.'

'You want to go home?' asked Harrington.

'No. No, I'll stay. I'm fine.'

'Okay, good girl.' Harrington waved over the priest. 'Time to do your thing, Father Bailey.'

'I'd advise against that, Keith,' said Nightingale.

'You saw what just happened,' said Harrington.

'But we don't know why it happened.'

Father Bailey took a dozen wooden crucifixes from his bag and handed them out. He offered one to Nightingale but Nightingale shook his head. 'Are you sure?' asked the priest.

'It's belief that defends you, not the trinkets,' said Nightingale. 'And sometimes even belief doesn't help you.'

'It's for the cameras, Jack,' said Harrington.

'Then it's wasted because I'm not appearing on camera,' said Nightingale.

'We'll blur your face in edit,' said Harrington. He took one of the crucifixes from the priest.

When he'd handed out all the crucifixes, Father Bailey went back to his bag and took out a flask of Holy water and a leather pouch.

'White sage?' asked Nightingale.

The priest smiled and nodded.

'Well good luck with that,' said Nightingale.

They heard several doors open and slam shut close by. A window burst inwards in the Murder Room, spreading glass everywhere. Then a chandelier smashed to the ground in the hall past the Murder Room, shattering. 'What the hell's going on?' said Frankie, trembling. She looked over at Harrington. 'Keith?'

'Lyle,' Harrington said. 'How many rooms have you got covered with static cameras and temperature sensors?'

'Eleven,' he said.

'What about the tunnels?'

'Nothing down there so far camera-wise, but we've got temperature sensors and movement sensors fixed up.'

'The tunnels?' asked Nightingale.

Harrington nodded. 'There's a series of underground tunnels beneath us that connect the buildings. We've got to check them out freehand. We'll have infrared body cameras.'

A loud rumble shook the floor like an earthquake. One of the floodlights toppled over and crashed on the ground, sending half the room into darkness. 'Camilla, come on! Tape them down!' shouted Harrington.

'Okay, okay!' Camilla quickly went about taping the remaining two floodlights, securing them to the floor. All around them things were smashing as disembodied voices howled and moaned. Lyle stared at one of the monitors. 'Guys, I'm seeing activity here!'

'Where?' asked Harrington.

'Everywhere! All the sensors are kicking off!'

On the monitors, furniture hovered in midair, then crashed into the walls, getting stuck or falling to the floor, then rising again. Doors opened and closed so hard that wood was splintering – they seemed to have a mind of their own, slamming unnaturally with lightning speed. Dark shadows moved across the hallways and disappeared. The Murder Room's lights flickered.

'We need to start recording now,' said Harrington. 'Come on Harvey, on me, now.'

Harvey leveled a camcorder at Harrington and counted down with his fingers. Three, two, one. Harrington took a breath and began speaking to the camera. 'We're here in Wentworth Asylum, where already paranormal activity has been picking up...' he stopped short as a powerful roar echoed up the stairwell. 'As you can see... and hear... tonight's show is going to be unlike anything you've ever seen before.' A metal gurney rose up from the stairwell, hanging in the air. 'Harvey, get that! Get that!' The camera focused on the gurney, which stayed suspended, slowly turning on its left side, then its right. The crew watched nervously, ready to duck at a moment's notice. But the gurney simply went into free fall, bouncing down the stairs far below. But then a chair came out of nowhere and sailed through the air as fast as a bullet, heading for Harrington. It missed him by inches, slammed against a wall and fell to the ground.

When the camera refocused on Harrington, his face had paled. 'We're going to exorcise Wentworth Asylum with the help of Father Bailey, Camilla, Ben, Harvey, Lyle, Frankie and myself. Pray for us, viewers, and prepare to see the truth.' He took a breath and then continued. 'While we investigate what is happening here, my assistant Rachel Wood is in the hospital with one of the survivors of a recent attack here that left two young people dead, apparently attacked with an axe. The question we need answered is whether Susan Grimes is responsible for this.' He looked around, then shouted at the top of his voice. 'Susan Grimes, are you there? Can you hear me? If you can hear me, show yourself!'

There was banging and crashing in the stairwell, but no reply.

'It's going crazy down in the tunnels!' shouted Lyle.

'We'll go down there then,' said Harrington. 'Someone fix up Jack with a camera.'

'I'm not being photographed,' said Nightingale.

'It's a body-cam. It'll show us what you see and because it's infrared it'll pick up stuff that's invisible to your eyes.'

Camilla jogged over to Nightingale and clipped a small camera to his jacket, then ran a wire to a transmitter and battery pack that she slipped into his pocket. 'Good to go,' she said.

'I've got the feed,' said Lyle.

'Ben, you take Camilla and Harvey through the wards.'

'Okay.'

'Lyle and Frankie, you stay here and manage the feed.'

'But I want to go with you,' said Frankie.

Nightingale stepped forward. 'No, you were the first one that attracted activity,' he said. 'Best you don't move around.'

'He's right, Frankie,' said Harrington. 'You stay here with Lyle. All right. We're ready. Turn on your feeds.' They felt the cameras at their chests and switched them on. They put in wireless ear buds, connecting everyone on a shared communication network. 'One hour, guys,' said Harrington. 'You get injured, come back here to the salt circle and hang tight. You ready?'

The team nodded.

'Let's go.'

* * *

Rachel Wood stared at her screen. She was getting a feed from the infrared camera on Harrington's chest and the picture was dizzying as he headed downstairs into the tunnel system that ran between the asylum buildings. She didn't like what was happening, and wished they would call the whole thing off.

She could hear the priest muttering in what she guessed was Latin, and there were bangs and crashes off in the distance.

'Oh no, oh no, oh no,' said Ronnie from the bed behind her.

'Don't worry, Ronnie, they'll be fine,' she said.

'Oh no, oh no, oh no,' he repeated, louder this time.

Wood twisted around, about to reassure him, when she saw the figure in the far corner of the room, advancing towards Ronnie with an axe held high. Ronnie had his arms up to protect himself but flesh and bone would be no match for the heavy axe.

It was a woman, her dark hair hanging over her face, wearing a grey stained and torn hospital gown. Her feet were dirty, her toenails yellowing, and there were dozens of small scabs on her legs, like insect bites that had healed badly.

'Help me, p-p-please, Rachel,' stammered Ronnie.

Rachel stood up quickly and her chair fell back and hit the tiled floor with the sound of a gunshot. The woman paid no attention to the sound but kept walking towards Ronnie, the axe above her head. Her fingernails were like talons as they gripped the handle of the axe. Her feet made soft plopping sounds as they hit the tiles.

'Rachel, p-p-please…. help m-m-me…'

Wood looked around for something to use as a weapon. The only thing she could see was a bottle of water but it was on the table on the other side of Ronnie's bed and she couldn't reach it.

'Leave him alone!' she shouted, but the woman ignored her. She raised the axe and with a grunt brought it down hard. Ronnie jerked back and the axe head buried itself into the bed where his feet had been. He was squealing now, pulling his legs up to his chest. The woman lifted the axe again. Wood grabbed her computer terminal and threw it at the woman as hard as she could. As it flew through the air it ripped its plug from the electric socket and the screen went blank. At the same moment the woman vanished, the axe along with her.

Ronnie collapsed into a sobbing heap and Wood hurried over to sit next to him. She put her arms around him and held him tightly.

A nurse opened the door and glared at Wood. 'What's going on?' she asked. 'What was that noise?'

'Nothing,' said Wood as she comforted the teenager. 'It was nothing.'

* * *

Jack Nightingale ducked just in time to miss a wooden pole that was flying towards his head. He avoided being impaled by inches. Harrington gripped his shoulder. 'That was a close one. Are you okay?'

Nightingale nodded. 'Yeah.' Father Bailey was reading from the Bible and waving prayer beads in the dank air. Suddenly his purple stole wrapped around his throat and choked him. He clutched it, gagging, but Nightingale swiftly undid the stole and removed it from his head. Father Bailey thanked him and continued reading the prayer, but Nightingale could tell from his voice that he was afraid.

They were in the tunnels now. The only light came from their flashlights. The corridor was narrow, and it was hard to breathe. The floors were made of dirt, and sometimes they passed through huge ponds of ice cold water that stank like feces. They'd lost contact with the rest of the team several minutes ago when their wireless ear buds began to burn inside their ears. They took them out and flung them in the water, cursing.

Their progress was made up of several minutes of silence, followed by total chaos. Walls shook. The ceiling splintered and caved in. Various sharp objects periodically flew at them. For whatever reason, the activity worsened the deeper they went into the tunnels. Father Bailey splashed holy water on the walls, where it steamed and bubbled as if thrown into a hot pan.

Something sloshed in the water up ahead, and they froze. A low, deep growl filled the corridor, echoing off the walls and chilling their bones. The corridor grew freezing cold. Ice crystallized over the surface of the water.

In the light of their torches they saw the figure of a woman, holding an axe above her head as she walked towards them.

Father Bailey frantically resumed his prayer. Harrington raised his crucifix and joined him. 'In the Name of the Father, the Son, and the Holy

Spirit, may the angels of Heaven be sent forth to protect us as we go forth as God's servants to do His will. Defend us O Lord from all the powers of darkness; protect us with your holy angels from the attacks of the evil ones. I come in the Name of Jesus, under His authority, under His banner, and under the protection of His Blood.'

Nightingale shook his head at the futility of it. Whatever was coming towards them, it wasn't possessed.

The priest and Harrington continued to speak, but Nightingale could hear the uncertainty in their voices. 'In the Name and by the authority of Jesus, and by the power of His Precious Blood, I hereby bind and make it known to all spirits not in the worship of God that you may no longer exercise dominion over this place! In the Name of Jesus, I command you to stop all evil activities and attacks now!'

The woman brought the axe down and the three men jumped back. It hit the dirt floor with a powerful thudding sound. 'Lyle, are you getting this?" shouted Harrington, but without his earpiece he had no way of knowing if he had been heard.

And then the figure vanished.

* * *

Ben, Camilla and Harvey had tried to ignore the wild cackles that filled the wards they passed through. But they couldn't ignore the sounds, especially not Harvey, who was coming apart at the seams. He sobbed as a horrible voice filled his head. 'Faaaaaatty. I'm talking to youuuu. Hey faaaaaaattyyyyyy. Why are you so fat, fatass? Why are you so ugly and disgusting, you big ball of meat and blood and filth! Fatty? Are you listening to me? Fatty fatty fatty! I'M TALKING TO YOU!'

Harvey sank to his knees, sobbing. Camilla had been reading from a copy of the Bible that Father Bailey had given her and dashing holy water on the walls. She stopped and knelt beside him. 'Harvey, just go back to the circle, okay?'

Harvey shook his head. He was whimpering. Pleading. 'Stop saying that. Please stop saying that!'

Camilla frowned. 'Stop saying what?' she asked. 'I was just trying to help.'

'Please stop!'

'Harvey…'

The voice in Harvey's head coaxed him to murder his friends. 'Kill them, fatty, and I'll let you live. Kill them and I won't eat your flesh. Your ugly, stinking, fatty flesh! See that piece of metal? Pick it up. Pick it up and stab her in the eye. Rip it out and watch her bleed. Fuck her! Kill her! Do it now!'

'No!'

'I said do it now!'

'NO!' Harvey jumped to his feet and took off down the ward. Ben and Camilla rushed after him. 'Harvey, wait!'

* * *

'I'm going back to the control room,' said Harrington. 'If we've lost communications they might not be getting our video feeds.'

Nightingale was staring at the ground where the axe had hit. 'Okay, sure,' he said.

'You should come with me.'

'I'm going to stay here,' said Nightingale, shining his flashlight along the floor of the tunnel.

'Father Bailey?' prompted Harrington.

'Can he stay with me?' asked Nightingale.

'Okay, whatever,' said Harrington, who turned and jogged away, his feet sounding like faces being slapped.

Nightingale shone his flashlight along the tunnel floor. There was a difference in texture, and he scraped his heel over the floor. There was a wooden hatch there, he realised. About three feet square. Close to where he'd first seen Susan Grimes. There was a metal ring set into the hatch but it had rusted and was packed with dirt and he couldn't lift it up. He stamped on it and the wood creaked. He stamped on it again, harder this time, and was rewarded with a splintering sound.

'Father, give me a hand,' he said. 'Or to be more accurate, a foot.'

The priest joined him in stamping on the hatch, which began to splinter and crack under the onslaught.

* * *

Frankie Mays looked over at Lyle Brooks. 'I'm not getting any sound, are you?'

Lyle was staring at the screens, his brow furrowed. 'I'm losing vision, too. Three of the static cameras have gone dark. I've lost Nightingale and Father Bailey.'

'What about Keith?'

'I've got his camera but no sound. He's running. I've tried talking to him but I don't think he can hear me.'

'But we're still recording, right?'

'I think so.'

Double doors burst open at the far end of the room, making them jump. It was Harvey, trembling as if he was being electrocuted. Harvey fell to his knees, gasping for breath. 'Harvey, what happened?'

'She's coming, she's behind me!' shouted Harvey. He got to his feet, started to run, but then collapsed again.

'Who's behind you?' asked Frankie.

Then the double doors burst open again. There was a woman in a stained hospital gown with long unkempt hair holding an axe above her head. Lyle and Frankie jumped to their feet.

The woman ran across the room, shrieking like a banshee, and swung the axe down on Harvey's head. It split like a ripe watermelon and brains and blood splattered across the floor. Frankie screamed, and Lyle felt his insides turn liquid as he wet himself in terror.

* * *

After a dozen or so hard kicks the hatch sagged on one side. 'Come on, nearly there!' said Nightingale. He and the priest continued to stamp down, and with each blow it splintered even more. Then it dropped free and crashed onto the floor below. Nightingale shone his flashlight through the hole. There was a small room underneath them. 'I'm going down,' he said.

'Do you think that's a good idea?' asked Father Bailey.

'It has to be done,' he said. He held out his flashlight. 'Hold this.'

Father Bailey took the flashlight and shone it through the hatch as Nightingale lowered himself down. Nightingale's feet touched the floor and he let go of the hatch. The priest gave him the flashlight. 'Would you like some Holy water?' he asked.

'No, I'm good,' said Nightingale. He shone his torch around. It was a room, barely eight feet by eight feet, the ceiling so low that he couldn't stand upright. In one corner there was a line of bones and a skull on a threadbare blanket that looked as if it had been chewed by rats. In another corner there were a dozen small skeletons of long-dead rats and mice. There were more than a dozen hospital exercise books in a pile next to a stub of a pencil.

'I need you down here, Father Bailey,' he said.

'What is it?'

'There's something you need to see,' said Nightingale.

* * *

'Please, no, don't,' begged Lyle, backing away from the terrifying figure that was moving towards him, the axe held high above his head. He couldn't see her face, it was covered by her straggly hair, but he could hear her screaming. Lyle fell over his chair and he hit the ground hard. Off to his right he could hear Frankie Mays sobbing. He tried to get up but before he could move the woman was standing over him. Lyle threw up his hands but there was nothing he could do to stop the axe head embedding itself in his face.

* * *

The priest lowered himself down the hatch. His robe caught on the hatch and ripped, but Nightingale reached up and helped him through. Father Bailey stood with his head bowed, breathing heavily as he looked around.'

'What is this place?' he asked.

'She was hiding here, all on her own,' said Nightingale. 'Sneaking out at night for food, maybe. Eating rats, insects, whatever she could find. It was probably an old storage space but she used it as a place to hide.'

'Why? Why would she do that?'

'She was crazy. Or she went crazy, while she was here. What chance did a child have growing up in here? If she wasn't crazy when she came in, she would be after a few years.'

He picked up one of the exercise books and flicked through it. It was full of childlike scribbles and attempts at writing, as if it had been done by a five-year-old. On the front of the book was SUSAN in clumsy capital letters.

He put down the book and picked up another. The writing was still in capital letters, but now they were smaller and neater. There were drawings, too. Of animals and trees and cars and boats and all the things she would never see while she was locked up.

He picked up another book. The drawings were more complex and darker. There were Satanic symbols and Latin phrases. There was mirror writing, too, still Latin but reversed. He showed it to Father Bailey, who fumbled inside his robe for a pair of reading glasses before peering at the pages. 'My God,' he whispered. 'What sick mind could possibly have written this?'

* * *

Camilla and Ben burst through the double doors and into the control room. They saw Harvey Cooper dead on the floor in front of them. Camilla covered her mouth with her hands. 'Oh no, Harvey, no.'

Ben walked across the room and saw Lyle Brooks on his back, his face an unrecognizable mess. Then he heard soft sobs coming from under one of the tables. He bent down and saw Frankie Mays, curled up and crying. 'Frankie, what happened?' he said.

She opened her eyes and looked at him. Her mouth moved soundlessly.

'What happened?' he repeated. 'Who did this?'

Her eyes widened. 'Behind you,' she whispered.

'What? What did you say?'

'Behind you!' she screamed.

Ben turned just in time to see the axe cutting through the air. It hit him square on the top of the skull and split it in half. He was dead before his body hit the ground. Under the table, Frankie began to sob again.

* * *

Father Bailey looked at Nightingale over the top of his reading glasses. 'This is Satanism, devil-worship,' he said.

'Yes, I know,' said Nightingale.

'But if she was in this asylum for her whole life, how could she have learned about these symbols? And the Latin. How could she have learned Latin, or learned how to write in mirror-writing?'

'Someone showed her,' said Nightingale. 'Or something.'

'I don't understand,' said Father Bailey, closing the exercise book. 'What do you think happened?'

'I think she was visited,' said Nightingale. 'Or she invited something in.'

'Something?'

'A demon. An entity. Something took over her.'

'So she was possessed?'

Nightingale shook his head. 'It's not possession when they are invited in. Whatever it was took over her body with her consent.' He took the book from the priest and showed him the Satanic symbols and the writing. 'There is no way she could have known how to do this. Something did it for her.'

The priest looked down at the bones. 'But she died, right?'

Nightingale nodded. 'Looks like it.'

'Poor child.'

'Well, to be honest, from the look of the bones I would say she was an adult when she finally died. I'm guessing that whatever took over her body had a long run. And when she died, it was able to continue on without her. What's out there isn't Susan Grimes. It's something else.'

Nightingale piled the books on the floor, took out his Zippo and set fire to them. He straightened up and then pointed at the bones.

'You need to douse them with Holy water. And say the prayer of exorcism.'

'You keep saying this isn't possession.'

'It isn't. But it was. And I think the bones are the key. So long as the bones are here and intact, the demon can roam the earth. Can you do it?'

'Of course,' said Father Bailey. He sprinkled Holy water on the bones, then began to recite the exorcism prayer from memory as the room filled with smoke from the burning books. 'In the Name of Jesus Christ, our God and Lord, strengthened by the intercession of the Immaculate Virgin Mary, Mother of God, of Blessed Michael the Archangel, of the Blessed Apostles Peter and Paul and all the Saints, and powerful in the holy authority of our ministry, we confidently undertake to repulse the attacks and deceits of the devil. God arises; His enemies are scattered and those who hate Him flee before Him. As smoke is driven away, so are they driven; as wax melts before the fire, so the wicked perish at the presence of God.'

He sprinkled more Holy water on the bones and they began to sizzle and fizz.

* * *

Harrington staggered into the control room and gasped when he saw the devastation there. All the monitors had been smashed and the tables and chairs had been scattered around like unwanted tours. There was blood everywhere and he bit down on his lower lip as he saw Harvey's bloodstained corpse. He staggered forward and gasped when he saw what remained of Camilla. Her arms had been chopped off and blood was still trickling from the wounds. Her eyes were wide open and stared sightlessly.

* * *

The prayer went on for a full two minutes, and after each verse Father Bailey sprinkled more Holy water on the bones

The end of the prayer required Nightingale to join in, and like the priest he said the words from memory.

'From the snares of the devil,' said the priest.

'Deliver us, O Lord,' said Nightingale.

'That Thy Church may serve Thee in peace and liberty.'

'We beseech Thee to hear us,' said Nightingale.

'That Thou may crush down all enemies of Thy Church.'

'We beseech Thee to hear us,' repeated Nightingale.

Father Bailey poured the last of the Holy water over the bones. There was a flash and a thunderous bang and then there was nothing on the blanket other than a dusting of fine powder.

'Is it done?' asked the priest.

'I hope so,' said Nightingale.

* * *

Susan Grimes – or at least the demon that had taken her form – raised its axe and brought it down towards Harrington's chest. Harrington rolled over just in time to avoid the blade and it thudded into the floor. He scrabbled backwards but the axe crashed down again, with less power this time so that when it hit his hand it made him scream in pain but didn't sever it. Harrington kicked out with his legs but missed. His chest was burning and he felt as if all the strength had seeped from his limbs. The axe went up in the air and this time he knew he was simply too tired to get out of the way. He resigned himself to a painful death, though at least it would probably be quick. 'Our Father, which art in Heaven…' he began, then suddenly there was a brilliant flash that blinded him and a faint cry from somewhere above him. He blinked to clear his eyes and when everything had come into focus again his attacker had gone and there was a strong smell of burnt flesh in the room. He sat up and looked around, unable to believe that he was still alive. He found himself looking at Frankie Mays, hiding under a table. 'What happened, Frankie?' he asked, but her eyes were blank and she didn't reply.

Suddenly the building shuddered. A chandelier crashed to the floor. Windows burst inward. Wood beams split in half and fell apart, bringing the ceiling down around him. Wentworth Asylum was destroying itself from the inside out. That was when the pain from his injured hand kicked in, as if it had been burned in oil.

'Come on, Frankie, we have to go!' he shouted.

She shook her head and curled up into a foetal ball.

'Frankie!' he shouted.

Slates and bricks were crashing around him.

'Frankie! Come on!'

A massive beam crashed down onto the table above Frankie, crushing it and her. Harrington turned and ran.

* * *

In the hovel where Nightingale had found Susan's bones, deep fissures appeared in the ceiling and walls as the room began to break apart. Nightingale felt a deep rumble beneath his feet like an earthquake. 'We have to go!' he shouted at Father Bailey, but the priest was already trying to claw his way through the hatch. Nightingale pushed him up and through and then the priest was running away down the tunnel.

The smoke from the burning books made it hard to breathe as Nightingale dragged himself up through the hatch. He got to his feet and ran as fast as he could through the dark. He burst into a long-abandoned kitchen. Everywhere he turned walls were caving in and the ceiling was showering down on him. He stopped short as a two-hundred-pound ceiling beam smashed on the ground at his feet. Shielding his eyes with his hands, he stepped over it. Glimpsing a shard of moonlight through the dust and debris, he went for it. He climbed through the window and rolled over on the ground. Stars winked in the night sky, welcoming him back to the land of the living. Not far enough, he thought. He had to get farther away.

'Nightingale! Over here!' Harrington was huddled in the center of the courtyard, clutching a mangled hand. Running full tilt, Nightingale made it to him just as the very foundation of the buildings was blown out. Wentworth Asylum came crashing down on itself in free fall, first the cafeteria, then the main building and the buildings to the right where Nightingale had come from. They watched as a monstrous debris cloud flew in the air and rained down on them, glass tinkling on the ground. To Nightingale, it sounded like the entire Earth was devouring Wentworth Asylum. The buildings settled into a huge pile of rubble, and the commotion around them stopped. Sirens were coming towards them. 'It's over, isn't it?' gasped Harrington, rolling onto his back, still clutching his injured hand.

'I hope so,' said Nightingale. He sat down heavily, pulled out his cigarettes, and lit one. 'I really hope so.'

* * *

Nightingale caught an early morning train back to New York. He was happy to leave the city behind and hoped that he would never have to return. Before he had left for the station he had watched a TV news report of the destruction of Wentworth Asylum. It had talked about a gas explosion and a fire. There was no mention of the team from The Truth Is Out There, which Nightingale figured was probably down to pressure from Joshua Wainwright. There was nothing in the two newspapers he had bought at the station – the Philadelphia Daily News and the Philadelphia Inquirer – but that was to be expected because they would have gone to press while the asylum was still burning. The big question was what would be in the papers the following day, but Nightingale would be back in New York by then.

His phone rang. It was Wainwright. Nightingale answered. 'Well, that worked out quite well, didn't it?' said Wainwright.

'Define "well" for me,' said Nightingale.

'No live transmission for a start. And nothing in the way of recorded material, from what I understand. It was all destroyed in the fire.''

'A lot of people died, Joshua.'

'Well, yes, there is that. But then, looking on the bright side, that leaves fewer witnesses, doesn't it.'

'Every cloud,' said Nightingale.

'You sound depressed.'

'I've been to Hell and back,' said Nightingale.

'Yes, but not literally. A few days R&R and you'll be fine. Go crazy with my credit card, my treat.'

'How's Keith?'

'Not good, I'm afraid. He was a sceptic for so long and now…'

'He's a believer?'

'It shocked him to the core. He's going to need a lot of therapy.'

'And I'm sure you'll get it for him.'

'He's being taken care of as we speak,' said Wainwright. 'He's being looked after in a nice little sanitarium outside Cleveland. He'll be fine.'

'You're all heart, Joshua. What about the priest? Father Bailey? Last time I saw him he was running for his life.'

'He didn't make it out, I'm afraid. I guess his boss had his attention elsewhere.'

Wainwright chuckled and ended the call. Nightingale took out his cigarettes but the frosty look from the matronly woman sitting opposite him was a reminder that smoking wasn't allowed on trains. Or pretty much anywhere in the US of A. He put the cigarettes away, closed his eyes, and tried to get some sleep.

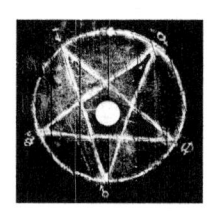

THE DOLL

Jack Nightingale had hardly had a moment's rest since coming to America. Busy, busy busy. Joshua Wainwright was always calling him away on new cases – Florida, San Francisco, North Carolina, Boston. But Wainwright had said he was going to be out of the country for a couple of weeks and that he wouldn't be needing Nightingale for a while. Finally, Nightingale could do what he wanted, go where he wanted – and it just so happened he wanted to go on a paranormal tour of the East Coast. He thought since America was to be his adopted home, he might as well make the best of it and he could think of no better way to acquaint himself with the paranormal workings he was to investigate than to see them firsthand.

He rented a Dodge Charger and drove to the south shore of Long Island, where he watched the Amityville Horror house from his car while parked outside 112 Ocean Avenue. The house had been the site of a grisly mass-murder in 1974, when a troubled young man named Ronald DeFeo had used a .35 caliber rifle to murder his entire family while they slept. He shot his mother, father, two brothers and two sisters, claiming he'd heard voices in his head telling him to do it. The next year George and Kathleen Lutz moved into the Dutch Colonial with their dog and Kathleen's three children from a previous marriage. The Lutz family fled the house after only twenty-eight days, claiming to have been plagued by malicious paranormal phenomena, including that of a demonic pig-like creature with glowing red eyes.

Sitting in his Charger and smoking a cigarette while the rain came down on the windshield, Nightingale saw nothing out of the ordinary, nor did he expect to. The current homeowners said they'd encountered no paranormal phenomena since moving into the house ten years ago. But he was glad to see the site of one of the best horror legends in North America.

Next he drove three hours in the rain along I-95 to Clinton Road, New Jersey, the most haunted road in America and also the road with the country's longest traffic-light wait at five minutes, which Nightingale experienced firsthand around three that afternoon. He smoked a cigarette while he waited, flicking ash out the window. The autumn rain had let up and the sky was grey and overcast. Thin pockets of sunlight fell through the clouds and illuminated patches of road, a two-lane highway bordered by trees growing so close he could reach out the window and touch the foliage. He was going to Gettysburg Battlefield in Pennsylvania, the Bell Witch Cave in Tennessee, the haunted Myrtles Plantation in Louisiana and ultimately the St Augustine Lighthouse in Florida. What better way to cap his road trip than to travel to a haunted lighthouse in the tropics?

He frowned as he realised he'd been at the lights for at least five minutes. He checked his watch: 3:07 p.m. He was hoping to reach Gettysburg just before nightfall, where he would stay in a tavern and visit the infamous battlefield by moonlight. He tapped his fingers impatiently on the steering wheel. It was three and a half hours' drive to Gettysburg, so he'd better leave soon.

Another minute passed. The lights stayed on red.

'All right,' he muttered. 'This is bollocks.' He flicked his cigarette out the window and hit the accelerator. Immediately he had to slam on the brakes as a motorbike careened out of the woods, almost colliding with his car, and sped past him. The driver, wearing tight black leathers and a black helmet with the tinted visor pulled down, tossed a bulky trash bag in the road before accelerating away.

'What the hell's going on?' muttered Nightingale. He was breathing hard. He realised there was a narrow woods path to his left disappearing into the dark of the forest. The motorbike must have been waiting there, but waiting for what? For the lights to change? Nightingale let the car idle as he eyed the plastic trash bag in front of his car. What came to mind was something he'd read about Clinton Road, that it was a dumping ground for serial killers. Curiosity got the better of him. He put the car in park and got out. Kneeling on the ground, he rummaged around the bag in search of the opening, found it and opened it wide. As he saw what was inside he jumped backward and yelped.

Staring up at him from the bag were two black, soulless eyes. As he looked more closely, he could see who they belonged to: a small porcelain doll in a faded white dress with a black button in the center. A tangled mop of dark hair fell down her shoulders, and her cheeks were blushing pink. The doll was in a sitting position in the bag, as if it had righted itself when it landed. He'd seen dolls like that before. Old Russian dolls in antique stores from the late 19th century. They were quite valuable. Why then was someone trying to get rid of it?

He put the doll back in the bag and set it on the side of the road in case the motorbike driver decided to come back for it. Then he got into his car and prepared to drive off, but a quick movement in the bushes to his right stopped him. Something had just run into the trees. He got out of the car and stood, waiting. A little girl was giggling in the woods.

'All right,' he said, quite loudly. 'Whoever's there, come out now.'

The giggles came again, spritely and childlike, and he could hear tiny feet pattering the wet leaves and kicking through the underbrush as they went deeper into the woods. He went in after her, the forest dreary and silent. Bright maroon and yellow leaves were still wet from the rain, dripping into his hair. The air smelled fragrant of earth and pine needles. He glimpsed movement in a copse of trees up ahead and thought he could just barely make out a small dark head darting under a tree branch, then disappearing.

'Hey, kid!' he shouted. 'Are you lost? Wait! Come here!'

No answer. Sighing heavily, he ran several paces and stopped. Sitting upright against a tree was another doll. It looked identical to the first one. 'You've got to be joking,' he muttered, facing the woods. 'Hey! Where'd you go?' he called out. 'You left your doll behind!'

There was no movement in the trees. An eerie silence fell over the forest and all he could hear was his own heavy breathing and the gentle patter of raindrops. 'Is anybody out there!' his voice echoed in the forest, coming back to him. When there was no reply he took a deep breath. 'Fine. I'm calling the police!' It was an empty threat, he knew. He doubted the police would be interested in a doll in the road and an unseen kid in the woods. He wasn't even sure there had been a kid.

He reached for the doll but suddenly felt a chill crawl up his spine, as if he was being watched. He shivered and picked up the doll. It had hardly any weight and looked quite worn and old. Its eyes were dark, very dark, and its porcelain face was dirty and cracked in places. Why would some kid drop a doll and take off into the woods like that?

Shaking his head, he made his way back to the road, planning to set the doll on the roadside next to the other in case the owner decided to come back for it, but Nightingale stopped in his tracks. The doll that had been in the road was gone, the plastic bag splayed open, revealing nothing. A horrible thought occurred to him: that the doll he was holding was in fact the same doll that had been in the bag; it had got up and run into the woods, giggling all the while. And now he was holding it. In his hands. He shook his head. No, he thought. Not possible. He tossed the doll on the roadside where it fell in a knotted heap. Then he got in his car and drove away.

Smoking as he drove the next several miles down Clinton Road, Nightingale couldn't shake off the feeling that he was being watched. His thoughts kept coming back to the doll, which had given him the creeps, but he didn't know why. Who had tossed it there in the road, and why? And who had run into the woods? If it had been a little girl, he'd seen no footprints or anything to show that she had been there. Just the doll.

Maybe it was all his imagination. Not the doll, obviously. The doll had been real enough. But maybe the running kid was just his mind playing tricks on him. It had happened on Clinton Road, so maybe that was what had spooked him. He'd heard stories of Clinton Road. Legends of ghosts, satanic murders, witches, and bizarre creatures. People strongly warned against traveling the road at night. There were bizarre disappearances, reports of strange lights, even 'The Iceman' Richard Kuklinski, the infamous mob hitman and serial killer, had used Clinton Road as a dumping ground for his victims. The murder that ultimately led to his arrest was that of a man found with ice crystals in his blood vessels, leading pathologists to the determination that the victim had been frozen, giving Kuklinski his nickname.

Four o'clock was approaching and the sun was already hanging low, though Nightingale couldn't see it because tall trees shrouded the road, casting it in perpetual darkness. A sign announcing the turnpike came into view and briefly filled Nightingale with relief. But then, coming to a small crossroads, he again felt the sensation that someone was watching him, his skin prickling around his neck, gooseflesh crawling up his arms. He glanced in the rearview. The doll was in the backseat, watching him with cold, dead eyes.

Nightingale slammed on the brakes and almost lost control of the car.

The Charger skidded, then spun as he fought to gain control over the wheel, finally coming to a stop after turning a full hundred and eighty degrees. Nightingale threw open the door and got out, ignoring a honking truck as it passed him from the other direction. He peered in the backseat. The doll was gone. He opened the door and ducked inside, inspecting the seats, the floor, everywhere – the doll wasn't there. Had it ever been there? Was his imagination playing tricks on him again?

Nightingale was sweating. He rubbed his forehead with the back of his arm and took out his packet of Marlboro. 'Bollocks,' he said, pacing nervously around the car. 'You're not mad. The doll was right there, I saw it! And now it's gone. How? What in hell is going on here?' Another car passed him from the opposite direction and he realized he was talking to himself. So what? People talked to themselves when they were alone all the time, didn't they? What did it mean, that he had fallen off his rocker and started seeing dolls? No. The doll was real, no question. He'd held it in his own two hands, although now he wished he hadn't.

It was three hours to Gettysburg, he thought. He'd better find himself a cup of coffee and try to forget the whole thing. He'd be all right, he told himself. He just had to get on the road and get to Gettysburg.

He'd be fine. That's what he told himself, anyway.

* * *

Nightingale arrived at Gettysburg's Olde Inn around 7:30 p.m. An 18th century Georgian mansion, the Olde Inn boasted a restaurant and pub on the first floor, just what Nightingale needed after such a long – and strange – journey.

He paid for his room at the front desk and was directed by a short stout lady named Martha to the suite at the end of the hall on the second floor. 'Are you Australian?' she asked, her dyed blonde hair an afro, her jowls quivering.

'British,' said Nightingale.

'Here on vacation?'

'Sort of.'

She took him to his room, which was spacious with a high ceiling crisscrossed by smooth mahogany beams. Period furniture with red and pink upholstery was packed into the room, and Nightingale nodded with approval when he saw the great bay windows with a view of Lincoln Square below, golden street lamps lighting up passersby with umbrellas in the steady rain. Across the square he could see the David Wills House where President Abraham Lincoln had signed the Gettysburg Address.

'No smoking,' said Martha, arms crossed. 'And I don't think I need to tell you that we don't want any callers in the middle of the night, of either sex. You got me?'

'Callers?'

'You know, callers. Visitors.'

'I'm not planning on having any visitors of any sex,' said Nightingale.

'Just so you know,' said Martha. 'And if you want to smoke, please do it away from the hotel entrance. Capiche?'

Nightingale fought back a laugh. Talk about small town hospitality. 'Capiche,' he said. With that Martha grunted and turned on her heels, leaving him alone in the room. The day just kept getting stranger, he thought. He unpacked his things, then went downstairs for dinner. He forsook the restaurant in favor of the bar, where he ordered a Corona and fish and chips. Martha was prowling the restaurant with a permanent scowl on her face, dropping dishes in front of patrons so hard that food bounced off the plates and landed on the table linen. She didn't stick around to apologize or help clean it up, either. Nightingale figured she was having a bad day. Or maybe a bad life.

Nightingale sipped his Corona and went through the events of the day. The Amityville Horror house, looking regal and majestic on Ocean Avenue, was now just another neighborhood McMansion with a Lincoln parked in the driveway. And then Clinton Road. Now that was the real terror. That was what really set his mind reeling. What happened back there was bizarre. He'd never experienced anything like it before, nor did he want to again. One drive along Clinton Road was enough for him, he decided. He was definitely not going back.

The door to the restaurant opened, interrupting his thoughts, and an attractive dark-haired woman dressed in motorcycle leathers came into the room. Her face was oval and her eyes were narrow and serious, as though she were on a mission and knew exactly what the outcome would be. Her skin was porcelain smooth and pale, making her dark eyes stand out austere and beautiful in the solemn face. She moved gracefully, almost sensually, her leather pants creaking as she took a seat next to Nightingale and asked for a bourbon.

Nightingale didn't believe in coincidences. He hadn't believed in them when he'd worked as a cop, and he believed in them even less now that he worked for Joshua Wainwright. Things generally happened for a reason. So he wasn't prepared to believe that it was a coincidence that only hours after meeting a motorcyclist on Clinton Road a motorcyclist would sit next to him in a hotel restaurant. She was carrying a black full-face crash helmet. Nightingale's memory wasn't great at the best of times and the motorcyclist he'd met on the road had sped away so quickly that he hadn't gotten a good look at him. Or her. And he couldn't remember what colour the helmet was. So maybe this was a totally different motorcyclist. Maybe. But then that would have been a coincidence, and he didn't believe in coincidences.

The bartender, a gruff man with a potbelly under a black shirt and the tattoo of a snake coiling up his neck, set down her bourbon without a word. The woman brought it to her pink lips and downed it without wincing, then pushed the shot glass forward and asked for another.

'Long day?' quipped Nightingale. He'd been picking at his chips after finishing his meal; now he pushed the plate aside and drank the rest of his

Corona, which had turned warm.

'You could say that,' she said without looking at him. 'What about you? Long day, or do you always drink alone?'

'I tend to drink alone,' said Nightingale, 'and it just so happens I've had a long day as well.'

She turned to look at him for the first time. 'English?'

'Yes ma'am.'

She was really quite beautiful. Dark hazel eyes, he saw, full pink lips slightly upturned, unblemished skin with tiny brown freckles on her cheeks and chin. 'How so?' she asked.

'How so I'm English?'

'How so you've had a long day.'

What came to mind was the doll, but Nightingale smiled. 'I've been on the road all day. I'm on a road trip of sorts. Acquainting myself with haunted America, so to speak.' He waved at the barman for a fresh Corona.

'Ah,' she said, the hint of a smile on her lips, 'so I guess I don't need to ask what brings you here to Gettysburg.'

'Only the most haunted battlefield in the world,' he said, grinning. 'Hey, I didn't catch your name.'

'I didn't give it.' She sipped her bourbon.

'Well, I'm Nightingale. Jack Nightingale.' He offered his hand and she took it.

'Sandra White.'

'And you're a biker?'

'What gave it away?' she said, and laughed. 'Yes, I'm a biker.'

The barman returned with a bottle of Corona and a slice of lime stuck into the neck.

'What's with that?' asked the woman. 'The lemon?'

'It's a lime.'

'So what's with the lime?'

'It keeps the flies away.'

'Say what?'

Nightingale grinned. 'That's what they say. It's a Mexican beer and it's hot in Mexico and there are a lot of flies. Flies don't like limes so if you stick a piece of lime in the neck it keeps the flies away.' He pushed the piece of lime down into the bottle with his finger. 'That might be apocryphal. Anyway, it tastes good.' He raised the bottle and took a drink. 'And what brings you to these 'ere parts, miss Sandra?' he said in a fair imitation of a southern drawl, causing her to raise her eyebrows.

She looked over her shoulder, then back at him. 'I have my reasons,' she said. 'Besides, we just met, and I don't normally talk to strangers.'

'Never understood the logic in that. We were all strangers at one time or another. If you follow that philosophy you'll end up a hermit in the woods.'

Sandra cracked a smile. 'Good point. So tell me, Mr Nightingale, since we're not strangers anymore, why is it you're so interested in exploring "haunted America?" What's the attraction?'

Nightingale shrugged. 'Just a hobby of mine.'

'Seems like a pretty weird hobby to me. It's not like collecting baseball cards.'

She drained her glass and waved for another bourbon. The unsmiling barman refilled it for her.

'Do you want to play a game, Nightingale?'

'I see we're on last name terms already,' said Nightingale.

'Well, do you?'

Nightingale shrugged. 'Depends on what you have in mind.'

'All right, how about this, I'll tell you something weird about me and you tell me something weird about you. Deal?'

Nightingale thought for a moment. 'Sure,' he said. 'Fire away.'

Sandra scooted her stool closer to Nightingale and leaned in close. She looked around conspiratorially, then whispered, 'I'm being haunted by a demon.'

Nightingale choked on his beer. From across the room, Martha gave him a sour look as if to suggest that bad manners were a product of the English. He cleared his throat. 'Sorry. I thought you said you were being haunted by a demon.'

Sandra's expression didn't change. 'I did. What's the matter, you don't believe me?'

Nightingale was now sure that her sitting next to him hadn't been a coincidence. She was there for a reason. 'Are you putting me on?' he asked.

'No.'

'It's not funny. Saying stuff like that. It's not funny at all.'

'Of course it's not funny. I'm not trying to be funny. I'm telling you the truth. I think something horrible has been haunting me for some time now, something demonic, but not anymore. At least… not as of today.'

'What are you talking about?' asked Nightingale, though deep down he already knew.

'Haven't you been listening to me?'

'Yes, but I feel you're not telling me the whole story.' What had started as a playful exchange had grown deadly serious, and Nightingale didn't like the transition.

Sandra looked sad, even crestfallen. 'I'm sorry, I thought I could talk about it but now I'm not sure I can. That's weird enough though, right?'

Nightingale nodded. 'Hell, yeah.'

'Your turn,' she said. 'Tell me something weird about you. Or about something weird that's happened to you.'

He shrugged. 'To be honest, nothing weird has ever happened to me,' he lied. 'I suppose what I'm doing now might seem weird to some people. I grew up watching horror movies in England and now that I've relocated to America I want to check out some of those places. The Amityville Horror house, for one. And now the Gettysburg Battlefield. They're just fascinating to me. The mystery. Is that weird?'

'No, not really. So you were in Long Island, then. Was that today?'

'Yeah.' He motioned the bartender for the check. 'And then you drove all the way here?'

'That's right.' He was pretty sure that she already knew that. She was playing him, but he wasn't sure why.

The bartender printed the check and set it down on the table in front of them. Nightingale paid for them both and left the bartender a generous tip for not having butted in during their bizarre conversation.

'See anything weird along the way?' prodded Sandra. She was staring at him now, and Nightingale decided he didn't like the look in her eye at all. For whatever reason, he felt like he was being interrogated. This was no longer a game, and now he just wanted to leave.

'No,' he lied. 'Not a thing.' He stood up. 'Sandra, it's been a real pleasure. Maybe I'll catch you again tomorrow?' He left without waiting for an answer, and all the way to the door he could feel her eyes burning into his back.

* * *

Nightingale decided he'd visit Gettysburg Battlefield in the morning instead of at night when it was dark and gloomy and the moon was hidden behind clouds. He was dog-tired, and it had been a long and eventful day. He needed his rest. At the door to his room he fished in his pockets for the key, found it, and unlocked the door. He immediately wished he'd gone to see the battlefield instead, because what he saw in front of him paralysed him with dread: sitting upright in his bed, past all the wreckage of his ransacked room, was the doll. All around were tattered pillows, slashed walls with gouges taken out, broken lamps, torn sheets and what looked like blood puddled on the wooden floor. The doll, completely still at first, now slowly turned its head toward Nightingale in the doorway, opened its mouth, and let out a high-pitched child's giggle. 'Ashes, ashes, we all fall down!'

Portraits and paintings crashed to the floor and Nightingale fell backward against the wall. From the stairs, Martha chuckled. 'What's the matter? Had too much to drink?'

'Come here!' said Nightingale. 'Someone's... someone's broken into my room!'

'Oh, nonsense,' said Martha, stomping to the door. She gasped, then fixed Nightingale with a poisonous glare. 'You sick son of a bitch.'

'It wasn't me! Someone broke into my room!'

'Tell it to the police,' she said, taking out her cell phone.

'I didn't do this!'

'No? Who did, then, since you're the only one with the key?'

'You've got a key, right? The hotel must have a spare.'

'You think I'd do this? You're crazy.' She took the phone away from her face. 'Now we can do this one of two ways. I can call the police, have you taken to the station and sue the balls off you, or we can settle up right now.'

'Settle up?'

'Uh huh. I'd say five grand ought to do it.'

'You're joking.'

She waved her cell phone in front of his face. 'Do I look like I'm joking, smartass?' Nightingale said nothing. Martha went on, 'So what's it gonna be?'

Nightingale wrote her a check for five thousand dollars. She let him pack up his belongings, including the doll, and leave, warning him that if he ever showed his face at the Olde Inn again, there'd be trouble.

He clutched the doll firmly by the neck. He tossed his stuff in the Charger and walked in the rain toward the woods. When he was deep enough in the woods that he couldn't see any light from town, he went about digging a hole with his hands, scraping away sodden leaves, damp earth and mud until he cut the tips of his fingers on the cold granite rocks beneath the first layer. He was soaking wet now and his hands were bleeding, but he didn't care. He would not be beaten. Not by a doll.

When the hole was deep enough he threw the doll into it, said an exorcism prayer and covered her with heavy stones. Then he piled the earth back over it, stamped on it and rolled a large stone over the top.

Nightingale left the woods and checked into a hotel across the street from the Olde Inn. The proprietor eyed his bloody hands suspiciously but said nothing. Nightingale fell onto his soft bed and went to sleep.

* * *

Horrible nightmares plagued Nightingale all through the night. He dreamed of the doll sitting on his chest while he watched helplessly, paralysed by an unseen force, as it wrapped its tiny porcelain fingers around his throat and began to squeeze. It giggled madly while his eyes popped out of his skull and he fought to gain control over his body. He woke up gasping, clutching his throat, which felt bruised and sore. Looking down at his chest, he saw three long claw marks cut deep in his flesh. He rolled out of bed and searched the room for any sign of intrusion, for any sign of the doll, but there was none. An ambulance siren called his attention to the window. He looked out and saw an ambulance pull up behind two police cars parked outside the Olde Inn. He threw on some clothes and went to find out what had happened.

The potbellied bartender and several other staff stood outside forlornly, some of them crying, some of them covering their mouths and slowly shaking their heads while a stretcher was wheeled down the steps of the Olde Inn. The body on the stretcher was covered by a white sheet. Blood had stained the top of the sheet. The bartender swore when he saw the blood.

'What happened?' asked Nightingale.

'I can't believe it.'

'What?'

'Martha, man, she's dead. I just can't believe it. I mean, I know the old bat was a pain in the ass, but still. She wasn't too bad. And now she's gone? Just yesterday I caught her bitching out a customer like any old Saturday night. It's just so surreal.'

'What happened to her?' asked Nightingale. The stretcher was loaded onto the ambulance and pushed inside. A solemn-faced EMT closed the double doors.

'She lost her head, man,' said the bartender, scratching his sideburns. 'I mean literally. Her head was ripped off. Can you believe it? Lost her fucking head, man. No sign of forced entry. Her door was locked from the inside. Jacky, one of the morning servers, went to see if she was okay because Martha's always the first one up and about, getting work done. Say what you want about her attitude but the woman never missed a day of work in her life. Anyway, Jacky knocked on the door real quiet and waited for a response. Nothing. Knocked harder. Still nothing. She had to go get Earl and have him use the spare key to open the door. And you know what they found?'

Nightingale shook his head, though by then he had worked it out.

'Martha in her white evening gown, sitting on the bed like she was waiting for her morning tea or something, only her head was gone – cut clean off. Can you fucking believe that, man? I feel like we're in the twilight zone right now.'

Nightingale stepped back, feeling sweat break out on his forehead. She was sitting upright, he thought, just like the doll. Sitting upright on the bed. He had to get out of there. He had to get out of there fast.

'Hey, man, you okay?' asked the bartender. 'You look like you're in shock or something.'

'I am.'

'Well,' said the bartender. 'Join the club, I guess.'

* * *

Nightingale entered the woods holding his rosary beads tight in his hand. He retraced his steps from last night and came back to the place where he had buried the doll. In his pocket was his old battered Zippo and in his coat was a small bottle of lighter fluid he had picked up at the store on his way there. He was going to burn the damned thing and send its wicked soul back to hell.

He found the large rock marking its makeshift grave and rolled it off, then took a fat stick and used it to dig. It didn't take long to reach the stones he'd placed over the doll. Maybe it was a fluke, he thought with a fleeting hope. Maybe the doll had nothing whatsoever to do with Martha's death. Maybe someone, a sadistic patron with a grudge, perhaps, had climbed into her window late last night and cut off her head. Maybe that's all it was. Maybe it was a coincidence.

But it wasn't.

Because Nightingale's stick suddenly struck something fleshy and hard, and when he picked out some of the rocks he almost threw up from revulsion: he had just come face to face with Martha's severed head. Her mouth was agape, her eyes wide and bloodshot.

* * *

Nightingale didn't wait around to be questioned. He was the lone Englishman who'd been kicked out of the establishment for trashing his room, and he'd had to pay Martha five grand to keep her from calling the cops. It would be easy enough to believe that he had gone back to the hotel to get his check and had killed Martha in the process. Nightingale was sweating as he walked to his car, trying to look unassuming. As soon as he got into the car, Nightingale took out a packet of Marlboro, his hands shaking. He slid a cigarette between his lips and lit it. Nightingale exhaled a plume of smoke and closed his eyes. When he opened them, more people were milling about the Olde Inn up the street. Leaning against a motorcycle was Sandra. She was watching him.

He waved at her and she walked towards his car. She looked frightened. He rolled down his window when she approached. 'Get in,' he ordered.

She seemed confused. 'My bike, it's just over there…'

'I don't care where the hell your bike is, I said get in.'

Sandra nodded and got into the passenger side of the car. Nightingale started the engine and drove silently onto the street. Many eyes were on him now. Questioning eyes. He drove slowly down the road, passing the Olde Inn and all its confused bystanders, some of them pointing fingers at him as he passed.

'Where are you taking me?' asked Sandra quietly.

'I don't know yet,' he said. 'But first you're going to tell me why you threw that doll in front of my car. Then you're going to tell me where I can find it.'

* * *

They were driving through the woods now, away from Gettysburg. The sky was already darkening with the threat of rain. The road was narrow and flanked by trees. No cars had passed them from either direction for several minutes.

'I didn't know it would turn out like this,' said Sandra.

'You must have known something like this would happen.'

'I just wanted it away from me. Off my back.'

'And what, you chose me at random?'

Sandra nodded. 'I'm sorry.'

'What were you thinking? What if I'd been a single mother with two children?'

Sandra shook her head. 'No,' she said. 'No way. I'd never do that.'

'But you'd do it to me, a stranger you'd never even met. For someone who says she doesn't even talk to strangers I find it bloody weird that you're so eager to put a curse on them.'

'It wasn't like that!' she cried. 'I didn't know what would happen. I just didn't know what to do anymore. I thought maybe if I put it by someone else, someone stronger than me, more capable, maybe then the doll would leave me alone.'

'That's a shitty thing to do to anyone, Sandra.'

'I was at my wit's end. I didn't know what else to do.'

Nightingale shook his head. 'There's more to it, isn't there? You didn't just drop the doll and ride off into the sunset, did you? You came to the Olde Inn and started asking me those questions. You wanted me to spill the beans and admit that the doll had started haunting me, is that it? So that you would know you were in the clear? That was why you went through all that palaver of asking me if anything weird had happened.'

'Sort of, but I was going to help you. If you'd told me it was haunting you I'd have fessed up and told you everything. But you didn't.'

'Of course not! I'd sound like a crazy person!'

She smiled thinly. 'Maybe we're both crazy.' She sighed. 'Anyway, you said nothing about it so I figured maybe you just drove around it, hell, maybe you ran over it, and nothing happened. Maybe someone else picked it up. Maybe a truck ran over it and destroyed it. I didn't care. I just thought the doll was gone for good.' She bit down on her lower lip. 'And then Martha died.'

'She didn't just die, Sandra. Someone – or something – cut her head off. What is that doll? Where the hell did it come from? How did you get it? Give me answers, Sandra. You owe me that, at least.'

She sighed and wiped a tear from her eye. 'My grandmother brought it home with her about six months ago. I live with her and my mother, at least... I did. They're dead now. Anyway, my grandmother said she bought it at an antique shop in New Jersey. You should have seen the way she talked about the wretched thing. Her eyes were all glazed over and she looked, I don't know, crazy. She began taking the doll everywhere with her. To the grocery store, on her walks, she kept it in bed at night. My mom and I thought it was bizarre, that maybe gran was finally losing it. But then we started finding blood on the floor with no indication of how it got there. We started seeing scratches on the walls and I began having horrible nightmares and waking up with scratches on my chest. Pretty soon my mom and I couldn't sleep. I looked up the antique shop and discovered that on the same day my gran said she picked up the doll, the owner suddenly got sick and two kids who'd visited the shop died in a car crash on their way home. This was on the very same day she brought it home with her.'

Nightingale rubbed the bridge of his nose. 'Your mum and your grandmother, you said they're dead. Did the doll…'

'Yes,' said Sandra, looking away. 'It killed them both. Murdered them. First my gran woke up one day with her eyes all bloodshot and crazy, muttering nothing but, "She's come to take me home, she's come to take me home," then she slipped out of the house at the first opportunity and walked straight into the freeway. They said it was an accident, that she'd forgotten to take her medication or something, but I knew better. Not long afterward I found my mom in the bathtub with her wrists slashed to the bone. My mom never had a suicidal thought in her life, yet there she was. Dead.'

'Shit,' said Nightingale. 'I'm sorry.'

'Then it came for me. The doll would disappear and reappear in strange places. I would hear it running around the house at night. I'd find dead cats and birds on my doorstep, their entrails cut out, and bloody kitchen knives in the sink. I was terrified.'

'Did you go to a priest?'

'Of course I did. I went to several.'

'And?'

'And they said I must be grieving over the deaths of my family, then they recommended I see a psychiatrist.'

'I'm sorry. But you can see why they might not believe you.'

'Jack, I didn't want to shove this burden onto somebody else. I just wanted to see what would happen. Selfishly, yes, I wanted someone else to be in this with me. I didn't want to be on my own anymore. I just wanted their help. Your help. Anyone's help. I just couldn't deal with it on my own anymore.'

'Did you try to destroy it? Burn it?'

'More times than I can count. I doused it with gas and tried to set it on fire. It wouldn't light. I weighted it down with rocks and tossed it into the river. It came back. And always when it came back, it came back with a vengeance. It would punish me, try to kill me but stop at the last second.'

'What do you mean?'

'I mean it would choke me until I passed out but stop just in time to let me live. I mean it would throw me around the house until I couldn't move anymore.'

'I'm sorry, I don't mean to sound rude, but—'

'But it's a tiny little doll, so how could it hurt me, a grown woman, right?'

Nightingale nodded.

'I don't know how but it's impossibly strong, stronger than any man I've ever met. It's like there's some massive force behind it, some ten-foot-tall monster exercising its strength through the doll.'

'You're probably a lot closer to the mark than you think.'

She frowned. 'What do you mean?'

He waved away the question.

'Did you ever find out its history?'

She looked at him. 'No.'

'Well, I guess we're going to New Jersey.'

She reached over to touch his arm. 'You're going to help me?'

'I haven't got much choice, have I?'
'Of course you do.'
'No,' he said. 'I don't.'

* * *

Night fell. With it came the rain, huge torrential sheets of it that smashed the windshield so violently Nightingale worried it would cave in on them. They passed very few cars on the road, seemingly delving deeper and deeper into a monstrous forest with no end in sight. There were no houses, no shops, no gas stations, no cars lining the road. The lack of human habitation unsettled him. He flicked on the high beams and glanced over at Sandra, huddled in her seat and looking out the window at the wash of trees and yellow fields drifting by.

Nightingale figured he might as well get a conversation going, to pass the time if nothing else. 'Got a boyfriend?' he asked.

'I had one,' she said. 'But he left.'

'How come?'

'Ever the gentleman, aren't you Nightingale? But seeing as you're so nosy, my ex left because he thought I was going insane.'

'The doll?'

'Yes, the doll.'

'You know, I got the feeling the doll was trying to set me up for Martha's murder.'

'I'm sure it was.'

'Anyway, I was just wondering because…' He stopped, sitting up in his seat and leaning forward to peer through the windshield.

'What is it?'

'A car,' he said hesitantly. 'It's driving on our side of the road.'

'What?'

Sandra leaned forward and looked out the windshield. A dark black car was coming down a hill several hundred meters away. Because of the rain, their visibility was severely limited, but the car was definitely in their lane.

'What the hell is it doing?' she asked.

Nightingale took his foot off the gas. He applied the brake and the car slowed. 'I don't know. But I don't like it.'

'Pull over.'

The car was closer now, and it appeared to be speeding up.

'No. It could still slam into us.'

'Pull over, Jack.'

It was less than a hundred meters away and they could hear the powerful engine revving up as it raced toward them. Whoever was behind the wheel knew exactly what they were doing.

'Pull over!'

Headlights filled the car, blinding him. Nightingale slammed on the brakes, turned left. The car skidded sideways, burning rubber on all four tyres while the approaching car came barreling toward them. The Charger slipped into the opposite lane, still sideways, and just as the car was about to smash into them the headlights and the car disappeared. The Charger spun rapidly as Nightingale ripped up the handbrake and righted the wheel, keeping them from launching down one of the banks and into a tree at forty-five miles an hour. The Charger came to an abrupt stop. Rain pecked the hood of the car.

Sandra peered down the road. There was nothing there. The road was empty. 'It wasn't real,' said Sandra, breathless.

'No.'

'How is that possible?'

'I don't know.'

They sat there for a few minutes, trying to catch their breaths. A car passed them. Then another. Nightingale started driving again, this time much more slowly. He didn't bother starting another conversation, he concentrated on his own thoughts.

* * *

Nightingale was so shaken by what had happened on the road that he kept his speed below fifty, which is probably what saved his life less than an hour later when the Charger's power steering failed and the car went off the road, sped down a deep incline and smashed into a towering oak tree at the edge of the forest. If they had been going any faster, they would have been dead for sure. As it was they were shaken, bruised, but okay. He called the American Automobile Association and after ninety minutes had passed a bearded man in a Carhartt jacket hitched the Charger and took them the rest of the way to New Jersey without further incident. He dropped them at a hotel where they had no intention of staying, then drove off, promising repairs the next day.

Nightingale wanted nothing more to do with the car and he phoned the rental company, told them what had happened, and said he wanted to cancel the contract.

Sandra fished out her smartphone and called a taxi. Minutes later a chubby man sporting a five o'clock shadow and greasy black hair pulled up to the curb in a yellow cab. Sandra gave him the address of the antique shop. 'That one over on 8th?' he asked, chewing a toothpick. 'It's closed. Been closed six months.'

'We know,' said Sandra firmly. 'Take us there anyway.'

'Can you stop off at a general store or something on the way?' asked Nightingale. 'Somewhere that sells flashlights.'

Twenty minutes later they were standing in front of a redbrick building on the corner of Hart and Melrose, a quiet and shady part of town where young kids in baggy jeans sold weed on the sidewalks and where rusty cars snaked along the streets blaring hip hop music. They had a flashlight each. Two streetlamps flickered and gave out as they approached the front door. Above the door was a large painted sign that read ANTIQUES AND CURIOS and stuck to the door was a small printed sign that said 'CLOSED DUE TO ILLNESS. THANK U FOR UR BUSINESS OVER THE YEARS.' Nightingale tried the door. Locked. He knocked but there was no answer, not that he expected one. 'Let's try around the back,' he said. They walked down the side of the building where they found a window with a pane missing. Nightingale stuck his hand in and unlocked it.

He looked at Sandra expectantly.

'What?' she said.

'Ladies before gentlemen,' he said.

'You want me to go in first?'

'To be fair, you look fit but I'm no lightweight so I'm not sure you'll be able to boost me in.'

'But if I'm inside, how do you get in? And more importantly, how do I get out?'

'I'm hoping you'll find something in there that I can stand on,' he said. 'Now come, let's not make this any harder than it needs to be.'

He hoisted Sandra up and she climbed inside.

'Are you okay?' he shouted.

'Define okay?'

'Just get me something I can step on.'

A few minutes later a stool appeared at the window and he pulled it out. He placed it on the ground and used it to climb through the window to join her. It was cold and musty, and the unpleasant smell made him wrinkle his nose. Turning on his flashlight, Nightingale saw thick layers of dust accumulated on furniture and knickknacks around the room. He could see his breath feathering in the cold air. Sandra hugged herself in an attempt to keep warm.

Nightingale walked around, inspecting placards detailing the various antiques. 'There must be a card catalog around here somewhere,' said

Nightingale. 'We need some information on the doll.'

'Wouldn't he have given it to my grandmother when he sold it to her?'

'Not necessarily.' Nightingale hadn't wanted to admit it, but he had his doubts about how Sandra's grandmother came in possession of the doll. There was a nagging suspicion in the back of his mind that told him Sandra's grandmother hadn't purchased the doll at all; that maybe the doll found its way into her grandmother's keeping of its own accord. He doubted something so dangerous would be kept on display, ready to be sold. The doll had power over people, especially over the grandmother, that much was certain. Had it tricked her into taking it home?

They went to the front of the building and Nightingale found a card catalog beside a cash register covered in dust and cobwebs. There were hundreds of cards and his heart fell - he didn't even know what to look for. What kind of doll was it? How old was it? Where did it come from?

'What the...?' said Sandra, shining her flashlight on a door at the other end of the room. 'This is weird.'

'You use that word a lot, you know.'

'No, seriously. Come take a look.'

Nightingale went over to her. There was a door with a laminated sign that said, 'OCCULT COLLECTIBLES. $5 ADMITTANCE. ASK FOR EARL.' Sandra frowned. 'What's that all about?'

Nightingale tried the door but it was locked. He went back to the cash register and began shuffling around the papers and rummaging inside the drawers beneath it.

'What're you doing?'

'Looking for something.'

'For what?'

'This,' he said, holding up a gold key with a paper card attached to it. 'Occult Collectibles,' he said, reading off the card. He went over and unlocked the door, which creaked open on ancient hinges. A burst of cold air ruffled their clothes, chilling them to the bone. The room was full of strange objects - human skulls painted gold, old vellum books with Latin writing on their spines, strange bygone relics of gargoyles and imps cast from bronze and carved from soapstone. Lining the walls were crude paintings of devils, as well as frayed tapestries depicting winged serpents eating men whole. Each of the items carried with it a small placard announcing its date and location of origin followed by a brief summary. There was a brown walnut box with a hinged lid lined with red velvet. Inside were a wooden stake and hammer, a small vial of holy water, a gun with six silver bullets, and a long thin dagger with a crucified Christ for a hilt. 'A vampire hunting kit,' said Sandra. 'How useful.'

'Check this out,' said Nightingale, shining his flashlight on a tall wooden case with a glass door. The door was open, with a key sticking out of the lock. Beneath it was a placard that said, 'DANGER! ABSOLUTELY DO NOT OPEN!' The case was empty. Nightingale picked up the placard hanging from the door and read it aloud. 'In here resides the Russian Killing Doll, said to be cursed by an ancient evil. There is no known origin of the doll, nor any manufacturer's label, official papers, or identifying characteristics. It was given to me by a Russian émigré, a priest who claimed to have come into possession of the doll after discovering it in a forest glen in his native Sovetsky. To his detriment, he felt an overwhelming urge to bring the doll home with him – I repeat, DO NOT OPEN THIS DOOR NO MATTER YOUR INTENTIONS. The priest's wife and three children were murdered, and try as he might, he could not escape the clutches of this horrifying creature. At last he traveled to Rome, where he consulted a Roman Catholic priest who built a specially-made box designed to house (but not destroy) the evil residing in the doll. Together they captured it and locked it away in this box, where it has remained ever since. It moves from time to time, but can't get out. It has been known to attract unwitting people, drawing them in, but luckily I have always been here to supervise. Again, DO NOT OPEN IF YOU

VALUE YOUR LIFE! PLEASE!'

Nightingale set down the card. 'I think we've found our doll.'

'No,' said a gravelly voice from the doorway. 'I think it found you.'

Sandra dropped the vampire hunting kit and it crashed to the floor, spilling its contents. Nightingale grabbed a heavy iron gargoyle off the mantel and held it like a baseball bat. 'Who the hell are you?' he asked.

An old man was standing in the doorway hooked up to an oxygen tank. His face was grey and sunken, and wisps of white hair shot up from his head in all directions as if he'd stuck his finger in a light socket. He was skinny – unnaturally skinny – and he slumped against the doorjamb, breathing heavily and with great difficulty. 'Didn't mean to scare you. But seeing how you're in my shop, I'm keeping the apology.' A clear plastic tube ran from the tank, around his neck and up to his nostrils.

'Earl?' asked Sandra.

Earl nodded, his breath coming to him in gasps. 'That's my name.'

'You own the shop?' asked Nightingale.

Earl nodded. 'Though it's not a shop anymore. There's nothing for sale here. Now what are you doing in here? Stealing anything here won't end well for you, trust me on that.'

'We're not here to steal anything,' said Nightingale, putting the gargoyle back on the mantel. He pointed at the case. 'What's with the doll. Someone let it out, didn't they?'

Earl nodded again, but this time he strained to speak. 'Couple of kids come to look at the occult museum one fine Saturday afternoon. Same as always. Nothing special. I show 'em around, tell some stories, but then some tough fella decides he wants to impress his girlfriend. Gets the key from behind my desk, opens the case and takes her out while I'm talking to an old granny. Starts playing with the doll, making crude gestures. Things like that. I wise up and go to take the doll from him before it's too late, but before I can this kid falls on the floor, choking to death. I'm about to grab the doll when his girlfriend screams at me to call an ambulance, so I do. I do it fast. Doesn't matter,' he shook his head, looking infinitely sad. 'By the time I get back, the doll and the old granny are gone. I imagine it got hold of her somehow. That's what it does. Kid's all right, but on his way home he crashes his car into a tree, killing him and his girlfriend. That night I get real sick, sicker than I've ever been in my life. Get taken to the hospital, they tell me I've got cancer.' He snapped his fingers. 'Just like that, overnight. The little bitch was getting back at me for keeping her locked up all these years. And I suppose that's what brings you here, isn't it? She's after you, isn't she?'

'The doll?' asked Nightingale. 'Yes.'

'I knew it,' said Earl. 'I could feel it in my bones.'

'How do we find her? How do we find the doll?'

'You don't,' said Earl. 'She finds you.'

There was a loud crash somewhere in the building and Sandra screamed. Then there was the sound of shattering glass. Then a flurry of tiny footsteps shuffled upstairs.

'Like I said, she'll find you,' said Earl. 'If you're here, she's here.' He smiled, showing yellow stubs of what once had been teeth. 'I've been waiting for her to come back. Waiting a long time.' He pointed at the box. 'Grab that and come with me.' With that he turned and shuffled toward the sound of feet running down the stairs. A child giggled in the darkness. 'Come on, you old bitch. I'm not afraid of you,' Earl muttered. 'I'm too darn old to be afraid of anything.'

Nightingale grabbed the box and followed Earl, Sandra hot on his heels. They were just in time to see the old man get thrown against the wall, then the doll, unimaginably quick, climbed up his torso while his head swayed dizzily from the impact, and coiled the oxygen tube around his throat, squeezing and giggling maniacally all the while. It gave a quick tug and snapped his neck. Earl's head lolled to the side and he stared sightlessly at the ground.

Nightingale rushed at the doll and tried to close the box around it but it hopped off the old man and somehow tackled him to the ground. He dropped the case and began wrestling with the doll, which had a vice grip around his throat. It was singing in a little girl's voice. 'Ring-a-round the rosie, a pocket full of posies, ashes, ashes, we all fall down!'

Sandra grabbed a heavy wooden cane and swatted the doll off him. It flew through the air, landed on its feet, and growled at her. Nightingale lay gasping on the ground. The doll charged Sandra, smashing into her feet and knocking her over. Then it began pounding her head with its fists, making thumping sounds as if its fists were made of iron.

Nightingale screamed at the doll. 'Hey! Get off her!' He stood up and held out his hands. 'Come on, pick on someone your own size, why don't you?'

The dolled laughed manically and stepped away from Sandra.

Nightingale had his arms outstretched as if planning to catch it with his hands. 'Come on,' he said. 'Here I am.'

'So keen to die?' said the doll in a little girl's voice. It began to sing as it walked slowly towards Nightingale. 'Ring-a-round the rosie, a pocket full of posies, ashes, ashes, we all fall down!' At the end of the rhyme the doll ran full pelt towards Nightingale, its little shoes clicking on the wooden floor. Nightingale stepped backward, half falling and half jumping behind the case, landing with it between his legs. He grabbed for the door, felt the doll smash into the wood, then slammed it shut. He turned the key and locked it. There was movement inside the case for a minute but then it grew deathly still. Inside, the doll stood placidly behind the glass, its dark eyes looking out, not moving.

'Is it over?' asked Sandra, sitting up. Her lips were split, her nose was bleeding and one of her eyes was closed.

'I hope so,' said Nightingale.

'What are you going to do with it?' she asked.

'Put it somewhere where no one will ever find it,' said Nightingale.

* * *

Joshua Wainwright and Nightingale sat in the back of Wainwright's limo, parked outside a large warehouse along the bank of the East River in New York. Wainwright was smoking a cigar and drinking Scotch from a crystal tumbler. Between them was the wooden case, the doll standing inside it like any ordinary collectible. Nightingale held the key uncertainly between them.

'I'll take that,' said Wainwright, nodding at the key.

'Joshua, I mean it. Do not open this box. Ever.'

'I won't.'

'I'm serious, Joshua. That thing is very, very dangerous. You let it out, everyone around you will die.'

'I hear what you're saying, Jack. Don't worry. Where I'm keeping it, no one will ever open it.' He took the key from Nightingale and slid it into his pocket.

They got out of the limousine and went up to the warehouse. Nightingale carried the box, holding it tightly, the glass door facing his chest. Two armed security guards stood either side of the entrance and a multitude of CCTV cameras stared down at them. Wainwright placed his eye in front of a biometric scanner and the huge metal doors swung slowly inward. One by one lights flickered down the aisle, revealing row upon row of massive shelves reaching up to the ceiling – shelves that housed tens of thousands of antiquities.

Nightingale looked around as he walked with Wainwright, the box clutched to his chest. 'What is all this stuff?' he asked.

'Just stuff,' said Wainwright. 'Stuff that's better kept here than loose in the outside world. Don't worry, nothing ever leaves here, Jack.'

They walked down the center aisle and Wainwright directed him to a bare shelf near the center of the building. He had Nightingale set the case with the doll on the shelf. The doll stared out through the glass door with cold, lifeless eyes. There were other boxes nearby. Some contained dolls. Others contained figures and statues. One contained what looked like a one-eyed teddy bear with fangs. Nightingale shuddered and it wasn't because of the blistering air-conditioning.

'We're done,' said Wainwright.

They left the doll behind, walking back down the center aisle. Wainwright switched off the lights and they went outside where Wainwright punched a code into the keypad, sealing the doors shut with a muffled clang. Wainwright nodded at the armed guards and walked back to the limousine. Nightingale followed.

Far behind in the darkness, the doll lifted its hands, and touched the glass.

THE MANSION

Jack Nightingale took a long pull on his Marlboro as he relaxed in the plush back seat of Joshua Wainwright's stretch limo. They were on the highway. Ahead of them was a cluster of tall wooded mountains painted an array of Autumn colours. On either side of the road was a proliferation of red oak and mountain ash, their leaves getting blown off the branches and dancing along the highway. Two of these leaves – one gold and one maroon – flew into the windshield and became stuck under the windshield wiper. Wainwright's driver and bodyguard, Hans, a fat brooding German with a Roman nose and thick bushy eyebrows, cursed under his breath and tried the wipers to get rid of them – to no avail.

Nightingale chuckled as he smoked his cigarette. Wainwright was sitting next to him, shivering. 'Sorry,' said Nightingale, flicking what was left of his cigarette out and rolling up the window. 'I don't notice the cold.'

'No problem,' said Wainwright. He was wearing tight-fitting jeans, lizard-skin cowboy boots and a checked shirt. On his head was a NY Yankees baseball cap. The man was worth several billion dollars but that was rarely reflected in his clothing. The gold watch on his left wrist was worth several hundred thousand dollars, Nightingale knew, but other than that a casual observer would assume that Joshua Wainwright was a young working class black guy with a flashy watch. 'So, as I was saying before you needed a nicotine hit, the man you'll be helping is David Warner the second. I need you to clean this up quickly and quietly, though you shouldn't have any trouble keeping it quiet. Warner lives on ten thousand acres of pristine wilderness and his mansion is a veritable fortress.'

'And as for quickly?'

Wainwright sighed, settling back in his seat. 'We have a pending merger between companies, Warner and I, but he's been dragging his heels since day one, which was about two years ago. Between you and me, Warner is off his rocker. He's sixty-five but his mind resembles that of an eighty-year-old with Alzheimer's. On a good day he's fine, ready to sign the papers and move forward with me and the board; on a bad day he doesn't know how to tie his own shoelaces. That and he's a stubborn old bastard. He doesn't want to shift the company but he knows the whole board is behind me, and it's only a matter of time. I don't think he likes me much, but if we can sort out the problem he has, hopefully we can change that.'

'And his problem?'

Wainwright sighed. 'David Warner is convinced he's being haunted. There's a ghost in his house. That's what he says.'

'What sort of ghost?'

'I don't know. I haven't been into details. But I'm hoping that whatever it is, you can get rid of it.'

'But if he's as mad as you say he is, maybe he's imagining it.'

Wainwright frowned. 'You're not saying you don't believe in ghosts?'

Nightingale shook his head. 'I believe in ghosts, sure, but true hauntings are very rare. You know that.'

Wainwright tossed a thick manila envelope in Nightingale's lap. Nightingale opened it and flicked through the stack of hundreds. 'Half now, the other half when you get rid of that damned ghost.'

Nightingale frowned. 'This isn't an exact science, Joshua. I can't even guarantee that I can get rid of the ghost. I don't even know if it is a ghost.'

'Well, you've got five thousand dollars at the other end to help you figure it out. You'll do it, Nightingale. I have no doubts. Do you have everything you need?'

Nightingale patted the black nylon overnight bag next to him. 'I'm good. So tell me about David Warner the second.'

'He's a captain of industry, an absolute Renaissance man of business and finance. His grandfather, Frederick Warner, had made his fortune in the oil business, his empire second only to John D. Rockefeller's. In the early 19th century David Warner's father used the family fortune to break into various areas of finance; he was said to have been present at the fateful meeting on Jekyll Island off the coast of Georgia, the precursor to the foundation of the Federal Reserve. Since then the Warner family has gone on to become one of the wealthiest and most ruthless business dynasties in the world. David Warner the second alone is worth over $40 billion.'

Nightingale raised his eyebrows. 'Wow. And the haunting?'

'It all came out at a board meeting that I attended last week. He turned up bleary-eyed and disheveled, his suit was frayed and rumpled, his eyes were bloodshot. He was a mess, Jack, clearly something was very wrong. He barely uttered a word the whole time, and it wasn't until the end of the meeting that he finally admitted he was losing sleep over a ghost.'

'He said that?'

'Out loud. To the whole board. I cut him short and we ended the meeting, but I made sure I had a few private minutes with him before he left. That's when I got the full story. Two years ago a ghost or demon infiltrated his house and has been wreaking havoc. But only recently did the activity grow more dangerous with priceless furniture and art getting smashed to bits and fires starting in odd places, threatening to burn the entire house down, all 70,000 square feet of it.'

'Did he describe the ghost?'

'He was vague. I'm not even sure if he's seen a ghost.'

'A poltergeist, maybe? Just physical manifestations of the presence?'

'That's what I was thinking. But we both know that poltergeists usually involve young girls and not old men.'

Eventually they pulled up in front of a wrought-iron gate at the edge of a forest, the sun already close to setting. 'This is where we drop you off,' said Wainwright.

'You don't want to see him?'

Wainwright shook his head. 'He said I wasn't to go to the house. He's agreed to allow you in, but he doesn't want me there. Call me when it's done.'

'Terrific,' said Nightingale. He grabbed his bag, climbed out of the limo and lit a cigarette as it drove away.

He waited until the limo had disappeared into the distance before walking over to a brick guardhouse. A guard shone a flashlight into Nightingale's eyes. 'Jack Nightingale,' said Nightingale. 'I hope I'm expected.'

'ID please,' said the guard in clipped tones that suggested he was former military. Nightingale handed over his driving licence and the guard compared it to his face then noted down the details on a clipboard before handing it back. 'This way, Sir,' he said, and showed Nightingale through the guardhouse and out of a side door. He pointed towards the mansion in the distance. 'There you go, Sir. You'll find another security officer close to the main house.'

Nightingale turned up the collar of his raincoat and walked a few hundred meters in the imposing shadow, craning his head each time he heard rustling in the woods. Night birds began singing their soft songs.

Twigs snapped under his Hush Puppies. Up ahead he saw another guard box, this one small and squat with a streetlamp glowing beside it. Inside was a pale night watchman wearing grey overalls and a grey baseball cap and sporting a black goatee. Under the bright glare of fluorescent lights Nightingale saw him intently studying a magazine. He reached the window and the man quickly shoved the magazine under a stack of papers – a corner of the cover peeked out to reveal a woman's long, naked leg.

The watchman stammered. 'Shit,' he said. 'You spooked me.'

'Sorry about that,' said Nightingale, fighting back a grin. 'Didn't mean to... interrupt anything.'

'Oh no, no interruptions here. Jerry said you were coming but I didn't know you were gonna creep up on me like that.' The man shivered, nudging the magazine further under the stack. 'Gets weird out here at night, you know?'

'Sure,' said Nightingale. 'It is a bit spooky. It's not haunted is it?'

'Not that I know of. There's a bad atmosphere, that's certainly true, but I guess that's down to the owner. He's a bit...' He left the sentence unfinished.

'It's okay,' said Nightingale. 'I'm not a friend. I'm a hired hand.'

The man leaned forward and lowered his voice. 'It's like there's a black cloud over the place. It's always gloomy and depressing. And that's Mr Warner in a nutshell.'

'Have you worked here long?'

'Eight years.'

'And has he always been like that?'

The man shook his head. 'No, to be fair up until a couple of years ago he was just fine. He's getting on, I guess.' He tapped his own forehead. 'These days he's not quite right, you know?'

'Yeah, I heard.'

The man leaned back. 'Anyway, go on ahead. Mr Pike is waiting for you.'

'Mr Pike?'

'Yeah. The butler.'

'Right,' said Nightingale. He continued down the pebbled drive.

Through a curtain of pine trees he caught random glimpses of bright golden light, then he rounded the corner and saw the mansion for the first time. It was the largest house he had ever seen. The mansion, perhaps neo-Gothic, stood a hundred feet high with tall pointed turrets and sculpted chimneys. The mansion was made of stone, its façade dominated by bays and arched windows. Marble stairs led up to a portico which boasted four marble beams that looked straight from the Pantheon. Above Nightingale's head, two ravens sprung from the eaves and flew out in the gathering dusk, their bodies carving dark shadows across the moon.

'I see you like the house,' said a sharp voice up on the portico. Coming down the steps was a short man in dark trousers, a waistcoat, and a tailcoat with gold buttons. His face was pale and bony, almost skeletal, and his eyes were sunken and beady, shining out like obsidian pools. But they were friendly.

'Yes,' said Nightingale, glancing around at the opulence and splendor. The mansion stretched for hundreds of meters on each side. 'There must be fifty rooms in this place.'

'A hundred,' said the butler matter-of-factly. He reached the landing and offered Nightingale his white-gloved hand. 'George Pike.'

'Nightingale. Jack Nightingale.'

Pike smiled. 'Pleased to make your acquaintance, Mr Nightingale. Now, let me help you with that bag.' Pike deftly took the bag from Nightingale and began leading the way up the marble stairs. 'It was built during the Gilded Age,' he said with a wave of his hand, 'as a summer residence for Mr Warner's grandfather Frederick. They call it Marble Manor.'

'Catchy,' quipped Nightingale, coming up to the shaded portico. Ravens squawked behind him. He felt the wind rustle his collar as a large gust blew into the trees and made their boughs whisper. More leaves fell and swirled about. 'Is that an Irish accent you have?'

'I used to be Irish. Came over with my mum during the Troubles. Been here ever since.'

Nightingale studied him. The man looked middle-aged, with grey hair slicked back from his gaunt face. But the pallor of his skin suggested he was at least sixty. He hid it well.

Pike pushed open the double doors, ushering Nightingale into a sprawling marble chamber with burgundy runners on the marble floors and carved pilasters up the walls. Through the glass-domed ceiling Nightingale caught glimpses of the moon and the stars twinkling in the night sky. The chamber was dominated by carved plastering of nymphs and devils and cherubs. There were halls on the left and right, and in front of them a large hall going straight through a twin staircase with stone banisters. Pike led Nightingale to the staircase on the right.

He set up Nightingale in a 'room' at the north side of the mansion, but the room was more like a house. There were actually four rooms, each with high ceilings, crystal chandeliers, and various items of antique furniture. Nightingale's bedroom boasted a marble fireplace with logs already burning and a canopied four-poster bed which looked like it could host the entire British royal family for a sleepover. Dotted around were vases of freshly-cut flowers, filling the rooms with their sweet scent.

Pike gestured to the bathroom at the end of the hall and invited Nightingale to freshen up, promising to return in an hour to bring Nightingale down to the dining room, where he would meet Mr Warner over supper. With that, the little man disappeared, leaving Nightingale alone.

Nightingale went to the bathroom and looked in the mirror. He could do with a shower and a shave but right now he wanted to explore.

He left his room and turned right into a long, narrow passageway. It seemed to stretch the entire length of the mansion, and he couldn't see the end of it. On the left were bedrooms – dozens of them, unlit, obscured by dust – presumably abandoned for years. After all, you'd need at least twenty families to even remotely fill this place, thought Nightingale. On his right were arched windows looking out on the dark forest from four stories high. He could see vast stretches of woodland going on for miles, only stopping at the base of the tree-covered Adirondack Mountains.

The long corridor came to an end at a dark chamber with a spiral staircase. Nightingale descended a flight and stopped at a landing where he could see golden light peeking through cracks in a door. He pushed through, coming into a library with mahogany-paneled walls teeming with bookshelves.

In the center of the library he saw a desk with photographs and went to it. There were photographs of what was presumably a young Mr Warner in a dapper suit standing alongside his bride, a gorgeous blonde with a bright smile. There were pictures of them on a cruise in clear blue waters and lazing on the beach under palm trees.

While he was inspecting the photograph of a young man who looked similar to Warner, one of the photographs rose up, hovering in the air, and slammed down at the edge of the desk, showering Nightingale's feet in glass. He stepped back and cursed out loud.

Books started falling off shelves, then rising up in the air. They swirled and flung themselves in all directions, shattering glass vases and a couple of whisky decanters. Furniture rose to the ceiling and fell crashing to the floor. Chairs were upturned as if kicked and in the middle of the room a tornado of a hundred books swirled round in a circle while the lights flickered and the walls groaned inward.

Nightingale stood in the midst of the mayhem, awestruck. Then a door opened and all of the hovering books, chairs and lamps fell at once, thumping to the floor in tangled heaps.

'Why, would you look at that,' said a nasally voice. 'I see you've met our ghost.'

David Warner the second was not an attractive man, not by any standards. His pig's nose was permanently upturned, and his grey hair was swept awkwardly over his head to conceal a glaring bald spot. He was short and stooped, and when he spoke, he seemed to despise each word as if it tasted of bile. 'You were supposed to remain in your room until called upon.'

'Sorry,' said Nightingale, still shocked by what had happened. 'I didn't know the place was off limits.'

Warner waved his hand dismissively. 'Not off limits. Private's more like it. Ever heard of privacy, Mr Nightingale? Or do you just traipse around wherever you like?'

'I'm a private investigator,' said Nightingale. 'That's why you hired me. To investigate.'

That seemed to sober his host. Warner straightened up a little. 'And what do you make of this scene then, Mr Investigator?'

Nightingale looked around. 'Well, I'd say you've got a serious problem on your hands. Judging by the level of activity, you might have a poltergeist, maybe even of the demonic variety.'

Warner smiled thinly, revealing an array of crooked, yellow teeth. 'Lovely.' The smile disappeared just as soon as it arrived. 'Come on,' he barked. 'My supper's getting cold.'

Nightingale bent to pick up the photograph of the man who resembled Warner and set it back on the desk.

'My brother Thomas,' said Warner. 'He went missing years ago.' Warner led Nightingale out of the library. 'About forty years ago my father got a call from a stranger announcing they had his son. My brother. They wanted money, and that was that.'

'That was that? You mean your father never paid the ransom?'

'All I know is my brother never came home again. Did my father pay the ransom?' He shrugged. 'Perhaps. But not likely. He despised Thomas just as much as I did. That boy was a queer through and through, and he had no business being born into such a fine, blue-blooded family such as ours. He should have been put up for adoption when he was a child. It would have saved us all a great deal of trouble.'

'Queer? Nightingale frowned. 'You mean gay?'

The old man turned on him, scowling. 'You're here to investigate the ghost, not my family, so keep your damned nose out of it,' he snapped. 'Understand?'

Nightingale said nothing and he watched the old man's cheeks quiver as he descended the stairs. 'So,' he said, trying to strike a friendly tone, 'how long ago did the activity begin?'

'Not yet,' barked the old man. 'Wait.'

Nightingale looked at him, confused. 'I'm sorry?'

'I'd rather you didn't ask me anything until I've had my first cocktail.' He walked away and Nightingale followed him.

Several minutes later they were in a cavernous dining room with stone Romanesque walls and arches painted white. The only source of light came from several candelabra positioned around the dark oak dining table. A chandelier hung over the center of the table, illuminating a plump middle-aged Italian woman with dark hair and olive eyes. She bent over the table, setting china on the white tablecloth. From the doorway Pike said something to her in Italian and she flushed, immediately racing to the kitchen through a set of double doors and returning with a glass decanter full of water. She filled Warner's glass as he sat down opposite Nightingale.

'From our artesian well on the grounds,' said Warner proudly. 'We had a man come here once to assess the quality of the water and he said it was among the purest in the country. We do all of our cooking with it. David Rockefeller can go to Hell with all of his heart transplants, I'm going to live to a hundred and fifty.'

Just then Pike came out shaking a frosted cocktail shaker and looking bored. He poured clear liquid into two martini glasses, handing one to

Warner and one to Nightingale. Warner took a large drink from his without ceremony and then shouted in the direction of the kitchen: 'Alena!'

The Italian maid popped out of the kitchen, her dark hair matted to her sweaty face, her eyes alarmed. 'Yes?'

'The hors d'oeuvres!' said Warner.

'I sorry, meester Warner. I bring them.'

'Well stop talking to me then and bring them!'

'Yes, yes,' said the woman, bowing quickly and leaving the room.

Nightingale took a big gulp from his martini, then another.

'So,' said Warner, gazing at him from across the table. 'You're a Limey?'

'I'm British, yes.'

'Wainwright says you're a permanent resident of the States these days. Why's that... trouble back home?'

'No,' lied Nightingale, taking another sip from his martini. 'Just personal preference.'

'Ah, you like America better.'

'I didn't say that. It's a much bigger country,' said Nightingale. 'So, naturally, there's more work for me here.'

'When did you become a private investigator?'

It seemed less a conversation now and more an interrogation. 'A few years ago.'

'Back in England?'

'Yes, back in England.'

'Typically private investigators have some background in criminal justice. Am I wrong?'

'Nope.'

'What was yours?'

'I was a hostage negotiator. I talked suicides down from tall buildings. Things like that. Look, I'd much rather learn about the case, if you don't mind. That's why I'm here, isn't it?'

The Italian maid brought a platter of half-shell oysters on a bed of ice. She set down two glass dishes of champagne mignonette to accompany them. 'You're not going to let me eat all of these by myself, are you? Come on! They're fresh off the coast of Maine.' Warner picked up one of the shells and loudly slurped its contents. Juices dribbled down his chin. 'I have a guy who brings them straight from the Portland pier. They're delicious.'

Warner's grey chin glistened with oyster juice, and in the candlelight his eyes looked feral and mad. 'So ask me about the ghost,' said Warner, slurping another of the oysters, 'anything you like. I don't want you to leave without sending that thing back to hell. I haven't had a good night's sleep in two years and I'm positively terrified, if you want the truth of it.'

Nightingale took one of the oysters. 'Afraid for your life?'

Warner shrugged. 'More afraid for my possessions than my life. That thing is a maniac! You saw what it did to the library. It's ruined forty thousand dollars' worth of art and antiquities this month. This month!'

'You said you haven't been sleeping well for two years. Is that when the activity began?'

'Thereabouts.' Warner paused to call for Pike, who returned with a new, full martini shaker. Pike poured generously in both glasses and disappeared to the kitchen.

'Anyway,' said Warner, 'it's been a bloody mess ever since. Little things went on at first. My suits went missing and I'd find them later in bizarre places.'

'Like where?'

Warner's eyes widened. 'Like on the roof, for one! And scattered about the grounds. A caretaker found them thrown about in the bloody trees! At first we all thought it had been some burglar, naturally, but honestly, what type of burglar steals fifty grand worth of suits and tosses them about in a fit like some carnival clown? None, is the answer to that.'

'Strange,' murmured Nightingale.

'Yes, it was strange. But then it graduated to breaking things, which went from strange to infuriating. Small things, to start. Water glasses. Mirrors. Flower vases. Then the large costly items like my private collection of impressionistic art and my father's rare books in the library, which I ultimately had removed and donated to the Smithsonian.'

Warner slurped another oyster. 'I had a marble Rodin,' he said, looking deep into a candle flame. 'It was given to me by Jacob Rothschild as a housewarming gift. Worth a fortune, if you consider twenty million dollars a fortune.' He scoffed. 'It was tossed out of a fourth-story window and broken to pieces on the driveway. Reduced to an ugly scattering of white dust and chalky rock, like bits of bone.'

'Twenty million dollars?'

'Smashed to pieces.' Warner waved his hand. 'Part of me says it's all just stuff, but it's my stuff, and that ghost is fucking with me.'

'Do you think it's the ghost of someone you know?' offered Nightingale. 'Perhaps someone you've wronged in the past?'

'I haven't hurt anybody. I pay my staff more than fair wages and give them paid holidays. They eat the best food that money can buy. But don't take my word for it. Pike!'

Moments later Pike came into the room and bowed. 'Yes, Mr Warner, how may I help you?'

'Pike, have I ever wronged one of my staff?'

'Is this a trick question, sir?'

'No. Just be truthful for my guest here.'

Nightingale tried to speak but Warner raised his hand. Pike looked from guest to host. 'No, Mr Warner. Certainly not in my opinion.'

'Thank you. You may go.'

Warner faced Nightingale, smiling triumphantly with yellow teeth. 'See?'

Nightingale smiled without warmth. 'Now that's settled, would you mind telling me if there are any particular areas of the house where the activity seems greatest?'

Warner pinched his chin, which still gleamed with oyster juice. 'Come to think of it, yes. The wine cellar hosts its own assortment of odd goings-on, though I can't attest to them personally, you understand.'

'Why not?'

'I don't go down there anymore.'

'No?'

Warner shook his head. 'Much too cold. Unnaturally cold, if you ask me. And I always get a sensation of dire dread down there, as if something horrible is about to happen to me. The help retrieves the wine for guests. I don't drink it. Too many sulfites and too much sugar. I aim to outlive them all, you remember. And I will. I most certainly will.'

'So you have a wine cellar but you don't drink wine?'

'Good wine is an investment that's hard to beat, Mr Nightingale. And I offer wine to my guests, of course.'

He hadn't offered Nightingale any wine, but then Nightingale wasn't a guest, he was there to do a job.

'Anywhere else that seems particularly haunted?' asked Nightingale. 'By that I mean cold spots, scratching in the walls, upside down crucifixes and scents of sulfur or rot?'

Warner wriggled his pig's nose. 'No, none of that. The activity is everywhere.' He squinted at Nightingale as if he was having trouble focusing. 'Haven't you been listening to me?'

* * *

After dinner, Nightingale stood on the balcony of his room in the dark, watching the moon and smoking a cigarette. An owl crooned in the darkness, and every once in a while he saw a large shadow vault from the trees and soar wraith-like across the moon, blotting it out. The food had been amazing. As Warner had explained several times, the chef used to work for a two-star Michelin restaurant in France and the girl who prepared their dessert had studied under Wolfgang Puck. The one downside was that there had only been water to drink.

Down below a door opened and a man walked out. It was Pike, struggling with a heavy wooden crate, which he carried down the marble stairs and set in the back of a small car. On his return journey Nightingale could see his chest heaving from the effort. He must have caught the glow of Nightingale's cigarette because he looked up, smiled, and waved. Nightingale waved back.

* * *

The next day, Nightingale woke to the sound of a knocking on his door. He grabbed a robe and opened it to find Pike, holding a breakfast tray. He wished Nightingale a good morning, placed the tray on a table, and left Nightingale to enjoy his eggs, bacon, pancakes and freshly-brewed coffee. Later Nightingale showered and shaved, pulled on clean clothes and spent the morning scouring the mansion in search of clues or activity, but he found nothing out of the ordinary. He decided to go down to the wine cellar to have a look around. In the kitchen he found Alena hunched over the sink, washing up. Her face was sweaty and she seemed to be muttering something to herself in Italian.

'Do you know where I can find a flashlight?'

She looked up and frowned. 'Flashlight?'

Nightingale mimed holding a flashlight and clicking the button.

'Ah, yes!' she said excitedly. She rushed to the next room and came back with the remote control to the television. 'Yes?' she said, trying to hand it to him.

Nightingale smiled. 'No, I'm sorry, that's not what I meant.'

'Is there anything I can help you with, Mr Nightingale?' Pike was standing in the doorway, immaculate in his tailcoat and pomaded hair. His eyes gleamed like black marble.

'Yeah, I was just telling Alena here that I could use a flashlight.'

Pike went to a kitchen drawer, took out a flashlight and gave it to Nightingale.

'Ah...' said Alena. 'Torcia elletrica.'

'What do you need that for?' asked Pike.

'I'm going down to the wine cellar to take a look around.'

Pike gave him a bemused smile. 'There are lights down there, Mr Nightingale.'

Rather than explain the number of cases where the lights went out and he was left scrambling in the dark while something demonic chased after him, Nightingale said nothing. 'Want to come along?' he offered.

'No, no. You go ahead. I haven't been into the wine cellar since all the crazy stuff started. If we need wine, I usually get Alena to fetch the bottles.'

Alena frowned at the mention of her name and shook her head. 'No, no,' she said. 'I no go.' Pike smiled thinly and gestured toward the sink and she went back to the washing-up.

'Really?' said Nightingale. 'I thought I saw you carrying a crate of wine last night.'

'No,' said Pike. 'Those were cleaning supplies.'

'Heavy cleaning supplies.'

'They were, yes. Am I under some sort of scrutiny?'

Nightingale didn't answer the question and headed for the cellar. At the top of the stairs he flicked the light switch and the lights flickered on. Coming down the stairs, he could see that the entire cellar was full of wine racks. He pulled out one of the bottles. It was a Château Lafite. Nightingale wasn't a wine fan, he was much happier with Corona, but he recognised the name. He put the bottle back. The next rack was filled with Château Mouton-Rothschild vintages. The one next to that contained several dozen cobweb-covered bottles of Château Margaux, another name he had heard of. He supposed the collection was worth a fortune.

Nightingale noted that while the bottom half of the foundation was exposed fieldstone, the top layer was fresh brick, as if it had been installed more recently. Illuminating the rows of wine were flickering filament light bulbs the color of amber.

He felt a rush of freezing cold air around him. Above his head, the electric whir of the filament bulb buzzed louder. The light grew in intensity, so bright it seemed blinding. Then it exploded, shattering glass down on Nightingale's face.

'Shit!' he said, quickly rubbing glass out of his closed eyes. He heard more light bulbs do the same thing: buzz loudly, then explode, down the line from rack to rack. He shook the glass out of his hair and carefully opened his eyes.

There was only one light left in the room.

'Hello?' His voice echoed in the still air. 'Who did that?'

The light bulb buzzed like a bumblebee and glowed, but it didn't burst.

He touched the base of his eye where a small glass shard poked out. He pulled it free. 'Who did that?' he called. 'I want to know. I'm not here to harm you, I just want some answers.'

Silence.

Toward the rear of the wine cellar, the lone light bulb buzzed. He couldn't see anything in front of him so he took out his flashlight and turned it on. His breath came out in small clouds. He walked slowly toward the light.

'I'm a friend of Mr Warner's. Well, not a friend exactly – actually I think he's a nasty prick. Do you agree?'

Nothing.

'He hired me to find out what was going on. To 'send you back to hell,' to borrow his expression. Only, I don't think you're from hell. I think you're from here, that you've been sticking around to tell us something.

Did something terrible happen to you?'

The light went out, came back on.

Nightingale stopped. 'Was that a yes?'

The light flicked off and on.

'See? We're getting somewhere. Okay, let me think. Yes or no questions... Did you know Mr Warner?'

The light flicked on and off.

'Did he hurt you?'

Nothing. The light stayed the same. That was his first guess. That Warner had hurt somebody and they were getting back at him somehow.

'Are you a man?'

Nothing.

'You're a woman?'

The light flicked off and on again. As Nightingale drew closer to the light he felt a dramatic drop in temperature all around him. Tiny icicles formed in his nostrils. He stood just below the light bulb now. He faced a rack of Rothschild Grand Cru dating back to the early 1960s. Many of the bottles were gone or missing, and what bottles remained were slick with frost. He picked one up. It was frozen solid.

'Why these bottles?' he asked.

The light blinked. Slowly at first, then rapidly. Wine racks began to shake. Bottles slipped out and smashed to the concrete floor. Whole racks reeled over, filling his ears with the cacophony of broken glass. The lone light bulb above him blinked madly but didn't burst, and the racks began to settle, slowly, as if the ghost was running out of energy – or patience.

In a moment all was still and silent again in the cellar. Nightingale stood in the midst of broken glass and puddles of wine the color of blood.

* * *

Warner was not at all happy when he found out about the catastrophic destruction dealt to his wine cellar. They were eating a dinner of duck confit when Warner began drunkenly chastising Nightingale for the episode in the wine cellar, hinting that he had been the cause of the destruction.

Nightingale sat and ate his duck and waited for Warner's outburst to subside. Eventually Warner calmed down and resumed eating. 'Anyway,' said Warner, 'I'll be away on business for the next two days. I expect this thing to be all wrapped up by the time I get back. Do I make myself clear?'

'With all due respect, Mr Warner, I can't just magically snap my fingers and make the ghost disappear. I'll do my best, but I can't guarantee it'll be finished by the time you get back. This is a process, and I take it seriously.'

Warner raised an eyebrow. 'How much is that weasel Wainwright paying you?'

Nightingale shrugged. 'Ten grand, if I get rid of the ghost.'

'I'll double it. Hell, I'll quadruple it if you get rid of it, plus a bonus if I'm satisfied. I just want it out of my house. Destroying my wine, that's the last straw. Have you any idea how much those bottles were worth?'

'A lot,' said Nightingale.

'Yes. A hell of a lot. And this isn't the first time. Bottles are always being broken down there. You need to take care of this, Mr Nightingale. And quickly.'

'I'll do my best,' said Nightingale.

'No,' said Warner, waving his knife in Nightingale's face. 'Do better than your best. Just get it done.'

During dessert they discussed the nature of good and evil. Smears of chocolate mousse hung from both corners of Warner's lips as he droned on about it. 'You're misinformed,' he said snidely, 'the utmost good comes from self-satisfaction and vice, and anybody who tells you otherwise is a damned fool. Why do you think there are so many poor people in the world? It's because they're weak-minded fools, afraid to grasp at what they want, afraid to work for it. They don't take chances. They don't make anything of themselves. Instead they suckle off the rich, the same people who give them jobs, the same people they blame for their plight. They're weaklings looking for a patsy, that's all they are and that's all they'll ever be. Vermin.'

'I'm guessing you voted for Trump.'

'You think this is funny?'

'Yes I do. I really do.'

His face reddening, his jowls quivering, Warner said, 'Then you're just like the rest of them. Sick in the head and weak. And one day your kind will be wiped off the face of the Earth.'

'Don't forget, Mein Fuhrer, we've got the numbers,' said Nightingale. 'What's that American expression? You'll be shit out of luck.'

Warner lurched from his chair, grabbed a steak knife and slammed it down on the table, embedding it in the wood. 'You ungrateful little shit! You fucking limey twat! Do you know who you're speaking to! Do you know who I am! Do you?'

As he screamed, spittle flew from his mouth and sprayed the table, droplets hitting Nightingale's face and sprinkling his martini glass. Nightingale slowly wiped his face with his napkin, ready to defend himself if Mr Warner decided to come any closer with that knife. Pike came into the dining room, his face creased with alarm.

'Mr Warner is everything all right? Sir?'

Warner glared at Nightingale for a moment. But then he seemed to wake from a sort of trance. Shaking his head slowly, he stood up and straightened his rumpled suit. 'You must forgive me, Mr Nightingale. I haven't slept much and I'm irritable. I think I'll go to bed now.' He was a completely different man now from the man who just a few seconds earlier had been ranting and raving.

Pike took Warner by the elbow and led him from the dining room. Nightingale sighed and shook his head. Looking down at his martini glass, he saw droplets of spittle floating on the top. He grimaced. What a waste of a good drink.

* * *

Later that night Nightingale roamed the moonlit grounds, listening to the night birds and smoking a cigarette. He was trying to decide whether he should stay or go. He knew if he stayed he would potentially face more abuse from his host. If he left, he faced backlash from Joshua Wainwright. He had never known a man to be such a complete and utter bastard and even his obvious senility was no excuse. But Wainwright paid his wages and the first job he walked away from would probably be his last. He had no choice other than to stay.

In the moonlight the mansion resembled an austere castle with its pointed turrets and stone walls. Nightingale glimpsed a few lit bedrooms, but most were dark and uninviting. He realized there were no windows in the basement and wondered if the staff had cleaned up the mess and replaced the light bulbs. His mind drifted back to the ghost. A woman. But who? He made a mental note to interview the staff and ask them about previous female workers who might have died on the premises.

He finished his cigarette and flicked it away. He had already spotted the tree he wanted, and he went over to it. It was just over five metres tall, with a cluster of stems coming up from its base. The bark was light brown, smooth and scaly, and the branchlets were light orange brown with the occasional white dot. The leaves were turning their autumnal yellow with rusty spots and in a few weeks they would probably be on the ground. It was Hamamelis virginiana, the common or American witch-hazel, just what he needed. He broke off several branchlets and put them in his pocket.

On his way back to the house he heard a muffled cry in the wind and stopped. He listened. There was silence for a moment, but then the cry came again, soft and faint, like a scream underwater.

'Who's there?' he called.

The wind picked up, whistling in the trees, and died. He heard the cry again 'Who are you? Can you hear me? Are you in trouble? Are you hurt? Please, tell me your name!'

The cry came again, closer this time.

'Who are y—'

He felt a hand on his shoulder and wheeled around. It was Pike. 'Who are you talking to?' he demanded.

'No one,' said Nightingale.

'You were calling.'

'It's nothing. Do you want something?'

Pike clutched Nightingale's arm. 'We have to go. Warner's been hurt.'

'Hurt? How?'

'The thing attacked him. Nothing serious, but he's asking for you. I'll explain on the way.'

As they hurried to Warner's room Pike told him the story: while Warner was delivering his nightly orders to his butler, a giant Monet painting lifted off the wall by unseen hands and smashed down over his head. Pike had moved away just in time, narrowly escaping the sharp edge of the hard wooden frame, but Warner had not been so lucky. Nightingale now found the old man in hysterics, sobbing and yelling from his bed with a bloody gash in his forehead.

'You… lousy… bastard!' he stammered at Nightingale.

Nightingale frowned. 'What? Why me?'

'This thing is ruining my fucking life and you're not doing a damn thing about it!'

'I'm working on it,' said Nightingale. 'I'll sort it out. But maybe it would be best for you to leave for your trip early. You should go first thing tomorrow. You're obviously not safe here.'

Warner nodded. He was confused, possibly in shock, staring off into space as if he glimpsed some other world there. Pike gently took Nightingale by the arm and led him from the room.

'He's just under a lot of stress,' he said. 'This ghost thing, it's really messing with his mind.'

'I get the feeling there's more than that going on,' said Nightingale. 'I think he's got medical problems. The mood swings, the temper. Mental health issues maybe.'

'His doctors want him in for tests,' said Pike. He shrugged. 'But you can see what he's like. He doesn't listen to them. He doesn't listen to anybody. But the ghost thing, you need to take care of that. What is it you people do, séances? No, that's not right – exorcisms. I saw a film about it. Can't you exorcise the thing from this house?'

'I wouldn't exorcise a ghost, certainly not one seeking help,' said Nightingale. 'What we need to do is to make contact with it and see what it has to say.'

'Are you serious?'

'That's how to deal with a ghost. Exorcism is for possessions and in this case no one has been possessed. This is a spirit and generally spirits have an agenda. Once you know what that agenda is…'

'It sounds like hocus-pocus to me,' said Pike.

'We'll see,' said Nightingale. 'Look, why don't you join me in my room for a few minutes. I could use your help with something.'

'With what?'

'You mentioned a séance. A séance needs a group of people but there is another way.'

Pike looked uncomfortable. 'I'd rather not.'

'I could ask your boss to get you to help.'

Pike's eyes narrowed. 'That sounds like a threat, Mr Nightingale.'

Nightingale smiled and patted the butler on the back. 'Of course it's not. I just need your help for a few minutes, that's all.'

They went into Nightingale's room and Nightingale waved Pike to sit down on a sofa. Then he picked up his bag, unzipped it, and took out a wooden board.

'What the hell is that?' asked Pike.

'An Ouija board.'

'They're kids toys,' said Pike.

'There are toy versions, true,' said Nightingale, placing the board on the coffee table in front of Pike. 'But in my opinion kids shouldn't be allowed anywhere near them. Talking boards have been around for centuries, and they're definitely not toys.'

Pike looked down at the board. It was a large square of oak that had cracked across the middle. The words YES and NO were printed in faded silver letters in the top corners and the letters of the alphabet embossed in gold in two rows across the middle of the board. Below the letters were the numbers zero to nine in a row, and below them the word GOODBYE.

'Parker Brothers made a kids version in the US, very similar to this one,' said Nightingale. 'But this predates their version by at least a hundred years. It's an antique. Very rare.'

'And you carry it around with you?'

Nightingale shook his head. 'I was told this was a haunting,' he said. 'So I came prepared.' He reached into his bag and took out five blue candles, each in a small brass holder. He spaced them around the board. 'Do me a favour,' he asked Pike. 'Could you bring some flowers and put them on the table?'

Pike nodded and did as he was asked, carrying two vases of flowers over and putting them on either side of the board.

Nightingale lit the candles with his cigarette lighter, then reached into his bag again and pulled out everything else he would need, including an old ivory planchette, distilled water, herbs and consecrated sea salt. From his pocket he took the witch-hazel twigs.

'Do you have crystal glasses or crystal bowls?' he asked Pike.

Pike fetched four crystal ashtrays and two crystal beakers and Nightingale poured water into one of the glasses and salt and herbs into the ashtrays, before arranging them on the table. Pike sat down on the sofa again, clearly bemused.

Nightingale put the witch-hazel twigs into the other glass and set it on the opposite side of the board to the water, then he lit the candles with his cigarette lighter.

Pike picked up the planchette. It was made of ivory that had yellowed with age. 'You've obviously done this before,' he said.

'It's a tool of the trade,' said Nightingale. He took it from him and placed it in the centre of the board. 'Now, this is important. You need to visualise a white light all around the table.'

'A white light?'

'The whiter the better. The sort of light you get from a fluorescent bulb. No matter what happens, you keep thinking about the light.' Nightingale pinched some sage from one of the ashtrays and sprinkled it over the candles one by one. He rubbed some on the board and the planchette, then he sprinkled lavender and salt over the board. 'Ready?' he asked Pike.

'Ready for what?'

'Just do exactly as I say,' said Nightingale. 'And keep visualising the light. Place your fingertips on the planchette.' Pike did so, but slowly, as if he feared it would burn him. Once he was touching it with both hands, Nightingale did the same. Nightingale took a deep breath and began to speak in a low but strong voice. 'In the name of God, of Jesus Christ, of The Great Brotherhood of Light, of the Archangels Michael, Raphael, Gabriel, Uriel and Ariel, please protect us from the forces of Evil during this session. Let there be nothing but light surrounding this board and its participants and let us only communicate with powers and entities of the light. Protect us, protect this house, the people in this house and let there only be light and nothing but light, Amen.'

He nodded at Pike. 'Amen,' repeated Pike.

Nightingale looked up at the ceiling. 'We're here to talk to the presence that is in this house,' he said. 'Are you there? Please, talk to us.'

The planchette twitched under their fingers.

'This is a safe place,' said Nightingale. 'You are safe here. I want to communicate with the spirit that resides in this house, the same spirit I encountered in the wine cellar and the same spirit that just smashed a painting over Mr Warner's head. If you're here, please introduce yourself.'

There was silence for a few moments, then the crystal chandelier above their heads began to shake gently, its lights flickering. The planchette vibrated abruptly, moving to the center of the board, but Pike pushed it down.

'Hey,' said Nightingale. 'Not so hard.' Looking up, he said, 'Are you here with us now?'

The planchette slid to YES.

'Right,' said Nightingale. 'Are you female?'

YES.

'This is bollocks,' said Pike. 'You're pushing it.' He took his fingers off the planchette but Nightingale shouted at him. 'No! Keep touching it! I'm not playing any tricks. We're actually getting somewhere.' He looked around for signs of the ghost. 'What's your name?'

The planchette began to move. M-A-R-

Suddenly the planchette veered off to the left, almost leaving the board. 'Did you just move it?' asked Nightingale.

Pike shook his head. A bead of sweat flew off the man's forehead and dropped onto the board. The chandeliers shook. 'What's that?' asked Pike. 'What's happening?'

'Keep visualising the light,' said Nightingale. He looked up at the ceiling. 'You didn't complete your name,' he said. 'Could you do that for me now?' He looked down at the board. The planchette went for the letter M but then forcefully shifted direction. This time Nightingale thought for sure he felt Pike move it. 'Pike, what are you doing?'

'What?' said Pike.

'You moved it.'

'No I didn't,' said Pike. He took his fingers off the planchette and stood up. 'This is ridiculous. I'm done with this. It's not working.'

As he stood up the crystal chandelier swayed and uprooted itself, slamming on the ground mere inches from him. Light bulbs burst. Lamps soared across the room, exploding into walls. Furniture rose high in the air and shot across the apartment like bullets. The Ouija board hovered in the air and slammed against the wall before falling to the floor.

Then suddenly everything was still again.

'I'd say it works just fine,' said Nightingale.

* * *

Nightingale decided that he needed local information on the house and its occupants, and the best place for that would be a local bar. He asked Pike what there was in the way of transport and the butler took him to an immense garage full of two dozen spotless, priceless cars. 'Take your pick,' said Pike. 'Except for the Jags. Mr Warner doesn't let anyone touch those.'

Nightingale eyed the cars – vintage Porsches, Ferraris, Aston Martins, Jaguars – and settled on a 1960 Ferrari 250 GT Berlinetta, cherry red.

'Fine choice,' said Pike.

Minutes later Nightingale was roaring out of the driveway, ignoring the speed limit signs, feeling slightly better than he did before. He found a pub, a new building with fake wood siding and a shaded veranda glowing with Christmas lights. Being a Saturday night, loads of people were inside, and he could hear the muffled thunder of Rock 'n Roll music as he stepped from the Berlinetta. He went inside, sat at the counter and ordered a Corona with lime. The bartender, a husky woman with dry brown hair and shiny red cheeks, eyed him reproachfully. 'You're not from around here,' she said, setting a beer coaster in front of him. She took a Corona and lime wedge from the refrigerator, cracked open the beer and set it on the coaster. 'You English?'

'I am indeed, you got me.'

She smiled, revealing a black hole where her two front teeth should have been. 'Knew it.'

'Thanks for the beer,' he said, looking around. He noticed at least a dozen people shamelessly staring at him. 'Looks like you're not used to strangers popping in.'

'Nah, not really. Are you just passing through?'

He took a sip of beer. 'No, I'm staying. For a few days.'

'Where at?'

'You know David Warner the second?'

'Sure. The king of Manhattan.'

Nightingale tipped his bottle. 'His house.'

The bartender smiled again and Nightingale found himself staring into the chasm beyond her missing teeth. 'No!' she said.

'Yep.'

'That guy?'

Mimicking the average American cowboy, he said, 'Yes ma'am.'

'What for?'

'I'm helping him with something.'

'Well, I can't say I know the man personally, because I don't. But boy, have I heard some stories. That guy goes through more staff than these fellas do their Budweisers.'

'That's funny, he said he was good to his staff. But what do I know?'

'What a crock! He said that? Of course he wouldn't admit to it. What billionaire would?'

'I don't know many billionaires.'

'You and me both, honey. But I can tell you firsthand it's a lie. Just looking around, I know of at least six fellas used to work there. There's some hedge-trimmers, a groundskeeper, a security guard, hell, even a cook!' She looked over Nightingale's shoulder. 'Hey, Arnie!'

A tall bald-headed man in a blue button-down shirt looked up from a billiards table. 'Hey what?'

'You used to work for king dipshit over on the hill, right?'

'Who, Warner?'

'That's the one.'

'Yeah, used to.' He glanced at Nightingale. 'Why?'

'What do you think of him?' asked the bartender.

The man shrugged. 'He's a scumbag.'

She turned away from Arnie and faced Nightingale. 'And there you have it. A scumbag.'

'But how come? What did he do?'

'Gee I don't know, honey, take your pick. There's plenty of stories. He's just a mean old goat, mostly. But there are more than a couple folks in here who'd say he killed that Caldwell girl.'

Nightingale froze. Alarm bells rang in his head. 'I'm sorry, what?'

'The Caldwell girl. Oh, right, I forget you haven't been here that long. I'm surprised they didn't tell you about it up there. Mary Caldwell. She went missing, what was it, two years ago? Hasn't been found since.'

'Two years ago, you say?' Nightingale was taking out his wallet.

'That's right.'

He put a twenty dollar bill on the counter and got up. 'Thanks for the chat.'

The bill disappeared in her ample cleavage. 'Hey, anytime. See you around.'

'Yeah,' said Nightingale, opening the door and stepping out into the cool mountain air.

* * *

Pike woke Nightingale the following morning with a breakfast tray and a copy of the local paper. 'Are you going to get rid of the ghost today?' he asked as he placed the tray on a table.

'I hope so,' said Nightingale.

'Do you need anything?' asked the butler.

'Internet access,' said Nightingale.

The butler frowned. 'How does that help?'

'I need information about a girl who went missing some time ago,' said Nightingale. 'Mary Caldwell.'

The butler rubbed his chin. 'Mary? She left.'

'According to the locals, she disappeared.'

Pike shrugged. 'Staff come and go. Usually they work out their notice but occasionally they just leave.'

'You remember Mary?'

'I suppose so. She was a maid. We have dozens here at any time.'

'Did the police investigate?'

'Not really.'

'Not really?'

Pike looked pained. 'Her parents kicked up a fuss at the time, but it was a storm in a teacup.'

Nightingale poured milk into his coffee and sipped it. 'Weren't there suggestions that Mr Warner was involved?'

'Tittle-tattle,' said Pike. 'The locals have too much time on their hands. They do love to gossip.'

'So, a computer?'

'The library,' said Pike. 'There is wi-fi throughout the house though it's password protected because Mr Warner doesn't like the staff using it.' He took a pen from his pocket and scribbled a ten-digit number onto the paper. 'That will get you online.'

Nightingale thanked him, then ate his eggs, bacon and pancakes before heading to the library. He found a computer in an alcove and sat down, logging in with the code that Pike had scribbled on the paper.

He went to the local paper's website and soon found details of Mary Caldwell's disappearance. Mary was a young girl in her twenties with chestnut hair and bright blue eyes, a pink-lipped smile and perfect teeth. She was beautiful. Just a girl working a summer job and trying to pay her own way through university. The parents, a married couple from a few towns over, gave grief-stricken statements, begging for Mary to come home, if she was alive. Nightingale printed off one of the articles that contained the girl's picture.

'What are you doing?'

He turned around. Pike was standing behind him.

'Just looking into the Caldwell girl story.'

'She left two years ago, what has she got to do with what's happening at the house?'

'That's when things started to happen,' said Nightingale. 'The disturbances started shortly after she went missing.' He held up the print-out. 'And there's her name. Mary. That's what the spirit was trying to tell us through the Ouija board last night. M-A-R. The spirit was trying to spell out MARY.'

'You don't know that.'

'No, true. Not for sure. But it's worth looking at. So where is Mr Warner?'

'He left early this morning. For the airport. Why?'

Nightingale ignored the question. 'What's his number?'

'Why do you want to talk to him?'

'Just give me the damn number, Pike.'

'Fine, fine. I was just curious.' Pike recited Warner's cell phone number and Nightingale dialed it into his phone. It started ringing. 'Is there something I can help you with?' Pike asked, hovering. Nightingale waved at him to go away.

Warner came on the line. 'Hello? Who's this? Hello?'

'It's Nightingale. Listen, I need to know if you've got a floor plan of the building. Ideally with the renovations you did to the foundations two years ago.'

'What do you want with those?'

'I don't really have time to explain. Do you have them or not, Warner?'

'The architect's drawings are in the library.'

'I'm in there now. Where would I find them?'

Warner gave Nightingale directions and he found a set of bound plans in a cupboard under a collection of old maps and charts.

'Are you going to be able to get rid of whatever it is, Mr Nightingale?' asked Warner.

'I certainly hope so,' said Nightingale, and he ended the call.

He took the bound plans to his room and placed them on a large table, open at a page that had a drawing of the floor plan of the whole ground floor of the mansion. He went over to his bag and took out two white church candles that he set on the table. His raincoat was hanging on the back of the door and he went over to it and reached into the pocket. He pulled out a small brown leather bag. The bag was several hundred years old but the leather was supple and glossy. Nightingale placed it on the table, then went through to the bathroom. He had already showered that morning but he filled the massive claw-foot bath with hot water and bathed again, twice, before taking a white robe from one of the wardrobes and slipping it on.

He went back to the table and lit the candles before undoing the leather thong that kept the bag closed. He slid out a large pink crystal, about the size of a pigeon's egg, attached to a fine silver chain. He closed his eyes and said a short prayer as he held the crystal pressed between his palms. When he had finished he opened his eyes and let the crystal swing free on its chain. He pictured a pale blue aura around himself as he took slow, deep breaths, then he slowly allowed the aura to spread out until it filled the room.

He repeated Mary Caldwell's name over and over again as he held the crystal over the article he had printed from the newspaper's website. For a minute or two it remained motionless and then it began to slowly move in a small clockwise circle over the sheet of paper.

He continued to repeat Mary's name as he moved the crystal over the floor plan. The crystal stopped spinning for more than a minute but as he moved the crystal over the plan it began to move again, spinning slowly. The closer Nightingale moved the crystal to the wine cellar, the faster it spun. 'I've found you, Mary,' whispered Nightingale. A gust of wind blew out both candles and Nightingale shuddered.

* * *

Nightingale took off the robe, dressed and hurried down to the wine cellar. He went to the brick wall above the fieldstone foundation and rapped it with his knuckles but all he did was hurt himself. He went off in search of something to knock with and found Alena in the kitchen. He mimed using a hammer and she pulled a wooden mallet from a drawer that looked as if it was used to tenderise steak. Nightingale shook his head and held out his hands. 'Bigger,' he said. 'Grande!'

'Grande?'

'Grande. Bigger.'

She nodded and took him to a storage room filled with tools. Nightingale grabbed a pickaxe. 'Perfect,' he said. He frowned as he tried to remember the Italian for flashlight. 'Torcia elletrica,' he said eventually and Alena smiled.

'Torcia elletrica,' she said, and pulled one out of a drawer.

He thanked her, then went back to the wine cellar and tapped the pickaxe against the brickwork until he found a section that resonated like a bell. He smashed the pickaxe at the brick wall and it crumbled inward. He hit it again, breaking through the wall. Four more smacks with the pickaxe opened a meter-wide hole with an empty space inside.

He put down the pickaxe and shone the flashlight into the hole. He saw nothing but crumbled brick and earth. But then his eyes adjusted and he saw an earthen wall, eroded over time. Sticking out of it was a small portion of white cloth. He tugged at it but it held firm. Standing on his toes, he seized the corner of cloth in both hands, and tugged.

Bits of mud and soil dislodged from the wall and crumbled over his hands, but a six-inch section of the cloth came free. He found himself holding onto a skeletonized human wrist.

'I'm going to have to ask you to come out of there,' said a voice behind him. It was Pike. Nightingale did as he was told, squirming awkwardly backward out of the hole, his hair peppered with dust and dirt. Pike stood in front of him, pointing a gun at his chest. He was in his butler's outfit, minus the tailcoat.

'You killed her,' said Nightingale.

'It was an accident.'

'What, and then you accidentally bricked her up?'

'I had no choice. They'd have put me in prison.'

'Not if it was really an accident.'

'I pushed her. She fell against a rack. It was over in seconds.'

'Then you should have called the cops and explained.' Realisation dawned and he pointed a finger at Pike. 'She caught you stealing wine, is that it? Even if they didn't do you for murder, the thefts would put you behind bars.'

'It was a perk of the job. The guy before me did it. Warner pays shit money, you take what you can. All the staff do it.'

'And you were selling the good stuff?'

Pike shrugged. 'A bottle or two.' He waved his gun at the racks. 'He's not going to drink one percent of this.'

'So you were stealing, she caught you, and you killed her?'

'She pushed me. I pushed her back. It was an accident.'

The newly-installed light bulbs in the cellar began to buzz and glow. One of them burst. Then another. Soon the light bulbs were blowing up everywhere, showering them with glass and plunging them into darkness. Pike looked around, muttering, 'What the…'

The breath was suddenly wrenched from his lungs as Nightingale barreled into him. They smashed into a wine rack, knocking it over and falling to the ground with it. The gun discharged and a bullet embedded in the wood beam above them. Pike punched Nightingale in the gut, rolled on top of him, and wrestled the gun away, pointing it at his head. Nightingale struck the gun just before it went off, sending a bullet ricocheting off the concrete beside his ear.

Nightingale grabbed hold of Pike's wrist, craned the gun barrel upward, and pressed down on Pike's forefinger. The bullet went through Pike's left eye and exited the top of his skull. He fell limp on top of Nightingale.

Nightingale threw Pike's body off him and sat upright against a rack, gasping for breath. He took out his cell phone and started to dial Wainwright's number, but something glowed in the hole in the wall, and he froze. Then he watched, mesmerized, as a ball of glowing white light exited the cavern in the wall and drifted into the cellar, hovering for a moment as if in salutation, before shooting straight up through the ceiling and disappearing. The few remaining lights which had been flickering went still and silent, and he felt as if the spirit of Mary Caldwell was finally at rest.

* * *

Nightingale walked out through the wrought-iron gates. Wainwright's stretch limo was waiting, white smoke feathering from the exhaust. Hans the driver heaved himself out of the driver's seat and opened the rear door for him, relieving him of his bag as Nightingale slid into the back.

Wainwright was smoking a massive cigar and holding a tumbler of malt whisky. He raised the glass in salute. 'Job well done, Jack,' he said. 'Warner has signed the contracts, the deal is done, and boy is he grateful.'

Hans slammed the door shut and put Nightingale's bag in the trunk before shoehorning himself back into the driver's seat.

'Good to know,' said Nightingale.

'Seriously, Jack, this couldn't have gone any better.'

'Well, Pike being dead is a wrinkle we could have done without.'

Wainwright shook his head. 'Actually, no. If he'd stood trial and started talking about the ghost, all sorts of questions would have been asked. This way, a violent criminal got his comeuppance.' He sipped his whisky. 'My people cleaned things up?'

'It's as if it never happened. Just make sure they give Mary a proper burial.'

'They will. They'll do the same with Pike, the last thing we want is for his malevolent spirit hanging around.' He raised his glass. 'The perfect ending.'

Nightingale chuckled as he settled back in his seat and took out his cigarettes. 'And of course, in the great tradition of mystery stories, it was the butler that did it.'

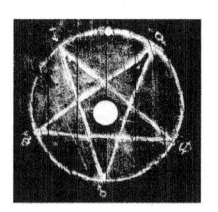

WRONG TURN

Jack Nightingale had never been a great fan of SatNavs, or any form of technology that relied on electrical power. Power cuts happened and batteries died and if you were relying on electricity for communication or for your location and it went down then you were up the proverbial creek without a paddle. The Ford Escape he'd rented at Charlotte Douglas International Airport didn't come with a SatNav as standard, he had to pay extra, and it was the last one they had and the blonde girl with too much make up who had handled his paperwork had apologised and said that the last person who had used it had reported having problems with it. They were going to have it looked at but if he really wanted a SatNav she would let him use it. She offered him a twenty per cent discount but money wasn't the issue, Joshua Wainwright was picking up the bill.

The airport was busy – it was a gateway to the Caribbean and most years was in the top ten US airports ranked by passenger traffic and aircraft movements. The rental car outlet was packed with holidaymakers and businessmen. Night was falling by the time Nightingale had reached the counter and the blonde girl had greeted him as if she was reading from a script. Nightingale took the SatNav and asked for a map but they had run out. The blonde girl apologised again. 'We've been worked off our feet today,' she said.

Nightingale told her not to worry. Anyway, Joshua Wainwright had made it clear that his destination wasn't shown on any map, instead he'd given Nightingale the coordinates to tap into the SatNav.

The SatNav came in a black pouch with a holder connected to a beanbag thing that sat on the dashboard. It took Nightingale the best part of fifteen minutes to work out how to connect it and another half an hour before he managed to input Wainwright's coordinates. According to the electronic miracle he was an hour away from his destination.

It was dark when he eventually drove out of the airport and headed west towards the Nantahala National Forest. According to Wainwright, the man he was going to see lived on an estate on the edge of the forest, on an estate that was so private it was not shown on any maps. It was Wainwright who had told him that Nantahala was a Cherokee word meaning Land Of The Noonday Sun. Wainwright had explained that some of the gorges in the forest were so deep that they were only touched by the sun when it was directly overhead. The rest of the time they were in darkness.

The SatNav took him along Route 74. After a few miles Nightingale muted the sound because the spoken instructions were annoying. It was a man's voice and there was a note of disapproval when he gave instructions as if he wasn't impressed with Nightingale's driving skills.

The SatNav took him north on the Interstate 26 and then it took him off the highway and onto a smaller road that wound through woodland with no street lighting or road markings. That was when his SatNav started playing up. He wasn't sure if it was because the equipment was faulty or if the trees were interfering with the signal but every few minutes the screen would flicker and his position would jump away from the road on the screen so it looked as if he was driving through the trees. Nightingale muttered under his breath. He was already late and without the SatNav he had no idea where he was going. He put the sound back on. 'Come on, matey, where the hell am I?' he asked out loud.

The screen went blank and Nightingale swore. It flickered and the map was there but there was no indication of where the car was. 'Please don't do this to me,' he said, easing his foot off the accelerator. The car's location appeared briefly on the screen but it showed him a half a mile away in the forest.

He cursed again and pulled over at the side of the road. It was in complete darkness and he hadn't seen another vehicle for the best part of twenty minutes. The headlights of the SUV cut through the blackness and illuminated the trees either side of the road. He groped in his pocket for his cell phone and cursed again when he saw that he had no bars. No signal. He tried calling Wainwright anyway but the phone wasn't lying, he had no signal. He put the phone back in his pocket and drummed his hands on the steering wheel. He figured he could probably find his way back to the airport and see about getting a replacement SatNav, or even switching rental companies. But then he'd be a day late for his meeting. He could try driving on, but that was going to be hit and miss. He had a vague recollection of the route, and certainly most of that route entailed sticking to the road he was on. There was a right turn when he got closer to his destination, he remembered that much, but not much else. And if he did drive on, maybe the SatNav would kick in again. And even if it didn't, there had to be places where there would be cellphone coverage. Failing that a filling station or a motel, somewhere where he could make a call to Wainwright. He pressed his foot down and started driving again.

The road twisted and turned and he had to keep his speed below thirty most of the time. Being lost was bad enough, but if he had an accident with no way of calling for help, an inconvenience would very quickly turn into a full-blown nightmare.

The road started to climb up a hill and he groped for his phone, figuring that the higher he got the more likely he was to get a signal. The SatNav screen had frozen now. He looked down at the screen of his phone. No bars. Suddenly light flooded his windscreen and blinded him. He braked and tried to keep the car on the road. A massive truck roared by, the slipstream buffeting his SUV. His night vision had gone completely and he slowed right down. He cursed again and banged the SatNav with the flat of his hand. 'Turn right in one hundred yards,' said the disapproving voice.

'Are you kidding me?' snapped Nightingale. The screen was still blank but he hadn't imagined the voice. He continued to crawl along but then saw a road off to the right. There was a sign pointing down the road and two words. WILLOW CREEK.

Nightingale indicated even though there was clearly no one else on the road for miles and made the turn. The road was narrower than the one he'd just left and the trees seemed even closer together and thicker, their branches almost meeting overhead. The headlights still cut through the night like yellow cones but the road twisted and turned so much he could never see more than a few hundred feet ahead.

He banged the SatNav again. 'Come on, mate, some help, please.'

According to the digital clock on the dashboard it was half past nine, about the time that he had expected to arrive at his destination. He couldn't be far away, he was sure of that. But by the look of it there weren't any houses around.

The road forked ahead of him and he slowed. There were no markings in the road and no signs and no indication of which was the continuation of the road he was on. Right or left? There was no way of knowing which was the main route, both roads appeared identical. He banged on the SatNav again but it remained sullenly silent.

Nightingale decided to go right but he kept the speed below twenty miles an hour just in case he had to go back. The road was narrower than it had been, and the trees denser. He drove for the best part of a mile and then in the distance saw a road off to the right and a sign opposite. He slowed and looked at the sign. WILLOW CREEK.

Nightingale frowned. That was the same sign he'd seen earlier. But he was miles away from the last one. He rubbed his chin. Straight on or turn right? He banged his hand down on the SatNav but it was no help and the screen stayed dead.

'Willow Creek sounds as good as anything,' he muttered and turned right, shaking his head as his hand automatically flicked the turn indicator. He drove down the road and again it twisted so much that he was reluctant to go above twenty miles an hour.

The trees were now so close to the side of the road that often leaves brushed against the doors as he drove. There were potholes and cracks in the road surface and the car rattled and bucked. He ignored the lanes and drove in the centre of the road. The branches of the trees interlinked overhead, blotting out any view of the sky. He was starting to get a very bad feeling about what was happening and regretted his decision not to drive back to the airport. But that ship had definitely sailed, he had no idea how to retrace his steps and his only hope now was to find Willow Creek. The fact that the place had a name suggested that someone lived there and hopefully that someone would have a working phone or a map.

The road dipped down sharply and he put his foot on the brake, keeping his speed at twenty miles an hour. There was a long, slow turn to the right and then he reached a T-junction. There were no signs, no way of knowing which way he should go. He slammed his hand down on the SatNav so hard that it fell off the dashboard and clattered to the floor. Nightingale didn't bother retrieving it, the device was worse than useless. He decided to go right and after five minutes of driving he figured he had made the correct choice because the road widened and the trees started to thin out. He grinned when he saw a building ahead, with lights on in all the windows. It was a hotel, he realised. A large, modern, six-storey brick building with a large sign above the entrance – WILLOW CREEK HOTEL.

There was a large car park behind the hotel but after driving around for a couple of minutes Nightingale realised there were no spaces. He drove out of the car park and drove up to the main entrance. There was a sign there that warned 'SHORT TERM PARKING FOR GUESTS ONLY' and Nightingale parked in front of it. He headed inside. There was a large reception area and it was packed with several dozen people milling around, their conversations melding into a gentle buzzing noise like a hive of bees that had been disturbed. To the left was a large table manned by three pretty girls in black jackets under a sign that read 'CONVENTION REGISTRATION'. There were three lines of people waiting to register.

The main hotel reception desk was to the right. There was only one receptionist on duty, a bald man with thick-lensed spectacles wearing a white shirt and a black waistcoat with gold trimming. 'Welcome to Willow Creek Hotel,' he said in a mid-Western drawl as Nightingale approached. 'If you're here for the convention you can do all your registration at the convention desk.' He pointed across the room.

'I'm not with the convention,' said Nightingale. 'I'm lost, can I use your phone?'

The man shook his head. 'I'm sorry, all the lines are down.'

Nightingale took out his phone and looked at the screen. Still no signal. 'Do any of the phone companies have a signal out here?' he asked.

'I'm afraid not,' said the man. 'It's the terrain.'

'So where can I get a signal? I really need to make a call.'

'If you drive ten miles east you can usually get a signal, but it's weather dependent and they say there's a storm coming and that's always bad for reception.'

Nightingale sighed. His day was going from bad to worse. 'Do you have a room?'

'I'm so sorry, we're fully booked. There's a convention. Every room has been sold for three days.'

Nightingale rubbed the back of his neck. 'Is there a sofa I can sleep on? Anything?'

'I'm sorry. No. But let me just check your name.'

'Nightingale. But I haven't booked. I didn't know I'd be here.'

The man's fingers tapped on the keyboard and he smiled. 'Jack Nightingale?'

Nightingale frowned. 'Yes.'

'There's a standard room in your name. Booked and paid for. And you are pre-registered.' His smile broadened. 'Problem solved,' he said. He handed Nightingale a keycard and waved at the elevators. 'Have a pleasant stay, Mr Nightingale. Your welcome pack is in your room.'

'My car is in the short term parking area out front,' said Nightingale. 'Am I OK to leave it there?'

The man winced as if he was in pain. 'No, I'm sorry. You'll have to move it.'

'But your car park is full.'

'Yes, the convention opened today and most of our guests have driven here. If you take your car across the road you'll find another parking area. It's not lit, I'm afraid, but it's quite safe out here. We are literally miles from anywhere.'

Nightingale thanked him and went outside. He got into his SUV and drove away from the hotel and across the road. A narrow dirt track cut through the trees and Nightingale drove slowly down it. Even on full beam the headlights barely illuminated the way, the darkness seemed to simply swallow up the light.

To his right he saw a dozen cars parked in a clearing and he turned and drove through the trees until he reached them. He parked and climbed out. He opened the rear door to take out his overnight bag before locking the vehicle. It was pitch dark and he stood where he was as he waited for his night vision to kick in. An owl screeched off to his left and overhead the leaves of the trees whispered as a night wind blew through them.

He started to walk to the track, his Hush Puppies crunching on dead leaves and twigs. He heard a rustling to his left but when he stopped so did the noise. The owl screeched again and he turned up the collar of his raincoat against the chill wind that was blowing against his back. From where he was standing he couldn't see the hotel, nor could he see the parked cars. It was as if he was alone in the forest. Off in the distance, something howled. It wasn't a dog, or a coyote he was sure of that. It sounded large and fierce and threatening and he started walking quickly in the direction of the hotel. He heard the rustling again to his left so he broke into a trot and then a run and didn't slow down until he broke through the trees and saw the road ahead of him. He hurried across the road and looked over his shoulder before he entered the hotel. There was nothing behind him. Just the trees.

He pushed open the glass doors and walked into the lobby. On the way to the elevators, Nightingale walked past a display of garish paintings of clowns, more than a dozen lined up on a wall. They were clumsily painted, the clowns were caricatures with smeared make up and evil eyes. A small group of men and women were drinking beer and studying the paintings. At the far end of the display was a man, presumably the painter, sitting at a table with a pile of brochures. He was a heavy-set man with a thick moustache and cold eyes that stared unblinkingly ahead. The man's face was familiar. A woman in a blood-red dress walked up to the man and handed him a twenty dollar bill. He picked up a brochure, smiled, and said something to her. She giggled, answered, and he scrawled on the cover of the brochure with a Sharpie pen and handed it to her. She clasped it to her breast, thanked him, and walked away.

Nightingale frowned and tilted his head on one side. He could just about make out the title on the brochure. KILLER CLOWNS by JOHN WAYNE GACY.

Nightingale's frown deepened. Gacy was a serial killer and rapist who had killed at least 33 boys and men in and around Chicago. He strangled almost all of them and buried 26 of the bodies in the crawlspace under his home, allegedly so that he could spend more time with them.

Nightingale looked back at the paintings. He could see a price tag on the one closest to him. Twenty thousand dollars. What sort of sick mind would buy a painting done by a serial killer, he wondered. Gacy had been given the nickname Killer Clown because he worked as an entertainer at children's parties dressed as a clown called Pogo while he carried out his murders.

He walked over to the man at the table. He was back staring into space, the Sharpie gripped in a large, clammy, hand. Nightingale put his overnight bag on the floor and picked up one of the brochures. The main picture was of one of the paintings on display – a clown with huge red lips and a silver tear trickling down a white cheek, wearing a small gold crown perched on a crinkly green wig.

The man grinned up at him. He had thin, bloodless lips and yellowing teeth and his eyes were as cold and hard as splinters of ice.

'Five bucks, twenty if I sign it,' said the man.

Nightingale took out his wallet and gave him a twenty-dollar note.

'Who shall I make it out to?' asked the man.

'Jack,' said Nightingale.

The man scrawled on the cover and handed it to Nightingale. 'Have a nice day, Jack,' he said.

As Nightingale took the brochure from him the smile vanished and the eyes stared straight ahead again.

As he picked up his bag and moved away, Nightingale looked down at what the man had written. 'HAVE A KILLER CONVENTION.' And underneath was his signature, an almost illegible scrawl that looked uncomfortably close to John W. Gacy.

As he reached the elevator, Nightingale looked over his shoulder. The man was signing another brochure, this time for an elderly man in a

Mickey Mouse baseball jacket. John Gacy was executed by lethal injection at Stateville Correctional Centre near Chicago on March 13, 1994. So what was that sick bastard doing signing on his behalf? Nightingale shuddered. His elevator arrived and he got in. As the elevator doors closed, the man turned to look at Nightingale, raised his hand and waved, his face a blank mask. Nightingale shuddered.

He took the elevator up to the fifth floor and walked along a gloomy carpeted corridor to his room. He used his keycard but a red light showed and the door refused to open. He tried again. Red light. He tried a third time, muttering under his breath, and a green light winked on. He pushed open the door and stuck his card in a slot on the wall to operate the lights. He hung his coat on a hook on the door before looking around.

It was a standard hotel room, nothing more and nothing less. A bed that could just about be described as a double, a television on a bracket opposite the bed so that it could be turned towards a small table and two chairs by the window. The curtains were open and he went over and looked out, He had a view of the car park and the trees beyond.

He had a quick look into the bathroom. There was a bath but it was less than four-feet long, with a shower unit and a glass screen that was spotted with white stains. There was a glass shelf above a small sink on which were two plastic-wrapped mugs and small tubes of shampoo and body wash.

He tossed his bag onto the table by the window and placed the signed brochure on top of it. There was a folder there with WELCOME PACK in large letters and underneath in smaller type – THE CONVENTION THAT NO ONE IS TALKING ABOUT. Nightingale frowned. That was a mistake, surely? How could that be a selling point. Somewhere a printer was taking money under false pretenses.

On top of the pack was a laminated badge on a blood red lanyard. There were just six words on it. JACK NIGHTINGALE. DELEGATE. ACCESS ALL AREAS. He rolled up the lanyard and pushed it into his trouser pocket, then picked up the phone and dialled room service. He was about to place an order for a club sandwich and a couple of bottles of Corona when the man who answered the phone told him that room service wasn't available because of the convention but that he could go down to the restaurant or bar.

Nightingale just wanted to eat and sleep but the urge to eat took precedence and so he headed downstairs. The restaurant was busy and he couldn't see a free table, and anyway he didn't feel like eating alone surrounded by diners so he headed for the bar. There were a dozen small tables along one side, a line of booths at the end, and a long bar that stretched the whole length of the room with two dozen barstools. There were only three drinkers on the stools so he found a space and sat down. The barman was a balding bruiser of a man with bulging forearms wearing a shirt with a ruffled front and a slightly skew-whiff black bow tie. He had a name tag with ERNIE in capital letters. 'How are we this evening, Sir?' he asked.

'A bit confused, but a drink'll hopefully sort me out,' he said. 'Have you got Corona?'

'Of course, Sir. With lemon or lime?'

'Lime if you have it.'

'Glass?'

'Absolutely not,' said Nightingale.

Ernie grinned. 'A purist,' he said. He flicked the cap off a bottle of Corona, shoved a wedge of lime down the neck, and put it down in front of Nightingale. Nightingale picked it up and toasted the bartender. 'First today.'

The bartender winked and went over to serve another customer. Nightingale sipped his beer and pulled over a menu. The bar served a club sandwich but it also did a steak sandwich and he was trying to decide between the two when a man slid onto the stool next to him. He was tall and thin with an angular face and greying hair. The man nodded at

Nightingale. 'Corona?'

Nightingale nodded.

'I've never liked that Mexican beer,' said the man.

'It's an acquired taste,' said Nightingale.

The man held out his hand. 'Charles Cullen.'

'Jack Nightingale.'

'Speaker or fan?'

'Fan, I suppose.' He looked sideways at the man. 'Wasn't that the name of the Angel Of Death? Charles Cullen? No offence.'

'None taken,' said the man. 'They always say I look nothing like my photographs.'

Nightingale fought to keep from showing surprise. Charles Cullen was a nurse who confessed to killing forty patients in New Jersey in the eighties and nineties and was imprisoned for life. The police reckoned the forty he confessed to were just the tip of the iceberg.

'You're English?' said Cullen.

Nightingale nodded.

'I'm on a panel tomorrow with one of your countrymen,' said Cullen. 'Harold Shipman. Do you know him?'

'The GP?'

'GP?'

'It's what we British call our doctors,' said Nightingale.

'That's him,' said Cullen. 'Dr Harold Shipman. Wow, that guy. They reckon he killed what, 250 people?'

'That's what they say.'

'Came close to my record,' said Cullen. 'I did three hundred.' He winked. 'Well, maybe a couple less but who's counting?'

'And you're on a panel?'

Cullen nodded enthusiastically. 'We're talking about medical murdering,' he said. 'There's been a lot of interest.'

'I'm sure,' said Nightingale. He sipped his beer thoughtfully. Harold

Shipman was indeed one the world's most prolific serial killers. He was sentenced to life imprisonment in January 2000 and just four years later hanged himself in his cell at Wakefield Prison. So if Harold Shipman was dead, how was he going to appear on a panel with Charles Cullen?

He opened his mouth to ask Cullen a question, but before he could say anything two middle-aged women with permed hair and matching trouser suits rushed over with mobile phones at the ready. 'Mr Cullen, can we take selfies with you?' gushed one.

'Of course you can, ladies,' said Cullen, beaming with pleasure. He stood up and the women held out their phones and pouted as they posed.

Nightingale waved at the barman and ordered a club sandwich and French fries. The barman smiled apologetically. 'Our kitchen is really backed up,' he said. 'It'll be forty-five minutes at the earliest.'

'That's fine,' said Nightingale. 'And can I charge it to my room? Jack Nightingale. Room Five Two Three.'

'No problem,' said the barman.

More fans had congregated around Cullen and one over-excited woman almost knocked Nightingale off his stool. He stood up to give them more room, then decided to go outside for a cigarette. He took out his pack of Marlboro as he walked out into the cold night air. He looked around but he appeared to be the only smoker so he walked a few paces from the entrance, slipped a cigarette between his lips and lit it with his Zippo. He breathed a contented plume of smoke up at the cloudless night sky and watched it disperse as he wondered exactly what the hell was going on. A long-dead serial killer posing for selfies with adoring fans. Another executed killer signing autographs and selling his art. In a hotel in the middle of nowhere. A hotel that he had stumbled upon by accident but which appeared to know that he was coming. None of it made any sense though he had a feeling that Joshua Wainwright had something to do with the unnatural series of events.

He looked at the woodland opposite. He could make out the track leading to the carpark but the vehicles weren't visible. He shuddered at the thought of walking into the darkness to retrieve his SUV but knew that he wouldn't be going anywhere until the following morning. He took out his phone and looked hopefully at the screen but there was no signal. He waved the phone in the air but it made no difference.

A good-looking man with dark brown hair walked out of the hotel and grinned when he saw that Nightingale was smoking. 'Have you got a cigarette, buddy?' he asked.

'Sure,' said Nightingale. He tapped out a Marlboro and handed it to him, then lit it.

The man blew smoke contentedly up at the sky. 'I hate this whole non-smoking thing,' he said.

'You and me both,' said Nightingale.

The man held out his hand. 'Ted,' he said.

'Jack.' The two men shook hands.

'When did smoking become such a sin?' asked Ted.

'They'd make every vice illegal if they could,' said Nightingale. 'I hear they're planning to tax fattening foods now.'

Ted blew another plume of smoke. 'It was a serious question,' he said. 'When did it become illegal?'

'Two thousand and six in the US, I think,' said Nightingale. 'For a while it stayed legal in casinos but they stopped that a couple of years later.'

'Health Nazis,' said Ted. 'Why do they do that? Why do they stop people doing what makes them happy?'

Nightingale shrugged. It wasn't a question he could answer.

'When was Prohibition? Nineteen twenty until nineteen thirty-three, right? Banning alcohol makes as little sense as banning cigarettes. At least they came to their senses on that one.'

'Because everyone ignored the law,' said Nightingale. 'It would happen with cigarettes too if everyone just carried on smoking.' He shrugged. 'Trouble is, most people are against it now so you'd be fighting a losing battle.'

Ted chuckled. 'I've never had a problem breaking the law,' he said.

Nightingale looked across at him and realisation dawned. 'You're Ted Bundy,' said Nightingale quietly.

'I sure am,' said the man. 'Do you want an autograph? A signed picture? I've signed a hundred today but always happy to do one more for a fan.'

'No, I'm good, I'm not here for the convention.'

'I thought everyone was here for the convention,' said Ted. 'That's what this is about, isn't it?'

'I don't know,' said Nightingale. 'I took a wrong turn.'

Ted chuckled. 'I think pretty much everyone here has taken a wrong turn,' he said.

That was certainly true of Bundy, Nightingale knew. He was one of America's most prolific serial killers, raping and murdering more than thirty young women in the 1970s. He decapitated several of his victims and kept their heads in his apartment, and often had sex with the corpses long after death.

'So I'm giving a talk at breakfast,' said Ted. 'Will you be there?'

'I guess so,' said Nightingale.

'You don't sound sure.'

'Like I said, I'm not really here for the convention. I'm just passing through.'

'We're all passing through, Jack.' He blew a pretty good smoke ring and nodded with pride.

'You know you're dead?' said Nightingale.

Ted smiled carelessly. 'We're all dead, Jack. If you think about it.'

'I'm not dead.'

'Not now, no. But in a hundred years, you are. Maybe you'll be dead in fifty. And fifty years ago you weren't alive and when you think about it, not being alive is pretty much being dead, right?'

Ted raised an eyebrow and smiled. 'Do I look dead to you, Jack?'

'No,' said Nightingale. 'You don't.'

Ted held up his cigarette. 'If I were to touch the end against my skin and it burned, that would show what? That I'm alive?'

'I guess so, Maybe. Maybe not. I'm not sure.'

'You don't seem sure of anything, Jack. That accent, where are you from, Australia?'

'England,' said Nightingale.

Ted nodded. 'I've never been but I hear good things.' He took a long draw on his cigarette and blew smoke up at the night sky. 'What year is it, Jack?'

'You don't know?'

He shrugged. 'I'll be honest with you. I know who I am but I don't know where I am and I can't remember what I did yesterday. I remember waking up this morning and today has been a blast, but I can't get any of the TVs to work and I've no idea what's happening in the world.' He took another pull on his cigarette and pressed the lit end into the palm. He yelped and then cursed and held out his hand. There was an ugly burn in the middle of his palm. 'That fucking hurt,' he said.

'I can see that,' said Nightingale.

'So what does that mean?'

'I don't know,' said Nightingale. 'Sorry.'

Ted flicked the remains of his cigarette away. 'Guess I'll see you inside,' he said.

'Guess you will.'

Nightingale smoked his cigarette as he watched one of America's most notorious serial killers walk back into the hotel. A serial killer who was executed in the electric chair at Raiford Prison in Florida, on January 24, 1989.

He finished his cigarette and went back into the lobby. A line had formed outside a set of double doors and people were filing in. A poster announced the four speakers who would be on a panel that would be discussing 'DINING WITH THE DEAD – CAN YOU EAT THE EVIDENCE?'

Nightingale stared at the poster in amazement. There were four head-and-shoulder photographs of the four panelists and he recognised them all.

Top left was a sandy-haired man with a straggly moustache. Jeffrey Dahmer. He had raped, killed and dismembered seventeen young men and boys in the 1980s, often keeping their body parts in his fridge. He'd been sentenced to life but had been beaten to death by another inmate in the Columbia Correctional Institution in 1994. Nightingale scratched the back of his head as he stared at the photograph. If Dahmer was dead, how was he going to speak at a panel at the Willow Creek Hotel?

The man pictured in the top left photograph was also quite definitely dead. Albert Fish had raped, murdered and eaten countless children in the early 1900s. He was executed in the electric chair in Sing Sing Prison in 1936.

The only woman on the panel was Leonarda Cianciulli who murdered three girls in Italy at the start of the Second World War. She turned the bodies into tea cakes that she ate herself and served to her friends. She was sentenced to thirty years in prison but died behind bars in 1970.

The photograph on the bottom left of the poster was a Russian. Also dead. And also a prolific killer. Andrei Chikatilo murdered and mutilated more than 50 women in the former Soviet Union in the 1980s. He was executed by firing squad in 1994.

Nightingale frowned. It made no sense. A panel made up of four dead serial killers, talking to a room full of what? Fans? That's what conventions were for, right? For fans to meet their heroes?

The last of the line were filing into the room. Nightingale went over to the two doors. There were two blonde girls in black suits standing guard and they smiled brightly. 'Can we see your badge please?' asked one.

Nightingale remembered the badge in his pocket and he took it out. They inspected it and waved him through.

There were fifty or so people already sitting down on lines of chairs that had been arranged facing a cloth-covered table. There were four high-backed chairs behind the table and four name-cards matching the faces on the poster outside.

Nightingale sat down at the back. There was a buzz of anticipation in the room and as the only door was behind them, heads kept turning. A young woman carried a tray of water bottles and glasses to the table and arranged them by the name cards, and a man in a black polo-neck and black jeans was checking the microphones on the table.

More fans came in and took their places. Several were taking photographs of the table even though there was no one there. An elderly man came in with an aluminium walker to which an oxygen bottle had been attached. He had clear plastic tubing running the oxygen to his nose and walking was clearly an effort. He sat on the back row, next to the aisle, took several deep breaths and then turned to give Nightingale a thumbs-up. Nightingale nodded at the man, who must have been in his nineties.

Over the next few minutes the room filled up and eventually every seat was taken. Most of the audience were white middle-aged men, but there were women too, and some who didn't look long out of their teens. From the way they were dressed they came from the full spectrum of the social classes. Some of the men wore expensive tailored suits, others tracksuits with gold chains around their necks. There was a man wearing mechanic's overalls and another in the uniform of a well-known courier company. A woman in her seventies who had clearly gone through several rounds of plastic surgery over the years and whose forehead was Botoxed to a shiny finish sat wearing a Chanel suit with a matching handbag perched on her lap. Next to her was a near-obese young blonde woman with a pinched face and acne-scarred cheeks who was wearing stretch pants and a low-cut leopard-print top that showed off almost twelve inches of cleavage. Both burst into applause when the doors opened and the four panelists made their way down the aisle towards the tables.

All four kept their heads down and avoided eye contact as if they were over-awed by the reception they were getting. A man had taken centre stage and was holding a microphone, gesturing at the audience to clap louder. It took Nightingale several seconds to realise who the man was. Like Nightingale, he was a Brit. Fred West. A short man with curly black hair and thin lips that curled back into a snarl as he watched the four panelists take their places. Over a period of twenty years Fred West and his wife Rosemary tortured, raped and killed more than thirteen girls and young women and buried several in and around their Gloucester home. Rosemary West was serving a life sentence but Fred West had hanged himself in his cell while awaiting trial in 1995.

Jeffrey Dahmer poured himself a glass of water and sipped it. Albert Fish sat back, folded his arms and for the first time smiled at the audience. Leonarda Cianciulli placed her hands on the table and interlinked her fingers as she said something to Andrei Chikatilo on her left. The Russian nodded and they both laughed.

Eventually Fred West motioned for quiet and the applause died down. The next hour was one of the most surreal of Nightingale's life. West introduced the four panelists, detailing their crimes to applause and cheers. Then he announced that the session would be a Q&A, with the audience asking whatever they wanted. Nothing was off limits, he said, though the theme was officially about eating your victims, something all four panelists had done in the past.

As soon as he asked for questions a flurry of hands went up. West moved around the audience, holding the microphone and prompting for clarification if the question wasn't clear. Most of the questions were perfectly clear. The audience wanted to know what it was like to eat human flesh, whether it tasted better raw or cooked, which parts of the body were tastiest, what were the health risks (absolutely zero said Albert Fish), how long body parts could be stored in a fridge, how did freezing affect taste and texture (better not to freeze said Dahmer), could body parts be preserved with salt, what could be done to mask the smell of a decomposing body. The questions came thick and fast and many members of the audience were taking notes, either scribbling in notebooks or tapping away on tablets.

The old man sitting along from Nightingale was staring at the panelists wide-eyed, chuckling from time to time and once laughing so hard that he almost choked.

The session went beyond its allotted time and there was no let up in the questions but eventually Fred West had to bring it to a close, causing a collective groan from the audience, followed by thunderous applause and a standing ovation as the four panelists left the room. Hands reached out to touch them as they walked by, and Dahmer grinned and gave out high-fives all the way to the door.

Nightingale sat stunned, trying to take in what he'd seen, and eventually a hand patted him on the shoulder and a man in a black suit told him he'd have to leave. Nightingale looked around. The room was empty and two women were removing the name cards and microphones from the table. Nightingale mumbled an apology and headed out. The lobby was packed and John Gacy was signing brochures and pocketing twenty dollar bills as if there was no tomorrow.

Nightingale went over to the bar and slid onto an empty stool. Ernie grinned when he saw him, and reached under the bar and pulled out a tray on which there was a plate covered with a stainless steel dome. He put the tray down in front of Nightingale and removed the dome with a flourish. Nightingale looked down at the toasted club sandwich and a neat pile of French fries. He lifted up one of the slices of bread and wrinkled his nose at the pieces of white chicken that made up the top layer of the sandwich. All he could think about was what Dahmer had said about his victims - they'd tasted like chicken.

'You okay?' asked Ernie.

'I think I've lost my appetite,' said Nightingale.

Ernie replaced the cover. 'How about I keep it behind the bar in case you change your mind?'

'Sounds like a plan,' said Nightingale.

Ernie put the tray under the bar. 'Another Corona?' he asked.

Nightingale nodded and Ernie opened a bottle, shoved a slice of lime down the neck and placed it in front of him.

A heavy-set man in a leather jacket plonked himself down on the stool next to Nightingale and ordered a whisky on the rocks. 'Make it a double,' growled the man. 'To hell with that, make it a treble and go easy on the rocks.'

Ernie gave the man his drink and he immediately gulped half of it down before wiping his mouth with the back of his hand. 'What's up?' he asked Nightingale.

'Not much,' said Nightingale.

The man looked at the Corona bottle. 'Fucking Mexican beer,' he said. 'I thought Trump had put a stop to that.'

'I think he's happy enough with the beer, it's the people he doesn't like.'

The man nodded. 'That's the truth. But I tell you Buddy, without the wetbacks I wouldn't make half the money I do. I own a landscaping business and I can tell you one thing about Mexicans and that's that they know how to work. They make shit beer, though, and don't get me started on the food.' He stuck out his hand. There was a large gold ring on one finger and a thick gold bracelet around the wrist. 'Luke McVie,' he said.

Nightingale shook the hand. 'Jack Nightingale.'

'Speaker or delegate?'

'Delegate.'

'You going to the auction?'

Nightingale frowned. 'Auction?'

McVie grinned. 'Hell, yeah. It's the main reason I'm here.' He pulled a printed leaflet from his pocket and slapped it onto the bar.

Nightingale looked down at it. There was a headline across the top – TIRED OF THE CHASE? BUY YOUR VICTIM TO GO.

Underneath there were three photographs. Two girls, one young man. The girls were a blonde and an Asian. The boy was in his teens with styled hair and frightened eyes. To the right of each photograph was a short description.

There was a line of type across the bottom. AUCTION STARTS AT MIDNIGHT PROMPT IN THE FIRST FLOOR ROOSEVELT MEETING ROOM.

McVie tapped the Asian. 'That's the one I'm going to bid on,' he said. 'I love Asians. I love to hear them scream.'

He reached out to pick up the leaflet but Nightingale beat him to it. He read it again, from top to bottom. Victims for sale? To the highest bidder? He looked up at McVie, open-mouthed.

'I know, sexy little thing, isn't she? And they have a room in the basement for you to do what you want, and they dispose of everything afterwards. Or they'll pack it up for you to take away. These guys really understand customer service.' He took the leaflet from Nightingale's hand and stuck it back in his pocket, drained his glass and snapped his fingers for another.

'How did you find out about the convention, Luke?' asked Nightingale.

McVie looked across at him. 'Same way as always,' he said. 'They find you, right? You do what has to be done and then one day you get the call.'

'And what has to be done?'

McVie grinned. 'You know as well as I do, Jack. You have to prove yourself before you get an invite.' He frowned. 'You got an invite, right?'

'I was registered and booked in so I guess so.'

McVie's eyes narrowed. He moved his head closer to Jack's and lowered his voice. 'But you've killed, right?'

Nightingale nodded. 'Yes,' he said, and that was the truth.

McVie smiled and leaned back. 'There you go, then,' he said. Ernie returned with his fresh drink. 'McVie nodded his thanks. 'Put it on my room,' he said. 'Five Two Seven.' He gulped down his whisky and looked at his watch. 'Think I'll head up now, grab me a seat at the front so I can get a better look at the merchandise.'

'I'll come with you,' said Nightingale, picking up his Corona.

They walked to the elevators and went up to the second floor. There were four men in dark suits standing by the doors that led to the meeting room. There was a sign above the door – AUCTION TONIGHT - DOORS CLOSE AT MIDNIGHT PROMPT. NO WEAPONS INSIDE.

One of the men was holding a portable metal detector and he ran it over McVie before nodding him through. Nightingale stood with his arms at his side while the man waved the detector up and down. It beeped over Nightingale's right jacket pocket and he took out his Zippo lighter. The man nodded and gestured at the door.

The room was already half full and McVie had found a seat in the sixth row. There was an empty seat next to him and he waved Nightingale over. Nightingale sat down and sipped his Corona.

A low stage had been built at the end of the room and on it were three metal boxes, each seven feet tall and a little over two feet wide. Nightingale knew immediately what was inside. The two rows of air holes top and bottom were enough of a clue. McVie licked his lips at he stared at the boxes. 'How fucking cool is this?' he asked.

'Pretty cool, yeah,' said Nightingale. He had a sick feeling in the pit of his stomach and the warm beer wasn't making it any better.

The seats were filling up and there was excited chatter all around Nightingale.

Fred West appeared and walked down the aisle to the front where he took up position in front of the metal boxes. There was a quick round of applause, and West beamed and nodded. He flashed a thumbs up at a young woman in the front row who was wearing an indecently short skirt.

When the applause had died down, West put the microphone to his fleshy lips. 'Ladies and gentlemen – and yes, I am glad to see so many women here tonight – our Master of Ceremonies tonight needs no introduction. He was named the Freeway Killer after raping, torturing and killing twenty-one boys and young men across California in just two years. Described as "the most arch-evil person who ever existed" by the prosecutor at his first trial, William George Bonin tells me that he killed another fifteen young men that the authorities never found out about.'

The audience burst into applause and the clapping became even more enthusiastic when a lanky man with shoulder length greasy black hair and a drooping moustache walked towards the podium. He was wearing mismatched denim, a light blue Levi jacket with darker Wrangle jeans. He turned and raised his hands in the air in a victory salute as the audience cheered.

Nightingale knew that Bonin had been executed by lethal injection at San Quentin State Prison on February 23, 1996, but the man revelling in the applause looked alive and well. He took the microphone and patted his hand for quiet.

The audience settled down and Bonin put the microphone to his lips. 'What a great crowd! Give yourselves a big hand, guys, you deserve it!'

The audience went wild, cheering and clapping and stamping their feet as Bonin strutted up and down like an evangelist spreading God's word.

Once the applause had died down, Bonin put the microphone to his lips again. 'Well, we all know why we're here,' he said. 'There are three lots to be auctioned. Only one of them is my type, I have to say, but there is something for everybody, I'm sure you'll agree. The organisers assure me that all three are virgins, never been touched, with no tattoos or unsightly marks. We all know how important good skin is, am I right?'

The audience cheered as Bonin grinned and nodded.

'So let's get right on with it. And just so we all know, all bids are final and are to be paid in cash. Cash is king, right? And only cash will do. This is one occasion when Amex will not do nicely and Mastercard won't cover the priceless items we have on offer. So, let's open the door to box number one.'

He turned and pointed at the box to his right. It swung open slowly even though there was no one standing near it. Inside the box was a young girl with a ball gag in her mouth. She was wearing a pink t-shirt and cut-off jeans and her wrists were manacled above her head. She struggled as the box opened and there were tears running down her cheeks. Her hair was long and blonde and matted with sweat across her forehead.

Bonin walked over and stroked the girl's cheek. 'Isn't she lovely?' he crooned. 'Sweet sixteen, plucked from outside her school in Baltimore just three days ago. She's been well fed and was washed just before she was put in the box. Perfect in every way.' He turned back to the audience. 'Now, who will say a thousand bucks? And believe me folks, that's cheap for quality merchandise like this.'

Several dozen hands shot up and Bonin pointed at one. 'A thousand,' he said. 'Who will say twelve hundred?' The same hands shot up. The bidding was fast and furious and within thirty seconds had hit five thousand dollars. Then six thousand. Then ten thousand.

Nightingale wanted to bid to save the girl from the fate that awaited her, but he only had a couple of hundred dollars on him.

The bidding carried on and didn't slow down until they got to twenty-thousand dollars. Bonin managed to get the final bid up to twenty-three thousand and five hundred dollars, offered by a man mountain in a red and black checkered shirt with a grey beard that reached his expanding waistline.

When Bonin announced the final winning bid, the big man jumped up and pumped the air with hands the size and colour of hams.

Bonin closed the door on the young girl. 'Your prize will be taken down to the basement where you can make yourself acquainted. There is a range of tools down there but you are welcome to take anything in that you require. You will have complete privacy, though we have arranged for video recording facilities if that's what you want.'

McVie leaned closer to Nightingale. 'I bought all my own gear with me,' he said. 'Got some great stun guns. One of them is long and thin, perfect for...' He chuckled. 'Well, you know, right?' He punched Nightingale on the arm. 'Say, Jack, you wanna come down and play with the Asian girl? Maybe go halves?'

'Not my type,' said Nightingale. 'But thanks for the offer.'

'Boys, huh?' said McVie. 'Well, whatever floats your boat.' He punched Nightingale's arm again.

Two men in black suits appeared with a metal dolly that they used to pick up the metal box. They trundled it off to the side and down to the doors. The big bruiser in the checked shirt followed, rubbing his hands together.

Bonin was talking again, describing the contents of the second box, a teenage boy in a soccer uniform. Like the girl he was gagged and bound. There was a damp patch at the front of his shorts. He'd wet himself. Bonin laughed as he pointed out the wet shorts. 'You can smell his fear, can't you?' said Bonin. He leant closer to the trembling boy and sniffed, then sighed. 'The nectar of the gods,' he sighed. He turned to the audience. 'How about we start at two thousand for this young buck?' he said, and hands shot up.

Nightingale got up to leave but McVie grabbed him. 'Where are you going, Jack?'

'I need a new beer,' said Nightingale holding up his empty bottle.

'No readmissions,' said McVie.

'That's okay, I prefer to catch my own.'

'Seriously?' McVie waved the leaflet. 'These are prime victims.'

'Knock yourself out,' said Nightingale. He pulled his arm away from McVie's grasp and patted him on the shoulder. 'I'll be at the bar.'

He walked towards the door and a man in a black suit moved to block his way. Nightingale smiled and raised his hands. 'I know, no readmissions,' he said.

The man nodded. He had a square chin and a nose that looked as if it had taken several punches in its time. He opened the door for Nightingale and closed it after him.

Nightingale stood in the corridor, wondering what to do. Calling the police was out of the question, but even if he could make the call he doubted that anyone would believe him. He went over to the elevators and stabbed the up button. He dropped his Corona bottle into a bin and on the way up to the fifth floor he took out his cigarettes though he waited until he was in his room before lighting it.

He went over to the window and looked out over the car park. The window was open and a breeze blew in, ruffling his hair. He blew smoke out through the gap, frowning thoughtfully. What room was McVie in? He took a long drag on his cigarette as he tried to remember what McVie had said to the barman. Five Two Seven? He opened the window and looked along the wall to his left. There was no ledge, the wall was perfectly flat, no way to get along to McVie's room that way and even if he could there was no guarantee that his window would be open.

He flicked his cigarette through the open window, then he let himself out and into the corridor. He walked slowly to McVie's room and looked up and down. There were no CCTV cameras that he could see, and it was after midnight so he doubted there would be any members of staff around. He stood in front of the door and gave it a kick. The lock was flimsy and the wood splintered. He kicked it again and the door flew open. Nightingale stepped inside, closed the door and peeped through the spy hole, his hands on the wall. He watched for a full two minutes before he was satisfied that no one had heard him, then he turned around and surveyed the room. It was a mirror image of the one he had been booked into. He found McVie's equipment in the bottom of the wardrobe in a hard-shell suitcase. There were three stun guns, a selection of bladed weapons ranging from a machete to a scalpel, various ball gags and handcuffs and several whips and paddles. There was a gun, too. A Glock that looked almost brand new with thirteen rounds in the magazine. Nightingale's heart was racing and he sat down on the bed, staring at the contents of the suitcase. He lit another cigarette and smoked it down to the filter as he considered his options.

Part of him wanted to just walk away but he knew that if he did that then three innocents would die, and die horribly. But there was no one he could call for help, which meant anything he did he'd have to do on his own.

He flushed the last of the cigarette down the toilet, checked through the peephole that the corridor was clear, then hurried back to his room with McVie's suitcase. He put on his raincoat, and put a stun gun in either pocket. There was no holster for the gun but he was wearing a belt so he stuck the weapon in that. The machete was almost two feet long and a vicious weapon but he couldn't see any way of carrying it. It came in a leather scabbard with a leather strap and he tried hanging it around his neck but it was too obvious. Then he had the idea of hanging it down his back. The tip of the handle was reachable if he stretched and his collar and tie hid the strap. He checked himself in the mirror and with his raincoat collar up there was no sign of the weapon.

There was a commando-type knife with a six-inch blade in a nylon scabbard and he tied that to the inside of his left arm with the handle just below the wrist. Another knife, with a serrated edge had a plastic scabbard and he put that in the right hand pocket of his trousers. Then he tucked away a handful of ball gags and sets of handcuffs.

He checked himself in the mirror. Good to go.

He let himself out of the room and went along the corridor to the elevator lobby. When the elevator came he got in and he looked quizzically at the buttons. There was no basement. He pressed G for ground and went down to the lobby.

It was still busy but Gacy had left his table and the stack of brochures had gone. There were stairs to the right of the table, leading down. Nightingale wandered over and pretended to look at the clown paintings. When he was sure no one was paying him any attention, he slipped down the stairs. There was a set of doors at the bottom of the stairs, guarded by a man in a black suit. His head was shaved and there was a thick rope-like scar across his neck. He jutted his chin at Nightingale. 'You can't come in here,' he said.

'I've got an invitation,' said Nightingale. He reached into his pocket and pulled out a stun gun. Before the guard could react Nightingale had pressed the prongs against the scar and pulled the trigger. The man convulsed and fell to the floor. Nightingale opened the door and dragged the unconscious man through.

He was in a concrete-floored corridor with half a dozen doors leading off to the left. He knelt down, handcuffed the guard's wrists behind his back and fitted a ball gag into his mouth. Then he used the stun gun a second time, just to be on the safe side.

He listened at the first door, but heard nothing. Then the second. Still nothing. He walked down the corridor to the far end. On the right was a set of elevator doors, presumably for a service elevator. He figured they had already brought down at least one of the metal boxes, maybe more. He had to move quickly.

He went over to the door nearest the elevators and pressed his ear to it. He could hear a man's voice. A deep growl. Nightingale pulled the Glock from his belt and knocked on the door, hard. There was a peephole in the door so he stepped to the side. There was the sound of a bolt being pulled back and the door opened a few inches. It was the man in the checked shirt and he didn't look happy at being disturbed. Nightingale rammed the gun under the man's chin and pushed him back, his left hand slamming against the door. The man staggered back and Nightingale kicked him in the chest then back-kicked the door closed behind him.

'What the fuck!' shouted the man and he took a step towards Nightingale.

He stopped when Nightingale pointed the gun at his groin. 'Get down on your knees or I'll blow your nuts off!' shouted Nightingale.

The man started to do as he was told but before he had got down Nightingale stepped forward and smashed the butt of the Glock against the side of his head. The man's eyes rolled up and he fell forward, his face smashing into the concrete floor.

Nightingale looked around the room. The girl in the pink shirt was shackled to a wooden rack. The ball gag was still in her mouth and while her face glistened with tears it didn't look as if the man had hurt her.

To the left was a wooden table on which were laid out a range of knives and cutting tools, twice as many as were in McVie's suitcase. There was a small key and Nightingale picked it up. He went over to the girl and motioned for her to keep quiet before taking the gag out of her mouth. She gasped for breath as she watched him warily. 'Listen to me, honey,' he said. 'I'm here to get you out of here, but you have to help me, okay?'

She nodded hesitantly.

'Good girl. Now what's your name?'

She swallowed. 'Jayne. With a Y.'

'With a what?'

'With a Y. J-A-Y-N-E.'

Nightingale smiled. 'Okay, Jayne with a Y. I'm going to undo your chains but when I do I need you to stay calm. No running off or screaming. There are two other people we need to help and we have to stay down here until everyone is safe. Do you understand.'

'I want to go home,' she said, her voice trembling.

The big man on the floor started moaning. Nightingale tucked his gun into the belt of his trousers, pulled out a stun gun and gave the man two long shocks to the back of his neck. He went into spasm and then lay still. Nightingale went back to Jayne. 'I know you want to go, but we have to rescue everyone. You aren't the only prisoner. There are two more. Now can you help me, honey?'

'I'll try,' she said.

'Good girl.' He unlocked the manacles and she stepped forward, walking unsteadily. Nightingale gave her the stun gun. 'I need you to stay here just for a minute.' He pointed at the man on the floor. 'If he moves again, press the prongs against his neck and pull the trigger. Keep doing that and he won't be able to hurt you.'

She nodded and bit down on her lower lip. Close up, Nightingale realised she wasn't much older than sixteen.

He pressed his eye against the peephole to check that the corridor was clear, then hurried out and grabbed the unconscious guard. He dragged him back to the room, pushed open the door and hauled him inside.

Jayne looked at him fearfully as he closed the door. 'Good girl,' he said. 'We're getting there.' He picked up the gag that had been in her mouth and used it to gag the man in the checked shirt, then handcuffed his wrists behind his back. He stood up and wiped his sweating hands on his raincoat.

'Okay, I'm going to be gone for a few minutes…'

'Take me with you, please!' she said.

'I'm just going down the corridor to see who else is here,' said Nightingale. 'You stand guard over these two. If they wake up, zap them. Can you do that for me?'

Jayne nodded.

'Good girl. Now lock the door behind me. When I want to come back in, I'll knock three times, followed by two times. Tap tap tap. Then tap tap.'

She nodded. 'Three times. Then two times.'

He winked, then headed out, pulling the door closed behind him. He waited until he heard her slide the bolt back before moving along the corridor to the next room. He put his ear against the door. He could hear a boy's voice. Nightingale couldn't hear the words, but it was clear from the tone that the boy was pleading for his life.

He held the Glock and knocked on the door. He moved away from the peephole as he heard footsteps. The bolt was drawn back and the door slowly opened. Nightingale stepped forward, pushing the door and aiming his gun, but his jaw dropped in surprise when he saw it was the Botoxed woman in the Chanel suit. She opened her mouth to scream and Nightingale reacted instinctively, grabbing her scrawny throat with his left hand and pushing her into the room. She snarled and clawed at his face with fingernails the colour of dried blood He rammed her against the wall but she continued to fight like a trapped animal, kicking at his shins and raking her nails down his left cheek, drawing blood. He slammed the gun against the side of her head and she collapsed onto the floor.

Nightingale closed the door, breathing heavily. The boy was lying on a table, naked. His soccer outfit was in a pile in the corner of the room and the woman had used rope to tie his hands and feet to the legs of the table. The gag had been removed and he was sobbing. There didn't seem to be any marks on his body though from the look of the surgical implements on a tray at his side, that wouldn't have been the situation for long if he hadn't intervened. He undid the boy's bonds and helped him sit up. 'What's your name, son?' he asked.

'Robbie.'

'I had a good friend called Robbie,' said Nightingale. 'Where you from?'

'New Jersey.'

'Okay, well we'll have you back in New Jersey with your parents in no time at all,' he said.

The boy sniffed. 'I live with my aunt,' he said.

Nightingale gave the boy his soccer uniform. 'Then we'll get you back with your aunt,' he said.

The ball gag that had been in the boy's mouth was on the floor. Nightingale picked it up, fastened it in the unconscious woman's mouth and then used a set of McVie's handcuffs to bind her wrists behind her back. Then he carried her over to the box and dumped her inside before slamming the door and lowering the box to the floor with the door facing down. Even if she came around she wouldn't be able to get out.

Robbie had finished dressing and was standing by the table, trembling.

'It's going to be all right, Robbie,' said Nightingale. 'Just stay close to me, okay?'

The boy nodded. 'Okay.'

'Good lad.'

Nightingale checked the peephole to make sure the corridor was clear, then pulled the door open and ushered Robbie along to the room where Jayne was. He tapped on the door as he'd arranged and she drew back the bolt and opened it.

Nightingale gestured for Robbie to go into the room and as the boy did as he was told, the elevator doors rattled open. There was a man in a black suit holding a dolly with the third metal box. In the corner of the lift was McVie. He grinned when he saw Nightingale, but the grin vanished when he saw Robbie and Jayne. 'What the fuck's going on, Jack?'

The heavy let go of the dolly and reached inside his jacket. He had a gun in a nylon holster and he grabbed it. Nightingale couldn't afford to have shots fired, the lobby was only one floor above them and if anyone heard the noise they'd be sure to come down and investigate. He groped behind his back and grabbed the handle of the machete. It slid out of its scabbard with a soft whisper. The heavy's eyes widened when he saw the wicked blade and he started to yell but Nightingale was too quick, driving it into the man's throat. Blood spurted down the man's chest and his mouth worked soundlessly. Nightingale twisted the blade and more blood gushed out. The gun fell from the man's hand and clattered on the floor of the elevator.

McVie bent down to pick it up. Nightingale pulled the machete from the heavy's throat and brought the blood-splattered blade down on McVie's skull, splitting it open like a ripe watermelon. McVie slumped to the floor, his head a red glistening mess.

Nightingale stood staring down at the two bodies as blood pooled around them. He dropped the machete and opened the metal box. The Asian girl was gagged and bound, her eyes fearful. She couldn't have been much older than sixteen. 'I'm here to help you,' he said. 'I'm going to take your gag off, don't scream, okay?'

She nodded.

'My name's Jack,' he said as he undid the gag.

She gasped as he pulled the ball out of her mouth. 'Thank you,' she whispered.

'What's your name?' he asked as he undid the ropes that bound her wrists.

'May-lee,' she said, tearfully.

Nightingale helped her out of the box. She was wearing tight blue jeans and white top that was stained with sweat. Around her neck was a thin gold chain with a circular jade pendant.

He took her to the room where Jayne and Robbie were and knocked on the door. Tap tap tap. Tap tap. The bolt slid back and Jayne opened the door.

'This is May-lee,' he said, pushing her into the room. 'Take care of her while I get sorted out here.'

'I want to go now,' said Robbie.

'I know, but I need to empty the elevator.'

'I'll help you,' said Robbie.

'It's messy,' said Nightingale.

'I don't care.' Robbie joined Nightingale in the corridor. He seemed stronger now. Harder. But he was still just a kid.

'Okay,' said Nightingale. 'Come on.'

Together they dragged the two bodies out of the elevator. Nightingale closed the door of the box and used the dolly to maneuver it into the corridor. The floor was sticky with wet blood and slivers of brain matter.

Once he'd moved the box out of the elevator, he fetched Jayne and May-lee. They hugged each other and were both shaking. He ushered them into the elevator with Robbie and pressed the button for the ground floor.

He nodded at the machete. 'Robbie, grab that. Just in case.'

Robbie bent down and picked up the machete. The elevator rattled to a halt and the doors opened. The corridor outside was empty and Nightingale breathed a sigh of relief. There were double doors to the left and a fire exit to the right. He took his car keys from his pocket. 'Can any of you drive?'

All three shook their heads. Nightingale gave the keys to Robbie. 'Okay, now listen to me and listen good. I need you to go out and cross the road, There's a track that leads into the woods, directly opposite the hotel. When you're sure no one can see you, head down the track. There's a car park on the right. My car is a Ford Escape, a blue one. Get in the car and wait for me.'

'Where are you going?' asked Robbie.

'I have to deal with the people here,' said Nightingale.

'Please come with us,' said Jayne, close to tears.

'I won't be long,' said Nightingale. He gave Jayne a stun gun. 'You know how to use this,' he said. 'But try not to confront anyone.'

She took it but he could see that she was scared.

'Have you got one for me?' asked May-lee.

Nightingale nodded and gave her another of McVie's stun guns.

Nightingale pushed the lever that opened the fire exit. He didn't hear an alarm go off. He stepped outside into the cold night air. He pointed to the right. 'That way,' he said. 'Wait until you're sure no one is looking then hurry across the road. You'll see the track. Don't forget, it's a blue Ford Escape.'

The three teenagers nodded but stayed rooted to the spot.

'Go!' said Nightingale.

They hurried away.

Nightingale pulled the door shut. He pulled the gun from his belt and headed down the corridor to the double doors. He opened them cautiously. There was another corridor with doors at the end and a door off to the left. There were windows in the doors and he peered through. It was the kitchen. There didn't appear to be anyone there but he pushed the door open cautiously. It was spotless, the staff had obviously cleaned up and gone for the night. There were three large gas stoves to the right, a walk-in fridge to the left, and a line of metal storage units and cupboards under a stainless steel worktop between them. Nightingale hurried to the stoves and turned all the gas burners full on. There were eighteen in all and within seconds the air was full of sickening fumes. Nightingale held his breath as he hurried over to the storage units. He pulled open the doors. There were cans of food, packets of seasoning, jars of spices, then he saw what he was looking for – several rolls of aluminium foil. He pulled out one of the rolls and ripped out a sheet of foil several feet long, He clumped it into a ball as he rushed over to one of two microwaves, a large industrial model. He opened the door, tossed in the ball of foil, then set the oven to its maximum setting – 800 watts - and the timer to as far as it would go – thirty five minutes. The microwave began to whirr and the ball of foil rotated.

Nightingale was forced to take a breath and his head swam as the gas fumes hit him. He ran to the door, knowing that he had only seconds before the foil began to spark. He pushed the double doors open and ran down the corridor to the doors that led to the lobby. Just as he pushed the second set of doors open, the kitchen exploded and a ball of flame blew him out across the lobby. People began screaming in terror and two men in black suits ran towards Nightingale. 'What happened?' shouted one.

'I don't know,' said Nightingale.

Both men looked towards the kitchen, then back at Nightingale. The man nearest him spotted the gun sticking in Nightingale's belt. 'What the fuck?' he spat, reaching inside his jacket for his own weapon.

Nightingale pulled out his gun and shot the man in the chest. As he slumped to the floor, the second heavy backed away, holding his hands up. Nightingale turned and ran for the lobby door. People were screaming and running away from the smoke that was billowing out from the kitchen.

Nightingale crashed out of the lobby and ran across the road. He heard yells behind him. Two men in black suits were in pursuit and they had guns. Shots sparked off the road and he whirled around, dropped into a crouch and fired twice, putting two shots in the chest of the heavy closest to him. As the man fell to the ground, Nightingale shot the second man in the face. Blood and brains splattered across the road as the man staggered back then his legs collapsed and he went down. Nightingale was already running towards the dirt track. He heard more shouts behind him and took a quick look over his shoulder. Half a dozen men and women were chasing him, screaming for his blood.

He left the road and ran into the woods. His Hush Puppies slipped on the dead leaves on the track and stray branches clawed at his face. There was just enough starlight to see by but he couldn't make out the car park. His breath was coming in ragged gasps and his chest was burning. He had his finger off the trigger so he wouldn't accidentally fire the Glock if he stumbled.

There were more screams behind him but he couldn't run any faster - if he fell it would be all over. He looked to his right and caught the gleam of a car windshield. He slowed, then saw a gap in the undergrowth and the parked cars behind. He pushed through a bush and gasped with relief when he saw his SUV.

He pulled open the door, saying a silent prayer that the teenagers he'd rescued would be inside. They were, cowering together in the back seat.

'Keys!' said Nightingale. Robbie handed him the keys and Nightingale started the engine. As the headlights clicked into life he saw a dozen figures running towards him, arms flailing, mouths open as they screamed. Nightingale slammed the vehicle into gear and stamped on the accelerator. The car leapt forward. Two men in motorcycle jackets threw themselves onto the hood, eyes filled with hatred and lips curled back into animal snarls.

The two girls in the back screamed in terror. Nightingale accelerated. His wing mirror smashed into the face of a middle-aged woman and she staggered back and fell to the ground as he sped towards the track. He wrenched the steering wheel to the left and one of the bikers rolled off the hood, swearing at the top of his voice. Nightingale looked in his rear view mirror and saw the biker roll over on to his back and then go still.

He turned onto the track and flipped the headlights onto hi-beam. There were more than a dozen delegates running towards him and there wasn't room to avoid them even if he wanted to. He slammed through them, the hood of the SUV crunching bones and splattering flesh. Just before he reached the road he stamped on the brakes, throwing the second motorcyclist off. He hit the accelerator and drove over the man. Bump. Bump.

He reached the road. The hotel was well ablaze now with smoke pouring from most of the windows. The lobby was burning and through the glass doors he could see men and women running around in terror as they burned.

'Take the next right,' said the SatNav.

'Seriously?' shouted Nightingale. 'Now you're talking to me? Too little, too late, matey.' He looked over his shoulder at the teenagers in the back. 'Seatbelts,' he said. He turned the wheel to the left and sped off down the road. The speedometer read forty. Then fifty. Then sixty.

'Make a U-turn when possible,' said the SatNav.

Nightingale ignored it. He just wanted to put as much distance between himself and the hotel as he could.

He kept his foot pressed down on the accelerator. The road turned sharply to the left and he started to brake but he was too slow and the SUV started to slide to the right and then he lost control of it and it bucked across the grass verge and slammed into the trees. Everything went black.

* * *

'Jack?' The voice sounded far away and Nightingale figured if he ignored it, it would go away. He was warm and comfortable as if he was wrapped in cotton wool and he didn't want to move or talk to anyone, he just wanted to sleep. 'Jack!' The voice was insistent but he kept his eyes closed. He wanted to stay in the warm soft place because nothing could hurt him there. 'Jack, come on! Wake up!'

He could see light through his closed eyelids and he could hear more sounds now. Mumbled conversations, rapid footsteps, and a beeping. Once he became aware of the beeping it got louder and louder and even before he opened his eyes he knew he was in hospital.

He blinked and immediately pain lanced through his head and he cursed.

'Language, Jack, there are ladies present.'

Nightingale turned his head and winced as his neck screamed in pain. He took a deep breath to steady himself. Joshua Wainwright was sitting in a chair in the corner of the room, chewing on an unlit cigar. He was wearing snakeskin cowboy boots with fanged snake heads on the tips, tightfitting black jeans and a New York Yankees sweatshirt and baseball cap.

'Don't mind me,' said a woman's voice and Nightingale turned to see a pretty Latino nurse in pale blue scrubs checking a drip that was connected to his left arm.

'Sorry,' said Nightingale. His throat was bone dry and speaking was an effort. The nurse realised his distress and gave him a bottle with a straw. He sucked water and swallowed then nodded his thanks.

'How's he doing?' asked Wainwright in his soft Texan drawl.

'Just fine,' said the nurse, checking the equipment that was monitoring Nightingale's pulse. 'The doctors say he can go home tomorrow.'

'What happened to me?' asked Nightingale.

There was a television on the wall facing his bed, a news show with the sound muted. A tickertape headline across the bottom said that the Dow Jones had opened ten points lower.

'You were in a car accident,' said Wainwright. Nightingale turned to look at him and a sharp pain shot through his hip. He gritted his teeth. 'Do you want more painkillers?' asked Wainwright.

'I'll be okay,' said Nightingale. He took a deep breath and released it slowly. 'I could do with a smoke,' he said.

Wainwright held up his unlit cigar and chuckled. 'You and me both.'

'How bad is it?'

'Broken arm, a lot of bruising around the face, but you had your seat belt on and the air bags did their job. You'll be fine.'

'How did the accident happen, do you know?' asked Nightingale.

'They found your car embedded in a tree. It was pretty bad but the airbag saved you.'

Nightingale looked at the screen and frowned. There was a picture of a burning building and below it the headline – SIXTY BELIEVED DEAD IN HOTEL FIRE.

'Sound,' said Nightingale.

'Say what?'

Nightingale pointed at the television. 'Sound.' Wainwright realised what he wanted and he reached for the remote and boosted the volume. A male reporter was explaining what had happened as firefighters fought the blaze. Flames were flickering around the sign above reception – WILLOW CREEK HOTEL.

The fire had supposedly started in the kitchens and spread quickly throughout the hotel and many people were trapped in their rooms. Firefighters had been slow to get to the scene because the phones hadn't been working, said the reporter. The hotel had been full because there had been a convention of internet travel agents at the time.

'Travel agents?' said Nightingale.

'That's what they're saying,' said Wainwright.

'So I didn't imagine it,' said Nightingale. 'I thought...'

'What? What did you think?'

'I thought I'd crashed the car and the hotel was just a.... a nightmare.'

'No. It was real enough.'

'The kids? Are the kids okay?'

'They're fine,' said Wainwright. 'Back with their families.'

Nightingale frowned. 'Did you send me there, Joshua? Was that what happened?'

'No one can send you there,' said Wainwright. 'You have to find it yourself.'

'But you put me in the area, with a faulty SatNav?'

Wainwright shrugged but didn't answer.

'They were expecting me,' said Nightingale. 'I was registered.'

'You fulfilled the criteria.'

'I've killed people, that's what you mean?'

'Well you have, haven't you?'

'That's not the point. I'm not a bloody serial killer.'

'To be strictly accurate, Jack, you are. You've killed several people over a period of time and that is pretty much the definition of a serial killer.' He saw Nightingale open his mouth to argue and he held up his hand. 'I'm not saying you're on a par with Ted Bundy or Jeffrey Dahmer, of course you're a totally different animal. But so far as the convention organisers were concerned, you satisfied their criteria.'

'You set me up, Joshua. Why didn't you tell me what I was letting myself in for?'

'If you'd gone in knowing what was going on, the organisers would have spotted you immediately. You had to go in as a blank canvas. By the time they realised you weren't one of them, it was too late.'

'And who are the organisers?'

'That I'm not sure of,' said Wainwright. 'But I do know there are at least two of them and that they're demons from Hell intent on causing mayhem here on earth. The only way to scupper their convention was to get you in under their radar and that meant you had to go in as an innocent. I'd apologise, but I'm sure you can see that all's well that ends well. That convention needed stopping. It went against the natural order of things.'

'And you couldn't brief me first?'

Wainwright looked pained. 'You had to stumble across it. You had to be in the wrong place at the wrong time.'

'What about the guys I shot? They didn't all die in the fire.'

'I had that taken care of, Jack. Look, all's well that ends well, don't sweat the small stuff.' He patted Nightingale on the shoulder. 'And there's a bonus for you, when you get out.'

'I could have died, Joshua.'

Wainwright waved dismissively. 'Could've, would've, should've,' said Wainwright. 'I'm going to order some food in, are you hungry?'

'I could eat.'

Wainwright patted him on the shoulder again. 'Good man. I'll have it brought in, I've never been a fan of hospital food.'

Printed in Great Britain
by Amazon